REBORN

THE GUARDIAN ODYSSEY
BOOK 1

ELLA CLARKE

Black Rose Writing | Texas

ISBN: 978-1-68433-320-2 (Paperback) 978-1-944715-45-8 (Hardcover)
PUBLISHED BY BLACK ROSE WRITING
www.blackrosewriting.com

Printed in the United States of America
Suggested Retail Price (SRP) $19.95 (Paperback) $24.95 (Hardcover)

Reborn is printed in Chaparral Pro

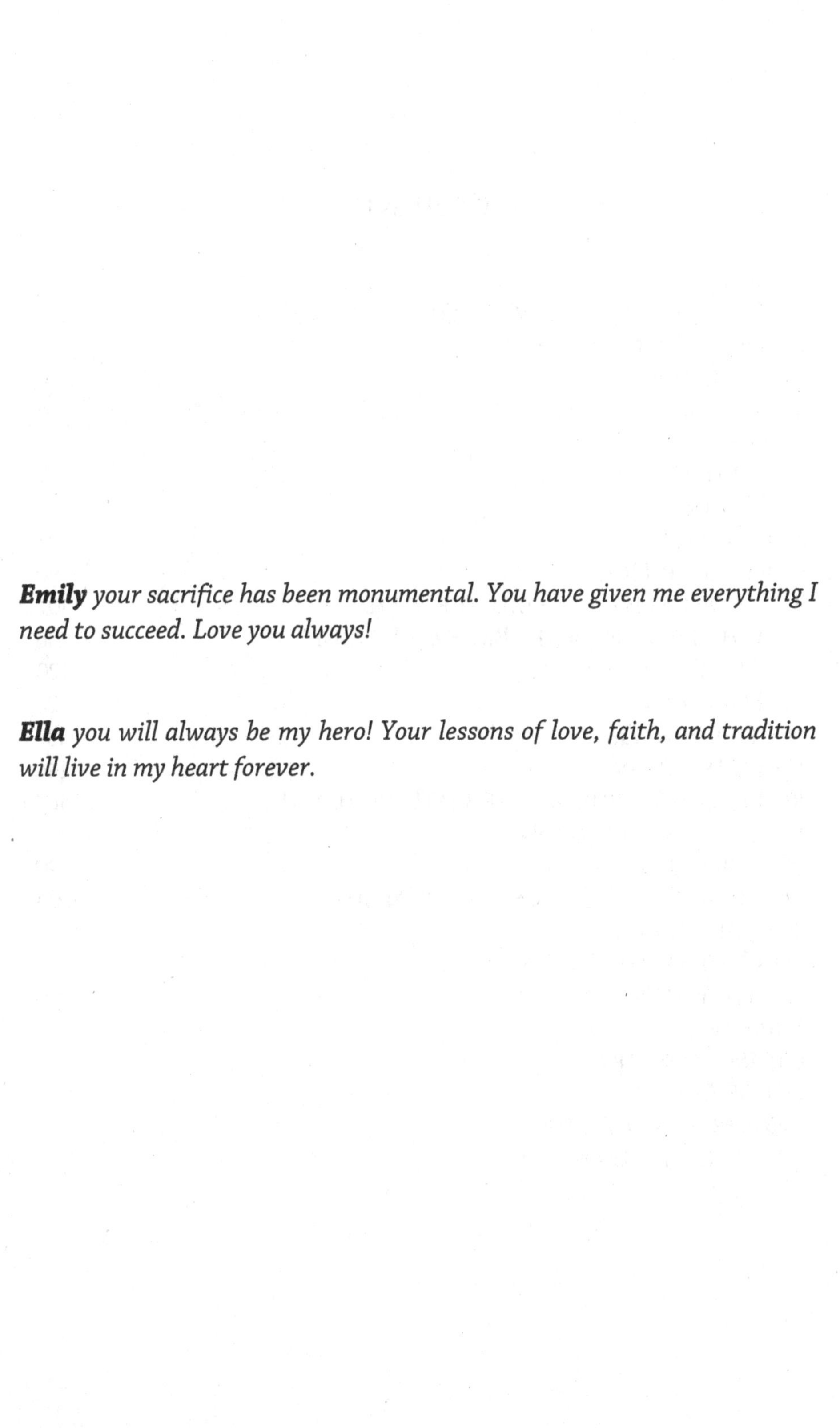

Emily your sacrifice has been monumental. You have given me everything I need to succeed. Love you always!

Ella you will always be my hero! Your lessons of love, faith, and tradition will live in my heart forever.

Contents

REBORN

Preface

And he dreamed that there was a ladder set up on Earth, and the top of it reached to heaven; and behold, the angels of God were ascending and descending on it!

The seven gateways from Empyrean to the Earth must be protected always, for they each have been opened by the Legion and are now heavily utilized by the Dominion on every continent. Only two of them have been conquered and resealed by the Guardian—Atsal and Zalal. Until victory has been declared in the five, the Guardian shall rule the gated cities, taking watch over the seed.

What is mankind that you are mindful of them, and human beings that you care for them? (Psalm 8:4)

1

You Were Serious about That?

The darkening sky provided little cover to shield me from the humans in pursuit. Sweat ran down my brow, stinging my eyes, and the fetid stench of garbage mixed with human flesh filled my nostrils as I ran through the back alleys of the downtown district seeking escape. Being in Danvers is like living in the left armpit of hell. I've had nothing but grief since I arrived in this wretched place. I curse the day I agreed to this sentence, and Yah is definitely on my shit list for forcing my hand.

I peered over my shoulder as I ducked into the doorway of one of the small buildings, not knowing if I'd shaken the pack of delinquent teenagers. If Yah had not taken my powers before dumping me in this hell hole, I would have been able to cloak myself. As much as I despise earth, my job was to serve and protect. Not sure how I am supposed to do that with no damn powers.

"Where did that little prick go?" I heard one of the guys say as they drew closer. I pushed further into the darkness. My black camouflage tee and combat boots should provide some cover. Not that I was afraid of the humans. Even without my guardian powers, I would be stronger than these mere mortals. I just wanted to avoid the confrontation...for now anyway.

"He's got to be around here somewhere. We'll find him." Another of the boys barked as they ran past my hiding place. I waited until the streets were silent before slipping out of the doorway and heading in the opposite direction of the pack.

Hopefully, I got a better look at the boys than they did me. If not, becoming a student at Danvers High soon would be a huge problem. I caught sight of an athletic jacket before I had to make a run for it. So, whether they were current or former students, this activity would fall under the jurisdiction of my new team.

The group was trouble, I knew it. It was just a matter of proving that they were up to no good. I couldn't ignore the shady deal I'd inadvertently witnessed in the alley on Cherry Street. Anytime you combined naive teenagers with older thugs wielding weapons and probably drugs, it was definitely bad news. The trouble I get myself into when I'm bored! Yah needs to disclose my new assignment already. Sheer boredom had me wandering the streets doing spontaneous recon when I happened upon this crew.

Definitely didn't think that I would come across such suspicious activity in a quiet non-descript town like Danvers, Massachusetts. If only I could have gotten a little closer, I would have been able to positively identify both the kids and the adults. Can't really make a report without solid evidence. Despite my quick escape, I would let the team know what I saw once I caught up with them later. The guys should be finished up at the school in a little less than an hour, but I didn't want to head that way yet, as the delinquents were headed towards the high school. I needed to kill a little more time to avoid possibly bumping into that crew again, and they needed a time-out.

Where to go? What to do in this small dismal town in the early evening? That's how I got in trouble in the first place...wandering. I couldn't wait for Reuel to get my enrollment at Danvers High completed, so I'd have something to occupy my time. The rest of the team was actively engaged as high school students. Raza and Angelo, the "twins," were sophomores, and Malachi was enrolled as a senior. Reuel was working it out so that I could be a senior as well. At least I would only have to endure one academic year as a high school student.

As I headed down Maple Street, I spotted Goodies and decided to stop in and try to warm up. It had rained earlier, making the air damp and cold. Goodies Ice Cream Parlor was one of the local town favorites. It was a rather quaint little shop with a 1950s theme. The joint reminded me of a scene straight out of *Happy Days*. Hadn't that show been canceled for like three decades? The entire place screamed Sock Hop. The bubblegum-pink chairs sat on top of a black-and-white checkered floor, and there was just enough royal blue splashed around to make you wonder if Joan Cleaver had been the interior designer. The locals seemed to get a kick out of it, so what the hell? When in Rome...

I took a seat at the counter in hopes of being served quickly.

"What can I get you, kid?" the gruff, overweight man I recognized as Gus asked from behind the counter.

It was going to take some time for me to get used to folks thinking of me as a child.

"Vanilla chai tea," I responded. Gus looked at me with a raised eyebrow as if I had spoken some foreign language.

"What?" I couldn't help but have an attitude.

"Vanilla chai tea, huh?" Gus smirked.

"Am I missing some joke? What's the problem?" I glared at the human. I couldn't believe I'd had to entertain this kind of nonsense for more than two centuries now.

"Most kids that come through here don't even know what chai tea is, let alone order it." Gus laughed. "You're new to Danvers, aren't you? I've seen you in here with Nathan Belling, right?"

No one in town called my guardian Reuel. Not sure why the aversion to his name. Humans like to keep things as simple as possible, I guess. Reuel was not an everyday kind of name. I had a feeling that anything too out of the ordinary in this one-trick pony town brought on way too many questions. So "Nathan" was just easier.

"Right?" Gus inquired again when I didn't answer.

Here we go, the nosey small townsfolk making small talk. "Yeah, he's my...father." I still had problems spitting that one out. Gus gave me the one-raised-eyebrow look again but shrugged his shoulders and turned to get my tea.

I understood the skeptical look this time. Everyone in town questioned the authenticity of our little family, as we looked nothing alike. Every time I caught a glimpse of my reflection, I wondered who was staring back at me. Danvers, Massachusetts, is not exactly the most popular place in the country for "people of color." Hell, the town is more than ninety-seven percent white—everything else is considered "other." As if it were not bad enough to just be human, I had to be an "other" on top of it? I'm beginning to think Yah wants to be certain I don't fit in anywhere.

At first glance, most folks would think I was black because of my complexion. But, as with all angelic beings, my eyes are a brilliant green—jealousy tends to bring out this signature trait. My features appear very slight: narrow nose, thin lips, definitely screaming *other* in combination with the complexion and shoulder-length, dark curly hair that I wear in twisted locks—a six foot, three inch, muscular, seventeen-year-old *other*. Whatever happened to blending in?

"Here's your tea, kid. Can I get you anything else?"

"I'm good. My name's Kendi." *Stop with the "kid" nonsense already.*

"Kendi...now there's a name you don't hear every day." He chuckled as he turned for the kitchen. "Nice to meet you, kid. Let me know if you need anything else."

I sat for a while enjoying my tea. The parlor was quiet. There were only a few folks scattered about. I noticed an elderly couple in the corner, eyeing me suspiciously. I guess it would have been too much to ask for Yah to make my appearance a little less conspicuous. I wanted everyone to just leave me alone, but in this form, I kept drawing the wrong kind of attention.

I slid five dollars on the counter to take care of my tea and the tip before getting up to leave. An old lady shifted uncomfortably in her seat and pulled her purse just a little bit closer as I passed her booth. I couldn't help but laugh. What a freakin' joke! What did she think I would do? Snatch her purse and run for it? I just had a five-minute conversation with Gus, identified who I was, and who I lived with, what the hell? Reuel was one of the most prominent lawyers in town. I guess around here, "a book is judged by its cover." Oh, well.

The JV football game should be about over, so I figured I'd wander that way to hook up with the guys. Maybe we could find something to get into for the evening that didn't involve cussing out the good townsfolk.

I headed north on Maple Street toward Danvers High. As I rounded the corner onto Locust Street, I bumped into a wave of students making their daily pilgrimage downtown. I hadn't realized it was so late. I walked faster to catch the guys, making sure that I was still aware of my surroundings. Force of habit. I hated having to walk everywhere, but since the four of us were currently sharing the Range Rover, and they were the ones in school, I was ass out. But at least I wouldn't have to walk home today if I hurried.

Approaching the school, I noticed a group of guys heading in my direction. Three of the boys wore the school's athletic jacket—football players. The group was being obnoxiously loud and immediately drew my attention. Could my luck be any worse? At least two of the boys were from the pack that I had ditched earlier. Damn.

I dropped my eyes and continued toward the parking lot, hoping to pass them without incident. No dice. The trolls recognized me instantly.

"Hey, Taylor, isn't that him?" one of the football players inquired.

"Yeah. That's the little punk," another of the guys responded with a sarcastic laugh.

The largest guy in the group had no intention of letting me pass. He tapped the boy next to him and then began whispering something else to the entire group that was too low for me to hear. The three football players shifted their tight-knit formation, spreading across the sidewalk, making it impossible for me to get around them. The fourth and smallest of the group hung back, looking a bit confused. He was a new addition to the pack.

I was only about a hundred feet from the group at this point, so I stepped into the street to avoid them. The group followed me.

I tried to remain composed. Although at this point, I was beginning to get irritated. Most humans automatically rubbed me the wrong way and this gang was really pissing me off. "What's up?" I said as I gave the cordial head nod and tried to pass, not letting on that I knew who they were.

"That's exactly my question, dude. *What's up?*" the leader of the group sneered at me. "What were you doing down on Cherry Street earlier?"

"Not sure what you're talkin' about, man." My temper was on a short-lit fuse.

"Bullshit. Not many folks around here that look like you, bro." He was in my face now.

If he thought I was going to be intimidated, this fleshling had it all wrong. I didn't cower to vermin. I ignored the big guy and attempted to step around them again.

This time, he grabbed my arm and spun me around.

"What the hell?" I snapped, not believing this human had the audacity to put his hands on me. My free hand automatically curled into a fist, as I no longer tried to control my anger.

"I said, 'What were you doin' down on Cherry?'" He was snarling through clenched teeth. "Yo, Taylor, man, leave him alone! Don't start anything," the small guy in the back pleaded.

"Shut up, Xavier. Don't be such a little wuss. I'll start whatever I want. You of all people should remember that I don't like nobody in my business. Nobody! And we certainly don't need any outsiders messin' things up." Taylor hissed.

The other three guys enclosed me in a circle, and Taylor let go of my arm so that he could get in my face. The teen was taller than me when we stood toe to toe, and I didn't like his bulky mass so close to me. He smelled of stale pepperoni and rancid grease. Humans were so disgusting.

"I said, what were you doin', homie?"

"Get the hell out of my face, *homie*." I was seething.

Just then, one of the guys shoved me from behind. My face slammed into Taylor. Ouch. That hurt. Flesh and bone. Could this possibly suck any more?

Taylor pushed me out of his space.

"That's some attitude you have there. You may want to check the numbers, boy." The comment came from behind me.

I corrected my balance and pushed Taylor out of my way, trying to pass. He stumbled into the fence behind him. Just then, I was grabbed from behind on both sides. I let my elbows fly as a few choice words slid through my teeth, but I was not able to free myself from the two monstrously sized teens.

Now that I was restrained, Taylor became brave enough to throw a punch. He landed a sharp jab to my stomach. The air whooshed out of my lungs, leaving me breathless. But I was able to use the momentum of the punch to take out the guys behind me.

With them on the ground, I swung at Taylor, connecting with his face. The resulting blow made an audible crunch as my fist connected with his jaw. What I didn't expect was the pain the punch caused to my hand.

"Damn it!" I howled, pulling my hand back.

"Get him bros!" Taylor commanded.

I found myself scrapping with a mob. A fist connected with my nose and mouth simultaneously, and the pain was like nothing I have ever experienced. My vision was suddenly blurred, and I could taste what I could only assume was blood in my mouth. My feet were swept from beneath me, and I was on my back. The teens went from punching to kicking and stomping at me as I flailed uselessly on the ground. Someone landed a shot to my ribs. I felt the snap of the bone and hollered in pain. Another foot landed in the side of my head, and everything started going black. I could feel the blood oozing from above my left eye.

"Rick, Corey, come on, cut it out. He's had enough," Xavier pleaded. "Taylor, we're gonna get caught, man. Come on, let's go!"

"Xay! What's going on? Stop it!" I heard a feminine voice call from a distance.

"Oh my god, leave him alone! What are you idiots doing?" The voice sounded as if it were getting closer, but my perception was fading fast. At least the girl had distracted the boys to the point that they were no longer beating the crap out of me.

"Xay, let's go! If Mr. Theos catches you out here, you are so done for."

"Oh, back off, Elle. Mind your own business. This guy started it."

"Yeah, right, Rick. He looks like he's causing all kinds of trouble. You guys are such maggots." There was a round of laughter from the group as they dismissed the female.

"Xay, let's go right now. You can ride home with me. You don't need to wait for them."

"Go ahead, Elle. I'll catch up with you," Xavier promised. The other three guys had now turned their attention back to me with another round of taunting. The one named Corey leaned down to smack me in the back of the head.

"Got anything else to say, hard ass?" he snickered.

"Bite me," I moaned.

I felt another kick to the middle of my back as the group turned to leave.

"Let's get downtown, y'all, before all of the good parking is gone. The other guys are meeting us at Giovanni's," Taylor said. "I'll drive."

The mob left abruptly. I wanted to get up but wasn't sure whether this prison that Yah called a body would allow me. I wasn't left with anything that would have given me an edge in a fight. The extraordinary speed, telepathy, flight was all taken away from me in Empyrean's high court when I was sentenced. And, worse of all, I could feel pain!

I tried to sit up, but the dizziness was too much. I slumped back against the wet grass, letting the coolness soothe my swollen, stinging face. My head hurt, my mouth and my eye were full of blood, the ache from my ribs was excruciating, and my face felt as if it were twice its normal size. So, this was what an ass-whipping felt like. I chuckled to myself and then winced as the action caused my ribs to throb.

"Hey, man, you okay?" It was Xavier.

I wiped the blood from my eye and looked at the idiot. What a completely asinine question. I knew that there was no possible way that I looked okay. I closed my eyes, hoping he would just go away.

"Xay, what are you doing? Let's get outta here before someone sees us. Mom will kill you if you get in trouble again!"

"Get back in the car. I'll be right there," Xavier said anxiously. "Do you need a ride somewhere, man? It won't be too smart for you to stay out here like this. You're sort of a sitting duck if Taylor and the guys double back. You don't want that kind of attention, dude." He sighed. Xavier was trying to be helpful, but it was a little late for that.

My head was spinning to the point that I thought I'd be sick. I tried to open my eyes, but Xavier's voice faded out into the blankness that consumed me.

2
'TIL DEATH DO US PART

Suddenly, I could hear new noises in the background—the sound of a car pulling up and stopping nearby, and the sound of another group of people approaching. With some relief, I recognized the voices.

"Hey! What's going on?" It was Raza.

"Don't know, man. I found him like this—was just seeing if I could help out," Xavier lied. "You know him?"

"Yeah. He's our brother. What happened?" Malachi questioned. I could feel the group around me, so I opened my eyes.

"Like I said, I don't know. I will let you guys take it from here." Xavier turned and jumped in the car with the female that had broken up the fight. As the car sped away, it looked as if they were arguing.

"Kendi, are you all right?" Angelo asked, kneeling beside me. "Can you get up?"

I was lying on my side, so I slowly rolled to my knees, trying to stand. A sharp pain in my sides made it impossible to breathe normally. I struggled for a moment, panting and trying to catch my breath. I thought I was going to pass out again.

"Can you heal him, Mal?" Raza questioned.

Malachi reached out his hand and touched me, closing his eyes briefly. After a moment, he let out a sigh and slowly shook his head.

"Yah won't allow me. We need to get him to Reuel. He'll know what to do." Malachi was anxious.

"I'll be right back with the truck," Angelo said and headed off.

"Raz, grab that towel out of my gym bag. We need to try to stop this cut from bleeding." Malachi gently pressed the towel to my head and held it firmly.

"How are we going to get Kendi in the truck? He's in so much pain."

"Don't worry, I'll get him moved. You just watch my back, and I'll take care of Kendi."

I raised an eyebrow in disbelief—remembering the look on Gus's face. Why would Malachi cross the line and risk exposing the team to help me? It had been quite some time since I had been in his good graces. He was still pissed about my getting him demoted from the elite guard, and yet he seemed the most upset that I was hurt—must be the head injury.

Angelo pulled in front of us with the Range Rover, came around to the passenger side, and opened the back door.

"Is there anybody out here, fellas?" Malachi asked, glancing around quickly.

"No, there's a group just leaving the building. Whatever you are going to do, you better do now," Raza said as he looked back over his shoulder.

"Hold your breath, kid. This may hurt just a bit."

Malachi grabbed me around the waist, and I felt like I was flying for a fraction of a second. I did pass out this time, but when I came to myself, I was lying in the backseat of the truck, and the truck was in motion. My head was resting on Malachi's lap, and he was still holding the towel to my head.

"I think I'm gonna be sick," I moaned.

"Pull over, Ange, quick!" Malachi ordered.

I was out of the truck in an instant. Malachi held my waist while I was violently sick on the side of the road. If this is what it meant to be human, I should've opted out when I had the chance. I was in pain, sweating, dizzy, and nauseated. Why put me through all of this? Couldn't I just learn my lesson in my angelic form? Yah was getting a little carried away with this human thing.

The ruling judges were trying to destroy me...slowly and painfully. I knew it. They were probably watching and getting some sick satisfaction out of me getting my ass kicked today. Yah should have allowed them to end my existence that day in Empyrean and saved everyone a lot of time and trouble.

Reuel had said if I chose to accept my sentence, I would be made "almost human." Where in the hell was the "almost" in this picture? If I knew I would be entirely human and trapped like this, I would have chosen exile. Hell, the Dominion couldn't be that bad. Running with the fallen angels couldn't be any worse than this. Could it?

When we arrived home, Malachi told Raza and Angelo to go into the house to see if Renay was home. No need to freak out the housekeeper. We made every effort to be extremely discreet in her presence. We couldn't risk exposing who we really were.

Luck would have it she was not at home. It was Tuesday—shopping day. "You can move Kendi now. Coast is clear to the couch," Angelo reported.

Malachi had me inside in the blink of an eye.

While I was very grateful for his intervention, something suddenly dawned on me. Since when was Malachi able to teleport at will? Malachi had regained his angelic power, and I had lost *all* of mine. My existence was so unfair!

"Raz, grab a bucket from under the kitchen sink. Kendi still looks kind of green, and Renay will be a little irate if we let Kendi hurl on the couch. Angelo, call Reuel. Tell him Kendi's hurt. We need to know how he wants to handle this," Malachi instructed.

"You look a mess, kid," Malachi said, turning back to me.

"Gee, thanks. I would have never guessed," I spat sarcastically at him.

I tried to roll to my side away from him, but the sudden motion brought on another wave of nausea. Raz appeared just in time with the bucket, and I was sick again. As before, Malachi was there to help me.

"Angelo, did you get Reuel on the phone?" Malachi inquired as he wiped the sweat from my face.

"Yeah, he said he'd be here in five. He sensed something was wrong."

"Perfect. I don't like how Kendi looks. Something needs to be done quickly. I can't get this bleeding to stop."

After what seemed to be an eternity, I heard Reuel's car pull into the driveway. The last few minutes had been torture. He came in through the front door and crossed the room with deliberate urgency, kneeling by my side.

"Kendi, are you all right?" Reuel said as he visually examined me.

"Head hurts...dizzy...can't breathe...there's pain in my chest," I managed to say. The sharp pain in my chest was growing worse since the last vomiting episode. I think I moved too swiftly in my attempt to make the bucket and was almost certain that I had damaged something further.

"He probably has a concussion at the very minimum. This cut looks pretty bad too," Reuel assessed. "We need to get him to the emergency room so that a doctor can get a look at him. Let's take the Hummer so that we can all fit."

Reuel wasn't going to heal me himself? Why was everyone so dependent on humans all of a sudden? Hospitals? Doctors? What a joke! We could regenerate human tissue just by thinking about it if the need arose. Angelo, Malachi, and Raz stood close by. They seemed as confused as I was by Reuel's decision, and they looked as petrified as I felt.

"I'll pull the truck around. It will be easier to carry Kendi out through the front than through the garage," Angelo said as he grabbed the keys from the board.

"Reuel, are you sure about this hospital thing? Won't they find something...extra?" Malachi questioned.

"No, they won't. Yah made certain of that. Look at him! None of us has ever been made more human. They won't find a thing. Trust me."

The front door opened, and Angelo motioned for the crew to get going.

"How are we going to lift Kendi?" Raza questioned, talking around me as if I couldn't answer for myself. "He is pretty banged up."

"Good point. But how did you all get him in here in the first place?" Reuel looked at Malachi, who abruptly dropped his eyes. Reuel probably already knew the answer.

"Never mind, I'd rather not know." Reuel turned to me. "Kendi, do you think you could walk if we assist you?"

"Can try," I responded in Reuel's general direction.

Malachi came over to the couch to assist me in trying to sit up. Raz was at my feet, and Reuel came to stand in front of me. Angelo kept his distance by the front door—looking more unnerved than ever.

Raz gently swung my feet around to the floor as Malachi shifted me into a seated position. Reuel moved closer to assist me in standing.

As I stood, there was a sharp ripping pain in my chest and a correlating stabbing pain in my side—something was broken for sure. It was excruciating. I felt like I was drowning in my own body as something completely cut off my air supply. With the last of my breath, I let out a howl of pain. Reuel reached for me as my knees buckled, and my eyes rolled back into my head. The room spun, and the darkness began to overtake me. I collapsed back toward the couch, trying desperately to hold on to consciousness. Malachi caught me so that I would not hit the floor.

"Kendi! What's wrong? What's happening, Reuel?" I could hear Raza shouting above everyone else.

"I don't know. This can't be right...this is not supposed to happen." Reuel was confused. "Breathe, Kendi. I know it hurts, but try to breathe. I promise it will be all right."

Reuel's words were fading, as I continued struggling to get air into my lungs through shallow quick breaths. I was scared, and despite Reuel's words, panic was beginning to set in.

I could fight a tangible enemy, but what was I supposed to do with a body that was miserably failing me?

"H–h–help...me...," I gasped through clenched teeth, reaching for Malachi. I felt as if my chest were exploding.

Malachi grabbed my hand as I doubled over in pain and began coughing up blood.

"Reuel! What do we do?" Angelo shouted from across the room.

"Call 9-1-1!" he ordered as Malachi and Raz struggled to get me back onto the couch. I was almost as big as Malachi, and quite a bit larger than Raza. I gasped for air as Malachi supported my shoulders and my head, trying to clear my blood-filled airway.

The room was in chaotic motion as Angelo scrambled for the phone and then began shouting orders at the others.

"They need to know what kind of trauma Kendi suffered."

"Kendi? Kendi? Can you hear me?" Reuel was trying to get me to focus, but I couldn't seem to make my mouth work. My eyes were open—I think—but I couldn't respond. My brain seemed to have momentarily disconnected from my body.

"Tell them we think he was in some type of altercation, but we aren't sure. He's not responsive. His breathing is labored, he's coughing blood, and losing consciousness. They need to hurry!" Reuel shouted back.

"Kendi, stay with me. Can you tell me what happened?" Reuel was trying to get a response. I could feel his hands on my face, and hear his voice, but everything seemed so far away.

"I can't get a clear read on him. His thoughts are too jumbled for me to pull the details," Reuel was answering an unspoken question.

"The paramedics are already on the way. They're trying to get more information to patch through to the unit en route," Angelo shouted back.

"Reuel, what's happening? His lips are turning blue!" Raza screamed in panic. "You've got to help him. We can't wait for these mortals. You've got to ask Yah to help him. This is insane! Is this part of Kendi's sentence? Come on— he's dying! Can't Yah teach him how fragile humans are without this? This is too much! Help him, Reuel, please!"

"The woman says to lay Kendi flat on the floor and to not move him anymore since they don't know the extent of his injuries. She says we'll have to do CPR if he stops breathing, that Kendi could go into cardiac arrest!" Angelo was frantic.

I was vaguely aware of Reuel, Raz, and Malachi lowering my limp body to the floor.

"Keep an eye on Kendi. I can hear the sirens. They are almost here. I am going to talk to Yah."

"I can't stand by and do nothing. I'll be right back," Reuel answered in a hurry.

I felt as if I was floating; looking down at everyone in the room—even myself?

Raza was on one side and Angelo on the other. What was wrong with Malachi? He was slumped over me. He didn't seem to be conscious. Had he been hurt? What did I miss? Ange was trying to drag him out of the way so that Raz could take his place at my side. Raza leaned over me and put his ear to my face. He put his fingers to the side of my neck and then began shaking his head back and forth in response to some question that Angelo had asked. Raza proceeded to carefully place his hands in the center of my chest. What was he doing? It looked as if he was pounding on my chest—no, he was pumping and then breathing into my mouth. I didn't understand what was happening. I couldn't feel anything or hear anything. I felt so lost inside of myself.

The room grew dim, and I allowed my eyes to slide closed. I must have been dreaming because, suddenly, Eloa was with me.

"Kendi...what did you do?" Eloa questioned as she took my hand. "Why can't you stay out of trouble? Really, I don't know what to do with you," she said as she stroked my hair. Her hands were warm and felt nice against my face. My entire body was so cold now.

"You know, there are better ways to accomplish seeing me than getting yourself beaten half to death," she continued.

"I miss you, Eloa," was all that I could manage to say. Eloa was my best friend. The only one at home that I could truly depend on...no matter what. Just the sight of her made me long desperately for Empyrean.

"I know. I miss you too, but this is not the way to conjure up a visit. I need you to take better care of yourself. Please remember that you are not immortal now. Your current state is much more fragile than you are used to. You have to be more careful!"

All I could do was listen to her voice and stare into her beautiful face. Eloa was the epitome of Empyrean. I never deserved such a friend. She was the only one that understood me. She knew my heart, my desires, and my hopes. Eloa had always made my existence bearable.

"How did you know I was in trouble? Have you been assigned to watch me along with Reuel and the guys?" I inquired.

"No, I was walking the gardens near Merkabah when I overheard Reuel pleading with Shopar and Naqam for entrance into Yah's chamber. He was anxious, agitated. I knew something was terribly wrong. And then I felt your presence in Empyrean. It frightened me, so I came to meet you."

"I'm confused. Reuel is here? In Empyrean… inquiring of Yah? Why? How did I get here?"

I didn't understand what was going on? No one took on the guards of Merkabah, the Thrones, without being extremely desperate. Shopar was not so bad, but Naqam was a nightmare to deal with. What was Reuel doing?

"Kendi, I need you to listen to me. None of us know how far Yah is willing to go with your sentence. In all my existence, I have never known Yah to not let us intervene to ensure the safety of one of our own. I'm afraid for you. I need my friend to survive this sentence. Do you hear me?"

This dream was getting more confusing by the minute.

"I am listening to you, but I can't say that I understand."

"Seriously? You have been banned from Empyrean indefinitely. It's no longer in your power to perform astral travel. And I am forbidden from coming to you without express permission from Yah. I was not given permission, and you know I follow the rules. How do you think we are together right now, Kendi?"

I knew Eloa was speaking the truth, and it confused me further.

"Wait a minute. Are you saying that I came to you? I'm really here—in Empyrean? This isn't some weird whacked-out dream?"

"That is exactly what I am saying. Your spirit is separated from your body, and right now, you're human! There's only one way that you can be separated from your body, Kendi!" Eloa hollered.

"Yah wouldn't!" I sat up as the reality of the situation hit me. Would Yah seriously allow me to…to…die… as a mortal? I could barely think it—let alone say it.

"At this point, I don't know what to believe. Yah didn't block me from coming to speak to you, so I wanted to warn you, and send you back before it's too late. He is serious, Kendi, and you need to take this sentence seriously. Humans are some of the most fragile of Yah's creations. Without the right protection and the right care, they die. You are now subject to any and everything that can happen to a mortal—with no exceptions. The only difference is that you have the awareness of Empyrean and of who you are. Please take heed to my words, Kendi. You must go now."

"Eloa...wait!" But she was already gone.

My surroundings changed abruptly once again. There were new voices in the room. Unfamiliar voices mixed with the voices of those I knew.

"Please don't stop. Keep trying. You have got to keep trying. He promised... he promised," Reuel was pleading.

"We aren't giving up yet. Hit him again...clear!" My body was riveted with a strange electric jolt, and I felt it involuntarily retract and slam back into the surface beneath me. How weird? The feeling was not a pleasant one.

"We've got him! I have a rhythm...his pressure is rising. He's breathing— get that oxygen over here. We need to get him stable before we load him up," a male voice informed.

"Should I remove the syringe?" another voice questioned.

"No, leave it in place for transport. If his pressure slips again, we may need to get the chest tube in en route, but hopefully this will hold until we get to the hospital. We need that gurney, stat. We've got to go... now!"

There was an oxygen mask put in place to cover both my nose and mouth. It made breathing a little easier, but it still hurt like hell. I slowly opened my eyes. Everything was hazy. The furniture was pushed back to clear a space in the middle of the room. Reuel, my brothers, and now Renay stood on the far side of the room, watching. She had tears streaming down her face as she looked on, clutching a rosary in her hand and praying in Spanish. Reuel was comforting her. Angelo and Raza stood with Malachi, seeming to support his weight. He looked as though he were on the verge of collapse.

"Let's use the board and the neck brace. I want to stabilize his neck. He has some head trauma; pupils are fixed and dilated—possible concussion."

There were four guys gathering around me with a large board. Two of the guys were EMTs, and the other two looked like firemen.

I was in tremendous pain and didn't want to move. But at this point, I didn't think they were going to ask my permission.

"We need to minimize his movement. Roll him to his right side, and then slide the board under him. On three. One, two, three!"

My feeble attempt to brace myself for the discomfort didn't work. The pain was unbearable.

"Awwwwww!" I hollered involuntarily. Reuel and Malachi were at my side instantly. The EMTs adjusted me on the board and got ready to put me on the gurney.

"What's wrong? Why is he screaming?" Malachi demanded. "Kendi, you'll be fine, you'll be fine," he soothed. The emergency personnel ignored him and continued working.

"One, two, three, lift! Fasten the straps so we can get going. You can follow the ambulance. We're taking your son to Beverly Medical, Mr. Belling."

"Can I ride with Kendi?" Malachi wanted to know.

"Are you sure? You still seem a little shaky yourself. Can you hold it together? Upsetting Kendi will only make things worse," the EMT said.

"I'm okay. I'm good now, promise."

As the stretcher moved toward the door, I opened my eyes again to survey the room. Raz, Angelo, and Renay were clearing a path to the door. Malachi and Reuel moved alongside me with the EMTs, keeping a careful watch.

I was so tired, my eyes closed without permission. As the gurney was rolled outside, I could feel the cool air on my face. I felt the stretcher jostle slightly as I was loaded into the ambulance, and then the door shut abruptly. The ambulance was in motion, and the siren was blaring. The noise was rather irritating. I just wanted to sleep.

"Kendi, we need to start an IV. You'll feel some discomfort when I put the needle in. It will be over in a second," I was assured.

The EMT removed the oxygen mask from my face and replaced it with a clear plastic tube that went around my face and into my nose. Then I felt the first attempt to put the needle in for the IV. Moaning involuntarily, I looked toward the EMT who was working feverishly to get the IV started. On the other side of me, Malachi was shifting anxiously as my discomfort increased.

"Why is he hurting so much? Can't you give him something for the pain?"

Malachi was losing his composure. His eyes were wild and beginning to take on the glow that presented itself as we slipped in and out of our mortal and immortal configurations. Only I would recognize what was happening, but Mal needed to calm down before he lost control altogether. The ambulance was not big enough to contain him if he snapped.

"S'kay, man," I tried weakly to reassure him.

"We don't want to sedate him just yet. Kendi's lung is collapsed, that's why he is having so much trouble breathing. They will want to put in a chest tube as soon as we get him to the ER. We need him awake to better monitor his condition until we get there," the EMT explained to Malachi.

In that moment, the needle must have pierced my vein. I automatically recoiled, trying to pull my arm away. The EMT reflexively restrained me. My moan became a scream that strangled off as my breath left me again. I was gasping for air. I could feel my heart pounding triple time in my chest, as the pain once again escalated. The ambulance became a shimmer as the last of my oxygen stores ran out. An alarm of some type began blaring from the other side of the small compartment.

"Pressure's bottoming out again. He's headed for another arrest. Damn it!"

"Help him! What's happening?" Malachi hollered.

"He needs the chest tube; the syringe is not alleviating enough of the pressure around his heart. Kendi's heart is working too hard."

Malachi was no longer seated. He was leaning across the gurney toward the EMT. "Do something! You hear me...do something!" Malachi was gasping in desperation.

"Calm down, I am doing everything that I can to help your brother. Sit down! You're not helping matters any. Malachi, you promised to hold yourself together."

I could hear the scuffle as Malachi allowed the EMT push him back into a seated position.

"Stay there! I can't help your brother with you in the way." The pain in my chest ripped down my right arm. I arched up off the gurney, trying to escape the agony.

"Help me, Mal. Please...please...don't let me die," I whispered.

"Kendi! Kendi!" Malachi was screaming at me.

The EMT worked frantically as the ambulance sped up and then jerked to a sudden stop. "We're here!"

"Mark, get back here! We need to get him inside—stat. He's crashing!"

Air rushed into the ambulance as the doors opened. I tried to open my eyes, but they were so heavy. The darkness was too deep.

I could hear Malachi's anguished pleas as the stretcher was removed. "Don't die, Kendi, please don't die. I need you to fight this." It sounded as if he were sobbing.

"What's going on? What's happening? I thought he was stable?" Reuel was questioning. "They said his pressure bottomed out. He couldn't breathe, he was in so much pain...and then he passed out again." Malachi choked out. His voice was strained.

"Malachi!" Reuel shouted.

"We've got him, Dad. Go with Kendi," Raza responded.

"Hang in there, Kendi...hold on...please. They're going to fix everything. Just hold on, please." Malachi's pleas were fading but sounded as if they were coming from the ground. The darkness was pressing so heavily now that I wanted to just give up.

"One, two, three, lift!"

Bright lights were shining in my face. Someone was tugging on what was left of my T-shirt, and then the shirt was gone.

The voices became distant mumbles as I felt the burn of some foreign substance entering my veins.

My arm was being restrained above my head, and something cold and wet was applied to my skin. The medication was slowly seeping through my body, and I knew that I would be completely out in a matter of seconds. As I began to fade, I felt a sharp stabbing pain below my armpit. My initial reaction was to scream, but the darkness dragged me completely under before I could find my voice.

3
The Office

I woke up to an annoying beeping sound, to find that my right arm was somehow restrained. I was still groggy and more than a little confused. My chest felt like I had an elephant sitting on it, so it was hard to take a deep breath, but at least I wasn't in excruciating pain. There was an oxygen tube taped carefully to my face so that it was positioned snugly under my nose. I blinked several times, trying to make my eyes focus. The room was dimly lit, so it must have been sometime in the evening. As I surveyed my surroundings a little closer, I noticed the two needles in my right arm and the tubes that they were attached to. One was some kind of clear fluid. The other was obviously blood. I turned away quickly. The sight of blood in a bag freaked me out a little—especially since it was being pumped into my body.

"Hey there, kiddo. How are you feeling?"

Reuel was sitting next to the left side of my bed in a hideous green recliner. He had a book open on his lap, and his reading glasses on the end of his nose. He looked exhausted.

"Ummm...okay...I guess."

My voice sounded as if someone had scratched the inside of my throat with sandpaper. There was a pitcher of water sitting near the bedside; I motioned to it as Reuel got up from his chair.

"Can I have some water?" I croaked.

"Sure. I'll get it. You'll need to sit up a bit first, though."

Reuel moved closer to the bed so that he could reach the remote controls and began slowly raising the head of the bed. As he did, the spinning in my head intensified.

"Whoa...hold on."

Reuel stopped immediately. "Are you okay?"

"Yeah...a little dizzy is all."

"How is this?" Reuel helped me to sit up a little straighter and adjusted my pillows and then turned back to the pitcher.

"Better. Thanks."

"Take it slow with the water," Reuel said as he came closer and held the small white Styrofoam cup with a bendy straw in it for me to drink.

The water soothed my throat, but even at room temperature, it hurt my chest a little as it went down.

"Thank you."

"You're welcome. Try not to move around too much. They had quite a time keeping you still, hence the restraints. I've never seen anybody so uncooperative...even in semi-consciousness." Reuel chuckled.

"What did they do to me?" I questioned, starting to take in everything.

As I moved my left arm, I realized that something was protruding from my side. I moved my hand up toward the protrusion and noticed that I was taped up rather tightly. As I reached for the protrusion, Reuel grabbed my hand to stop me.

"Don't touch that, Kendi. It's the chest tube. It's keeping the fluid in your chest drained so that you can breathe. Your broken ribs punctured your right lung. You also have a minor concussion. I guess that incredibly hard head of yours finally did you some good. It could have been a lot worse," Reuel teased. "The doctors have kept you sedated. They felt it would speed the initial healing process. You were so worked up when you first got here, no one could get you to calm down. You wouldn't let anyone touch you. After the tube came out a couple of times and you had a third cardiac episode, Dr. Patrick ordered heavy sedation and put you here in the ICU," Reuel said, shaking his head as if he were trying to dislodge the memory.

I took a good look at Reuel then. He was worn out. There were dark circles under his eyes, and he looked as if he had been sleeping in his clothes.

"What day is it? How long have you been here?"

"It's Saturday. I never left, Kendi. I couldn't leave. Your condition was far too serious. I needed to be here in case I had to intervene," he said, looking away.

"Saturday? Really?" I was missing more than three days.

I sighed and then winced at the responding pain in my side. I put my head back on the pillows, closed my eyes, and tried to remember the last few days, but nothing would come. It was rather unsettling not being able to remember an entire block of time. I was a member of the angelic Host—a being created in eternity. How was it that I couldn't remember a mere three days? The pain in my ribs was growing worse, and I didn't quite understand why.

"Calm down, Kendi...you need to calm down. Slow your breathing, and it won't hurt so much."

Until Reuel got my attention, I didn't realize I was hyperventilating. I closed my eyes and tried to concentrate on breathing slowly. It helped. However, in response to my little episode, the heart monitor was now beeping loudly.

A nurse was through the door as soon as the alarm sounded. She assessed me quickly as she crossed the room to the monitor to reset it and to read the printout.

Then she turned to me and took my wrist in her hand, checking my pulse.

"How is your pain level, Kendi? On a scale of one to ten—ten being the worst?"

It caught me a little off guard that she knew my name, but I guess I'd been here long enough for all the shift nurses to know who I was.

"Seven...maybe," I said, trying not to clench my teeth. The pain was probably more like a nine now that I was fully awake. I just didn't want to be a baby about it.

She eyed me suspiciously and glanced again at the heart monitor.

"Are you being honest with me, young man? No need to be brave. Don't minimize your pain. We want to be able to keep you comfortable." She turned to Reuel. "Dr. Patrick instructed the staff to slowly decrease Kendi's sedation, but we still need to closely monitor and manage his pain level so that he continues to heal properly. He needs to stay still and not get too worked up."

"Understood, Gloria. I'll keep him calm," Reuel promised.

"Thank you, Mr. Belling."

"Please, call me Nathan," Reuel said with an inconspicuous wink.

"Nathan." Gloria smiled with a blush.

Reuel, or should I say, Nathan, was quite the talk among the ladies of Danvers—a young, single attorney who was new in town, and good-looking to boot. Nathan was tall, with an athletic muscular build, fair-skinned, with dark, thick hair and green eyes. The women around here would probably be throwing themselves at his feet if it weren't for the fact that he had four teenage boys. Although they admired him for his bravery to raise his four boys as a single dad, they were leery of taking on the challenge. A young father who had been tragically widowed only a few years into marriage, and four boys—one with "issues"—was a little bit too much to deal with on the dating scene. So, the women kept conversations with him friendly and flirtatious. Nothing more.

"I'll give you a few minutes with your dad, and then I'll be back with your pain meds. You need to rest." Gloria shot me a serious look before leaving the room.

I didn't respond. I just let her leave. I wasn't too crazy about the idea of going back to sleep. I had already missed so much that I couldn't remember. What the heck were they giving me in this place? Gloria seemed cordial enough, but I still didn't trust anything human. Hell, if it weren't for them, I wouldn't be here in the first place. But it was okay. I *would* see those four guys again, eventually. They may have won the battle, but now the war was on. Word to the wise, it's not in your best interest to start shit with someone who has eternity to retaliate.

"Kendi, enough!" Reuel cautioned. "You've got to remember that you are here for a purpose. Stop getting sidetracked. It's starting to take a toll on the entire team."

I nodded again. I had to work on keeping my thoughts in check while Reuel was around since he was the only one who could read them. I wondered briefly if he already knew what happened at school the other day?

"Yes. I do," Reuel responded to my meditation. "Your recollection was pretty vivid while you were sedated. Would walking away have been a crime? I agree that they were wrong, but sometimes you could try a little harder to be the bigger man."

"I tried to walk away, Reuel!" I snapped and then regretted it immediately. A sharp pain ripped through my chest, doubling me over.

"Damn it!" I winced through clenched teeth as I worked to catch my breath.

"Take it easy, son. We can talk about this later when you are more up for it. Your brothers will be here soon, and if you don't calm down, Gloria won't let them in. They are all very worried about you, you know. This little incident has thrown them for quite a loop." Reuel was obviously distraught over the memory of the last few days.

"It's been a hard time all around. Until now, I don't think I realized what I volunteered the team to endure when I agreed to be your guardian. Taking you on, with the severity of the sentence that Yah had imposed, has proven to be more complicated than I could have ever imagined. Most celestial beings don't have to deal with hurt, with pain, with the emotions that go with being mortal. It's not in our makeup to do so. To watch the horror in the faces of Raza and Angelo has been incredibly difficult. And Malachi is at his breaking point." Reuel was sitting in the recliner again as he spoke with his head in his hands.

"Don't get me wrong, Kendi. I have no regrets about adding you to the team...none whatsoever. I just didn't think Yah would subject us all to so much. I really wasn't prepared to help them through this is all, especially Malachi," Reuel continued.

"The guys figure if Yah will allow these kinds of human tragedies to happen to you, what will prevent the same kinds of things from happening to them? They were terrified that Yah was going to allow you to die. As a matter of fact, so was I."

I wanted to console Reuel since his anguish was my fault, but I didn't know what to say.

"Your body was shutting down right in front of me. It's happened to humans countless times during my existence, and if it wasn't their time, I simply intervened and saved them. But Yah would not allow me to help you. I felt paralyzed...completely helpless. The team pleaded with me to do something to help you, and I couldn't."

Reuel had tears streaming down his face. Unbelievable. It wasn't that we couldn't cry; it's just that it was extremely rare. The only immortal I had ever seen cry to this point was Eloa. It didn't shock me anymore when she would cry. It was just a natural part of her makeup...but Reuel? His reaction was completely foreign to me.

"Reuel, I'm sorry." I didn't know what else to say.

"No need to apologize," he said, pulling himself together. "Yah and I have come to an understanding. So now I'll be better prepared to handle whatever else may arise. He has returned some of my governing authority in dealing with you if I am willing to accept the penalties that may come with my decisions to intervene."

I guess the look on my face said it all. What exactly did "accept the penalties" mean?

"Don't worry about that right now. It will be fine...it has to be." Reuel seemed to be trying to convince himself. He redirected. "Kendi, has anyone ever explained to you the origin of the Guardian? Not what we do, but why we truly exist?"

I had heard bits and pieces of the story during my existence, but I can honestly say that I was never interested enough to inquire. I genuinely didn't care to hear the soliloquy right now either, but Reuel was having a moment, and I didn't want to ruin it for him.

"No, I haven't."

"I know you aren't up for much this evening, but I just need you to listen. Now is the perfect time for you to hear this for yourself."

I had only been awake for a few minutes, and already the fatigue was setting in. I leaned back against the pillows and turned in Reuel's direction so that I could listen to him tell the legend. I was tired enough to sleep, maybe even without the medication that Gloria had promised, but Reuel had certainly earned my attention.

"Go ahead, Reuel. I'm listening."

"I know you need rest, so I will give you the condensed version," he said with a smile. "Many millennia ago, there was a great uprising in Empyrean. Lucifer, Yah's chief Throne, decided that he no longer wished to serve, but instead wanted to be served. He convinced not only himself but also a significant portion of the angelic Host that he could exalt himself above Yah, thus, creating a whole new kingdom. Rumors surfaced in Empyrean that a war was imminent and that all the Host would be forced to choose sides. We were left with no alternatives. Either choose Yah or choose Lucifer. It was a very trying time. Members of the angelic Host that I had always existed with harmoniously were now power hungry and had visions of a different Empyrean—a divided kingdom with a different rule.

"The growing conflict made Empyrean a very difficult place to exist for quite some time. Yah was very patient with Lucifer. Some believed that Yah's patience was in hopes that Lucifer would rejoin the ranks and resume the duties for which he had been created. However, there were also those who believed that Yah wanted the rest of us to see who would choose to stand with Lucifer. All in all, it was obvious that Yah loved Lucifer and wanted to give him the opportunity to fix what he had done to disrupt the balance of Empyrean. Although mankind would like to believe that Yah has compassion for only them, Yah's hesitation in dealing with Lucifer's rebellion expeditiously proves that theory fallacious. Yah could have chosen to deal with Lucifer the instant he formulated his thoughts of jealousy and rebellion; however, he did not. We may never know the reason that Yah prolonged the rebellion. Sometimes, it's just not for us to know."

I had heard the ancients talk about the insurrection, but only in passing. I never knew it lingered and caused such torment among the Host. The look on Reuel's face as he continued with the story seemed to age him a century. He was lamenting a former Empyrean.

"Until Lucifer's defiance, the angelic Host all enjoyed sharing in the celestial duties as they pertained to both Yah and Empyrean. There was not the distinction in ranks and duties that exist today. The Thrones served the inner court with Yah. They were his chief musicians; not guards like they are now. The Cherubim, Seraphim, and Archangels all had access to Merkabah. We could enjoy Yah's presence at any time we wanted. There was no high court, no such thing as Shades or Sheol, no one patrolling the grounds or keeping watch for unauthorized activity. It was a totally different state of being back then—blissful. Lucifer's uprising created an alternate Empyrean—one with the need for guards at Merkabah."

I had to interrupt Reuel then. "Shades didn't exist?" I asked in shock.

My existence had always been governed by a healthy fear of becoming a Shade and being confined to Sheol for all eternity. Becoming a Shade was worse than the mortal equivalent of death. At least dying allowed for an afterlife. Being a Shade meant being confined to a state of nothingness; losing all essence and strength. It was the greatest fear of all the angelic Hosts.

Sheol was the place that these destroyed immortals resided for all eternity. It was a nightmarish, lonely wasteland of a place that some of the exiled angels were sentenced to guard. It usually drove them so insane that they would wind up joining the Dominion and serving Lucifer in an attempt for revenge because of Yah's judgment.

"No, Kendi. There was no need. There were no wars in which an immortal would be destroyed." Reuel continued.

"Lucifer created discord of the likes that I had never experienced. The peaceful Empyrean that we all knew and loved was coming apart at the seams as Lucifer successfully turned Seraphim against Thrones, Thrones against Cherubim, and Archangels against Cherubim. Jealousy and distrust had spread among the Host that never existed before Lucifer lost his way. Those who had chosen Lucifer's side made it miserable for those of us who refused to be part of the insurrection. There were secret meetings, scare tactics, and intimidation against the humblest of the angels. There were also rumors of attacks and fighting within the ranks of those that stood with Lucifer. For the first time, ever, fear was a dominant emotion in our home. We couldn't understand how Yah could allow what was happening and not take some type of immediate action, but at the same time, we were sure Yah had a strategy.

"Yah's patience was exhausted when Lucifer gathered together his army, the Legion, and planned a forceful advance on Merkabah. They had gathered near Kahal, arranged themselves in military formation, seven regimes in all, and marched to Merkabah, prepared to fight. When word reached Merkabah that the Legion was on their way to attempt to overthrow the castle, the Host that stood with Yah prepared for battle. Some seemed more anxious to fight than others. They had grown weary of being threatened and bullied by the Legion and wanted it to come to an end.

It was good to know that I wasn't the only one that tested Yah's limits. I shifted on the bed trying to find a comfortable position.

"The intended battle would have been unprecedented. How could we destroy those that we had stood in service with such a short time ago? This was the day that changed the complexion of Empyrean forever. The Host rallied in the courtyard of Merkabah, determined not to allow the Legion inside. However, Yah instructed us to allow the entire Legion inside the gates. We couldn't understand why he would not permit us to fight to keep them off the grounds and outside the gates. We were outraged that this kind of mutiny would be allowed to desecrate the sanctity of Merkabah's hallowed grounds. So, despite Yah's wishes, we prepared for battle. Led by Charam, we rallied in the courtyard, preparing to leave to defend Merkabah's walls against Lucifer.

"As we reached the gates, the first regimes of the Legion, led by Lucifer, were already entering the grounds. We held our position at the entrance of the courtyard near the castle. Neither side seemed to want to make the first move; however, the enmity that the preceding days had fostered was evident in the atmosphere. The grumblings quickly escalated into physical manifestations of the temperamental climate.

"The constitution of celestial beings has always been somewhat volatile, and the command that was generally practiced was completely absent on the day of the insurgency. The sky was blackened by the somber state of the Hosts. The wrath that exuded from the Legion demonstrated itself in the atmosphere in the form of boisterous thunder. The booming thunder was coupled with blinding lightning. The Host had to brace themselves against the walls of the castle as the wind blew in torrents. The effect of the change was imminent. Most of the Hosts were deeply saddened by the division that had occurred in Empyrean in this season of turmoil, and that sorrow brought the rain. I'd never experienced such a violent storm in all my existence and have not again since that day.

"Amid the ferocious storm, we braced ourselves for battle against Lucifer. And then as suddenly as the storm started, it ceased. We were in awe as the warmth and the brilliance of the sun touched our faces. And then it was clear. The congregation discerned that Yah had risen from his throne. We waited patiently for his entrance into the courtyard. Certain of those that stood with the Legion now wore expressions of regret. But they also realized that it was too late to change their stance. My heart ached for them. Every one of us in the courtyard, Host and Legion, knew that judgment was coming. The castle doors opened, and Yah advanced into the midst of the opposing forces. He moved deliberately and with undeniable authority. Yah considered the gathering thoughtfully for a moment and then turned to face Lucifer.

"As Yah began to address Lucifer, Empyrean shook violently.

"'Lucifer, you have served me well. Nevertheless, insurrection was never intended to have habitation in Empyrean. From this day until eternity, you will no longer call Empyrean your home. As it shall be with the third of my Host that stands with you today.'

"At Yah's words, the ground opened, and Lucifer and those that stood with him were cast down out of Empyrean. They fell like lightning from the heavens into the realm that we called Earth."

Despite myself, I shuddered as Reuel described the abruptness with which Yah dealt with Lucifer. I should have been toast by now, not just stuck in a human body with my angelic powers stripped. Maybe Yah was getting soft as the millennia passed...lucky for me. Reuel pretended not to notice my sudden distraction as he went on.

"Until this moment, none of our kind had ever entered the Earthen realm, and especially not in such magnitude. The heavens reacted. The troposphere was accelerated in an irreversible manner. The better part of creation on Earth was destroyed in an instant by the fall of the celestial beings.

"In the fall of the Legion, not only were the Earth's life forms destroyed but its original state also drastically altered. Lucifer was very strategic in his resolve to come against Yah and had devised an alternative plan if the battle was lost. As the Legion fell, the seven regime heads were instructed to tear portals between Empyrean and the Earth so that they would not only have passage back into Empyrean but also create an alternate realm for the Legion to dwell. A place that Lucifer would finally rule. This is how Sha'ar was created.

Lucifer intended to continue to grow his army and to create further discord in Empyrean.

"The Host didn't deem the gateways important in the beginning. They were merely an annoyance, as any of the angelic Host could handle the interruptions caused by the fallen angels' random appearances in Empyrean. We had come to expect encounters with certain members of Lucifer's army and were fully prepared to deal with them. Everyone had witnessed Yah's swift judgment of the transgressors, so there was no continued concern of another organized revolt.

"It was also during this time that Yah restructured the Host. Prior to the insurrection, we were all considered equals with different duties to attend to in Empyrean. Now, levels of distinction were instituted, and the Host was arranged in a martial configuration. The Cherubim and the Seraphim were promoted and became the only beings with direct access to Yah. The Archangels became Yah's messengers, and the Thrones were now the guards of Merkabah. No one was allowed entrance into Yah's throne room except at the direct summoning of Yah, or by the permission and escort of one of the Thrones. The Authorities were implemented to work closely with the Thrones to ensure that law and order were being upheld among the ranks of the Host. Lucifer and his Legion were designated Dominion, or fallen angels, and were now considered the enemy. Those of us that were not in any of these categories were given various other duties in the maintenance of Empyrean.

"We didn't fully understand the purpose of the changes, but of course, our trust was in Yah's sovereignty, so we settled into our new duties with enthusiasm. The Host had just begun to fully embrace the changes when Yah decided to replenish the Earth. Lucifer's focus shifted from causing problems in Empyrean to the destruction of the man that Yah loved. With the dissention and turmoil that Lucifer caused in Empyrean, Yah knew mortals would never be able to stand against the wiles of the Dominion without assistance. The office of the Guardian was instituted.

So, this was the dawn of my destiny. The beginning of the office that I despised with every fiber of my being. I dropped my head back onto the pillow as Reuel elaborated.

"The Guardian was the only office for which Yah initially took volunteers instead of making appointments. He knew the Guardian would not only be in constant battle with the Dominion but would also have to spend much of their time on Earth to fulfill their purpose. It was only those that had the true heart of Yah who volunteered to take on this office.

"As time went on and Lucifer's forces grew in strength, the need arose for Yah to create celestial beings that were designed specifically for the office of the Guardian. So, to preserve the destiny of mankind, Yah both sent and created an abetment. The Guardian became the most distinguished among the ranks of the angelic Host because we were officially the defenders of Yah's heart.

"The Guardian was strategically positioned in Earth to defend mankind in the regions nearest the gateways. The demonic activity in these regions was far more extensive than in any other area of the world. The attacks on the mortals in these areas caused great losses of Yah's chosen. Thus, Yah began to assign a Guardian to watch over certain mortals that were handpicked. These were the mortals that Yah needed to carry out his purpose on the Earth. Some were well known by the world, and others never came into any type of notoriety, but, because of the Guardian, fulfilled the purpose for which they were born. The Guardian was created not only to watch but also to intervene whenever and however necessary to preserve Yah's design.

"All those that had previously volunteered for the Guardian were given the option of stepping down if they found they could not fulfill the assignments to which they had been appointed. The rank of the Guardian is not for the fainthearted. The battles are constant. The strategy is ever changing. We must put ourselves in constant danger—always with the possibility of destruction. We are the only angelic rank that subjects itself to the perils of mankind.

"Because of the severity of our duties, many lost heart and were no longer functional; therefore, Yah began to create angelic Host specifically designed to carry out the role and responsibilities of the office. These newly created beings were designed with more empathy, more ingenuity, and a different array of powers than what is granted to celestial beings that serve in other ranks of the Host. This is because the Guardian serves a dual purpose. The Guardian was created to defend mortals against the Dominion and to defeat Lucifer and his regime heads. Defeating them would be the only way to successfully seal the gateways and trap the Dominion in Sha'ar; thus, cutting off their access to mankind. Sealing the seven gateways would have to occur prior to Yah fulfilling his promise to mankind. Five of the gates remain open today, sealing them is paramount."

Reuel was lost deep in his last thought—the battle for the gateways. He sat still and quiet with his head hung down, seeming to feel the weight of his own words. I allowed him his moment of reflection without interruption. It was difficult to think about what it meant to be a Guardian when all I wanted to do was opt out. But I knew opting out was not in the cards for me. I had not volunteered for this rank. I was created for it. So, for now, I was stuck with figuring out a way to cope with the hand that I had been dealt.

I wouldn't dwell on my plight tonight. I had put Reuel through enough in the last few days. I quickly shifted my thoughts away from the legend of the Guardian to my brothers.

"Where are the guys?" I asked as a distraction.

"Not sure. They should have been here by now. I'm sure Gloria's not going to allow you visitors much longer. Maybe I should give them a call."

I wasn't sure I wanted to see my brothers just yet. What was I going to say to them? I didn't mean to be such a selfish ass or to continue to put the team and myself in these ridiculous predicaments. But somehow, it always seemed to happen that way.

Just as Reuel pulled his cell phone from his pocket, I heard Raza and Angelo talking in the hallway. I motioned to him, and he returned the phone to his pocket.

"I better let Gloria know that it's okay for them to come in. She may need some convincing," Reuel said with a wink as he headed for the door.

I was seriously tense about seeing the guys, especially Malachi. It had only been a few days, but my last memories were of them looking on in horror as I almost died…from being a complete idiot…again.

The door cracked open. Raza and Angelo entered the room first, followed by Reuel and then Gloria.

"Kendi, man, am I glad to see you awake!" Raza beamed.

"Glad doesn't begin to describe it," Angelo chimed in as he crossed the room and sat on the foot of the bed.

Gloria rounded the side of the bed and checked the monitors. "Guys, I'll give you all ten minutes, and then I'm putting you out," she said to Raza and Angelo. "Kendi, I need to check your vitals, and then I'll be out of the way so that you can have some time with your family."

Before I could respond to anyone, Gloria had a thermometer in my mouth and was putting a blood pressure cuff on my arm.

"Pressure's a little high," she informed Reuel. "Not too bad, though. It's probably just his body's reaction to the pain. It should go back down once I administer his pain meds." She turned to leave the room.

"Ten minutes," Gloria warned as she went out the door.

"Hey, guys. How's it going?" My voice sounded incredibly weak. I wanted to rest at this point, and the pain meds were starting to sound quite appealing. I didn't like being all drugged up, but I wasn't a masochist either. My discomfort was mounting quickly.

It suddenly dawned on me that Malachi was missing. "Where's Malachi?" I inquired. I was feeling slightly better about my strained relationship with Mal because of how he came to my aid during this ordeal.

Raza and Angelo shared a look between themselves that I didn't quite understand but didn't answer. Raz stole a quick glance at Reuel, who abruptly looked away. They were having a silent conversation in which I was not included. It totally sucked that Yah had taken away my telepathy for this little experiment.

Just the other day, it was Malachi who seemed to be the most concerned. What happened? I know that I was out of it, but I distinctly remembered feeling awful about Malachi being so upset. Why did he even bother if he wasn't going to hang around to make sure that I pulled through? I had planned to thank him for being there with me although I knew it was difficult for him. I had thought that maybe this would be the turning point in our volatile relationship.

I was the reason that Malachi was stuck on Reuel's team. He had put a lot of faith in me as a junior Guardian—bad attitude and all—and had trusted me with his assignment. Yah wasn't interested in explanations when the assignment died. Malachi was punished for his lack of judgment and was demoted from the elite guard.

I guess my plan for a quick reconciliation was moot.

And this was my problem with the team thing. You start to care about the dumb stuff—exactly why I liked the hard-ass reputation. No one expected me to give a damn. No one expected compassion from me. I could deal with that. Stay indifferent, and no one can hurt you. But I let my guard slip when Malachi came to my aid, and now I was somewhat upset that he didn't bother to show up. I knew he was tired of bailing me out of all the shit I continued to get into but come on! Talk about Dr. Jekyll and Mr. Hyde.

"It's not like that, Kendi," Reuel said quietly as he read my mood change.

"Then you tell me, Reuel. Exactly *how* is it?" I demanded. I would never admit that I was hurt by Malachi's absence, though I wasn't sure why. I knew going into this assignment how he felt about me. There was no confusion on any part as to the animosity. So, why did I care so much?

Whatever the reason, I knew I didn't have the energy to figure it all out right now. For now, I was content being pissed off.

"I told you everyone was having a hard time with you being hurt—Malachi especially."

"Why? What's up with him?" I was growing angrier as Reuel defended Malachi.

Why was he having such a hard time coping? Hell, I was the one who had gotten my brains beaten out for just trying to do my job. "You'll have to speak with him yourself," Reuel responded.

"Whatever," I sneered rolling my eyes. I was in no mood to deal with this.

I turned my attention back to Raza and Angelo. It was amazing how two beings that looked so different could be so much alike. They were about the same height, five ten, but Raza was dark complexioned with short brown hair, darker than me even, and Angelo was as fair as Reuel with sandy-blond hair. Raza had the athletic build of a jock, and Angelo's physique was that of a long-distance runner. But these guys were Yin and Yang. They always moved in unison. They literally thought for each other. It was like they completed one another.

Angelo had a quiet disposition, and Raza was outgoing. Occasionally, Yah would create angels in this kind of pairing—angels who were dependent on one another for survival. It was a little weird to watch. It was like watching the same person in two different bodies. They were *really* brothers... celestial twins. There were several kinds of these pairings created by Yah. I think it was so that we would have some level of accountability.

"You look better, bro. How do you feel?" Angelo questioned from his position at the foot of the bed, as he eyed me carefully.

"I've been better, Ange, but okay, I guess." I was trying to be as truthful as possible without giving too much detail. In the back of my mind, I was wondering when Gloria would be back with the pain meds. The pain had escalated to the point where I was now sweating.

"What's been going on with you guys? Anything new at school?" Angelo and Raza exchanged another look.

"What?" I said with a raised eyebrow. "Tell me."

Raz began to answer despite the side glance Reuel gave him.

"Well, actually, you've been the big topic for the better part of the week."

I was surprised. "Me. Really, why?"

"Not you specifically, but the fight. The police came to the school to investigate what happened. They questioned that guy we found with you the other day—Xavier. He wasn't a lot of help, though. He's sticking to his original story. He told both the police and everyone else that he found you already beaten up and was simply trying to help when we showed up," Raz continued.

"How'd the police get involved?"

Reuel turned to me. "When we called the paramedics, we had to give them an explanation of how you had gotten hurt. With the extent of your injuries, the police were automatically notified. They want us to press charges."

All I could do was shake my head. This was getting out of control. Yes, those guys were jerks, and that Xavier was a little liar, but I wasn't a snitch. I was going to handle this my way. I still had to be enrolled at Danvers High after I recovered.

"You know I have already seen their faces in your memory, Kendi. I can identify all of them. Although, I still don't know exactly what happened," Reuel continued.

"No police, Reuel. I'm not going there."

"Kendi..."

"No, Reuel. It's over." I was exhausted and starting to get dizzy. I didn't want to talk anymore.

I let my head slump back against the pillows and closed my eyes to still the room.

"Angelo, go get Gloria. Kendi needs to rest. You guys can come back tomorrow," Reuel directed.

"Thank you," I whispered.

"Would you like me to lower the bed? You look like you need to lie down," Reuel observed.

I must have looked worse than I felt because Reuel didn't wait for my answer. He crossed the room and began to slowly lower the bed, then readjusted the pillows to make me comfortable. The door opened, and Gloria came in followed by Angelo. Gloria was carrying a small syringe in her right hand, and I immediately became anxious. I still remembered the attempt to start the IV in the ambulance.

Gloria appraised my reaction and responded accordingly.

"Calm down, Kendi. This is going into the IV, not your arm." The corners of her mouth twitched as she fought a smirk.

Great, now she thought I was a wimp too. Whatever. At this point, I just wanted to sleep.

Gloria proceeded to inject the medication into one of the tubes in my right arm. I could feel the sting of the foreign substance the instant it hit my body. I winced, and Angelo touched my shoulder in support. The effect of the medication was immediate. I could feel my body begin to involuntarily relax, and the drowsiness came.

"We'll see you later, bro. Get some rest," Angelo said as he and Raz headed for the door.

"See ya'," I slurred back.

"Not goin' home?" I questioned Reuel, who had moved next to my bed once again.

"No, I'll be here when you wake again. Don't worry."

"Not worried." I think I tried to smile, but I couldn't feel my face.

"S'up with Mal?" His absence was still bothering me. Even in semi-consciousness, I could feel the void created by Malachi not being here. Weird.

"He'll come around. Take it easy. Just rest."

I felt Reuel's hand on my head as I succumbed to the morphine.

4
School Daze

Another week, and a lot of patience later, I was released from the hospital. I was glad to be back at home where I didn't have to continue to put up so many pretenses. It was exhausting. Additionally, my irritation with big brother Malachi had reached an all-new high. After his initial pleas to ride in the ambulance, he never came back to the hospital. Raza and Angelo had come every day. Renay came a couple of times, though I could tell she was not quite comfortable. She brought me some of my favorite dishes so that I wouldn't have to eat that hospital garbage they were trying to pass off as food. And I literally had to put Reuel out by day five so that he could go home and get some real rest. Until then, he had been sleeping on that damn recliner in the corner of my room. Even that little lying punk from school, Xavier, tried to get in to see me after hearing that I had been hospitalized. I refused, of course. But no Malachi, not even once. What the hell?

Since returning home, he seemed angrier with me than usual. I decided not to pursue the reason why until I was sure that I could remain calm. The longer I had to tiptoe around Malachi, the more pissed off I became. If he wanted to hash things out regarding Uriel and his demotion, then we needed to get it out in the open and deal with it. Giving me the silent treatment was completely juvenile. Reuel continued to referee the two of us, trying to convince us to just sit down and talk it out, to no avail. Malachi was content with keeping his distance. As angry as I had become, distance was probably best.

Malachi was basically tolerating my presence. I got it. He didn't trust me. It was my fault that his last assignment was killed. He actually thought I gave a damn when he put me in charge that day, and unfortunately, he took all the blame for my blunder. He was punished harshly—losing his place on the elite

Guardian team. He was well on his way to becoming a permanent member of Uriel's "Navy Seals" before I came along.

Malachi didn't have to voice his lack of confidence in our relationship for me to understand his resentment in having to work with me again. What made matters even worse was that he was not given a choice. Being backed into a corner was never the approach to take if "cooperation with a smile" was the intended result. I was the poster child for that train wreck of a plan. The thing that totally confused me, though, was his reaction to me being hurt. Malachi was beside himself. And now, he was acting as if none of it ever happened. Talk about nuts!

During my recovery, Reuel completed my enrollment in Danvers High School. Yay me. I can't honestly say that I was looking forward to returning to campus after the incident with the football players, but I didn't have much choice. My temper was going to be an issue, especially now that I had a legitimate reason to be angry; hence, my hesitation. I didn't want to wind up letting the team down again by doing something stupid. The very thought had my stomach in knots.

I had one last check with Dr. Patrick the day I started school so he could clear me to attend. Reuel and I were headed over to Beverly that morning, and then he was going to take me to school. I had tried to convince him to let school wait for another day so that I could just ride with the guys, but he insisted on my attendance immediately following the appointment. I guess he was asserting his "parental authority." This teenager thing was starting to get on my nerves.

Reuel's knock on my bedroom door startled me. "Kendi, are you ready to go?"

"Ready as I'll ever be," I said, opening the door.

"Try not to sound so excited about your first day of school, kiddo," Reuel countered with a grin.

"Ha ha ha. Let's just go already."

Dr. Patrick had a private office near the hospital. The drive was not far from our house, and for that, I was grateful. Reuel had been trying to get me alone to talk about my issues with Malachi. I didn't want to talk about it. Malachi and I would have to hash this out on our own. Although I knew Reuel was just trying to be helpful, I wished that he would just butt out.

"It may help if you talk about it," Reuel interrupted my thoughts.

"Thanks, but no thanks." We were parking now. "Let's just get this over with so that I can move onto the next phase of my nightmare for today."

"Come on. High school won't be that bad. I thought you were bored and ready to start your assignment?"

"I guess I am. There's just a lot of other baggage to consider—now that so much has happened."

"Agreed. But you have the capacity to do this, Kendi. If you didn't, you wouldn't be here."

"Thanks for the vote of confidence. Hopefully, it has the trickle-down effect," I said with a grin, trying to make light of the conversation.

My appointment with Dr. Patrick didn't last nearly as long as I would have hoped. He gave me a quick once over, making sure that my lung sounds were good, checked my pain level and my range of motion on the side that I had broken ribs, and signed off on the release form for me to go to school. The only restriction I had was with contact sports, which I had no intention of participating in anyway.

I grew more anxious the closer we got to Danvers High. I needed more time to prepare for this. Although I was not sure what I could possibly do to get ready—not exactly the kind of thing that sit-ups and the right diet can take care of.

The parking lot was completely full when we arrived. Reuel was circling, looking for a space in front of the Dunn Wing. The main building was still under construction. The Dunn Wing housed all the seniors and administrative offices. So, the faculty had first dibs on this small lot, and the visitors got what was left over. Students had to park at the far end of campus until further notice.

"What are you doing? You can just let me out. I can find my way to the office."

"I know you can, but I would rather take you in," Reuel responded. "The last time you wandered around this campus alone, we wound up calling 911."

At first, I thought that he was joking or just being sarcastic, but Reuel's hardened expression told me otherwise. There was a definite undertone to his voice. His statement was not a request.

"I promise I won't stay long or embarrass you. I just want to make sure the appropriate people know you are here, and that you get your schedule, okay?" Reuel was attempting to be persuasive.

"Sure. No problem," I said with a roll of my eyes.

I was secretly relieved for Reuel's intervention. It wasn't that I was afraid to be back at the school, but I was worried about how I would react when I ran into Taylor, Rick, Corey, and Xavier. The school was not large enough that I wouldn't come across these guys in some form or fashion, especially in the tiny, temporary quarters that housed the seniors. Coming face-to-face with those jackasses would be inevitable. At least Reuel's forced presence would help me exercise some level of restraint— temporarily anyway.

A little more than three weeks had passed since the fight. The only physical evidence that remained was the pain from my healing broken ribs— which was in no way visible—and a small scar just above my left eye from the stitches. It was noticeable enough, but I had kinda gotten used to it. The mental scars ran quite a bit deeper. How could mere mortals get the best of me so easily? That weakness made me even more resentful of the position Yah had forced me into.

Anyway, now was not the time to be thinking about how much I detested humans, especially not on the day that I had to start my senior year with an entire campus full of them.

We didn't have any problems finding the administrative office in the makeshift Dunn building. The office was brightly lit with yellow walls and beige, speckled, commercial grade carpet. A counter successfully sectioned off a third of the front office. A small blond woman looked up over her glasses as we entered. The nameplate on the desk read "Lillian Parnell." Mrs. Parnell was the office administrator, I assumed. She was a frail old lady that looked as if a good stiff wind would blow her over. She wore a simple navy-blue dress with a pale-yellow sweater hung loosely around her hunched shoulders.

"Well, good morning, Mr. Belling! And this must be Kendi?" she squawked with delight.

Great, she was one of these morning people that exuded tons of excitement way too early in the day.

"Good morning, Mrs. Parnell," Reuel responded with his usual charisma. "Yes, this is Kendi."

"Good morning," I responded as cordially as I could manage. Why was everyone in such a great mood? Geez.

"Kendi, we are so glad to finally have you here with us at Danvers High. I certainly do hope you are feeling better," she added cautiously.

I just nodded.

Really? Was I going to get the sympathy treatment all day? I wanted to put the fight as far behind me as possible. Dwelling on it, or the guys that attacked me, would likely cause me to do something I would regret later. I needed to move forward. I had a job to do, and it was about time I started wrapping my mind around that so I could get the hell out this place as soon as possible.

The only thing I wanted more than this assignment being over was being back home in Empyrean—with Eloa.

From the corner of my eye, I could see Reuel's expression. It seemed to be one of pity, but too quickly he controlled what was bubbling to the surface for me to be certain.

"Do you have Kendi's medical release form?" Mrs. Parnell inquired.

"Certainly. Here you are," Reuel responded, handing the envelope to the feeble woman. "Wonderful! And here is your class schedule, Kendi. You are all set. There are seven periods.

You have six classes and a free period," she explained. "Please make sure each of your teachers signs this form and then bring it back to me at the end of the day."

"I'll do my best to show you where to go on this old map," Mrs. Parnell continued as she began writing on the map. "The construction project has everything in an upheaval, but all of your classes are on this side of campus. It should be fairly easy to find your way around."

She proceeded to trace the path from our current location to my first-period class—that was already more than half over. "Your English class is on the third floor at the far end of this building, and physics will be in the next building over on the first floor. Your assigned locker is on this hall here. The locker number and combination are on the back of your schedule." Mrs. Parnell continued through my schedule explaining how I should get to each classroom and marking them on the makeshift map.

"That should be all you'd need. Lunch is after the fourth period, and the cafeteria is here." She pointed at the map on the counter. "Would you like me to take you down to your first class and introduce you to Mr. Crum?"

"That won't be necessary. I think I can find my way." I attempted to smile at the old lady because I knew that she was just trying to be helpful, but she was talking to me as if I were a freaking five-year-old. Back off already.

Reuel nudged me from behind, noting his disapproval. "Thanks for all your help, Mrs. Parnell," I added to soften the sarcasm of my last statement.

"You are very welcome. Have a great first day."

Mrs. Parnell picked up the schedule and the map from the counter and handed them to me. "Mr. Belling, please let me know if you need anything further," she added with a smile.

"You have been most helpful. Thank you for getting us all set up," Reuel said.

We had turned to leave the office and were almost to the door when someone called to Reuel. "Ah, Mr. Belling, Kendi? I'd like to speak with the two of you briefly, if I may."

"Certainly, Mr. Theos," Reuel said, turning back to the office. Nicholas Theos was the principal at Danvers High School. He was a stern-looking man of obvious Greek descent. While I assumed that he was middle-aged because of his lack of hair, Mr. Theos had quite a muscular physique. He could easily pass for some type of athletics coach. His skin was a deep olive complexion, and he had extremely strong features. For a mortal, he was honestly a little intimidating—mob-like.

I said nothing as we followed Mr. Theos past the administration counter to a large corner office with mahogany furniture. He took his seat behind the desk and motioned for us to sit in the two burgundy leather chairs in front.

"Mr. Belling, I know we did not schedule a meeting this morning. I hope you don't mind the momentary interruption to your morning."

"Not at all, Mr. Theos. What can we do for you?" Reuel replied cordially.

"I just wanted the opportunity to speak with you again, in the presence of Kendi, prior to his starting classes today, regarding the incident that occurred last month. I want to ensure you both that the safety of our students is of utmost concern to both me and my staff."

Wow, this was going to be a long day if this sort of thing continued. I turned my head to stare out of the window as Mr. Theos continued speaking to Reuel. "Though you have decided not to press charges or hold the school liable for Kendi's injuries, I wanted to let you know that I am still pursuing an internal investigation. I did not take this matter lightly, and if I find out who was behind it, they will certainly have to deal with me. I will be keeping a close eye on Kendi, Mr. Belling. You have nothing to worry about."

"Thank you, Mr. Theos. We certainly do appreciate your diligence in this matter," Reuel began. "Starting school in a new place midyear is stressful enough, without the added pressure of this kind of incident. I have no problems leaving my son in your capable hands."

Can the floor open and just swallow me now? I didn't need Mr. Theos watching me like a hawk, or his staff checking up on me every two seconds. I was well prepared to handle whatever came at me now. There would be no more surprise attacks, for damn sure.

"We want you to feel safe here. Don't you worry about having any other problems," Mr. Theos directed at me.

"I am not worried at all. Thanks for the concern, though." I realized how sarcastic I sounded a little too late.

My tone caught Mr. Theos by surprise. He straightened up in his seat to give me the full effect of his stare.

"Very well then, Mr. Belling," Mr. Theos was addressing me now. "Would you like to explain to me what happened the day you were injured on my campus?"

Not really, I thought to myself but didn't answer aloud. Reuel nudged me again—this time with his foot under the desk.

"I really don't remember much from that day, Mr. Theos. I would just like to move on and not think about it anymore."

"You remember nothing?" Mr. Theos responded suspiciously.

"Not really...must be the concussion," I replied with a smirk.

I could feel Reuel's disapproval without looking in his direction, but I was certain Mr. Theos was getting my message loud and clear.

"All right then," Mr. Theos replied, pushing away from his desk, irritated with my attitude.

Not exactly sure what he expected. Did he honestly think it would be in my best interest to name names and start pointing fingers? Mr. Theos leveled his eyes on me and continued.

"Just so you know, Mr. Belling, I will not tolerate acts of retaliation of any kind at Danvers High, violent or otherwise, no matter what *your* justification. I will not allow my school to disintegrate into that kind of chaos. Do we understand one another?"

Now the principal was threatening me too?

I was formulating a not-so-nice answer to his demand when Reuel stepped in.

"Mr. Theos, I can assure you that Kendi is ready to put this incident behind him so that he can settle into his senior year. You will not have any trouble from him. Isn't that correct, son?" I could feel Reuel watching me without ever allowing my gaze to leave the principal's face.

"Absolutely. I am ready to move on, I certainly hope everyone else is as well," I challenged. "May I go to class now?"

My patience was wearing thin, and I hadn't even gotten to the part of the day that I counted on being the most difficult.

"Certainly. Mr. Crum is expecting you." Mr. Theos turned to Reuel and extended his hand. "Please let me know if I can assist you in any way during the school year. Thank you for allowing me a few minutes of your time."

The two of them settled into some meaningless dialogue about the lack of parking due to the construction project while we were escorted from the office. Right now, silence was my best defense. What was it with these humans anyway? Was it an automatic mechanism to try to intimidate? It certainly wasn't working. The only thing that it was accomplishing was pissing me off.

"Have a great rest of the day, Mr. Belling." Mr. Theos shook Reuel's hand again. "And sir, your class is that way. Please don't linger in the hallways."

Again, I didn't respond but waited for him to go back into the office before I turned to glare at Reuel.

"What the hell?"

"I know. Calm down." Reuel put a hand on my shoulder to calm me. I shrugged him off. "And this is how they treat the victim?" I snorted. "I'm under surveillance now because I was attacked at his school? This is bullshit!"

"Enough, Kendi. This could be over with if you would just come clean with what happened and point out the young men that were involved in the altercation. But you want to handle this your way, so this is the consequence. And I don't want any more trouble because of it. You are done with this, understand?"

Reuel was trying to be patient and persuasive at the same time, but I could see the anger stirring in his eyes. I decided to back down. I had enough to deal with in the next few hours. Taking on Reuel and that jerk of a principal was certainly not on my list.

"Fine. I'll see you later at home." I turned in the direction of my English class. "Don't want to *linger* in the hallways," I added sarcastically.

"Kendi."

"Okay, okay...going to class."

"Try to make the most of this, kiddo." Reuel turned and headed for the parking lot.

5
MEEP!

I followed the hallway to the end and took the stairs to the third floor as instructed by Mrs. Parnell. Approaching the door to Mr. Crum's classroom, I wished I had taken her up on the invitation to escort me for an introduction. I was now nervous and sweating. This human thing absolutely sucked.

I knocked lightly on the glass to get the attention of the slender young man standing in front of the class. He looked as though he could be one of the students. He couldn't have been older than his early twenties. Unfortunately, my interruption got the attention of the entire room. Some looked to the door in curiosity while others began whispering among themselves. Mr. Crum halted his lecture and came to the door.

"Ah, Kendi. I've been expecting you. Welcome to AP English literature," he said with a smile as I entered the room. "Class, this is Kendi Belling. Let's make him feel welcome."

Mr. Crum proceeded to hand me a couple of books from the end of his desk as well as a class syllabus. I handed him the form from Mrs. Parnell. He signed and handed it back to me.

"You can take any empty seat, Kendi. We are just wrapping up the introduction of our next reading assignment, *Heart of Darkness* by Joseph Conrad."

I headed for the first empty seat I spotted, anxious to be out of the spotlight. The seat was in the back-right corner of the room. As I hurried to the seat, I noticed some tentative smiles as I passed—mostly from the girls. The guys seemed to eye me suspiciously. However, as I passed the desk of one girl, she quickly glanced away. What was up with that? She didn't look familiar, but I did notice her beautiful hazel green eyes.

I took the seat one row over and two seats behind the elusive girl, who was now shifting anxiously in her seat— interesting, although distracting.

"Kendi, have you read *Heart of Darkness* in your previous studies?" Mr. Crum interrupted my observation of the nervous girl.

"No, I haven't." I briefly wondered what he would say if I told him that I had met the guy who wrote it.

The simple answer seemed to satisfy him, and he launched back into the end of his lecture. There were only about fifteen minutes left to class, and I'm sure he wanted to get to his intended stopping point for the day.

As Mr. Crum expounded on the motifs that would be part of our assignments in the next few weeks, I surveyed the students in the classroom. The class wasn't large—about thirty or so students. I guess this was the typical senior English class, nothing out of the ordinary. Several of the students continued to glance in my direction. Most would look away or smile sheepishly as they were caught staring. However, there was a blond girl, dressed in a cheerleading uniform, who continued to look in my direction. She didn't seem to care that I caught her glaring at me repeatedly. I had no idea who she was, or why she found me so intriguing. The girl was agitated to the point that the boy sitting beside her also began to glance in my direction. Their glares made me uncomfortable.

The bell sounded, signifying the end of the period. I stood, slowly gathering my things, as to avoid conversation with the other students. The girl with the hazel green eyes hurried from the room without as much as a glance in my direction. The cheerleader lingered, having a quiet conversation with the boy who sat beside her. The boy glanced awkwardly at the back of the classroom as she spoke. Whatever. Time to get to the next class. I finished gathering my things and turned for the door.

"Kendi...hi. My name is Robert Umeana." He extended his hand.

Robert was a gangly, skinny boy with dark, curly hair. "Hello, Robert. Nice to meet you." No need to not be cordial.

"You can call me Rob. Nice to meet you too. So, where are you from?"

"North of here," I responded with a smirk.

"I know how it is to be the 'new guy on the block.' I moved here from Connecticut in the middle of the year a couple of years ago...completely sucks."

"Definitely."

"What's your next class?" Rob inquired.

I pulled out my schedule. "Physics, with Mr. Woodard."

"Cool. Me too. I'll show you the way."

We stepped out into the crowded hallway. It was bustling with loud teenagers hurrying in every direction, some stopping at lockers to drop off books. This reminded me that I needed to locate my locker on the way as well. Rob was full of questions about me and my "family," and I was tired of making things up on the fly, so I decided to distract him with some questions of my own— namely about the blond cheerleader.

"So, who is the cheerleader in our English class?" I asked as nonchalantly as I could. Rob chuckled at my question, grinning.

"That would be Lauren Biondi. Noticed her watching you, huh?"

"Didn't everyone? What was that all about?" I was hoping to keep today low key. I was 0–2 in that department so far. Why couldn't I ever just fly *under* the radar?

"Not completely sure, but it could be several things. Everyone here's been a little defensive about strangers since the attack after the football game a couple of months back." He lowered his voice to a whisper. "Amber, the girl that was assaulted, is Lauren's little sister."

That's why the name sounded familiar! This incident was one of the reasons Yah allowed Reuel to enlarge his team. Reuel thought the assault was preternaturally influenced.

"Yeah, my brothers told me about what happened. But what does that have to do with me?" No need to tell the human I had stumbled onto Taylor's gang's shady dealings.

"Nothing directly, but..." He hesitated. "But what?"

"Although no one is saying anything, we all know Lauren's friends are the ones that jumped you." Rob hesitated again to gauge my reaction before he continued. "They were actually bragging about it at first. Talking about how they had kicked some guy's ass that had the audacity to step to them on their yard. It was annoying really. Not much of a challenge—three on one." Rob rolled his eyes. "Then the police showed up. Taylor and company weren't quite so smug when they found out that they had nearly killed Nathan Belling's son, and that someone was going to be arrested. Once the police became involved, the whole story changed to make it seem like everything was your fault. They started telling everyone that they thought you were a threat because of the way you were acting."

All I could do was shake my head. Unbelievable. When did they even have time to conjure this lie? No need to mention I knew exactly why that zoo crew jumped me.

"Is that how it works around here? If you're a stranger, a little different, you get harassed, your ass kicked, and folks think it's all right?" I accused. It pissed me off that a lie was so easily accepted by the masses here.

"Not at all, man. Danvers is a cool town… seriously. What happened to you sucks—big time— but I think it was more of you being in the wrong place at the wrong time than anything else." If only he knew.

Rob misread my expression and quickly tried to explain. "Taylor, Rick, Corey…they're a special breed—the privileged kids. They would never admit to being wrong. Especially not when it's easier to just not like you and try to make everyone else agree. Sorry to say, but you'll be fighting an uphill battle to get on their good side."

"Well then, it's a good thing I won't be trying." I pulled the class schedule from my pocket in order to get my locker information. "Hey, man, can you show me where this is?" Rob glanced at the schedule and began smirking.

"Damn, boy, if you didn't have bad luck, you wouldn't have any luck at all!" Rob was laughing out loud, literally.

"What's that supposed to mean?"

"That locker is on the jock's hall—the football players?" Rob said, raising his eyebrows meaningfully.

"Damn," I hissed, grinding my teeth.

"You may want to invest in a strong backpack, my friend," he said, shaking his head. "I don't know how much time you'll want to spend on that hall." He pointed it out as we passed the location.

I decided to hold on to my English books for now.

The farther we walked, the antsier Rob seemed to get. I was about to ask what was up when he finally blurted out what was bothering him.

"I might as well tell you now. Rick and Corey are in our physics class."

A knot formed in the pit of my stomach. My teeth automatically clenched, and my free hand curled into a fist. I knew I would have to see them again, but until this moment, I wasn't sure how I would react.

Now I knew. Instant anger.

The first bell sounded as we walked into the physics classroom. Mr. Woodard was at the whiteboard starting the notes for today's lecture and did not notice my approach. I intentionally avoided surveying the classroom, remaining focused on the short, overweight, balding man at the front of the room.

"Mr. Woodard?" I called to get his attention.

He was deep in thought and my call startled him. He jumped and turned slowly to glower in my general direction.

"I'm Kendi Belling. Mrs. Parnell asked that I get you to sign this slip."

"Oh yes." He attempted to straighten the scowl on his face. "I was expecting you, Kendi. I am Mr. Woodard." He held out his short stubby hand to me. "Let me sign that now or I will forget." We walked over to his desk where he signed the slip and gave me a packet of information and both my text and lab books.

"This class is at capacity. The only open seat is the one back there on the far left."

I turned in the direction he was pointing and noticed a group of students gathering on that side of the classroom. There were several guys and a couple of girls. Two of the guys wore letterman jackets. I froze.

Before anyone noticed, I controlled the rising panic. Human was human. Wouldn't I be better prepared to handle anything that would come my way now?

Were these even the same football players? I glanced at Rob. He gave me a sympathetic nod as he headed to his desk on the opposite side of the room. Well, that answered my question. Rick and Corey. Not sure what I was expecting from Rob...moral support maybe. At least I would have had someone to try to stop me from punching two certain jocks in the face.

I straightened up and headed for the seat Mr. Woodard had pointed out. I *could* do this without killing anybody. As I made my way to the seat, the small crowd of students began to disperse. The last of the crowd to move were the two football players. They moved slowly, leaving little space between themselves for me to pass, but I was not about to be intimidated. Turning sideways, I tried to squeeze through, but as I passed, one of the guys conveniently raised an elbow, hitting me in the ribs. I winced through clenched teeth, refusing to let the sound escape my lips.

"My bad, man...just stretching." Rick smirked.

"No problem." I exhaled, trying not to show the breathlessness that the small jab caused.

They continued up the aisle to their seats. As they turned, Corey chuckled, and under his breath, he added, "Meep!"

The small group of students within earshot immediately began to giggle.

I ignored them and took my seat, trying to inconspicuously massage my throbbing side. Mr. Woodard launched into his lesson about heat and the laws of thermodynamics. I tried my best to pay attention to the lecture and take notes, but something was going on to which I was not privy. Each time Mr. Woodard would turn his back to the class to transcribe notes on the whiteboard, I would be interrupted by an annoying chorus of teenagers throwing paper balls and echoing "meep" in syncopation.

What in the hell was *meep*? Whatever it was, these human children found it hilarious. After a few minutes, my entire side of the classroom had joined in on the fun.

"Thought he was meeped up? Can't believe he came back. What the meep?" the guy behind me chimed in.

"Leave him alone...he may meep himself!" the girl beside me added.

"I ain't cleanin' no meep off the floor!" someone else added from behind me.

That did it, everyone in earshot erupted in laughter. Mr. Woodard turned with a disapproving look, trying very hard to look authoritative.

"That's enough! I better not hear any more of that nonsense in this classroom. If you all are finished with the notes, start the 'Further Study' section at the end of the unit, as I will be including it in tomorrow's quiz."

The last word, *quiz*, brought an abrupt end to the giggling, which was quickly replaced by moans and complaints.

I just couldn't help myself.

"Who's the meep now?" I said loud enough for everyone in my vicinity to hear when Mr. Woodard turned to take a seat at his desk.

The girl in front of me yelped like someone had kicked her. Her outburst of laughter caused Mr. Woodard to look up from the desk where he sat flipping through a large textbook.

"Miss Dungee, would you like to explain to me what is so funny?" he asked as he pushed his over-sized glasses back up his nose.

"No, sir. Just something caught in my throat." Her attempt to turn the laugh into a cough was unsuccessful. Mr. Woodard shook his head in disapproval, clearly not amused.

When Mr. Woodard lifted his scrutiny, the redheaded girl turned to look at me.

"Good one," she encouraged with a wink and then turned back to her notes.

I was a little surprised, but I guess not everyone around here was a complete jackass. My add-on seemed to bring the little game to a close, and the class continued uneventfully for the remainder of the hour.

When bell rang, I decided to go to my locker to offload some of my books before calculus. I didn't care where the locker was. I was beginning to feel like a pack mule. As I gathered my things, the redhead turned to speak to me.

"You're pretty quick, Kendi, and funny too. I like that. I'm Lesley." I eyed her suspiciously, not knowing what to make of her. The rest of this room were complete buttholes, and I didn't have the time to figure out her intentions. Humans were just not my thing, and I wasn't in the mood to be chummy.

"Hi," I responded while continuing to throw my stuff together.

"Where are you headed in such a hurry? What's your next class?"

I sighed without answering or even looking at Lesley. I wished she would just take the hint so I wouldn't have to say what I was thinking out loud.

"You look bothered. Everything okay?" Lesley was studying my face.

"Can I help you with something, Lesley?" I snapped, rolling my eyes.

"Ooooh! You *can* speak in more than monosyllabic responses." She chuckled.

"Are you always this irritating, or is it just me you're trying to annoy the hell out of?"

"And a temper too. Looka there."

"Excuse me. I am going to be late for my next class." I grabbed my load and headed for the door with Lesley right on my heels.

"Come on, Kendi. Just making light of a bad situation. I know it can't be easy for you. New school, new surroundings, dumped into the middle of the semester, and I won't even bring up the *incident*." I could almost hear the quotation marks that she put on the *incident*. Just as we reached the hallway, Rob joined us.

"I see you've already met Lesley. She's okay, not usually this forward or intrusive, but she's cool," Rob added, throwing a quick glance at her.

"What? I was just trying to make conversation with the new guy." Lesley shrugged.

"Yeah, we've met." I continued up the hallway toward my locker. "Where're you headed, man? I have Spanish."

"Calculus and then criminal law. But I am going to dump these books off before heading over to math."

Rob looked at me nervously. "It's in the opposite direction from where I'm heading, but do you want me to come with you?"

"Naw. I'm good." If I got into anything, I didn't want to drag anyone else down with me. As humans went, Rob seemed okay.

"All right then. You headin' off campus for lunch, or are you hanging out in the cafeteria?"

"Hadn't really thought about it. I haven't seen my brothers yet, so I guess it'll be the cafeteria." I wasn't in the mood to walk anywhere.

"Cool. Later." Rob turned and headed up the hall with Lesley.

"I promise I won't be so annoying at lunch." She smiled and threw another wink at me over her shoulder. I just rolled my eyes.

It was getting late, and the halls were quickly thinning as the students hurried to their third-period classes. I approached "jock hall" cautiously, but there was no one around. Relieved, I went to the locker, got it open, and deposited the books. Turning up the hall, I remembered the schedule and map I had shoved into my English book. *Dammit.* I was already running late. Clumsily I fumbled with the combination lock, when I heard a familiar and unnerving laugh.

"What's the hurry there, meep?" Taylor and Rick stood about ten feet from me, laughing. My temper flared.

Would walking away have been so hard? I heard Reuel's words echoing in my head. I got the map and my schedule, closed the locker and started up the hallway.

Again, Rick stood his ground. Taylor followed suit. I stepped to the side without saying a word.

They let me pass without further comment or provocation. I couldn't believe it.

I suppose I should have let it go, but then it wouldn't be me, now would it?

"Meepholes," I snickered under my breath when I was far enough up the hallway that I was visible in the classroom windows.

I heard Rick encouraging Taylor to let it go... for now.

I walked into calculus just as the second bell rang. I went through the same routine I had in the previous two classes, and then settled in for another boring lecture.

I wasn't paying much attention to Mrs. Runey but spent much of the class recalling all that had happened in the first half of my morning—a lot to process.

The hour passed without incident. No one bothered me. For which I was extremely grateful. Calculus may very well become my favorite class. This trend continued in my criminal law class with Mr. Bradford. The class was smaller than the others. I guess there weren't very many seventeen-year-olds interested in criminal law. Maybe this wouldn't be as horrible as I had originally thought. The second half of the morning was okay.

By the time the bell rang ending fourth period, I was starving. I did wonder why I hadn't seen the guys yet. The twins were sophomores, and this was the senior building, so that made sense. However, I did expect to at least bump into Malachi. Everyone did use the same cafeteria, though, so I would find them soon enough.

Again, I tempted fate and stopped by my locker to deposit the last pile of books I had acquired—this time without incident. The halls were packed with anxious students who were either hungry or just overwhelmingly ready for a break in the monotony supplied by the morning's lectures.

I never thought I would be so excited about cafeteria food, but at this point, I think I would have eaten my shoes if they came in nacho flavor. The cafeteria was not hard to find. I just followed the crowd. Unfortunately, due to my detour, the line was quite long upon my arrival, but I could smell the day's menu just on the other side of the door. I waited impatiently as the line inched toward the door, and my stomach snarled.

"Kendi, there you are!" Lesley called as I entered the crowded cafeteria. She was waving her hands overhead as if trying to signal a plane or something. Rob was looking at her incredulously— probably embarrassed by her overenthusiasm. They were waiting for me at a table near the salad bar with their lunches already assembled.

I waved back at Lesley while scanning the cafeteria for the guys. There was no sign of them. The room was packed with students scrambling about to grab whatever it was they were planning to devour in the next few minutes, but the fellas were nowhere in sight.

"Looking for someone handsome?" Lesley sang looking up at me. I would have gone in the opposite direction if I'd noticed her approaching.

"Yeah, my brothers. Guess they had plans for lunch."

"Well, grab your lunch. You can hang with Rob and me. I think the rest of our crew had other plans today as well. We can grab a spot outside since it is nice. It gets pretty claustrophobic in here when it's crowded."

"No problem." I was already walking away from her, heading for the pizza line. I grabbed a couple slices, a soda, and Doritos, and joined Rob and Lesley by the exit. "Where to?" I asked.

"There is usually space over behind the gym," Rob responded.

It was nice outside, chilly, but the sun was out and provided just the right balance to warm it up. I was glad for the fresh air after being cooped up inside all morning with stinking teenagers. Doing this five days a week was going to take some getting used to.

Sure enough, there was an empty spot behind the gym. We found a place on the wall and began eating.

I was enjoying the blissful silence, but I should have known it would not last with Lesley there.

"So Kendi, what brought you to Danvers in the middle of the school year? I heard your brothers have been here a couple years. Why weren't you here with them?"

"Are you always so nosey, Lesley?" I asked without even looking up from my food.

"Only when I am interested." She smirked, putting extra emphasis on the word *interested*.

That got my attention, and I looked up to see that Lesley was literally gazing at me. Was she seriously attempting to flirt with me? This was new. I assessed her features quickly. Lesley was a petite girl with a narrow face framed by naturally curly, long, red hair. Her ice-blue eyes seemed out of place in her pale, freckled face. She had full lips that always seemed to be pulled up in a full grin when she was looking at me. Lesley's smile would be very pretty— her best feature—if she weren't so damned annoying. Since Lesley was determined to leave the bait dangling out there, I decided to bite. Hell, I was bored.

"And why are you so *interested*, Miss Dungee?" I gave her a wink. It seemed to work well for Reuel.

Lesley's reaction was priceless. I thought she would fall backward over the wall. I had finally brought her up short. She didn't know what to say. If I had known that a simple wink would shut her up, I would have done it a long time ago.

"What? Nothing to say? That's a first!" I chuckled having quite a bit of fun watching Lesley flounder. Rob laughed with me as he reached across Lesley to knucle bump me.

"Well, isn't this a cozy little group?"

I turned to see Corey, Rick, and Taylor standing behind us. Every time I let my guard down, these jokers showed up. My best defense with this crowd was to ignore them and create distance as quickly as possible. I rose from the wall to gather my stuff and head back inside. Of course, they were once again standing in my direct path. Rob and Lesley got up as well.

"Making yourself the welcome wagon, Lesley?" Taylor interjected sarcastically.

From the way he was looking at her, I surmised that he was much more interested in the fact that she was not hanging out with him than the fact that she ate lunch with me. Taylor was looking at Lesley like Lesley had been gazing at me a few minutes ago.

"Get over yourself already, Taylor. You guys ready to go?" Lesley pushed past the group and kept on going, highly annoyed and maybe even a little embarrassed.

Rob lightly tapped my shoulder to get my attention, which was locked on the football players. "Let's go, Kendi."

Corey moved over to block my path once Rob was past him. Rob turned to come back, but I shook my head ever so slightly. I didn't want anyone else involved in my mess. My gesture did not go unnoticed.

"Yeah, go on Rob. We'd like to have a chat with Kendi for a minute," Corey continued.

Rob hesitated and then slowly continued toward the cafeteria. He was intimidated by the oversized jocks— something I absolutely refused to be. I waited for Rob to be safely inside the building before I turned back to the three antagonizers with my stone-faced glare. No one moved. I raised one eyebrow and took a step toward Corey, making my intentions very clear. To my surprise, he backed up. However, Taylor took a step closer and began speaking in a low, menacing tone.

"We heard you met with Mr. Theos this morning? What was that all about? What did you tell him, Meep?"

Again, with the meep foolishness? I slowly turned to face Taylor.

Until now, I hadn't realized that Taylor was the only one of these boys bigger than me and he was only taller by about half a head. It still ticked me off that they could get the jump on me so easily during our first encounter. But I vowed that that would never happen again. Just thinking about it made me angry. This little game was getting old fast, and I wasn't going to stand here testing my patience any longer.

"Taylor, move. Now," I hissed.

Corey and Rick were looking anxiously over their shoulders. Lunch was just about over, and the yard had cleared quite a bit. However, the students that remained were not oblivious to our little confrontation.

"Whatcha gonna do, Meep? Get the shit kicked out of you again?"

Taylor and I were toe to toe.

"I promise I'll be the one doing the kickin' this time, ass wipe," I retorted, moving even closer to him. Taylor grinned, welcoming the challenge.

"Feelin' froggy? Leap, numbnuts." I taunted him with less than a foot of space between us.

Taylor pushed me, and my anger reached its boiling point. I'd had it with the entire school scene and these damn mortals for one day. I prepared to give Taylor the fight he should have had the first time. It didn't look like Rick or Corey was going to back him up this time. There were too many witnesses. Taylor would be on his own—just the way I wanted it.

Taylor swung first. I prepared to duck, but it wasn't necessary. Out of nowhere, Malachi was there. He had grabbed Taylor's arm mid-swing. Raza and Angelo also came into my peripheral view after a few seconds. They were moving much slower and more cautiously than Malachi.

"Not this time, Taylor," Malachi snapped as he pushed Taylor back a good two feet with very little effort. Malachi was bigger than Taylor, and Taylor noticed.

Taylor started back in toward us and then thought better of it when he noticed Raz and Angelo flanking me.

"I don't know you, Taylor, but I promise you this. What happened to Kendi before will *never* happen again. These are *my* brothers." Mal pointed to us collectively. "And if you have a problem with them, then you and I will have a major problem."

Taylor assessed the situation and, to my surprise, he, Rick, and Corey abruptly headed in the opposite direction.

And then I saw the reason for the sudden departure. Mr. Theos was crossing the lawn heading directly for us. The bell rang, signaling the end of the lunch hour.

"Kendi, don't say a word. Raz, Ange, go to class," Malachi demanded under his breath before Mr. Theos was within earshot. Raza and Angelo walked away as instructed, heading to their fifth-period classes.

"What's going on here?" Mr. Theos asked. Although his question was directed at Malachi, who was clearly in control of whatever the situation was, Mr. Theos was looking at me.

"Nothing, Mr. Theos. Was just checking on my brother. I was about to bring him to the office to get Mrs. Parnell to issue an excuse for the rest of the day. He is not feeling well. It's been a long day, and he needs to go home and rest. Kendi may have overdone it trying to be here all day."

I could have collapsed right there. The look on my face must have been priceless. The shock of Malachi showing up at the precise moment that I was about to lose it, taking control of the situation, and then bailing me out with the principal was just too much. Honestly, I think I did feel sick. My legs felt hollow as if I had been gut punched.

"I'm sorry you aren't feeling well, Mr. Belling," Mr. Theos directed at me and then turned back to Malachi. "Were you going to call your father?"

"Actually, I have a free period right now. I was going to take Kendi home myself. If that's all right?"

Speechless again.

"That will be fine. You can go. I will let Mrs. Parnell know to inform Kendi's afternoon teachers that he's taken ill and had to leave for the day."

Mr. Theos appraised my stunned expression. He placed a hand gently on my shoulder as if to steady me.

"Feel better, son," he said and turned back toward the Dunn Building.

"Let's go, Kendi, before you get me into some kind of fight too," Malachi chuckled.

I followed him to the car without a word.

"Are you still hungry or do you want to go home?" Malachi asked casually as he pulled out of the student lot.

"Nah, I'm good. Just drop me at home." What the hell? I couldn't deal with Malachi or anything else today. Enough already.

I stared blankly out the window, confused.

What the meep?

6
SARIELLE

Thanks to Malachi's intervention during my first day of school, I could stay at home for a couple of days. Reuel thought I needed the time to calm down and was grateful that the guys had stepped in to interrupt what was sure to have been another altercation. Mr. Theos was convinced I had taken ill, so there was no need for further explanation when I didn't show up for school the next day. Raza informed me that it was Lesley who had alerted the principal to the impending disturbance. I would have to find a way to thank her later. Another fight would have just made everything worse. Although, even if she hadn't intervened, I guess I still would have been in good shape because of Malachi.

Why couldn't my relationship with Malachi be normal, unstrained? It would make my life so much easier. He got along just fine with everyone else. With me, it was just aberrant. Malachi was coming to my aid more frequently, and at just the right time, it seemed. It was as if he had a sixth sense about what I needed and when. It was starting to freak me out a little.

After swooping in to save me from myself the first day at school, Malachi again reverted to his normal standoffish behavior. He acted as if he had done nothing special and that once again, I was the most annoying person in his universe. I wanted to ask him about what had happened, but I was too dumbfounded at the time. By the next morning, Malachi had let it go and was barely speaking to me again. It was only so far that I could expect Malachi's tolerance of me to stretch. I decided not to push my luck.

After my respite, I was riding to school today with the guys. At least I wasn't going to be escorted by Reuel again like some two-year-old. Although, I would have to go back to the office to get a pass for my classes after being absent for a couple of days. Hopefully, I would be able to avoid Mr. Theos and his probable third degree.

I dressed quickly then headed downstairs to grab breakfast before leaving.

"Hey, Kendi! Gonna try it again, huh?" Raza looked up from the table when I entered the kitchen.

"Yeah. I guess so."

"Things will be better today, don't worry," Angelo encouraged.

"I know. I'm cool," I lied.

Truth be told, the whole school thing made me anxious. Why did this have to be so difficult? Just give me my assignment already, so I can get it completed and move on to something else! No matter how hard I was trying, I couldn't seem to wrap my mind around this whole thing—this sentence. I was uncomfortable just thinking about it. But I had come to realize that my comfort level was not very high on Yah's list of priorities.

"You okay, Kendi? You seem a little nervous," Malachi commented from across the kitchen with a grin.

How the hell does he keep on doing that? Knowing that Reuel was the only one that could hear my thoughts made me feel better, but something else was certainly going on.

"Naw, I'm good. Where's Reuel this morning?" I realized he was missing.

"He left early to meet a client at his office. He seemed to be in a bit of a hurry," Angelo responded with a shrug. "Ready to go, guys?"

I grabbed a couple of pop tarts from the pantry as Angelo grabbed the keys off the board and headed for the door with the others.

The ride to school was short but comforting. The guys were really starting to grow on me. They took every opportunity to be encouraging. Even Malachi tossed in a "Don't worry about them; we've got your back."

We parked at the far end of the lot and began the long trek up to the buildings. "Hey, you guys wanna do lunch at Giovanni's?" Raz asked.

"Sounds good. Maybe it will keep Kendi out of a boxing match at recess," Malachi added.

"Ha, ha," I threw in his direction. Was he trying to be funny or just sarcastic as hell? I hated analyzing everything Mal said or did, but at this point, he had me on edge.

"Cool. See you guys after fourth period," Raz said as he and Angelo headed toward their side of campus.

Malachi and I headed toward the Dunn in silence. Being alone with him for even a few minutes made me uncomfortable. I didn't know how to handle Mal, and that bothered me. All things considered, he was pretty cool. I hated that I had screwed up our friendship, but I had no idea how to even begin repairing it. I pushed the thought to the back of my mind.

"Have a good one," Malachi called over his shoulder as we parted ways at the Dunn Building.

"You too."

Not wanting to be late, I hurried to the office to retrieve a pass from Mrs. Parnell and then headed to my first-period class. I figured it would be better to be early rather than late so that I wouldn't be the center of attention again. The class was still unsettled when I walked in. Mr. Crum was at the desk working on some last-minute notes but greeted me cordially as he signed my pass.

The students were gathered in small cliques throughout the room. No one paid much attention to me as I made my way to my desk. Good.

"Hey, man. How's it going?"

I turned to see Rob approaching. "Oh, hey, dude."

"Everything cool? Hadn't seen you for a few days."

"Yeah. I'm cool, man. Just wasn't feeling too great. That's all." I wasn't in the mood to get into all the details of my absence.

"Well, glad you're feeling better. You get things settled with Taylor and company?" Rob asked, pushing for information.

"I don't know if that's even possible." I rolled my eyes at the thought.

"Understood." Rob realized I wasn't about to elaborate any further.

The first bell rang, and Rob went to his desk. Mr. Crum called the class to order and began giving instructions regarding the week. I had done a great deal of thinking over the last few days and decided that I would throw myself into this school thing and make the best of a bad situation. Hell, I certainly knew more than any of the mortals around here. The material would be a cakewalk. I might as well become the star student that I was supposed to be since Reuel had signed me up for all advanced courses. I could be patient until my assignment was revealed.

I settled into my desk and pulled out a notebook, just as Mr. Crum began introducing the imperialism theme in *Heart of Darkness*. I was paying attention and taking notes when I was overcome by the strangest feeling that someone was watching me. I looked up just in time to see Lauren turning back to the front of the classroom. I had forgotten all about the nosey cheerleader. At least she was not glaring at me today.

Lauren wasn't wearing her cheerleading uniform, and without it, she didn't stand out. It took me a minute to realize who she was. She was a fairly average-looking teenage girl—in my opinion, anyway. She was the petite, blond-haired, blue-eyed, princess type. I figured Lauren for the overly pampered, spoiled kind that was used to getting whatever she wanted. I was sure she had her parents wrapped around her little finger, and hordes of friends clamoring to be in her inner circle. Typical. It probably wasn't fair that I already didn't like her, but whatever. She was close friends with the entourage of idiots who had pummeled me. So today, I met her glance without turning away. It was time for some other folks to start feeling uncomfortable because of *my* presence instead of the other way around.

Just as the second bell rang, the door to the classroom flew open. I looked up at the sound just as everyone else had.

"So nice of you to join us, Miss Breland," Mr. Crum greeted the latecomer.

The girl nodded sheepishly, embarrassed by being singled out, and hurried to her seat.

It was the elusive girl from my first day at Danvers High. I had been so preoccupied with Taylor and his crew that I had neglected to ask Rob about this girl, Miss Breland. I had not gotten a good look at her before aside from her amazing hazel-green eyes. It was as if she were deliberately hiding her face from me last week. Today was different. I was already seated, and she had to walk toward me to get to her seat, so I had the opportunity to study her as she came down the aisle. The girl had softly curled sandy brown hair that hung just past her shoulders, coupled with a very light caramel complexion that in no way gave away her ethnicity. She had a narrow nose, high cheekbones, and pleasantly full lips. Her long eyelashes perfectly accented those eyes. Miss Breland was tall for a female. She had to be about five feet ten. The black skinny jeans that she wore made her legs even more impossibly lengthened. The jeans were paired with a soft gray Angora sweater that hugged her petite frame. Just before she turned to take her seat, she looked up directly into my eyes and smiled shyly. She was a beautiful creature.

After Miss Breland's entrance, I had a very hard time focusing on Mr. Crum's lecture. I was far too curious about the girl and why she had gone through so much trouble to avoid me a few days ago. The hour passed quickly as I let my mind wander. Something about the girl reminded me of Eloa. Maybe I could talk to her—she did smile today.

If I introduced myself, I could find out why she seemed to be avoiding me last week. I was still consumed with thoughts of Empyrean, Eloa, and Miss

Breland when the bell rang. I looked to see if the girl would hurry from the room again. She lingered. I gathered my things with the intention of going over to introduce myself.

"Kendi, let me introduce you to another one of my friends." Rob had made his way over to my desk.

"Sure," I responded, a little annoyed because I didn't want to miss my opportunity to speak with my latest distraction.

To my surprise, Rob led me straight to the desk of the girl. "Kendi, this is Elle Breland. Elle, this is Kendi Belling."

Wow. Now I understood the hesitation. Elle. This was the girl who interrupted the fight last month—the girl who argued with Xavier. That's why the avoidance. But why? If it had not been for her interruption, I may have died that day. The idiots didn't even realize the physical damage Yah was allowing them to inflict. She may have very well saved my life. Maybe she felt guilty because she had not hung around to help. I would let her off the hook, let her believe I didn't remember she had been there. That would be the kindest thing to do.

"Nice to meet you," I said with a grin.

Her smile widened. "Nice to meet you too, Kendi."

"Come on, guys. Let's head toward the science wing before we wind up being late. Elle is not in our physics class, but her chemistry class is in the same direction," Rob continued.

As we headed toward physics, I couldn't help but strike up a conversation with Elle.

"Elle. Is that your real name or is it short for something?" I asked because I couldn't think of anything else to say.

"Why would Elle need to be short for anything? It's a pretty common name. Unlike *Kendi*. What kind of name is that? I have never even heard it before. But to answer your question, Mr. Inquisitive, Elle is short for Sarielle, but no one calls me that."

No one until now. She didn't know it yet, but conforming was *not* in my nature. "Well, it's nice to meet you, Sarielle," I said with a grin. She rolled her eyes.

I let the comment about my name slide. I didn't want to get into the meaning behind my name, "the loved one." I chuckled to myself. That was a tremendously long story that I had never shared with anyone except Eloa. I had no reason to share it with a mortal, and I never intended to do so.

We reached the hallway for our science classes, and Sarielle turned to leave. "What are you guys doing for lunch today?" Rob asked.

"Me and my brothers talked about going to Giovanni's. Y'all want to hang out?"

"Sounds good to me. Elle, you wanna help round up the crew?"

"Sure, Rob. I'll probably need to drive separately though. See you guys later."

"See ya, Sarielle."

The corners of her mouth twitched but she didn't respond. Sarielle walked into her classroom without looking back. Rob and I headed for physics.

"Hey, Kendi!" Lesley called from the doorway of Mr. Woodard's room. She danced into the hallway to meet us as we approached.

"What am I, chopped liver?" Rob retorted.

"I was getting to it, give me a moment, dang. I was just glad to see that Kendi finally decided to rejoin us." She was grinning up at me.

"Whatever, Lesley. Glad to know you were so preoccupied by my absence. Maybe I should disappear a little more often just to keep you entertained."

"That's not it at all. I hope you're feeling better. Seriously." Lesley was having a sincere moment. I figured this would be a good time to thank her for intervening a few days ago.

"Thanks for sending Mr. Theos to break up that madness the other day," I said, lowering my voice. "I appreciate it... really."

"No problem. Someone had to act rationally. There was way too much testosterone flying around out there. You certainly didn't seem like you were going to back down."

"I wasn't." I grimaced. I didn't want to think about it—especially not heading into physics class.

"Are you okay? You know your two buddies are in there," Lesley warned.

I didn't respond. Rob noticed my hesitation.

"You all right, man?"

"Yeah, let's do this," I said as we entered the classroom.

7

CONFESSIONS

I had a decent morning and was starting to get settled into my classes. No problems out of my "buddies" except a few angry side-glances that I could easily ignore. I had told Rob and Lesley I would meet them at Giovanni's after I met up with the guys. So, after fourth period, I went to my locker to deposit my backpack. As I turned to head for the parking lot, Rick, Corey, Taylor, and several other football players were coming down the hallway heading for the lockers. Really? What was it with these damn lockers and my timing? The backpack wasn't that heavy. I could have just carried it to lunch with me. Hell, we were driving to Giovanni's. I continued walking, looking straight ahead, as I didn't want any of them to notice my irritation.

To my surprise, the football players parted so that I could pass. I reached the end of the row of lockers and was almost at the open hallway again. I exhaled a sigh of relief—a little too soon. A strong hand came down on my shoulder and spun me around into the row of lockers. The metal closures slammed into my ribs on impact, and the pain radiated through my body.

"You are becoming a pain in my ass, boy," Taylor spat as he held me pinned to the lockers. I was still trying to catch my breath, which wasn't easy with Taylor's forearm pressed against my throat.

"If I get called in by Mr. Theos one more time because of you, it's your ass."

Let it go. Just let it go. I was working on keeping a lid on my temper. But Taylor was constantly pushing me. I had to find a way to bring his "reign of terror" to an end, but now was neither the time nor the place. It would have to be soon, though.

I pushed Taylor off of me, and he slammed into the lockers on the other side of the hall. I turned and continued up the hallway headed for the parking lot. As the adrenaline wore off, the real pain came. I wished these stupid ribs would just heal already, but I guess I would have to stop being punched in them for that to happen.

The truck was parked closer to my side of the parking lot, so I reached it before the guys did. Of course, it was locked. I wanted to lie down in the backseat for just a second to stretch out the knot in my side. No luck. So, I leaned over against the rear of the truck with my head down, rubbing my side, trying to get some relief from the throbbing around my lungs.

"Kendi, what's the matter?" I didn't hear Malachi's approach. I lifted my head from my arm.

A puddle of sweat had soaked into my sleeve. I pulled my arm behind my back as I spoke. "I'm fine, Mal," I huffed.

"You're in pain. What happened?" Malachi was surveying my immediate surroundings looking for the source of the trouble.

"It's nothing. I'll be fine in a minute," I said straightening up further. Raza and Angelo were approaching, and I didn't want them worried too.

"Kendi."

"I'm fine. Really," I said nodding my head toward the twins. Malachi turned and saw Raz and Ange and decided to let it go. "You guys ready to eat? I'm starving. Let's go," I said enthusiastically as Ange unlocked the car.

Malachi eyed me carefully but didn't say anything further.

Giovanni's was a regular lunch hangout in Danvers. The place was overflowing with teenagers when we arrived. I started scanning the crowd for Rob. I didn't know who all he planned to bring with him, but I wanted to claim a section that would be big enough for all of us. Most of the students were ordering to go, so the tables were open.

"Kendi, hey." I turned to see Rob coming through the door. With him were Lesley and Sarielle.

"Hey, guys. Y'all ready to order? It's crowded in this place."

"You all go ahead. I am waiting for someone else," Sarielle replied. Interesting. I hadn't been introduced to anyone else, but oh well.

The rest of us got in line. I officially introduced Rob and Lesley to the guys. Although they had been at Danvers High for over a year, the guys didn't know very many people. They were pretty content to hang out with one another, as their focus was pending assignments. Becoming attached to the mortals that we were bound to protect was not part of the job description. Reuel's team had unjustly been labeled as subpar—the screw-ups. It hadbecome an unspoken mission of this group of Guardians to become a "by the book" crew. Malachi was desperate to regain the respect that he'd lost when his assignment was destroyed on my watch.

We grabbed a couple of tables that had enough space for the eight of us although Sarielle had not come back into the restaurant yet. Everyone seemed to be getting acquainted quickly. The guys were easy to get along with. They were especially grateful that Rob and Lesley seemed to be looking out for me when they weren't around to do it. After a few minutes, I started to wonder where Sarielle had gone. We didn't have that much time for lunch. It would be time to go soon.

"Who's Sarielle waiting for?" I asked Rob.

He and Lesley glanced at each other and Rob looked to the door.

"Ummm. I think she invited Xay. He usually hangs out with us," Rob stammered.

"Xay? Do you mean Xavier? That little punk that hangs out with Taylor? Seriously? You've got to be kidding me." I got up from the table. I had successfully avoided Xavier so far, and after my little encounter with Taylor earlier, it would be wise for Xavier to stay away from me.

"Ange, Raz, you guys ready to go?" Malachi had gotten up when I did.

"Kendi, come on. Give Xavier a chance. He's a good guy. He was just in the wrong place at the wrong time," Rob tried persuading me.

"Yeah, right. Kinda like I was? Just in the wrong place at the wrong time. A victim. Poor Xavier. It's a good thing he didn't get his ass kicked too! Huh, Rob?"

Malachi grabbed me by the arm and pulled me away from Rob.

"Come on, Kendi. Let's go."

I headed for the door, not saying anything further to Rob or Lesley. I could hear the chorus of apologies and good-byes in process behind me, but I didn't care. Outside the air was cool and crisp. I inhaled deeply, trying to calm myself, only to be reminded by my aching ribs of the reason I was angry in the first place. I grimaced, shaking my head.

The guys joined me, and we headed for the car. For a day that started on a high note, this one was deteriorating rapidly. "Kendi, where are you going?" Sarielle and Xavier were coming toward me.

Angelo unlocked the door. I hopped in the backseat and closed the door without saying a word.

My actions would speak for themselves.

My brothers had learned when to give me space to calm down. The ride back to school was tense and quiet.

Because of our abrupt departure from Giovanni's, we had plenty of time before fifth period began, so, when we got back to school, we just sat in the truck with the radio playing. I put my head back against the headrest and closed my eyes. I should try to take a nap. Maybe the detachment would finish calming me down. I thought of Eloa and Empyrean—the only two things that seemed to bring me any level of peace these days.

"Raz, Angelo…you guys need to get to class," Malachi instructed the twins. "Leave the keys with me."

"See you guys later," Angelo said, turning away.

"See ya after school," Malachi responded when I didn't.

Malachi let the silence drone on for a few minutes before he couldn't take it any longer. I heard him shifting anxiously in his seat. "Mal, don't feel like you have to sit here with me. I'm good. You can go. I'll lock the truck when I get out." I didn't open my eyes.

"Are you going to tell me what happened earlier?"

"Does it really matter at this point?" I mumbled. "I'm pretty much damned if I do and damned if I don't around here. I can't win, no matter what I do."

"You know you're not in this alone. Don't you? If I didn't care, I wouldn't ask." I opened my eyes so that I could raise an eyebrow at Malachi.

"And *why* is it that you care all of a sudden, Mal?" I had nothing to lose by asking at this point.

"It's not all of a sudden, Kendi. I admit you can be a royal pain, but I have never *not* cared. I meant it when I told Taylor to back off."

"Well, Taylor and company have other ideas about what 'backing off' entails, unfortunately," I countered.

"I knew it. What happened?"

"Let's just say locker jams and broken ribs should never mix."

Malachi sighed. "Are you okay? Are you still in pain?"

"Not too bad. It's back to a dull roar. Nothing I can't handle," I tried to reassure him.

"You shouldn't have to handle it. Sorry, man. I'll have to keep a better watch."

"For what? Seriously, I'm good."

"Kendi, look. I know you can handle yourself, but remember, Yah placed you on a team for a reason. Why do you think we were all dumped together? This is certainly not my idea of fun. We have a job to do, and the only way to accomplish our task is to do it together—whether we like it or not."

"Well, you certainly have a point there," I agreed with Malachi wholeheartedly. We *were* stuck together for the duration. We would have to make the best of our situation, and that meant learning how to get along with one another. Malachi's mother hen behavior was starting to put me at ease with our relationship.

The bell rang. Lunch was over, but neither Mal nor I moved. We both had a free period after lunch, so there was no need to rush.

"You ready to go?" Malachi asked after another few minutes. "Sure. I could use some fresh air before heading to French."

We strolled to the area behind the gym to sit. The air felt good. The campus was rather quiet except for random students here and there. It was nice to enjoy the atmosphere uninterrupted. Malachi didn't bother me. He seemed to be enjoying the quiet time as much as I was. I leaned back against the wall and closed my eyes again. I found myself doing this a lot lately. I guess it was my defense mechanism—it was the only way I could block out the negativity that always seemed to come my way. If only I could forget about my temporary banishment from Empyrean, I would be more at peace. Not likely, but I could pretend for a few minutes. I was almost asleep when the silence was broken by my name being called from some distance away.

Sarielle was crossing the lawn toward us. But where was Xavier? I didn't trust the girl now. And I especially didn't like the company she kept. I didn't see Xavier anywhere, but that didn't mean he wasn't somewhere close waiting to pounce the second I let my guard down. I was suspicious, and not in a friendly mood.

"Kendi, Malachi?" Sarielle called again.

I was still hesitant. Malachi responded. "Hey, Elle. What's going on?"

"Malachi, I would like to speak with Kendi alone. Please?" Her eyes were pleading.

Malachi looked at me, wondering if I could handle the conversation. I nodded my head slightly. I was curious as to what she could possibly want to say to me that couldn't be said in front of Mal. It's not like she knew either one of us.

"See you in seventh period, Kendi. Be careful." Malachi walked back toward the Dunn Building, leaving me alone with Sarielle. Once he was out of earshot, I turned to glare at her. Whatever she had to say to me, I was going to make her work for it.

She took Mal's place on the wall next to me and exhaled slowly as if trying to calm herself.

Interesting.

"Kendi..." She paused.

"Sarielle?"

"Why do you call me that? I told you no one calls me Sarielle. Elle is just fine." She was trying not to be exasperated with me.

"You just answered your own question," I countered.

"What?" She was confused.

"I have never considered myself a 'no one.' I'm in a different category than your other acquaintances. Therefore, I'll call you Sarielle, as I refuse to be lumped in with your usual *friends*," I sneered at her.

I was no longer feeling generous and was ready to get this over with. "Now, what is it that you want to talk about, Sarielle?"

"You certainly aren't trying to make this easy for me."

"Why should I? I'm not feeling particularly generous at the moment." I scowled. The mortal was beginning to get angry herself.

"Fine. I'll just get to it then. I want to talk about Xay."

I rolled my eyes and stood up, ready to make my departure. I was not about to listen to anything that she had to say about that little coward. I took one step, and Sarielle grabbed me by the arm.

Her grasp was firm yet soft. I could have easily pulled away from her, but I allowed her to stop me.

"Wait, Kendi. I need you to listen to me. Xavier is not the person that you think he is. You are all wrong about him. He is a good person. You just need to get to know him.

"He feels horrible about what happened to you. All he wants is the chance to make it up to you."

Are you freakin' kidding me? She expected me to stand here and let her defend Xavier? She obviously didn't know me at all. Everything in my mind told me to snatch my arm away from her and be done with this entire conversation, but something else softened my reaction.

"Look, Sarielle. I'm not trying to hurt your feelings, so please let go." She did.

"Why are you so angry with Xay, and not me? At least he tried to stay and help you. Even when I didn't want to get involved." She was looking at the ground now with much of the same expression she held the first time I had seen her. Only this time, I knew what the look was—guilt.

Really? She just threw herself under the bus for Xavier! She didn't realize that I already knew she had been there, yet she was willing to tell me just so that she could defend Xay. I was still angry, but now I was also intrigued. This was not the kind of behavior I normally observed from mortals. Stunned, I turned to face her once again.

"I knew you had some cuts and bruises, but I didn't think you were hurt so badly. I would have never told Xay to leave you out there if I had known. I am not that kind of person either. I was just protecting Xay. I didn't want him to get into any more trouble.

"He's used up all of his chances with Mr. Theos. One more thing and he is out of here. I won't allow that to happen to him. He's my brother. I was just protecting him. He makes horrible decisions. I don't know what else to say other than I am horribly sorry. Be angry with me, not Xay. He tried to do the right thing."

"Wait a minute, Xavier is your brother?" I was certainly not going to let that piece of information slide. They looked nothing alike. He was short and stocky, probably no taller than five six or five seven, and was very fair complexioned. I honestly didn't remember much else about him other than his voice, which was annoying as hell. But that may just be me.

"Yes, Xay is my brother."

Sarielle began to cry. Damn. Why did everyone have to have such strong emotions in my presence? I wanted to be angry with her. I wasn't used to anyone pleading with me on an emotional level. And one thing I certainly had not gotten used to was dealing with my own human emotions. I somehow felt bad because I was the source of her tears. What the hell?

"Then, why didn't he do the right thing?" The response was softened by my internal struggle to be nice to her.

"Because of me, Kendi. Xay was trying to do what I asked. He didn't want to upset me," she stammered.

Sarielle was trying to pull herself together. She wiped the tears that were streaming down her cheeks with the back of her hand. It was trembling. Odd. It wasn't that cold out here. She must be really upset.

"He's my foster brother. We grew up together. I'm just used to protecting him." She was biting her bottom lip as it quivered. I would have to get the whole story about her "brother" another time. She was looking away from me, trying to hide her face. Now I felt bad about upsetting her. I took her by the hand and led her back to the wall to sit down.

"I didn't mean to upset you, Sarielle." This was the closest that I had ever come to apologizing to a human in my entire existence.

"It's not you, Kendi, it's me. I'm just glad I can apologize to you. I promised myself I would if I had another chance. I was so caught off guard when you walked into Mr. Crum's English class that I couldn't even look at you. I thought for sure you would recognize me. I was scared to death. I know you must have thought that I was a complete nut job." She chuckled. "I was so upset I had to leave school for the rest of the day."

"I know the feeling," I interjected.

"You have got to believe me. I would have never made Xay leave you. I would not have left if I had known that you were hurt so badly, even though we didn't know you. We are not like that...really. I am so sorry. Please forgive me. Please forgive Xay. We didn't know. I feel awful about the entire situation. You have got to believe that." Sarielle was pleading.

This conversation was incredibly hard for her. She was having trouble sitting still and was growing more anxious. Her face was flushed, and she was sweating. She held her hands together tightly—trying to disguise the fact that they were trembling as she continued.

"It wasn't until the next day when the police came here that we found out that you were in the ICU with a collapsed lung. Xay about lost his mind. He couldn't believe that you had almost died and that he didn't help you. That he didn't try to defend you. He wanted to come forward, but Taylor..."

Sarielle hesitated and stared off in the distance. She was again trying to control her emotions by biting her quivering lower lip.

"Taylor what?" I encouraged her to continue.

"Taylor is...dangerous, Kendi."

"Dangerous?" Not that I didn't already have an inkling that the guy was a complete dirtbag.

"He's the kind of person that preys on the weak—a user. He's persuasive and manipulative. He is usually the one at the root of all the trouble but always seems to come out with his hands clean. I tried to keep Xavier away from him, but I didn't do a very good job. Something happened. He won't tell me what, but Taylor has had Xay jumping through hoops the last few months. Taylor has something on him." She was shaking her head, visibly upset.

I didn't comment. This was a lot to process all at once. I had had more than a month to formulate an opinion in my mind about Taylor, Rick, Corey, and

Xavier. Changing my mind about any of them was going to take some doing, even with Sarielle's explanation. All I could think about was the fact that I had almost lost my life at their hands for nothing more than a cover-up. No, Xavier didn't take a swing at me. He didn't hold me while the others beat me, but he also didn't help me. And to me, it was the same thing as participation.

"Kendi, let me make it up to you. Let Xavier." Sarielle was looking earnestly into my eyes. My anger was melting away.

"I won't make you any promises right now, Sarielle. But I'll try. Okay?" I smiled at her to ease the tension of the conversation. She blushed, turning away.

"Isn't your next class French?" she asked, changing the subject.

"Yes. How did you know that?"

"Mr. Dubois sort of announced your arrival last week. He was expecting you, but you've been absent until today. Lesley told me what happened. I hate that they are still giving you a hard time."

"Yeah. Me too." I laughed. "Well, it's almost that time. I need to swing by my locker first. I guess I need to head in." I stood to leave. She did as well.

Sarielle wobbled a bit as if she were off balance. She leaned against the wall briefly to steady herself. "You mind if I walk with you?"

"No, but I'll warn you. I am kinda an endangered species around here. Being seen with me is not going to get you too many cool points," I teased as we walked.

"Well, that depends on who you ask."

"Oh, really now?" I questioned, looking at her sideways. "And what exactly does that mean?"

"Trust me, Kendi. Most of the girls would have no problem hanging out with 'your species.'" I laughed and thought of Lesley's reaction last week. I guess I would seem attractive to the female mortals. It wasn't like any of us were unappealing. Not sure if that was even possible. Angels were all created with a certain unique beauty. I never thought about it before because my choice was to dwell among my own kind. I'd never considered what a human might think of my looks.

Like I had done with Lesley, I decided to flirt. I wanted to see Sarielle's reaction. I was considerably more interested in how she would respond than Lesley.

"Most girls, huh? Does that include you?"

"I think you'll find that I am not, nor ever will be, 'most girls,' Kendi." She was smug.

Interesting. Didn't teenage girls want to be identified with everyone else? Humans had an innate need to be wanted—to belong to a larger group. Not many of them enjoyed being singled out, unlike the angelic Host. We don't care much about being needed or about belonging but about being recognized for our worth—our essence. This is the reason why becoming a Shade is such a tragedy in our world. Losing our essence is the loss of identity, of a persona— it is everything.

"And what makes you so different, Ms. Breland?" I asked with a raised eyebrow.

"Wouldn't you like to know?" she said with a smirk.

"Is that a challenge?"

"Perhaps."

Yes, Sarielle was interesting. She didn't know it yet, but I loved a good challenge. We walked the rest of the way in silence. No doubt sizing each other up—at least that was what I was doing.

We entered the classroom as the first bell rang. Xavier was in this class. Sarielle hadn't told me. She was probably afraid of my reaction. She went to sit in the seat beside him as I went to speak with Mr. Dubois. I had not been in this class before, so I had to take care of the preliminary junk. Mr. Dubois handed me the syllabus and my book. There were several open seats. One was on the other side of Sarielle. For two reasons, I went to the opposite side of the classroom. One, I didn't want to seem too anxious to get to know her, and second, I didn't want to test my tolerance of Xavier just yet.

As I settled into my seat, Mr. Dubois began firing questions at me in French. "Kendi, combien d'ans de français vous a pris?"

"Plusieurs ans, monsieur. Je parle français facilement," I responded.

"Excellent. Votre partenaire sera Sarielle. Elle est aussi couramment. Elle a besoin de plus d'un défi."

Even more interesting, Sarielle was fluent in French. Apparently, no one else in the class was enough of a challenge to be her partner. The upcoming weeks were to include in class exercises using assigned prompts to create real time dialogue with the other person. This would give me a convenient excuse to question her further. Why would she be fluent in French? I, on the other hand, was fluent in all of Earth's languages. We had to be able to communicate on every continent, although I couldn't explain it to Sarielle this way. I would have to come up with something before she asked.

I turned to see Sarielle's reaction to Mr. Dubois's announcement. She was just as curious as I was. We smiled at one another. This class should be fun. Some of the other students were watching our interaction in confusion—including Xavier. My guess was that the rest of the class was either at the beginner or intermediate levels. This could prove to be very accommodating.

The class went by quickly while I considered the possibilities. When the bell rang, all I could think of was the fact that I only had to make it through one more class before this long day would come to an end. Being human was both mentally and physically exhausting. My seventh-period class was local history with Sylvia Trapolis. She was a favorite among the students at Danvers, and many requested her class, I was told. This would be the only class that Malachi and I would share this year.

"Kendi, quel est votre prochaine classe?" Sarielle had come over to my desk. Was she playing along?

"Ma prochaine classe est l'Histoire Locale avec Mme Trapolis," I responded with a wink. Yes, this was going to be extremely fun.

"Vraiment? M'aussi." Sarielle grinned back at me. She had the same class I did. Xavier was cautiously approaching.

"Elle, do you want me to wait for you? I can't be late again. Ms. Trap will kill me." Damn. My enthusiasm went straight out of the window—two classes in a row? Really? "Ah, hey, Kendi," Xavier stammered awkwardly. For Sarielle's sake, I decided to be nice. I nodded in his direction to acknowledge his greeting.

"See you in class," I directed at Sarielle as I walked out of the room.

Malachi met me at the door of the local history classroom. He saw Sarielle and Xavier close behind.

"You okay?"

"Yeah, fine."

"Good. Come on, let me introduce you to Ms. Trapolis."

I followed Mal into the room where he introduced me to a statuesque woman with short, curly black hair and a warm, friendly smile. She welcomed me to the class and encouraged me to get the notes I had missed from my brother. As the class filled up, I was surprised that the whole gang seemed to be in attendance. Rob, Lesley, Sarielle, and Xavier had all filed in after me. I took the empty seat next to Malachi and got ready for class to begin. I consciously ignored the fact that Taylor's zoo crew was in this class as well. It was going to be bittersweet; the last class of the day, but also the class that I would have to exercise the most patience. The good thing was that Malachi was here with me. At least he wouldn't allow me to do anything too stupid.

Taylor walked in just as the bell rang. He glowered at me for a second and then thought better of it when he remembered Malachi to my right. I settled back in my seat and didn't even try to rearrange the smug grin that had spread wide across my face. Ms. Trap launched into a tale about Old Salem, and for the first time today I was at ease amid my troubles.

Yeah, I was deeply thankful for Mal's presence in this class.

8
DITCH DAY

After a couple of weeks, I had adjusted well to my high school routine. The classes were not much of a challenge, but I pretended to be enlightened in each one. We had a normal group that consistently hung out together, which included Rob, Lesley, Sarielle, and, unfortunately, Xavier. The guys tolerated him well enough. They seemed to have forgiven him for his part in the fight. I was not so generous. Although Xavier had gotten up the courage to speak to me on occasion, my response to him was little above tolerance. I wouldn't give him the opportunity to talk about how sorry he was, or why he didn't try to stop the fight. I didn't want to hear it. At this point, it was over. Unfortunately for Xavier, first impressions were lasting impressions.

Reuel constantly pointed out how quickly I had settled into school—apart from the few minor incidences the first week. He was glad that I was "trying" after putting up such resistance. I was just too exhausted to continue fighting with everybody. I had enough issues with Taylor and his cohorts to be unyielding to those who were only trying to befriend me. I had gotten used to the mortals that I allowed in my inner circle. Reuel didn't miss this either. He frequently questioned me about Rob, Lesley, Sarielle, and even Xavier. I would just shrug him off. I wouldn't justify my actions for every little allowance. I had different levels of tolerance for certain mortals. No more, no less. I didn't want Reuel to read anything else into it.

He constantly mentioned the relationship between Malachi and me, noting that we seemed to be getting along better. I was starting to feel like he was keeping a report card on me. Hell, this wasn't preschool. I didn't need daily reminders about my progress and my behavior. Most of all, it pissed me off because I felt like I was becoming predictable. Predictability wasn't me, ever. I was used to mixing things up, not complying.

To make matters worse, Malachi was making good on his promise to "keep a better watch" at school. It was becoming suffocating. Taylor and his friends hadn't been within a hundred feet of me in more than a week even though Mal and I only shared one class. I couldn't figure out how he was doing it. He would show up at just the right time or appear around the corner at the precise moment a confrontation seemed likely. The only good thing about it was, I was feeling significantly better—physically. Not getting punched or slammed into things was certainly helping my ribs heal more efficiently. However, Malachi's extra awareness was bothering me more every day. Had Yah given him access to my thoughts? Reuel assured me that this was not the case, and he didn't have a reason to lie to me, yet his assurances gave me little peace of mind.

I wasn't quite sure what to make of the relationship Malachi and I shared anymore. I no longer had a way of defining it. At least when our relationship was strained, I knew where I stood. I knew to steer clear of him. But now, he was becoming like a mother hen—overly protective. He would become illogically irate whenever it seemed as though I was putting myself unnecessarily in harm's way. His behavior had swung so drastically that it appeared that the boy had developed an alter ego of some sort. I'd given up on trying to figure Malachi out and decided to deal with it as part of his *new* personality.

Reuel was always the mature voice—continually reminding me that ignoring the elephant in the room would not make it go away. But I was not about to shake things up just when they had gotten settled. We seemed to be coexisting well, so why disturb the fragile balance—even if it was weird. Malachi didn't bring it up, and of course, I didn't either.

The latest excitement at school was senior "ditch day." As I understood it, it was a Danvers High tradition. It was the next day, but I had not heard what the plans were for the afternoon. Of course, I only talked about this when my brothers weren't around—especially Malachi. He would be completely opposed to any kind of activity that could lead to trouble. I, on the other hand, thought the idea was completely alluring. But I strongly advised the gang not to bring up any plans around my brothers if they expected me to be able to escape with them. School had become ordinary and boring. I was looking forward to ditch day spicing things up a bit.

"Hey, good-lookin'." I knew it was Lesley without turning around.

"Hey, Les. What's going on?"

"Not much. I think we've decided what to do for ditch day." She was giddily excited.

"Well, what is it? Hurry and tell me before we get to the cafeteria. I don't want to fight with Malachi about this."

"Still chicken about telling him you plan to ditch, huh?"

"Shut up, Lesley. Fear has nothing to do with it. What Mal doesn't know, he can't harass me about." Or do his damndest to prevent. "Got it? So, spill. Now."

"You can be such a grouch, Kendi Belling." She was all about the teasing today.

"Lesley."

"Okay, okay. Tomorrow is supposed to be unseasonably warm. So, we decided swimming would be a good idea."

"Swimming? We're gonna ditch to go swimming? That's just stupid. What pool is still open this late in the year?"

"I never said anything about a pool." Lesley had a huge grin spread across her face. "Give us a little credit for originality."

I was intrigued. I looked down at her curiously and waited for an explanation.

"There's a tradition to sneak into the Danvers Reservoir through one of the neighborhoods that backs up to the woods. There's a pump station on that end that makes for good diving. It will still be cold for swimming, and there is a bit of a current near the pump station, but hey, what's life without a few challenges? You in?"

"Well, it definitely sounds interesting. Is everyone else in?" I was curious who all had agreed to the plan thus far. It did sound a little crazy.

"Yep. You are the only one that I hadn't spoken to yet. It's like planning mission impossible to catch you without one of your brothers watching. Do they have a LoJack on you or something?"

"They just might," I responded, shaking my head. "So, are you in?"

I hesitated. While I certainly wanted to be *in*, I still had to figure out how to get away from Malachi. Everyone was ditching after lunch, but Mal and I had a free period together immediately after. There was no way he was going to stand by and let me take part in this event. A bunch of teenagers horsing around without proper supervision—in addition to illegal activity that included trespassing.

"I'll let you know in the morning."

"Aw, Kendi, come on," Lesley was pleading.

"Later," I threw in her direction walking away from her. We were entering the cafeteria, and my brothers were already there. The day was rainy, so the cafeteria was unusually crowded. Of course, Malachi was looking for me and noticed my abrupt retreat from Lesley. He was staring after her suspiciously.

"Everything okay?" Malachi inquired as I took my seat.

"Yeah. Fine. Why?"

"What's up with Lesley? You look like you were trying to get away from her."

"Aren't I always trying to get away from Lesley? She irritates the hell out of me. Today is no different. Lesley is being Lesley." I dismissed his question with a roll of my eyes. Malachi let it go.

We were at the table alone while everyone else gathered their lunches. This happened to be one of the days Renay was feeling overly generous and packed lunches for us. She knew the weather would be bad and was trying to spare us from another day of mediocre cafeteria food. Malachi leaned in to get our attention as he lowered his voice.

"Reuel needs us home right after school, something's up. He wouldn't tell me what it was, just that we needed to meet."

"That doesn't sound good," Raza commented.

"Well, let's not read more into it than we need to," Angelo reassured us. "Reuel would have gathered us immediately if it were that serious."

"Good point," Malachi added. "I just wanted to make sure that you all didn't scatter after school. Let's get to the truck and head home so that we can find out what is going on. All right?"

"Sure thing," I replied.

I knew Malachi was directing the "don't get scattered" comment toward me. I was the only one that went missing after school at times. There were several occasions in the last few weeks when I just needed time alone. I would opt to walk home so that I could stop off at Goodies, enjoy some tea and quiet time, and daydream about the season when I would finally be able to return to Empyrean. Not that I would partake in this indulgence today—it was raining—but I figure Mal just wanted to be certain that I would be in place for our first official team meeting.

When we arrived home, Reuel was in the living room waiting for us. He looked worried.

"Hey there, guys. Come on in and have a seat." He motioned for us as we entered the room.

"What's going on, Reuel? Is everything okay?" Malachi questioned.

"Well, I'm not completely sure yet. I needed to let you all know that the team is now on high alert until further notice."

My heart sank. High alert could only mean one thing—increased Dominion activity in our region, in Charon.

"Don't panic, Kendi. This is only an alert status, for now, not a warning. We just need to be more aware, that's all," Reuel responded after hearing my thoughts.

"Are you at liberty to share any details with us? What's happened?" Raza asked.

Reuel nervously scrubbed his hands through his hair. It seemed as if he were deliberating what information he should share. Not that he wanted us in the dark but because he wouldn't want us to carry the burden of worry. He would take that albatross upon himself.

Yes, he was the leader of our team, but Reuel had truly stepped into the father/protector role for all of us. This was a covering for which I was certainly grateful.

Reuel let out a heavy sigh.

"Kendi, your conclusion is accurate. There has been a significant increase in Dominion activity in our region over the last couple of weeks. We've been keeping an eye on the situation, but unfortunately, the problem seems to have escalated—not only have the Dominion increased in number, but Azrael has been sighted."

Azrael was a high-ranking member of the Legion forces—second in command only to Abbadon. This kind of strategic alignment was never put in place unless the Legion was planning to mount an attack of some kind.

Fear rose in the pit of my stomach. What did this mean? Full-scale battle was one of the things that I had avoided in my Guardian role. Of course, I'd had the same training that the entire Guardian received. We were trained by the best—the Thrones. I had been told that I had a natural proclivity for battle, but I certainly wasn't trying to test that theory any time soon.

"We need to be prepared for every eventuality, Kendi—including a full-scale battle," Reuel again answered my unspoken turmoil.

Full-scale battle. Were we ready for that as a team? Were we strong enough to stand against the Dominion alone? Reuel and Malachi were the only ones with actual battle experience of any kind, although, I have always been told that battle skills would come naturally when I needed them. I had no trust in myself—especially not after my recent pulverizing at the hands of mere mortals.

"Don't worry. We will be prepared to handle whatever comes. The Guardian is mounting forces of our own. We will not have to do this alone," Reuel assured us.

The aura of the room shifted somberly. The team was now in business-mode and trying to gather as much information as possible before Reuel shut us down.

"Who's coming to help?" Angelo wanted to know.

"When I left early a few days ago, it was in response to the Azrael sighting. I joined Uriel and his team to take him down, but we were not successful. Azrael is a strong, powerful being. The Thrones trained us, but Azrael *was* a Throne. Bringing him down will not be easy. More importantly, we need to find out why he is here."

"Uriel is here? Reuel, this has the potential to be explosive." I could hear the concern in Malachi's voice.

Uriel was the only other senior Guardian in the Earth realm that had a team. His team was rather large, always consisting of twelve direct members, and then those extensions that reported to him but were not considered members of the team—like Malachi had been. These extensions were in a sense auditioning for one of the twelve coveted positions on the most prestigious team the Guardian had ever assembled. These were the heavy hitters—the big guns. They were the Navy Seals of the Guardian forces. This was the opportunity that Malachi had lost when he was demoted as the result of my first debacle.

The last I heard, Uriel's team had been assembled in the Teshukah Region in Europe. For him and his team to have moved, something serious was about to go down here in Charon. It would be up to the Guardian to find out what it was and to defend as we were trained.

"Yes. Uriel, his team, and the extensions have all moved into the region and are ready to be engaged at a moment's notice," Reuel answered Malachi's question.

Malachi was staring intensely at Reuel. I assumed they were having a separate conversation. My suspicion was confirmed when both Raz and Ange looked to Reuel simultaneously. Reuel shook his head ever so slightly. I was being left out of this part of the conversation, and it made me even more nervous, but I pretended not to notice the silent colloquy.

The somber atmosphere made me feel like we were lamenting a death or something.

I decided to try to lighten the mood.

"Hey, Uriel is here to save the day. No worries, right?" I threw a wink at Reuel and tried to smile.

Reuel knew what I was attempting to do and chuckled in response. "Yes. The cavalry has arrived."

The conversation was effectively ended as Renay came in with grocery bags to begin preparing dinner.

By the next morning, the discussion of the previous evening seemed to have been filed away. Yes, we had a job to do, and by all estimations, that job would be intensified in short order, but we also had an appearance to uphold. So, we were back to business as usual. The ride to school was upbeat and lighthearted as it was just about every morning. I got the feeling Malachi was doing just what I had tried to do last night, protect the twins. It had become a natural mechanism for me to shield them from things that may worry them. It seemed almost criminal to shatter such innocence.

We said our goodbyes in the parking lot, and the twins headed to their side of campus. It wasn't until they were gone that I could see the mask lift from Malachi's face, and the genuine uneasiness of our current situation show through.

As we approached the Dunn Building, Malachi grabbed me by the arm to slow my pace. I stopped and turned to him.

"Kendi, keep your eyes and ears open today. Be careful," he said earnestly. "Time to step it up. When the Dominion gathers, not only are we at risk but so is everything that we are bound to protect. I know Reuel went along with minimizing the risk, but you and I both know it was for the twins' benefit."

"I figured. What was with the silent conversation between you, Reuel, and the twins last night?"

Malachi looked away, debating. After a few seconds of silence, I let him off the hook. "Never mind, Mal. I was just curious," I said with a shrug.

"Just be careful. Okay?"

"Don't worry, I will." I punched his arm, laughing. "You aren't afraid of

Azrael, are you?" I was trying to pull Mal out of this slump, but he remained focused.

"A healthy dose of fear may be just what you need."

"Point well taken. See you at lunch."

I walked away from him before he could say anything else. I knew the situation was serious but continuing to dwell on the difficult could be exasperating. I would deal with whatever when it came. I headed off to English, trying not to think about the meeting with Reuel. I didn't want to contemplate an impending confrontation with the Legion forces.

I walked across the lawn behind the gym, taking a shortcut to the side of the building where my English class was held. It was so nice outside; I decided to sit on the wall and enjoy the sun for a few minutes before going in. I wasn't ready to surrender my freedom just yet.

I couldn't help but wonder about the silent conversation from the previous evening. If we all had to be at the top of our game right now, why would the team withhold information from me? What benefit could it be to the team or me if I was kept in the dark regarding what we were about to face? I didn't understand, and it bothered me more than I wanted Malachi to know.

"Hey, Kendi, what are you doing out here?"

I looked up to see Sarielle coming toward me. There was a light breeze. Her sandy hair was blowing back from her face, accentuating her hazel-green eyes and the dimples that were revealed by her smile. I didn't want to be bothered, but I smiled in response—involuntarily. It was weird.

"Good morning, Sarielle."

"Are you okay? You look worried. More trouble with Malachi?" she said, putting a hand on my shoulder and taking a seat next to me.

"You got all of that just from my 'good morning'?" I said sarcastically, looking at her. I got defensive at her mention of Malachi. My relationship with Mal was no one's business but our own.

"Not really...just guessing. I figured whatever was on your mind was not about Taylor because you didn't look angry. You look concerned, not enraged." She laughed.

Sarielle was very perceptive for a human. I wasn't quite sure how this made me feel, though. It certainly piqued my curiosity. She seemed to know me well quickly. What bothered me more was why did I care? I was always unnecessarily honest with her.

"Yeah. I was just thinking about a conversation that I had with my father and brothers last night. That's all."

"You want to talk about it? Everything okay?" Sarielle pushed. What could I say?

Well, I just found out that we are in the middle of an invasion of demons—hellbent on the destruction of mankind—and by the way, I'm not really human but an angel, a Guardian, sentenced to Earth to protect the mortals I hate. And if I fail this time, it's my ass. That's all.

"Naah. Nothing major, just family stuff." I shrugged nonchalantly.

"You ditching today? That should take your mind off whatever is bothering you."

With the events of last evening, I had completely forgotten about ditch day. At this point, it would probably be next to impossible to get away from Malachi to participate in this little soiree.

"I don't think so. It's probably not worth the trouble," I said, shaking my head.

"Your brothers?"

"Pretty much." I got up from the wall. "Come on. Let's get to class before we're late."

We started into the building. Without breaking her stride, Sarielle grabbed my hand and entwined her fingers with mine. She said nothing to explain her action. Was she waiting for my reaction? Her touch startled me. I didn't know how I should respond, so I just went with it. Although the morning air was chilly, her hand was warm, and her skin soft. Holding her hand was somewhat pleasant. We walked in silence for a few moments. When Sarielle realized that I would not drop her hand, she wound her fingers just a little bit tighter.

"Kendi, please don't take this the wrong way, but you seem unhappy—a lot. Like you have the weight of the world on your shoulders."

"You have no idea," I mumbled.

"If you ever need someone to talk to, I'm here."

I stopped walking so that I could look at her. She was staring at the ground as if embarrassed. "Sarielle, you barely know me."

"What I know is that you try to act like you're this big tough guy, but underneath, I think you're...miserable."

Again, her level of perception shocked me. I thought I was putting on a good mask, especially here recently. I said nothing but began to walk again. We continued in silence until we got to the door of the building. She gently untangled our hands just as I opened the door. I wasn't ready to let go, as I found her touch comforting somehow. But I didn't protest.

The entire morning crawled at a snail's pace. I just wanted to be at home, in my room, where I could forget about everything going on, even if for only a few hours. Lesley was harassing me every time she saw me about not accompanying the crew to the reservoir. Earlier in the week, I was looking forward to it. I was only hesitant to say yes because I was trying to figure out a way around Malachi. But now, it seemed minuscule compared to everything else. Human entertainment was at the very bottom of my to-do list.

When I walked into the cafeteria for lunch, the first thing I noticed was Raza and Angelo sitting at a table with Lesley, Rob, Sarielle, and Xavier. Malachi was missing. I approached the table cautiously. Something was wrong.

"Hey, guys," I said, taking a seat. "Where's Mal?"

"Uh, he wasn't feeling well. Dad came and got him about an hour ago." Raz glanced at Angelo. My heart sank. There was no way Malachi could be sick. It was an impossibility. I was the only one that had to put up with that kind of human nonsense. And since I had recovered from the fight, I hadn't known any real sickness either. Yah hadn't gone that far.

If Mal was with Reuel, something had happened with the Dominion, and the situation was too large for Reuel to handle alone. As I lamented the probability, Lesley began kicking me under the table. I looked up into her excited eyes and the huge grin on her face. I could read her exuberance easily. No Malachi meant that I could sneak away for ditch day after all. The twins would never know. I could be back by the time school was out. Hell, at this point I might as well. I wouldn't be able to concentrate the rest of the day in classes anyway—knowing something was going on. No Malachi also meant Taylor would be free to start his crap too. Today would certainly be the wrong day. Distance from the school for the afternoon could be a good thing. So why not? I nodded slightly at Lesley, and her grin got even wider. I laughed despite my bad mood.

Even with the sun shining and the weather unusually warm, the cafeteria was packed. After further examination, I realized the crowd was mostly seniors. Hilarious. This must have been the designated rendezvous spot for ditch day—the place to pull together last-minute plans before heading out. The twins seemed out of place. I prayed they wouldn't notice. But I quickly pushed the thought aside since they always hung out with the upperclassmen because of Malachi and me.

Now was not the time to panic and attract suspicion. All I had to do was make it through lunch and send the twins on their way to fifth period, and I would be free to do as I chose.

When the bell finally rang, I rose to walk the twins outside. I wanted to know what was going on but had to get out of earshot of the mortals first.

"Do you guys know what's going on?" I asked, turning to Raz. "What happened?"

"Not really sure. I'll bet it had something to do with Azrael and Abbadon, though."

"If there is going to be a battle, Reuel is doing his best to keep it as far from Danvers as possible. They are attempting to push the Legion back. There must be something here the Dominion is looking to acquire. Reuel and Uriel are trying to find out what it is and why they want it," Angelo explained.

"It must be big for the Legion to take such a risk. If we wind up in a full-scale battle, both sides are certain to suffer loss." Raz shook his head.

"What could possibly make them take such a gamble?" I wanted to know.

"That's what we must find out," Angelo responded in a quiet voice. "Will you be okay for the remainder of the day with Mal gone?"

"Sure, I'll be fine. No worries." I brushed off Angelo's inquiry as casually as I could without giving them reason to be suspicious.

"All right, we'll see you after school then. We'll have to wait until then to find out what's going on anyway. Come on, Ange. Let's get to class."

With that, the twins headed for their fifth-period classes, and I was finally free to do what I wanted...at least until I had to be back in the parking lot before they could catch on to anything.

Back in the cafeteria, the crew was waiting anxiously to see if I would be able to leave campus after all.

"The prison door been sprung?" Lesley sang sarcastically as I entered the cafeteria.

"If you're going to be a pain in my ass for the rest of the afternoon, I'll take my chances with Taylor and his hood rats."

"Don't worry, man, we'll make Lesley behave." Rob laughed, putting his hands over Lesley's mouth as if to gag her. She pushed him away, frowning.

"Come on, guys. Let's get out of here and go have some fun," Sarielle pushed from the table.

"Sounds good to me." I went to her side before Xavier could claim the spot.

"Who's driving?"

I didn't want to push it by asking for the keys to the truck. Though I could drive, I rarely did. I had gotten a little spoiled being chauffeured around.

"I'm driving. Let's go, people," Rob responded, throwing a glance over his shoulder. Sarielle and I were a little more relaxed than the others since we were on a free period.

We all headed for the parking lot and loaded into Rob's truck. I grabbed the backseat with Lesley and Sarielle. I don't think Xavier trusted my calm enough to be that close to me. Smart kid. We turned out of the parking lot and headed toward the neighborhoods around Reservoir Drive.

"All right, somebody explain to the neophyte what's about to go down," Rob called from the front seat.

"Yeah, what's the deal with sneaking in through the subdivision anyway?" I directed towards Lesley.

"The Folly Hill subdivision overlooks the reservoir, but it's one of the ritzier neighborhoods in the area. The residents don't particularly like teenagers running through their backyards, especially since we are not supposed to swim out there anyway."

"Fishing is allowed, but not swimming," Sarielle added.

"Why is that?" I wanted to know.

"Well, the only real access that is kinda suitable for swimming is near the pump station," Rob threw in.

"So?"

"There's a strong current. After a couple of kids drowned, swimming was banned," Xavier explained, though he didn't turn to speak directly to me.

"Got it. Folly Hill's the shortcut. What's the long way in?"

"We could go in from Locust Street, but it's about a mile hike to get to the side of the reservoir where we can dive from the pump station."

"And?"

"It's through the woods, Kendi!" Lesley bellowed at me.

"I don't see what the problem is. What...with all that mouth, are you afraid of the woods? I thought you all were looking for some fun?"

"I'm in if the girls are," Rob laughed from the front of the car.

"Me too," Xavier added.

"No, I'm not afraid. I just don't like the woods!" Lesley spat at me.

"That's your story, and you're sticking to it, right, Les." Rob was cracking up now.

"Sounds like there's a story behind this. Do tell, Robert, my friend."

I was far too amused not to indulge in this entertainment at Lesley's expense.

Rob and Xavier were laughing so hard they were in tears. Sarielle was attempting to be supportive but was having a hard time keeping a straight face. Lesley was scowling out the window, trying to ignore the lot of us.

"C'mon. Somebody tell me!"

"Let's just say it involved a dog, a tree, and a skunk. Let your imagination fly!" Xavier was doubled over in his seat gasping to catch his breath through the howls of laughter.

"Shut the hell up, Xay! Why did you even bother to come? You swim like a rock." Lesley was truly angry now.

"Someone has to be the lookout for you water-loving idiots," Xavier said, wiping his face. "All right, guys. Leave Lesley alone. It's not her fault that she is equally hated by dogs and skunks alike." A giggle burst through Sarielle's lips, as she threw her arm over Lesley's shoulder. Lesley pushed her away, folding her arms across her chest and pouting like a five-year-old.

"Lesley spent a week bathing in tomato juice. She smelled like she wanted to be alone! And her mom still made her come to school!" Xavier roared.

"I would have ditched the entire week," Sarielle added.

"I do believe that's enough fun at my expense." Lesley rolled her eyes.

"What's the matter, Les? You can dish it but not take it?" I winked at her, successfully turning her pout into a grin. She stuck her tongue out at me.

"All right, guys—woods or Folly Hill? The turn is coming up."

"I still say woods." I turned away from Lesley's glare.

"C'mon, guys, where's your sense of adventure?"

"I'm definitely in." Xavier smiled. He would do anything to try to get on my good side.

Whatever. "Rob?"

"I'm down for whatever. It's the ladies that you need to be trying to convince, Kendi."

Sarielle was closest to me. I thought I could convince her easily enough if it weren't for Lesley's aversion to the new plan. But now, this could take some doing. I wished now that I would have taken the middle seat. I could have been quite a bit more persuasive if I had equal placement with both girls. I decided to start with the farthest and the hardest challenge.

"C'mon, Lesley. Don't tell me you dragged me out here just to back down on the real fun. There are three guys here. You think we would let anything bad happen to you? The five of us will stick together. You can't tell me you're scared."

"I'm not scared. I just don't like the woods," Lesley repeated. "But I'll go if Elle will." Lesley's words weren't particularly convincing. Sarielle glanced cautiously at her friend.

Sarielle would easily cave and take the blame for the group going the route of Folly Hill. I stepped in quickly, turning to Sarielle and looking her straight in the eyes.

"Sarielle, surely you wouldn't want to deprive me of the opportunity to fully experience my first ditch day, would you? This could have the potential to scar me for the rest of my young life. This is a once-in-a-lifetime experience. You wouldn't want to single-handedly ruin my adventure, now would you? You couldn't possibly do that to me."

The guys were very amused. Lesley was rolling her eyes in aggravation. "Laying it on a little thick, aren't you, Kendi?"

I didn't respond, but laid my head on her shoulder, took her hand, and looked deeper into her eyes.

"You couldn't break such a tender, fragile spirit... could you?"

"You're quite pathetic, Kendi Belling." She smiled. I winked at her. "Let's hit the woods, guys."

"Yes," I hissed in victory.

The guys chuckled in agreement. Lesley sighed quietly. Rob did a U-turn to head back the way we had come.

After a couple of minutes, we pulled onto the side of the road and eased onto what seemed to be a narrow gravel parking pad. There was a small pickup truck backed into the space with a large trailer hitch probably used to pull a boat. We unloaded and grabbed our backpacks for the short hike.

Lesley was right. The day turned out to be tremendously nice. The sun was high in the sky, and it was quite warm for mid-fall. The air was still—which was strange for this time of the year. There was usually some type of breeze even when the sun was shining. No breeze was probably a good thing, especially if we were going to get in the water later.

"You guys ready?" Rob called over his shoulder as he headed to the trees.

"Sure thing. Who knows where they're going? I am not up for being lost in the woods." I laughed and then glanced at Lesley, who was still standing next to the truck. She looked as if she were debating staying there until we returned. Xavier and Sarielle were already joining Rob. I turned back to get Lesley.

"Les, you aren't seriously scared, are you? Come on. I'm not sure what happened the last time, but I promise I won't let anything happen to you today."

She didn't look very convinced. Lesley stood rigidly with her hands balled into little fists, staring at the ground. I went to stand next to her.

"Look at me." When she didn't move, I put my hand under her chin and raised her head. She nervously looked away from me, avoiding my eyes, so I gently pulled her chin around forcing her to look at me.

"Les, I got you. Promise." I smiled, and it seemed to loosen her up a bit, although she was still hesitant.

"Kendi."

"I know." I smiled again to reassure her and took her hand. I was still not very well versed in human emotion, but the one look that I had successfully mastered was fear.

Lesley was scared to death.

"Let's catch up with the others. I'll be right here."

Yes, Lesley was annoying, but over the last few weeks, she had proven to be a friend. I didn't mind looking out for her because she had already done the same for me on more than one occasion.

Everything would be fine. What's the worst that could happen?

9

Reservoir Dogs

When we entered the woods, it was as if someone had turned off a light switch. The thick cover of the trees effectively blocked out most of the sunlight. My eyes had to readjust. From the top of the hill, I could see the vast lake that stretched out across the reservoir. But there was an enormous expanse of trees separating us from the water's edge. I took a few steps forward with Lesley in tow and then stumbled as the ground immediately slanted downward.

"Hey, you guys...wait for us," I called to Rob.

The forest was like another world. The air cool and damp. The ground was squishy—covered with lots of grass and moss which made for slippery footing. Lesley was now clinging to my arm instead of my hand just to stay upright.

"You okay?"

"Un huh." Lesley pulled closer to my side.

We caught up with the others. After about five hundred feet or so, the ground began to even out, though it never completely flattened. To make matters worse, it was full of divots, just large enough for a foot. The last thing I needed was a sprained ankle to try to explain to Reuel. The ground was also laden with roots and vines. I was having a hard time not tripping and taking Lesley down with me. Not breaking my neck was the goal; however, it was greatly encumbered by Lesley hanging onto my arm for dear life.

There was a small path worn into the woods that was barely a foot across. Though it was clearly visible, it was difficult to navigate. The route did not seem to bother Rob or the others. My guess was that teenagers frequented this route getting to the pump house. They were used to it. I was a little uncomfortable with the sky completely obscured. It messed with my senses. It was too quiet and too dark. No one spoke but concentrated on plowing through the trees to our intended destination.

Suddenly, Lesley stopped and stiffened at my side, dropping my arm. I turned to see what was wrong. Lesley's eyes were wide, her face ashen.

"Lesley, what's the matter?"

Her lips started to tremble, but she said nothing.

"Lesley!" I shook her, trying to get a response, and she turned to me. "D–d–don't you hear that?"

I listened for any sound coming from the darkness. And then I heard what had frightened her, the low growl of what could only be a dog of some kind. The sound was coming from behind us. I called to the others, who were about fifty feet ahead.

"Guys! There's a dog out here! We need to move it!"

Rob spun around and saw Lesley petrified at my side and ran back to assist.

"Lesley, sweetie, you have got to move. We are right here, but you've got to run," Rob pleaded with her.

I took one hand, and Rob took the other, and we began pulling Lesley along. She moved slowly—almost zombielike. Was she really that afraid of dogs?

The growling was getting louder. The growls were coupled with intermittent snarls and angressive barking. The animal was in persuit. I would be a lot more comfortable on top of the pump station just in case this dog was as angry as it sounded. I didn't want Lesley any more freaked out than she already was. We pulled harder, and Lesley began to run alongside us. I motioned to Rob to pull ahead so that I could get his back. If the dog did appear, I wanted there to be something in between it and Lesley. I had promised that I wouldn't let anything happen to her, and I wanted to keep my word. Rob turned when I fell farther back.

"Go! Sounds like the dog's coming up fast."

I could hear the paws of the animal as they struck the ground in pursuit. I stopped and turned to the trees, waiting for the attack. I wanted to see its approach rather than have the animal attack me from behind. I quickly searched the ground for a weapon and found a large stick lying at the foot of a tree.

As I leaned in to grab the small branch, the red glowing eyes of the dog appeared. It was snarling with fangs bared. The dog was large, black, and horribly mangy; this was not a pet of any kind. Since when were there wild dogs in Danvers? And what in the world was wrong with its eyes?

I grabbed the stick and turned to face the dog just as it lunged for me. I used the crude weapon to knock the dog to the ground mid-leap. It yelped loudly, but rolled over, got up, and came again. This was no ordinary dog. Something was off. The animal was far too aggressive. It was hunting. The dog leaped again. This time, the force of it knocked me to the ground. The thing was huge.

I grabbed the animal at the sides of its neck, trying to hold it off as it went for my throat. I used all my strength to push it away and jumped to my feet again. However, the stick was no longer in reach without having to turn away from the dog to retrieve it. The animal circled in front of me as I backed up against the wall of trees. I was trapped.

Just then, the still forest came alive with a gentle breeze. In the distance, I could have sworn I heard what sounded like a wind chime, but the growling of a second dog quickly interrupted my thoughts. Out of nowhere, a huge brown dog leaped into the small clearing where I stood.

What the hell?

I'm not sure which creature was more shocked—my attacker or me. The black dog immediately turned from me to break ass on the new intruder. I didn't hesitate to use the distraction to make my escape. I spun and sprinted down the path toward the others.

As I fled, I could hear the snarls and yelps as the dogs ripped away at one another. Then I heard the pursuit once again. I turned just in time to see the black dog lunging for my back. Though I tried to push myself faster, the dog caught me by the leg of my jeans. I went sprawling to the ground, kicking at the dog as it readjusted its grip, this time into my calf.

"Awwwwh...shit!"

I kicked at the animal with my free leg, trying to get away. At that moment, the brown dog emerged once again from the forest—teeth bared and ready for battle. I was released from the animal's grip and scurried to my feet. I could feel the blood running down my leg.

"Kendi!" I spun around to see Xavier running toward me. "Damn." He stopped short, eyes wide as he saw the hostile dogs.

"Go, go, go!" I hissed, limping toward him. Xavier glanced down at my leg, threw my arm over his shoulder, and pulled me down the path toward the rest of our group.

Thankfully, we were not far from the pump house. The rest of the crew was already safely on top. I nervously glanced over my shoulder to ensure the dogs were no longer in pursuit.

"Are you okay? Do you think you can climb?" Xavier asked as we got to the base of the pump house.

"Yeah. It probably looks worse than it actually is." I grabbed the ladder at the side of the little house and began to climb with Xavier at my back. Rob pulled me up over the top with Xavier pushing me from behind.

I lay on the roof for a minute, trying to catch my breath. The girls stared wide-eyed at my torn, bloody pant leg.

Sarielle came and knelt beside me. "Are you all right, Kendi?"

"I'm good. I'm sure it's just a scratch," I replied. I didn't want Lesley any more panicked.

"Not such a good idea to get in the middle of a dogfight."

I chuckled and sat up. "Les, breathe. I'm fine." She was still white as a sheet and didn't respond. "Will it help if I say you were right and I was wrong, that we should have gone through Folly Hill? You know you will never in life hear those words come out of my mouth again. Today is your only shot."

That brought a smile to her face.

"Can I get that in writing, Mr. Belling?"

"Not a chance. But you do have witnesses." I grimaced then took in the scenery. "So, this is what all the fuss is over," I said. I had to admit it was amazing. From the top of the pump house, you could see clear across the reservoir. The view was breathtaking. The sky was crystal blue, cloudless, and once again it was warm, and the air was dry.

"Beautiful, isn't it?" Sarielle responded.

"Yes, it is."

"Let me see that leg, Kendi," Sarielle added.

"Why, are you a doctor?"

"No, but I do have a first aid kit, smart ass." She grinned.

I rolled up my pant leg. The bite was superficial. The dog didn't have enough time to get a good grip on me. It still throbbed terribly as the dog had bitten into my calf muscle.

Sarielle cleaned the wound up with antiseptic. I wouldn't let her bandage it because we were about to go swimming. This made her angry.

"You are seriously still going to get in the water?" She was rolling her eyes at me.

"Absolutely. I didn't come all the way out here to watch you guys have all the fun." I smirked at her.

She wasn't amused.

"I see why your brothers watch you like a hawk. You're completely reckless."

"Ouch. That hurt." I made a mock-hurt face.

She smacked me in the back of the head and turned to the rest of the group.

"We're wasting time. It'll start getting dark, and we will have to leave. You guys ready to swim?"

"Sure thing," Lesley sang. She seemed to have recovered well. "Boys, be on the lookout so that we can change." The girls descended the side of the pump house.

I waited until I was sure that they were out of earshot before turning to Xavier. "Thanks for coming back for me."

"No problem. I've never seen dogs like that," he said, shaking his head.

"I think they may have been coyotes."

"Coyotes? Around here?" Rob questioned.

"I thought it was strange too, but I haven't been here long enough to know for sure. Doesn't matter what they were. We certainly don't need to go back to the truck that way, especially not with the girls, just in case those dogs are still lingering."

"Agreed. We can go back through Folly Hills. It will take about the same amount of time, but we'll only be in the woods a minute or two."

"Sounds good to me," Xavier agreed.

The girls reappeared in cutoff shorts and T-shirts, ready to hit the water. Rob pulled off his t- shirt and stripped off his jeans—he was wearing a pair of shorts underneath. He joined the girls at the front end of the pump house overlooking the water.

"I thought you were swimming?" Lesley inquired.

"I am...just giving you guys a head start." I smiled at her. My leg was throbbing horribly. It was going to take some doing to get my jeans past the wound, and I didn't want the girls around to witness the challenge.

"Xavier, you not swimming?" I asked. He was still seated next to me, watching the others.

"Swimming's not really my thing. I just came to hang out."

"What he means is that he can't swim," Lesley shouted from the edge of the wall. Before Xavier could respond, she hollered, "Cannonball!" and leaped into the water.

The others giggled and followed her, leaving me alone with Xavier for the first time since our initial meeting. I still wasn't sure how I felt about him, but I was glad he had come back for me. I might not have made it to the pump house on my own with a bloody leg and angry dogs in pursuit. There were a few minutes of awkward silence as neither of us knew what to say. We had no one to facilitate a conversation and until today had never spoken directly to one another. I had already thanked him for coming back for me; that was all I had.

"Kendi, I know you still haven't forgiven me for not helping you with Taylor, but I really want you to know how sorry I am about—"

I interrupted him.

"Just let it go." I didn't want to talk about it, hear about it, or be reminded of it. I turned away from him.

"Please let me finish."

I was so tempted to go join the others in the water, but I still had to get my jeans off. I was trapped for the second time today. Sighing, I turned to face Xavier again.

"I promise I didn't know how far Taylor was going to go. I thought he was just trying to scare you. I never knew he planned to get physical. By the time I realized what was going on, it was too late. And I was really in no position to confront him without—" Xavier stopped midsentence.

"Without what?" Maybe Xavier would tell me what Taylor had on him since Sarielle was not around. No dice.

He had his head hung down. When he continued, he acted as if he didn't hear my question. "I wanted to stay and help when I saw that you were hurt, but—"

I cut him off again. I knew he was struggling with implicating Sarielle. I guess she didn't tell Xavier that I already knew.

The only thing I hadn't figured out was what Taylor had on him to make him keep quiet for so long. Obviously, I wouldn't get that information today either.

"It's over. Don't worry about it." I got to my feet and pulled my pants off. I couldn't continue listening to Xavier fumble over an apology. It was a little late at this point, and he was only going to piss me off by not giving me the information I wanted.

"You gonna get in? Really? What about your leg?"

"Yeah. The cold water will probably make it feel better," I answered, moving closer to the edge.

The jump was a little farther down than I thought, but I could see the others bobbing in the water about a hundred yards or so out. I prepared to jump.

"Do you need some help, man?" Xavier was moving to the edge to assist. I ignored him as the still air came alive again. The breeze buffeted the treetops. As before, I heard wind chimes in the distance. Xavier didn't seem to notice.

"Did you hear that?" I inquired.

"Hear what?"

"Wind chimes."

"Wind chimes? Do they still make those?" He grinned.

I blew it off. It had to be either my imagination or coming from across the water in Folly Hill. One of the residents must have them hanging outside of a window or something. Maybe my ears were more sensitive than most humans'—even though Lesley had heard the dog before I did?

"Are you going to jump? You look a little...hesitant." Xavier was smirking as he misinterpreted my pause.

I rolled my eyes at him and jumped from the roof. On the way down, the wind caught my attention again, along with the ringing of the wind chimes. My feet sliced the surface, and I was shocked at the icy temperature of the water on such a warm day. No one had bothered to warn me. Some friends. However, they had warned me about the current near the pump station. It was indeed strong. As soon as my head broke the surface of the water, I was immediately dragged under again by the current. It was pulling me back toward the pump house. I didn't panic. I knew to swim parallel with the current until I was free, and then I could swim out to the spot where everyone else had stopped. Obviously, the current wasn't strong there.

The water was black and murky, making it very hard to see where I was going, but I could feel the current and knew I was headed in the right direction. It was easier to swim beneath the surface, so that is what I did until I felt the current release me. As my head broke the surface, I looked around to gauge my position in the water in relation to the others. They were about a swimming pool's length farther out in the reservoir. I decided to rest a moment before making the swim. The current had worn me out. I was swimming with one good leg.

As I rested in the water, several things happened at once. The wind blew, the wind chimes sang, and Xavier let out one short yelp. I turned in the direction of his cry, just in time to see his feet slide out from under him, his head hit the roof, and his limp body plummet into the water. I could hear the others screaming, but I was the closest to him, so I sprang into action without thinking.

Swimming back in toward the pump house was even harder than swimming away from it. I found myself being pounded and thrashed around in the water, not making the necessary progress in getting to Xavier. I popped my head up again looking for him and saw him flailing about fifty yards in front of me.

"Hang on, Xavier. I'm coming!" I choked as the water pounded my face.

I swam with my head above water now so that I could keep an eye on his location. He wasn't kidding about swimming not being his thing. Xavier didn't stand a chance against the raging current. It was difficult for me to stay afloat. He was sucked under again in just a few seconds.

"Xavier! Xavier!"

His hand popped out of the water just inside my reach, and I grabbed for him. I pulled him in towards me, but he was already panicked. Xavier clutched onto the collar of my T-shirt and began pulling me under with him. I should have taken the time to pull the shirt off—too late. Xavier was using it as his lifeline, and my attempt to save him was about to kill us both.

The frigid black water near the pump station was violent. I struggled beneath the water trying to get Xavier under control. My head broke the surface momentarily, and I could see that Rob had just reached the edge of the current. In the back of my mind, I processed that he would never make it in time. Xavier pulled me back under, and the salty water burned my throat as it went down. I fought to hold the breath in. Xavier's assault was becoming less intense. He wouldn't be conscious much longer. He was drowning.

"Kendi. Hang on! I'm almost there! Hold on to Xavier. Don't let him go. I'm almost there!"

"Malachi?"

"Yeah, it's me. Hold on to Xavier. Don't lose him!"

"But how…?"

"Reuel. No time to explain now. Just hang on to Xay."

"What's going on?"

"Just hold on, Kendi! Please don't let go of him! I'll get both of you—hold on!"

Things were starting to fade, but I grabbed Xavier and held on. I struggled to pull the two of us above water. My head broke the surface just in time to hear

Malachi's splash into the reservoir. Fighting to hold on to Xavier in the current, I leaned back gasping for a clear breath, with Xavier's limp body clutched under one arm.

Malachi and Rob reached us at the same time.

"Kendi, are you okay?" Malachi hollered.

I nodded weakly. "Get Xavier. We gotta get him out of the water. He's not breathing."

"I've got him." Malachi pulled Xavier into his arms and began side paddling toward the reservoir wall to the left of the pump house.

"Rob, help Kendi!" he ordered over his shoulder.

Rob grabbed my arm and began towing me out of the current. We followed Malachi as this was the quickest way out of the water. However, it was steep and heavy-laden with rocks. Malachi reached the side first and was struggling to pull Xavier the rest of the way out of the water.

"Kendi, can you get out?" Rob called as he lunged himself out of the water to help. "Yes. Go!"

I climbed up the rocks to the wall just as Mal and Rob hoisted Xavier over. The girls were right behind me. I assisted them over the wall.

"Oh my God, Xay! Help him!" Sarielle screamed, running for her brother. I caught her around the waist, pulling her to me, comforting her and trying to keep her out of the way. Malachi knew what he was doing.

"Shhhh. It's okay, Sarielle. Shhhh...he'll be fine." I held onto her tightly, stroking her hair, trying to calm her.

Malachi had rolled Xavier onto his back. His face was dead, his lips blue. Malachi straddled Xavier and began thrusting upward on his chest. Torrents of water sprang from his nose and mouth.

"Breathe! Breathe!" Malachi ordered. Nothing.

Mal repeated this action until no more water came. Still nothing.

Sarielle was sobbing frantically. "Xay, don't leave me. Please don't leave me." She was trembling with such force that I shook with her.

Malachi leaned forward, tilted Xavier's chin up, pinched his nose, opened his mouth, and blew in two full breaths. He waited a couple of seconds and did it again. This time, Xavier coughed. Water sprung out of his mouth. He rolled to his side and threw up.

"Xay!" Sarielle screamed, snatching away from me. She threw herself on the ground and wound her arms around his neck.

Malachi turned his attention to me. *"Kendi, are you all right? How's your leg?"*

"I'm fine, Mal. Really. How did you know where I was? That we were in trouble? I'm starting to believe I'm some kind of trouble magnet."

"Reuel located you. And today's trouble wasn't all your doing. You had a little help. I'll explain later. Right now, we need to get out of here."

I looked at Malachi with a raised eyebrow.

"What's going on? Why is my telepathy suddenly 'turned on'?"

"Reuel. Don't get used to it. I'm sure it won't be on for long... just long enough for us to get out of here. Let's put some hustle on this crew. Shall we?" I nodded.

"Xay, are you okay?" Malachi inquired.

"Yeah. I'm all right," he croaked. He sounded horrible, but he got to his feet and pulled Sarielle up with him. She looked as bad as he did. She was still crying and shaking. Xavier seemed unsteady on his feet and was not able to support Sarielle. Rob moved to her side, and Lesley went to support Xay.

"You all right, Elle? You don't look so good," Rob noted.

"I t–t–think so," she stammered.

"Let's get our clothes and get out of here," Lesley said.

We rounded the side of the reservoir to the pump house where the girls had left their backpacks and clothes. Rob and Malachi scaled the ladder to the roof to retrieve our bags. The girls began dressing. Sarielle seemed to be having significant trouble. Lesley was completely dressed while Sarielle had only managed to pull on a shirt.

Rob and Malachi descended the ladder, and Rob pulled a jacket from his bag and gave it to Xavier. I pulled my jeans back on and changed my shirt. Sarielle was still struggling with her jeans. Her hands trembled terribly.

"Elle, what's the matter? You okay?" Lesley inquired, moving toward her.

Sarielle didn't answer but continued struggling with her pants. Her face was flushed, her lips quivering. Xavier looked up at his sister, and his face crumbled.

"Elle? Elle!" Xavier quickly closed the space between them and took her face in his hands. "Elle, can you hear me? You with me, sis?" Sarielle seemed to focus on her brother's face for half a second, and then her eyes rolled in the back of her head, and she slumped forward, folding into Xavier's arms. Lesley helped him to lower Sarielle to the ground.

My heart sank. What was wrong with her?

"Where's Elle's backpack? Where's her bag!" Xavier was frantically searching the ground. Rob grabbed the bag and tossed it to Xavier. He tore open the front pocket and pulled out a small pink box, opened it, and took out what looked like a syringe. Xavier proceeded to push the hem of Sarielle's wet shorts aside and then jabbed the needle into her thigh. He grabbed her by the shoulders and pulled her into his arms.

"Elle. Elle, can you hear me?" He shook her slightly, pushing her hair back from her face. "Oh, God. Don't do this to me, please...Elle!"

"Is she okay?" Rob asked, kneeling next to them.

"I don't know yet." He shook Sarielle again. "C'mon, Elle. Wake up, please."

"I'm calling 911," Malachi said, pulling his phone from his backpack.

"Wait, Mal. I think she's coming around."

Sarielle's eyelids fluttered as she struggled to open her eyes.

"Elle? Honey, can you hear me?" Lesley said, holding her hand. Sarielle turned toward Lesley's voice and slowly opened her eyes.

"Lesley? Xay? What happened?" She looked around trying to make sense of her surroundings.

"You passed out. I had to give you a shot." She reached for her leg, still disoriented. "How do you feel now?" Xavier asked.

"Not so good. I think I may be sick."

"We don't need an ambulance, but we need to get her to the emergency room to get checked out," Xavier called to Malachi.

"All right. My truck is just beyond the tree line in Folly Hill."

"I don't think I can carry her," Xavier said.

"Rob, you help Kendi, and I'll carry Elle," Malachi said. "We need to get out of these woods, now."

Amid the chaos, I had forgotten about my sore leg. Rob came to my side so that I could lean some of my weight on his shoulder. Malachi scooped Sarielle up from the ground. Her head rolled and bobbed around until it found a resting place on Malachi's wide shoulder. She still looked as if she wasn't all the way there—like she would lose consciousness again at any moment. Lesley gathered up the rest of our things, and we headed for the path out of the woods.

Just as we broke through the trees into the backyard of some unsuspecting resident, I heard the wind chimes ring out behind me and fade away in the distance. Malachi turned slightly toward the sound.

"You heard that too?"

"Yes. I heard it."

"What the hell's going on, Malachi? What is that?"

"Kendi, you haven't been gone from Empyrean that long. Surely you haven't forgotten the sound of the Host. Reuel and I have been tracking activity in this area all day. The Legion is here, and so are the Thrones."

I leaned just a little bit harder against Rob's shoulder.

10
KNOWING IS ONLY HALF THE BATTLE

Just when you thought it was safe to go back into the water, think again.

When I woke up this morning, I fully expected the day to be abnormal based on our meeting with Reuel concerning the Dominion. What I had not expected was that the day would spiral out of control so chaotically. We had left school a little more than four hours ago just to have some fun, and now we sat in the emergency room of Beverly Medical Center waiting to see if Sarielle was going to be all right.

She had been semiconscious the entire way to the hospital. Xavier kept her awake by making her talk. He explained to Malachi and me that Sarielle had Addison's disease. It was a disorder that affected her adrenal function. Simply put, excessive amounts of stress could send her into a state of shock where her body would shut down due to the inability of her system to compensate. I guess seeing her brother drown and thinking that he was dead qualified as such an event. Thankfully, Xavier was there and knew exactly what to do to revive her. I couldn't recall a time when I felt more helpless, and I didn't like it.

Xavier had called Dr. Warner, Sarielle's endocrinologist, to meet them at the hospital. She agreed to do so without calling their mom until after she assessed Sarielle's condition. Apparently, they had been through this before. She also gave Xavier a once-over for the knot on the back of his head— courtesy of his fall—and determined that he was okay. No concussion. The doctor had also offered to check out my leg, but I refused. It had already stopped bleeding. The soreness was nothing I couldn't tolerate.

Sarielle was being given meds intravenously to stabilize her. We anxiously awaited an update on her condition. If she didn't rebound in an hour or so, Ms. Breland was going to be called. The doctor seemed to have a great relationship with both Xavier and his sister. They had obviously been through a lot together. There was so much about this girl I didn't know. She intrigued me, and I wanted the opportunity to figure out why.

After about an hour, Rob and Lesley said their goodbyes and promised Xavier that they would call him later to check on Sarielle. They had both seen one of these episodes before and were more confident than I in her recovery. They wanted to get home before either of their parents questioned their whereabouts. Malachi took them to pick up Rob's truck, which was still parked on the side of Locust Street. I was again left alone with Xavier. This time I had several questions.

"Do you really think Sarielle is going to be okay?"

"I'm sure she'll be fine. Dr. Julie would have ratted us out by now if she wasn't," he answered, smiling to himself. "Elle has a bad habit of scaring the hell out of me when I least expect it."

"Tell me about it. How long has she had this problem?"

"Pretty much all her life. As far as we know, she was born with it." Xavier shrugged his shoulders.

"This thing seems pretty serious. What happens when you're not around for one of these episodes?" I asked.

"Rob and Lesley know that Elle carries the medication with her—although they've never had to give it to her. Needles freak Lesley out, but Rob could have done it if he needed to. Elle makes me so angry sometimes. She's supposed to always wear a medic alert tag in case of an emergency like today. She refuses to wear it. She doesn't want to seem weak, or for people to treat her differently because she has a chronic illness. I think she's embarrassed, really," Xavier explained.

"Well, that's just...stupid." I didn't want to sound rude, but I couldn't think of a more appropriate word. "I would pick embarrassed over *dead* any day of the week and twice on Tuesday."

"You're preaching to the choir, dude. I've tried to make that point. No dice. I haven't given up, though. Since she's adamant about being stupid, I stay close in case she needs me. You saw firsthand how quickly she can get out of it. She wouldn't be able to tell anybody what is wrong with her."

"What was that you injected her with?"

"A synthetic steroid...It basically jump-starts her adrenal system."

"Have you had to do that a lot?" I wanted to know just how often her life was in jeopardy. "You didn't hesitate at all."

I was impressed with his levelheadedness. He had just drowned himself and still had the wherewithal to come to Sarielle's aid. No matter what I thought about Xavier, his love for his sister was obvious.

"Not a whole lot, but too often, if you ask me. I don't even think about it much anymore. The way I see it, it's give her the damn shot, or watch her die. It's not really a matter of choice, man." Xay was shaking his head, clearly disturbed thinking about Sarielle's illness. I decided to change the subject.

"Tell me something, Xavier. How in the hell did you fall into the reservoir?"

"I really don't know what happened. I was standing on the edge after you jumped in, I glanced up to see what the guys were doing, and..." He hesitated.

"And what?"

"I don't want to sound crazy, but I swear someone pushed me." He looked up at me, embarrassed.

"Pushed you?" I raised an eyebrow. "Boy, you were on the roof alone."

"I know, but that's the only way I can explain it. The wind had started to blow, but not hard enough to blow me over. I distinctly remember feeling like I was shoved."

I just stared at him. I didn't know how to respond to crazy.

"Of course, I did slam my head on the way down and knock myself unconscious, so what do I know?" He laughed at himself.

"Xavier," Dr. Warner called as she approached. He got up to meet her in the middle of the room. I followed although I wasn't invited. I couldn't help it.

"Elle is going to be fine. The nurse is helping her get dressed now so you all can go home. Straight home. She needs to rest. No more excitement today." The doctor looked back and forth between the two of us in warning. "I have doubled her cover meds for the next three days. Please help her remember to take them, Xay."

"No worries. I'm all over it, Dr. Julie." Xavier smiled. "Thanks for not calling Mom. She would have killed us."

"I'd be more worried about me killing you if you two don't stay out of trouble," she chided.

"I know. No more trips to the reservoir. Scout's honor." He threw up the three-finger promise.

"You were never a scout." Dr. Warner scowled.

"You caught that, huh?" Xavier laughed as the doctor embraced him.

"Get Elle home and to bed. Nice to meet you, Kendi," she added as she turned to leave. "Elle will be out in a few minutes."

I sighed in relief.

"I know, right? I feel like we dodged a major bullet."

"Several of them," I agreed.

Malachi returned to the hospital just as Sarielle was wheeled from the back. "Hey, sis. Ready to go home?" Xavier smiled at his sister, touching her cheek. "Definitely. Let's get out of here."

"Glad you're feeling better. I'll pull the truck up," Malachi said.

"Thanks, Mal—for everything," Elle replied.

"No problem." Malachi smiled and turned for the door.

"Sarielle Breland, you certainly know how to give a guy a heart attack," I said, giving her a quick once-over. Her color hadn't completely returned, and she still looked a little shaky.

"Sorry, Kendi. Didn't mean to scare you." She looked away, embarrassed.

I moved closer to the wheelchair, took Sarielle by the chin, and turned her head so that I could look into her eyes.

"There's absolutely nothing for you to apologize for. I'm just glad that you are all right. Seriously."

She blushed and looked away again.

"Don't worry about the heart attack. It was the second one of the day," I said, throwing a look at Xavier.

"Let's get you home. Doctor's orders."

We drove back to the school so Xavier could retrieve their car. It was a quiet drive. It had been a long day. Everyone was exhausted, and probably processing the events of the afternoon. Although most of the information I needed would have to come from Malachi once we were alone. Unfortunately, my telepathic ability didn't last much beyond the backyards of Folly Hill—Mal was right. So, I had to be patient.

As we pulled into the empty parking lot, Xavier dug around in his sister's bag until he found the keys to their car. He went to put their things in before he tried to move Sarielle. She had fallen asleep. I guessed these episodes took a lot out of her. Malachi noticed how lethargically Xavier moved and climbed out of the truck to help him.

When Sarielle collapsed, I guess we all forgot that Xavier had just been revived from drowning himself. He looked like hell but was trying to be strong for his sister. Xavier climbed into the driver's seat of their car, and Malachi came back to get Sarielle. When he opened the door, she startled awake.

"Sorry, I didn't mean to scare you," Mal apologized.

"You didn't," she lied. "Where's Xay?"

"There, in your car waiting for you. Ready to go?" Malachi extended his hand to assist her out of the Hummer.

"Get some rest, Sleeping Beauty." I winked at her, and she smiled. "And don't forget to take your meds." Her smile disappeared. Sarielle didn't want me or anyone else acknowledging her illness. I quickly changed the subject.

"Maybe we all can get together this weekend and do something. I'll talk to Rob and Lesley and let you know."

She nodded slowly, trying to rearrange the frown on her face. "Sounds good. See ya." She waved as Mal closed the door and helped her into the car with Xavier.

Malachi climbed back into the Hummer, and we sat in silence as we watched the little red Honda drive out of the parking lot. Once the car was out of sight, Mal slumped forward over the steering wheel, and let out a heavy sigh.

"You okay, man?"

He leaned back and let his head flop against the headrest with his eyes closed. "Yeah. Exhausting day. You?"

"Honestly, I've had better days." I thought about it for a second. "But I've had a lot worst too." We both laughed. "What the hell just happened?" I inquired.

"I don't even know where to start, brother."

"The beginning helps."

Mal was once again debating what to tell me, and what to conveniently leave out. "Reuel wants to meet. He asked that I wait until we are all together."

"It's that bad?"

Malachi didn't answer but started the truck and headed for home.

When we walked into the living room, Reuel and the twins were waiting for us. "Are you two all right?" Reuel questioned.

"We're fine, Reuel," Malachi responded.

"Can someone please tell me what is going on?" No more beating around the bush, no more silent conversations—I needed the truth.

"I know you're aggravated. Have a seat, and I'll tell you as much as I am at liberty to divulge," Reuel started.

Frustration gave way to nervousness as Reuel confirmed my suspicions. The team was withholding information.

But why?

"I am under orders directly from Yah. I will tell you what I'm allowed to and no more."

"Reuel?" Malachi's eyes were pleading. Reuel shook his head ever so slightly. Great, another private conversation.

"Kendi, sit down," Reuel repeated.

I was still standing in the middle of the room, wound too tight to even think about relaxing. I moved slowly to the chair facing Reuel and folded myself into the seat.

"Okay, I'm sitting. What's going on?"

I looked around the circle of what I now considered my family. Their expressions were strained.

"I told you yesterday that the Legion's activity in Charon had increased. And this morning, Uriel again contacted me. He and his team had been tracking Azrael's activity— without engaging him. We needed to find out the reason for the Legion's sudden descent in this area. For the last few weeks, Azrael has been sending emissaries to search. Uriel continued to watch from a distance, waiting for the Legion to reveal what they were after. A few days ago, we realized all of the Legion's surveillance had one thing in common." Reuel paused.

"What's that?" I looked around the room when he didn't continue, but everyone was still looking at Reuel, waiting for him to continue.

"What's the commonality, Reuel?"

Reuel looked up directly into my eyes. "Xavier Breland."

"Xavier? What in the world would the Legion want with Xavier?" The very sound of it was comical. I laughed.

"Xavier has been chosen," Reuel continued.

"Okay...so there are lots of mortals that have been chosen by Yah. That's why we are here, right? To protect the chosen." I shrugged my shoulders.

Malachi, who had never sat down, began pacing, agitated. Something wasn't right. "Kendi, he's been targeted by Abbadon. We believe it's because Abbadon found out that Xavier Breland...is your assignment." Reuel paused.

Gut punch.

This is what they were keeping from me! How long had they known? I thought we were supposed to be a team? A family? What the hell?

I could barely stand to be in Xavier's presence. I certainly hadn't been watching out for him, let alone protecting him! Did they not think this little piece of information would be helpful? Hell, it was only *my* very existence that was at stake. If Xavier died, it would also be the end for me. Yah had made it abundantly clear that this was my last chance. How could they keep this from me? I stood up, feeling as if the wind had been knocked out of me. I was confused. I didn't know exactly what emotion I should feel. I wanted to be angry, but fear won amid the onslaught of emotions starting to overwhelm me.

If Abbadon was targeting Xavier, *my* destruction was the goal. The big question was why? I had never gone head to head with any of the Legion so this couldn't be a vendetta of any kind. Thus far, I had only managed to piss off the part of the Host with whom I worked and interacted—including the Guardian and the Ruling Judges. And I couldn't forget Ophan—the one Throne that had been my friend before I betrayed him.

The two assignments I had lost were both direct results of Abbadon's involvement. I had tried to blow it off as coincidence, but something in my gut had always told me otherwise. Suspicion confirmed. What did Abbadon have against me? Why was he so hell-bent on destroying me?

Looking into Reuel's eyes, I knew he was reading my inner turmoil. His eyes were concerned yet resolute. There was no need to ask Reuel to explain what he knew about Abbadon. I knew this look well. The discussion was closed.

"He deserves to know, Reuel," Malachi demanded.

Malachi had stopped pacing. His face was rigid. His hands balled into tight fists. "He's not ready." Reuel was shaking his head.

"It's not fair to Kendi. How can he prepare for what's coming if we don't tell him?"

"Prepare for what?" My voice cracked. Malachi crossed the room to where I stood, taking me by the shoulders so that he could look into my eyes.

"Malachi...don't," Reuel pleaded.

Malachi shook me slightly to regain my attention. The twins came to stand with Malachi.

Although they had been silent, their actions were in clear support of him now. He continued. "Kendi, we are anticipating a battle in this region, soon. The Legion doesn't want this war as they know we will be ready. With the Guardian prepared, the Legion would lose a significant portion of their forces here. Abbadon doesn't intend to take that risk."

"Malachi. That's enough!" Reuel was on his feet. I ignored him.

I heard what Mal was saying, but I still didn't understand. What did all of this have to do with me? I was trying to put the pieces together in my head.

The only time the Legion battled with the Guardian, in the Earth realm, was to protect one of their gateways. There were only five of the seven gates left that had not been sealed—each one on a different continent. Only the Legion forces knew the locations of these gateways. However, Yah had created a higher breed of Guardian called Shoers. The Shoers were assigned the task of locating and sealing these secret passageways.

Sealing the gateways was the only way to contain the Dominion in the realm of Sha'ar. This would stop them from tormenting the humans we were bound to protect. Sealing the gateways would effectively end the infinite war that raged on between the angelic Host and the Dominion. Defeating the Legion in battle was the only way to successfully seal a gateway. A Legion regime head would have to fall. In Charon, this would mean bringing down Abbadon.

Shoers were the highest rank of the Guardian. Within the Guardian, we called these respected leaders *Eklektos*, which meant "chosen." The Shoers had been created and handpicked by Yah for the responsibility of closing the gateways. They were, for all intents and purposes, the saviors of the Earth. For without access to the Earth realm, the Dominion would not be able to use mortals as their pawns. The demons would become powerless against Yah. Unlike the rest of the Guardian, Shoers had an extrasensory perception so to enable them to identify the gateways. The special tactical ability of the Shoers allowed them to lead the Guardian forces into battle—directly into the heart of the Legion's strongholds.

I had heard stories about Shoers, both past, and present. The Eklektos were legendary. They were some of the most powerful beings created. Shoers were mighty warriors with great strength and impeccable integrity. No, they didn't always win, but they were still highly revered for acknowledging such a call and serving their time dutifully. No Shoer had ever been killed in battle as the remainder of the Guardian served as protectors for them. The Guardian protected the Eklektos with their very lives because of what they represented to Empyrean—the end of both the Legion rebellion and the torment of mankind.

It had taken me all of ten seconds to process what was happening. Malachi had said that a battle was imminent, which meant a Shoer had to be in the region. My legs began to shake. My body had drawn the conclusion before my mind got there. Abbadon's goal would be to avoid a battle against the Shoer and the Guardian forces. The best way to preempt the battle was to get rid of the Shoer. No Shoer meant no battle.

Malachi held my shoulders more tightly, waiting for me to fully understand.

"A Shoer has been sent to Charon?" I whispered. My question was more a statement, as I already knew the answer.

"Yes. Eklektos." Malachi answered firmly—making it clear that he was addressing me by title—my Yah-given position.

My head began to shake involuntarily from side to side as I tried to formulate the words with my mouth. It took several seconds for my body and my mind to reconnect.

"N–n–no...No...no. It can't be...I can't...How could he...?" Malachi released me. I began backing away from him. This couldn't be. I couldn't even wrap my mind around being a Guardian. I hated it. I hated Earth. I hated being here. I was no leader, no warrior, not worth being protected. Not at the expense of the team, my family. I couldn't do this. I wouldn't do this.

All I wanted was escape, but Yah had trapped me in this body. I couldn't even get to Empyrean. I needed Eloa. She could tell me what to do. She could help me. But I couldn't get to her. She couldn't get to me.

My legs shook violently, my stomach cramped, and tears poured uncontrollably down my face. My breath came in gasps.

Malachi took a step toward me, while Reuel and the twins looked on helplessly. I put up one hand to ward him off. I didn't want him to touch me. I didn't want any of them to touch me. I just wanted to go. I couldn't put together the words I needed to say. Only one would come from my lips.

"No...no...no!" I screamed as I bolted from the house. I had no idea where I was going. I just ran. My instincts wanted to take me to the skies where I would be free of this fleshly prison, but that was a luxury I was no longer afforded.

I could hear my name being called, but I ignored the sound and continued running blindly into the darkness. Perhaps the darkness would cover me. Maybe it would swallow me. At the moment, I didn't care. I just didn't want to be *me* anymore.

I ran for blocks until my legs betrayed me and gave way. I had no idea where I was, but trees surrounded me in the darkness. My mind relaxed. I felt covered. I fell into a tree for support, holding myself up as I gasped for breath. My stomach lurched, and I began to vomit. My knees eventually gave out too, and I allowed myself to collapse. The sobs racking me seemed to last for an eternity. The problem was I knew my reaction would change nothing. I had been handed a death sentence. Yah was putting one nail in my coffin at a time, and there was nothing I could do about it. But this time, others would fall— those closest to me.

Finally, I sat back slumping against the tree. The tears still weren't under control, so I put my head down on my knees and just let them continue to come. Eventually, I would cry myself out, or maybe Abbadon would find me here and just end this now.

"I would never allow that to happen," Reuel's voice startled me.

I looked up to find Reuel standing in front of me. I had not heard his approach, although he had probably been watching me the entire time. He *could* transform out of his human form at will. I couldn't imagine he would let me out of his sight without added protection, knowing I was a marked man.

"Kendi, you can do this. I have faith in you. The team has faith in you."

I just shook my head in disagreement. I could barely see Reuel through the blur of tears. He knew I didn't have the aptitude to carry out such an appointment. That's why he kept the information from me. I was sure of it. And he was right. I couldn't handle it. I wasn't ready. I never would be.

Sighing heavily, Reuel came and sat next to me.

"Your ability to carry out your assignment has nothing to do with my decision to withhold information. There were several other factors I needed to take into consideration. It's never been that I thought you incapable."

I just stared at the ground hoping I wouldn't be sick again. I didn't know whether Reuel's presence was a comfort or causing further stress.

"Kendi, look at me." Reuel placed his hand on my shoulder. I wanted to shrug him off, but my body was physically spent. Reluctantly I turned to face him. "You have been created for this moment, son. I have no doubt that you're well able to rise to the challenge. Have you not taken the time to think about why Yah gave you yet another chance instead of ordering your immediate destruction after your trial in Empyrean?" I continued to stare blankly at him. Reuel continued, "Why, Yah, would put you in a human body, allow you to live, feel, and nearly die as all mortals do? It was for this very moment. You were given the same grace as they are granted, Kendi—an opportunity to make a choice. It was all a part of Yah's master plan—a chance to accept his design for your life, to die to self; a chance to start with a clean slate, to be reborn. The alternative is to reject him and risk destruction."

"If the choice was mine, then why keep information from me? Did you not think I would need to know about Xavier so that I could protect him? Protect myself?" I scrubbed my hand across my face, trying to get rid of the tears.

"Honestly, my concern was for your physical capacity to handle all of this. You've been through so much in the short time you've been in Danvers. You're just starting to get your legs under you, so to speak. My fear was unloading too much on you too soon. I wasn't sure you would be able to handle the strain of it all at once. I have to admit that I've been quite a bit more protective of you than I anticipated." Reuel smiled though I could see the concern in his eyes.

I could see his point of view. I wasn't exactly handling the news about Xavier and this Shoer stuff with much composure—that was for damn sure. I wasn't sure what bothered me more; having to keep Xavier close for a prolonged period, or the fact that I had become a target for the Legion, along with anyone crazy enough to stand with me.

"How long have you known, Reuel? About Xavier? About my...position?"

"I only found out that you were targeted by the Legion a few days ago during my meeting with Uriel. I considered his counsel and decided that it would be best to work with his team to monitor the Legion's activity. It didn't take long to figure out that Charon was being overrun by the Dominion. We just couldn't seem to figure out what it was they were after." Reuel was agitated by the situation.

"I have yet to discover how the Dominion found out that Yah had appointed you as Shoer here. Not even I was privy to that information. Yet it was somehow divulged to the Legion."

Reuel paused, seeming to contemplate the possibilities.

"And Xavier?" I felt like Reuel was deliberately avoiding this part of my question. Reuel hesitated, and then let out another sigh. Yeah, he was reluctant to continue.

"We found out the same day you were attacked. Xavier was the only eyewitness that we knew of at the time, and Malachi was determined to find out what had happened by any means necessary. He was ready to go after the kid himself. Angelo and Raza had to physically restrain him. Yah gave me the information I needed when I went to Merkabah to intervene on your behalf."

Reuel glanced at me to gauge my response, but I had nothing left.

"Your reaction to Xavier was so incredibly severe; I didn't want to hamper your recovery by telling you. The team vowed that Xavier would be covered until you were able to handle the actuality of it all."

This explained why the guys seemed to have forgiven Xavier so quickly— why they allowed him in our inner circle even though he was involved in the fight. I sat quietly for several minutes trying to absorb all that Reuel was saying. It was a lot to process. The tears had finally stopped, although my stomach was still tied in knots. I think it was a combination of anger, fear, and denial. It would take some time for me to wrap my mind around all of this, let alone figure out an appropriate reaction. Right now, my goal was to get the answers I felt I needed—that I deserved— if I was ever going to be able to move forward.

"What happened today?" I asked, looking Reuel directly in the eyes. I needed to know he wasn't withholding anything else. I wouldn't be able to handle any more surprises.

Reuel stood and began pacing in the small clearing. He said nothing for several seconds.

"Please, Reuel," I begged at my breaking point now.

As Reuel paced, his resolve seemed to waver. He was battling with some internal conflict. "This morning we discovered your appointment and it being the reason the Legion had decided to move against you. Uriel and I had tracked the location of Abbadon, and we were watching him. However, we found that we too were being watched. So, I engaged Malachi. Abbadon had already pinpointed the location of the team at the school and was not expecting Malachi's involvement.

"Malachi was able to infiltrate a meeting between Abbadon and Azrael regarding the destruction of the Shoer. They wanted to be certain that the location of the gate remained hidden. Abbadon instructed Azrael to utilize the first opportunity to strike. And we didn't know which way they would attack. We didn't know whether they would come after you directly or take the easy route and go after Xavier. We couldn't allow either scenario to unfold."

Again, Reuel paused to examine my reaction. Once he confirmed that there was none, he continued.

"Malachi was beside himself by the time he got back to me with the information. He was frantic because you were at the school alone. He wasn't comforted by the presence of the twins. He knew they would be no match for

Azrael. I tried to assure him that you were fine, that you were in school, but he insisted something was wrong. To calm him, I searched for your location and found you. Not in French class but entering the woods near the reservoir. Malachi almost took the front door off the hinges when he tore out of the house.

"I continued to monitor your location through your thoughts and updated Malachi. I tried to keep him calm, letting him know that nothing out of the ordinary was happening. We were both worried but were fairly certain that you would be all right because he was so close to your location. That is until I heard the first wind chime."

"The Throne," I mouthed.

"Yes. A Throne close enough to your vicinity to be heard made me rather apprehensive. The Thrones usually remain aloof to the point of obscurity. They don't risk detection by the Guardian or the Legion. The other problem was that some of the Legion used to be Thrones. Azrael is such a creature. I couldn't be sure who was out there—friend or foe.

"Then the dogs came. Things began spiraling out of control quickly. I thought Malachi would wreck the truck trying to get to Folly Hill. I had calmed him down by the time you reached the pump station, only to have Xavier *fall* into the water. Malachi was ready to teleport from the Hummer straight into the water to help you both. There was no calming him at this point. I had to allow him to speak to you himself. He wanted to be certain that you knew help was on the way and that you would hold onto Xavier until he could get into the woods and teleport discreetly to the reservoir."

"I don't think I'd ever been so relieved to hear Mal's voice." I trembled slightly.

I wasn't sure whether the involuntary spasms were brought on by the bad memory, or from the wet shorts that I was still wearing under my jeans in addition to no jacket. It was dark and the warm day had given way to a rather chilly night.

Reuel pretended not to notice. So, I continued my questioning. "Why was Malachi so adamant about me learning the truth tonight? I never thought I would survive long enough to see him break rank like that— especially not for my benefit."

"A lot has changed for Malachi during this assignment," Reuel said, extending his hand to help me up from the ground. "You ready to go home? You've had a long, difficult day."

"Should I even ask you to explain what you mean, about Mal?" I looked up at Reuel, waiting for an answer.

He smiled.

"Let's go, Kendi."

I took his hand and allowed him to pull me from the ground. My legs were stiff and weak. They trembled as if they couldn't hold the weight of my frame. I took a step and stumbled, sure that I wouldn't be able to walk the distance home.

"We don't have to walk." Reuel draped his arm around my shoulder and, instantly, we were in my bedroom.

"Thanks," I said as I slumped onto the bed.

"Anytime. Take a hot shower. You'll feel better. I'll get Renay to bring up some soup. Eat and get some rest." Reuel left, closing the door behind him.

The house was quiet. I could hear the low murmur of the television and voices downstairs as I crept into the bathroom. I was grateful to be left alone. I'm sure it was by Reuel's mandate.

I'd learned the meaning of "overstimulation" in the last few hours, and I was not coping well. The hot shower did indeed help. My internal trembling seemed to have stopped.

When I returned from the bathroom, I found that Renay had left a bowl of chicken noodle soup on my desk. I scarfed it down and climbed into bed. I peered across the room at the clock—7:10 p.m. Still too early. It didn't matter. I was exhausted. I pulled a pillow over my head and effectively shut out the world for the rest of the night.

11

WHO'S AFRAID OF THE BIG, BAD THRONE?

The double doors banged open, and the Authorities were leading in Ophan.

What the hell was he doing here? I didn't want him to be involved in this mishap any further. It was bad enough that I had already taken advantage of his ignorance, and now he was being dragged into the high court to face this quorum of judges who were quickly transforming into an angry mob.

Poor kid. Ophan was confused as to why his presence had been requested. He glanced at me apologetically and then quickly returned his eyes to the floor as he was led to stand before the ruling eleven. Ophan was confused as to why his presence had been requested.

Ophan was very small in stature, and the Authorities towered over his slight frame. His dark locks hung loosely to his shoulders. The black luster was quite alluring against his contrasting white robe. Ophan's caramel-colored skin was luminescent, and his green eyes were brilliant in the dim light of the chamber. Ophan was beautiful—a magnificent creature to behold—not unlike the rest of the Thrones. Their luminous persona had everything to do with being in the direct presence of Yah. All the Thrones took on a certain incandescent aura that was somewhat mesmerizing.

Thrones were such mystical creatures. They rarely ever spoke unless directly spoken to, as much of their time was spent in worship. The level of worship that the Thrones personified took on a musical nature. As the winds of Empyrean blew, we could often hear the chimes that rang out from every Throne within earshot. It was the Thrones that filled Empyrean with the beautiful music of Yah.

Haamiah came forward to stand in front of Ophan. He appeared overly anxious to hear Ophan's testimony. Until this moment, I had assumed the judges already knew what I had done and were just trying to coax me into an audible confession.

"Ophan, I know that you are rather uncomfortable in this position, and I apologize to you for the necessity of your witness. However, would you please tell me and my fellow judges the nature of your relationship with Kendi?"

Ophan looked up at me and smiled graciously. "Kendi is my friend. He and I were introduced by Eloa, the angel of compassion."

Wow, I hadn't heard Eloa referred to this way in over a century. Eloa was one of the older celestial beings that still operated in a capacity that allowed her to interact with both mortals and immortals. It was said that she was created by the tears that Yah shed for his people. His level of compassion was so great that it was sealed in her heart for all eternity.

Ophan continued, "Because Kendi is Eloa's friend, he is also my friend."

I could hear the rumbles of disagreement behind me. Haamiah simply shook his head and continued. "Can you please share with me the request that Kendi asked of you prior to his being taken into custody by the Authorities?"

How could Haamiah possibly know about my request! No one knew about this—or so I thought—except Ophan and myself. I didn't even tell Eloa. First, because she would have talked me out of it. Second, because Eloa would have explained the rules to Ophan so that he wouldn't be used by the likes of me.

My body began to tremble involuntarily. I wasn't afraid for myself, but for Ophan. He was so innocent...so trusting. He had no idea that my request was illegal. In this moment, I realized that Ophan's innocence was about to be obliterated and that it was entirely my fault. I had completely and shamelessly taken advantage of him, and that was about to be revealed.

"Yes, Haamiah," Ophan chimed. "Kendi asked that I allow him to accompany me on my next assignment into Yah's inner chamber."

He didn't have a clue what was coming.

Haamiah leaned forward toward Ophan in anticipation. "Ophan, did Kendi not tell you that it was against the law for a celestial being other than a Throne to visit the inner chamber without being summoned by Yah himself? Did he not tell you that it was your job to guard the entrance to Merkabah, and to only grant access per Yah's command?"

Ophan's countenance fell. Understanding lit his expression, followed by the pain of betrayal. Ophan shook his head as if he were trying to clear the thoughts that now flooded his mind. From his place at the foot of the cathedra, he purposefully turned to meet my stare. I could see the agony in his eyes. The brilliance of his liquid green eyes had now hardened as if frozen in time. His aura had changed so fiercely by Haamiah's one statement that I wanted to crumble. I wanted to run, to hide, but his glare would not release me. I peered back at Ophan, yearning to retract the betrayal that had forced him into this reality: not all immortals were decent.

Ophan turned back to Haamiah and spoke through clenched teeth. "Sir, is anything further required of me?"

Ophan's face was stoic as he constrained himself to remain in his current form. The brilliance that we could see illuminating from Ophan's skin became a fiery semblance in Yah's presence. It was somewhat frightening to consider what he could do in this courtroom right now if he were not restraining himself. There was an astonishing amount of power contained in this being, and it was only out of reverence for Yah that he had humbled himself at the request of the judges.

Thrones were the closest to Yah and therefore endowed with authority that no other celestial being could even imagine. To walk among the rest of us, the Thrones had to harness most of their power. This was the reason no one dared to tamper with a newly created Throne. It allowed us a peek into their existence while they came to the knowledge of their true essence.

Awareness now filled Ophan's space. He had a full understanding of who he was and felt the apprehension that other Thrones had regarding coalescence with the rest of us. His heart was changed forever by my one exploit. The glimpse into the mysterious had once again been closed off to us all.

Everyone could see the visible change in Ophan's countenance. The courtroom had become silent as we took in the physical change that was taking place. The temporary cage in which he had harnessed his power was wearing thin, as Ophan was at his breaking point. No one dared move or even speak as we felt the power that exuded from this incredible being—potentially explosive. It was quite unnerving.

Ophan's patience was depleted. He turned around now to face Reuel at the front of the courtroom.

"If nothing else is required of me, Reuel, I will take my leave." Reuel simply nodded once. Ophan turned to descend the center aisle. He stalked past me, the seated judges, the Advocates, and the Authorities without a single glance. Our existence was no longer of consequence to him. Ophan pushed through the double doors and was gone. There was an audible sigh of relief from several places in the courtroom.

"Haamiah, have you lost your mind? What would make you summon a Throne into this proceeding?" Reuel bellowed once he was certain that Ophan was gone.

I rolled over, gasping awake. The sound of my heart hammered in my ears as I looked around the dark bedroom, feeling as though I were being watched. Everything was quiet, still. The beads of sweat rolling down the side of my face distracted me. I quickly wiped them away with the bottom of my shirt while I continued my surveillance. The last twenty-four hours had my nerves on edge.

Tonight was the first time that I dreamed of my time in Empyrean's high court and of Ophan—the Throne I had pissed off. The presence of the Thrones at the reservoir today must have triggered something in my subconscious.

My current situation sucked, and worse yet, there was nothing I could do about it. I would either have to live with it or die because of it...not much of a choice. I felt the tears begin to flow again. I didn't have the strength to care now. I fell back onto the pillows and pulled the covers back over my head.

12
THE TRUTH…HURTS

The sun was setting behind the trees when I awoke. I rolled over stiffly, trying to decide whether I would get up or not. I'd spent the entire day yesterday, and apparently most of today, in bed. No one bothered me, as far as I could remember. I vaguely remembered Renay leaving food on my desk at some point—although I never ate anything. My stomach snarled, and I looked over to check the desk. There was a sandwich, a bowl of sliced fruit, and PowerAde. I would have to thank Renay later.

I sat up, and my head spun. Once I felt steady, I crossed the room to the desk to try eating something. The fruit was still chilled. Renay must have been in here recently. I shouldn't be surprised that they were consistently checking up on me seeing that I was in such bad shape. Renay bringing me food was no doubt an excuse to make sure I wasn't hanging from the ceiling fan or something. I'm sure she was worried—especially since no one would have told her what was going on. She probably thought I had taken ill.

I picked at the fruit as I pondered all that Reuel had shared with me during my last conscious moments. Everything was so foggy. It all seemed like a horrible nightmare, but my mind knew it was all too real.

I was deep in thought when a light tap on the door interrupted my reverie. I hadn't answered yet when the door crept open.

"Kendi? You mind if I come in?" It was Malachi.

"Sure," I said without looking up from the desk. Why bother protesting? He was already in now.

"Are you feeling better?"

I shrugged. Truth be told, I didn't know how I felt. I hadn't gotten that far in the process yet. The extended sleep had been quite effective in making me numb to the entire situation. And I wanted to stay that way.

Malachi crossed the room and sat on the bed, watching me pick at the fruit.

"Aren't you hungry, man? You've been closed up in this room for almost forty-eight hours."

"A lot on my mind right now, Mal." I sighed.

"I understand. You want to talk about it?"

Malachi's question brought me up short. Did I want to talk about it? I still wasn't sure, but I knew I'd have to deal with all this sometime—soon. My silence wouldn't get any of the answers I needed.

"You've got to have a ton of questions," Malachi continued.

"That may just be the understatement of the year." I laughed to myself. Better to laugh than start the waterworks again.

I needed to plug the holes in Reuel's explanation. Despite his best effort to hide it, I knew he had given me an edited version of the truth, tailored to include only as much as he thought I was capable of handling. He was only trying to protect me, but I was tougher than he or even I realized. Yes, I would throw my toddler-esque tantrums, but in the end, I dealt with whatever it was I needed to handle.

Reuel's approach to this was driving me crazy. Just rip the damn Band-Aid off already. This inch-by-inch method was infuriating. I was constantly living in a state of fear, waiting for the other shoe to drop. I couldn't take it anymore.

I started with the easiest of my questions.

"You and the twins had a private conversation with Reuel the night of our team meeting. What were you all keeping from me?"

Malachi didn't hesitate to respond, which was encouraging.

"Reuel told us he thought the Legion had targeted you, and he mandated that we keep you safe. I wanted him to tell you exactly what was happening. We argued about the need for you to be brought up to speed. Raza and Angelo agreed with me, but Reuel was...unyielding. He didn't feel it necessary to cause you additional anxiety."

I would have to side with Reuel this time.

No, I didn't like being left out of the conversation, but now, knowing the context, I saw Reuel's reasoning. I wasn't in the right state of mind to deal with any of this. He had overruled everyone else's desire to have me in the know—for which I was grateful. I don't know how I would have reacted with just that small fraction of information. The ambiguity would have completely consumed me. Knowing that I was targeted by the Legion, without knowing why, in addition to everything else I was going through, would have been more than I could handle. And Reuel knew it.

"Reuel was right not to tell me. I'm not so good with the digestion of bad news. I'm sure you've noticed."

"Kendi, you've done better than any of us could have in the same situation. Yah's sentence is harsher than anything we could have ever imagined. It's brutal. Believe it or not, a large number of the Host is outraged with what you are being made to endure. And your recent appointment compounds the impossibility of it all."

Malachi was shaking his head as if to dislodge the thought. "Know that you have lots of sympathy among the Host. But sympathy doesn't allow anyone to feel what you are going through. Who would have thought Yah would resort to imprisoning one of the Host in this way? It's inconceivable."

Malachi shuddered as if his words triggered some bad memory. It was as if he were speaking from experience—like he had taken a long walk in the shoes I had been condemned to wear. Strange. I turned to face Mal as he continued to lament *my* situation.

Malachi was no longer looking at me but gazing into the distance as if caught in his own recollection of the events of Friday night.

"I felt so helpless. I could feel your desperation for escape from your human form, yet you had nowhere to go. The weight of it was crushing. I thought I would go mad—literally." His lips quivered as he spoke in a whisper.

Malachi had just articulated my exact feelings—the moment that I came to an understanding of both my assignment and my appointment. The words that he spoke now were the words that had escaped me as I fought to hold on to my sanity, as I stood shaking and crying in the middle of our living room. How was it that Malachi now described the event as if he'd lived it himself?

I had an overwhelming feeling that my recent revelation was still incomplete. The blood drained from my face.

Malachi continued as my stomach knotted painfully.

"I tried to come after you, but Reuel forbade it. He insisted on following you himself. It could have easily turned into a fight if not for the twins. You were trapped in a conundrum of human emotion, and I had exploded with the intensity of angelic volatility with no fleshly prison to hold me. It's a good thing Renay wasn't home. I nearly took down the living room in my tirade. That much energy in a closed in space ...not a good thing.

"Raz and Ang restrained me long enough for Reuel to finish subduing me. My body was grateful for the release. But my mind raced on, consumed by the inner turmoil that I had just caused you. You had gone over the edge, and I was the one who pushed you there.

"Kendi, I can't tell you how sorry I am. It was never my intention to cause you this kind of distress—this kind of pain. The instant the truth left my lips, I regretted telling you."

Malachi's head was bowed, shoulders hunched, as he seemed to curl in on himself.

I was processing his words, but more closely appraising his demeanor. Mal was a mess. What had happened to him in the last couple of days? His face was shrouded in a thinly veiled mask of composure that threatened to crumble at any moment. Something wasn't right. Malachi's reaction was something more than just a team member feeling sorry for me. What he was describing went far beyond mere sympathy. Malachi was being affected by this situation as if it were his own reality. Yes, the team had become extremely close over the last few months. They were indeed my family. But this was something more.

I rose unsteadily from the desk and slowly crossed the room to Malachi. He didn't look up at the sound of my approach. I placed my hand on his shoulder. He was trembling.

"Malachi, what is it?" He was scaring me. I could feel that "other shoe" looming overhead.

When exactly did Malachi become so sympathetic to my situation?

"Kendi." Malachi paused and turned to me. "I owe you an explanation. One that's long overdue."

My racing heart felt as though it would burst from my chest. I knew Mal would just finish ripping off the Band-Aid, finally. Maybe this time, I would just bleed to death, and this torment would end abruptly.

I allowed my hand to fall from his shoulder.

"We have never talked about my absence during your time in the hospital."

This was it. This was the conversation Reuel had tried to push us into for the last few months.

But what had changed to make him ready to discuss this now?

Maybe now, Mal had no choice.

I didn't say anything but just nodded slowly, waiting for him to continue.

"The entire team was distraught when you were hurt. We couldn't believe Yah had allowed your sentence to implode the way that it had. None of the

Guardian had ever been injured at the hands of humans prior to that day, so everyone, even Reuel, was at a loss as to how to manage the incident. It was horrific all the way around. So, I didn't notice at first—hell, no one noticed." Malachi chuckled, shaking his head.

Notice what? I had not expected him to bring up the fight with Taylor.

"You had been beaten so badly. I could barely believe what I was witnessing. Of course, all of us had seen firsthand the battery of numerous mortals—wars, car accidents, fires, natural disasters, you name it. We are not unaccustomed to seeing the human body ravaged, but never had we seen this kind of damage to one of our own. The team had a hard time watching your sentence unfold and become *real* for each of us on a personal level. But it was not until you collapsed here at the house that I realized I was more than just upset because you were hurt. I was...physically affected by it in a way that none of the others were.

"I didn't know what was happening and it frightened me. It was as if my entire being was transformed in a few short moments, and I was no longer my own. You and I became connected, Kendi, in a more tangible way. It was as if I were inside your body looking out. When you began to lose consciousness, I held onto you desperately, not just because I could see that you were dying—and you were—but also because I could *feel* your life slipping away. I felt as if everything that I am was being drained out of me.

"I couldn't breathe. A debilitating weakness overtook me. The desperation to cling to you, to protect you, was the most overwhelming sensation I had ever endured.

"It wasn't until you stopped breathing that the twins realized something was wrong with *me* as well. I had become completely unaware. The only thing I can liken the feeling to is being caught in the death-hold by one of the Dominion. It was a feeling of complete helplessness. It was as if I were paralyzed.

"I could see that you needed help. I could feel the desperation in the room as Raza began CPR, but I couldn't *feel* myself anymore. Angelo was trying to rouse me, but all that I could comprehend was crushing hopelessness—as if all purpose had escaped my existence. Like my essence was gone. I was petrified, although not for me, but for the part of me that was abating."

Malachi was visibly shaken as he recalled the event for me.

"I felt as if I were dying. Yet it was you who was slipping away," he whispered. "You crashed again when we arrived at the hospital. This time

Reuel was there to witness my experience. He didn't know what was going on with me, and you were in such a critical state that he didn't have the capacity to deal with me as well. Reuel reasoned that I was overwhelmed by your condition and that I just needed some time away from it all. So Reuel released me to go to Empyrean. He felt the time at home would give me the strength to better handle what the team was being made to endure.

"But I knew what I was feeling was more than just anxiety over what had happened to you. Never had I been able to feel what someone else was feeling. I could literally feel your breath stop and your heart slow until it was no longer beating as if it were happening to me. I could feel my essence begin to wean like it was being ripped away from me. I didn't feel like *me* anymore.

"I had felt this way only one other time. It was long ago when I was still a part of Uriel's guard. We were in the Teshukah region and engaged in battle with the Legion. Omniel stood as the Eklektos then. The battle was fierce, but it was clear the Guardian would not prevail. Uriel ordered us to retreat, and as I fled, Soqed pursued, and I was not prepared for the attack. Soqed caught me from behind around the neck and immediately incapacitated me. I found myself plummeting toward the Earth, locked in Soqed's death-hold. I was fully aware but was paralyzed and unable to do anything about it. I thought that my time with the Host was over and that my next stop would be Sheol. If it hadn't been for Uriel, I would be a Shade today—instead of Soqed.

"When you were dying, I felt as if I were in that death-hold all over again—like my essence was being taken. I didn't understand what was happening, but I did know that it was in direct correlation to your condition. Every time that you were revived, so was I. I was confused beyond belief. It was in Empyrean that I was given the explanation I needed."

What the hell? I had never heard of such an occurrence. I honestly couldn't remember much from the day of the incident with the football players after the guys found me, other than pain, not being able to breathe, and my encounter with Eloa. Her warning to me that day was still vivid in my mind.

I could vaguely remember how upset Malachi was, and how involved he was in trying to take care of me until Reuel arrived. I could also remember his irritation with the EMT in the ambulance on the way to the hospital, but beyond that, I was coming up blank.

Malachi had stopped talking. I presumed that he was waiting for me to process the information he had just shared. I continued to stare blankly out of my bedroom window to avoid Malachi's gaze while I tried to recall the events of that day.

I didn't know how to face him, or any of the team for that matter, knowing what they would have to endure because of me.

Malachi rose from the bed standing in front of me so that he could continue his explanation. "When I arrived in Empyrean, I was met by Tabbris, the Eklektos of Zalal. This surprised me.

"Although, I knew exactly who he was—who didn't? I had never had an actual conversation with one of the Eklektos, and especially not one that had been successful in sealing a gateway. He explained to me what I needed to know, what you need to know now. Tabbris interpreted the office of the Shoer and all that is connected to it. He then introduced me to Hozi, his Achim."

My head snapped up at the word. A shock ran through my body as if I had been tasered. I looked at Malachi with my eyes stretched wide—certain I didn't want to hear any more of this. Whatever it was that Malachi was trying to tell me was bad enough that he had withheld the information for weeks. This conversation would not end well.

It had been ages since I had heard the title *Achim* tossed around; and then, it was only in Empyrean. I never thought about the hierarchy of Empyrean during my time on Earth, especially since I did not consider myself an important part of it. Malachi knew this. Yet he brought it up now. As the knot in my stomach tightened, I raised a questioning eyebrow.

"For every Shoer, Yah has created an Achim—a brother. The Achim and the Shoer are created from the same essence, one mold. The pair is essentially one spirit with separate bodies. The Achim is older, created first, to prepare the way for the Eklektos. Once the Shoer is created, the Achim's destiny is set. There is no way to sever the connection without the destruction of both beings.

"I guess you can say that Yah didn't break the mold when I was created." Malachi chuckled softly.

I felt as if my legs would give out. What was Yah doing to me?

"The Achim is created to protect the Eklektos—even at his own expense."

I stared at Malachi while his words engrafted themselves into my very being. Suddenly I understood Malachi's actions over the last few months—his aversion to my presence. He distanced himself to deal with the onslaught of information and duty with which he had been burdened. Malachi had gone to Empyrean for a respite, only to find out that he had an albatross around his neck that he would never be able to get rid of. The same team member that had let him down, had treated him horribly, and felt perfectly justified in doing so was...his brother.

Malachi had every right to hate me. Right now, I hated myself. My knees began to shake. The room spun. It was hell knowing I had a death sentence looming overhead. I was incapable of adequately dealing with my own sentence. Rage was the prevalent emotion I dealt with on a regular basis. Was I now to swallow Malachi's damnation as well? He was tethered to me without any hope of reprieve. Everything that I did, or didn't do, would impact him. I was identified and marked by the Legion, and Malachi was in the middle of the bedlam.

My level of responsibility continued to mount—the challenges unfathomable. The damage I was sure to inflict would be colossal. This time, I would take down not only myself, but also my brother, and most likely the entire team with me.

"Malachi, I'm sorry...I'm so sorry," I whispered.

I shook my head trying to dislodge the hopelessness and the dread that was threatening to take root there. The tears today were unlike those that I shed two days ago. Today they burned with the shame of my failure, my unscrupulous approach to getting what I wanted, and with the disgust, I felt for disregarding all that I had been created for as trivial.

My human frame was not going to be able to endure much more. The last few days had proven to be the most horrendous of my existence. How was I supposed to reprogram myself from just wanting to be left alone to stepping into the most revered position among the Host—Eklektos?

Why would anyone choose me? This was surely the place in which Malachi should stand. He was noble and selfless. He was the one with integrity. I could see Malachi as Eklektos, but Yah would have to create another Achim. I wasn't even worthy of that role. How many times now had I let Mal down in my own selfishness? I turned away as I felt the breath catch in my chest and a sob broke through.

My only desire in this moment was escape. I couldn't think anymore. I didn't want to feel anymore. Not in this body. It wasn't meant to endure this kind of pain—this kind of weight.

Malachi's hand came down on my shoulder. The added weight enhanced my body's uncontrolled trembling.

"Come on, Kendi. Let's get out of here. Let's go home." At that precise moment, the release came. We burst from our cages and took to the heavens.

I could breathe again...even if momentarily.

13

EMPYREAN

I had forgotten what it felt like to have the freedom of the heavens as my playground. It had been months since my last release from my mortal body. I'm not sure why I was suddenly afforded this liberty now, but my guess was that Reuel feared I had reached the mental capacity of what I could handle in my human form without some sort of breakdown. He knew this respite was an absolute necessity. And it didn't come a minute too soon.

I was grateful for the release but still wanted to be alone. There was only one being I wanted to see—even in Empyrean. Eloa. The problem was that Eloa was essentially never alone. She had the type of aura that drew the other Host to her. So, upon arrival, I went to the gardens of Merkabah. It was a calming, solitary location—a great place to be alone. I knew Eloa would eventually find me there. The gardens were a place she frequented whenever she wanted an escape of her own.

Being home brought a joy that I had not experienced for some time now. No memories I could conjure of Empyrean did its beauty any justice. In comparison, Earth just did not hold the same allure.

I wandered the gardens for quite a while, allowing the contentment and tranquility of home to wash over me. However, it didn't take long to recall the reason for this brief reprieve. And even in my natural form, the weight of my predicament was a tremendous burden to withstand.

I continued to drift aimlessly through the gardens, desperately trying to keep my mind from focusing on my circumstance. After some time, I found myself in the innermost center. It was the place that Eloa and I often came to be alone; just being in our place brought an extra layer of comfort. In the center of the gardens, there was a small circular clearing with an array of flowers that were mesmerizing, the many fragrances soothing. I ambled to the smooth stone pew, sat down, closed my eyes, and allowed my mind to rest for the first time in what seemed like an eternity.

It wasn't long before Eloa found me in our place. I felt her gentle hand come down on my shoulder. "Kendi, it's good to see you. I've missed you." Her voice seemed to echo throughout the small sanctuary.

I opened my eyes, looking up into her radiant face. She smiled tenderly, comforting me further.

I smiled back at her as I took her hand and held it to my face. Not having any words to adequately express what I was feeling, I let the silence speak for me. I could be myself with Eloa. I didn't need any pretenses. It was refreshing to know that this had always been enough for her.

She remained silent as well, allowing me to enjoy her presence. I was so blessed to have a being like Eloa as my closest friend and confidante.

As I opened myself to fully appreciate both being in Empyrean, as well as in Eloa's presence, a sudden flood of other emotions overwhelmed me. I had never experienced such intense emotion in my angelic form. And for the first time in my existence, I cried as a member of the Host.

The tears that I had shed in Danvers, in my human form, were tears of dread, frustration, and hopelessness.

The tears that escaped now came from the innermost part of my being. They were a release. It was as if these tears were washing me, healing my brokenness, as they flowed. With each tear that fell, I felt a little bit lighter.

As quickly as the silent tears appeared, they stopped. If I had been in the presence of anyone but Eloa, I would have been bothered by the display of weakness. However, I was comforted in knowing that she was here to share this very private moment.

Eloa leaned in closer, placed her hand under my chin, and lifted my head, forcing me to look at her. She released my chin, and with the same hand began to gently wipe the tears from my face.

"Better?" she whispered.

I didn't answer, but I did feel better somehow. "Reuel and the others are looking for you. There is much for you to learn and so very little time." I nodded my head in agreement.

"Reuel sacrificed quite a bit to make sure that you would have this unscheduled time in Empyrean. He pleaded desperately with Yah to allow the respite. It wasn't supposed to happen this way. However, Reuel felt sure that you would succumb to the burden of your sentence without this reprieve. He is horribly frightened for you.

"To be honest, so am I. It pained me greatly not to be able to help you through the last few days. But Yah has been adamant about no one interfering."

Eloa's face was remorseful.

"Then why has he allowed me to come to Empyrean?" I questioned.

"It is part of Yah's deal with Reuel, part of the governing authority that he has allowed. But this interference will not be without consequence. He is taking a great risk by continuing to intervene for you. Yah is at the end of the grace that he will extend to Reuel on your behalf."

"Why does he continue to intervene? I wouldn't. Not for me...if I were in his place. Yah already knows how this ends. Let it play out already."

"Kendi, why can't you see the potential within yourself that we see? What Yah sees? What he knows?"

I shook my head in disagreement. All I could see were my mistakes, my mishaps, and the mayhem I was sure to cause while I was trapped by this appointment.

I let out a long sigh before rising from the pew. I knew my moments of solitude here would be severely limited—especially my time with Eloa.

"Thank you...as always."

I took her by the hand and pulled her up from the pew. I would go and find the team, but there was no reason why she couldn't come along. I didn't know when I would be allowed home again. We walked in silence down the trail toward the outer part of the garden. My guess was that I would find the team near Kahal. There was a training ground there that the Thrones used to instruct the rest of us in the art of battle. It was a place where I had spent countless hours daydreaming about ways to escape my role as Guardian rather than paying attention to the combat training that I was now so desperately in need of. As much as I hated the thought of battling against my own kind, I had to look at this time of training as necessary basic survival skills. I never thought that I would be in a "kill or be killed" scenario, but here I was.

The mere thought of stripping another immortal being of their essence and sentencing them to an eternity in Sheol made me sick to my stomach. Things shouldn't be this way. I never wanted to be trapped in the middle of the Host and the Legion, especially not with a target on my back and bulls-eyes on the foreheads of anyone close to me.

"Kendi, everything will be fine. Yah created you for this moment. I know it's hard for you to see right now but know that I believe in you. Your team believes in you," Eloa encouraged.

Formulating a rebuttal would be pointless. Eloa never allowed me the luxury of being negative.

I guess it's why I always felt better after having spent time with her.

We exited the gardens onto the path that led to Kahal. The path curved sharply to the right and was bordered by tall shrubs on both sides so that our view up the path was obscured. However, I could hear footsteps approaching. I figured Reuel had gotten impatient and had come looking for me. I took in a deep breath to steady myself for the encounter. I had not seen or spoken to Reuel since the "data download" a few nights prior.

"You can do this, Kendi." Eloa felt my sudden anxiety.

"I know," I responded as I exhaled, trying to smile.

We rounded the curve, and I immediately stopped, pulling Eloa to a halt with me. It wasn't Reuel that had come looking for me, but Tabbris.

"Kendi. Eloa." Tabbris greeted us with a nod of his head.

"Your Grace." I nodded in return.

"I will leave the two of you alone," Eloa announced releasing my hand. "See you soon, Kendi."

I watched Eloa disappear up the path before turning my attention to Tabbris. He made me nervous, to say the least. I had successfully managed to avoid the Guardian that were in the higher ranks—until now. I wasn't sure how to interact with him.

"Do you mind if I accompany you to Kahal? I would like to speak with you for a moment before joining the others."

"Not at all, Eklektos," I lied. "What can I do for you?"

"Reuel felt as though it would be a good idea for you and me to speak. He was rather concerned with your reaction to your appointment. I must say; I was worried myself once he replayed it for me. How are you feeling now about being appointed the Shoer of Charon...any better?"

I didn't know what the politically correct answer was, so I decided to be honest. Tabbris probably wouldn't understand my angst any better than the rest of the Host who insisted on giving me these pep talks, but at least he would know about the weight of the appointment.

"Not at all...I'm scared to death," I replied, shaking my head.

To this point, all I had ever heard was that the appointment was such a great honor. Yah would not bestow it on just anybody.

The office demanded great respect.

My appointment would change that point of view— quickly. Thanks to my unscheduled visit to Empyrean and the impromptu training session at Kahal, it wouldn't be long before my position was made public knowledge. If it hadn't already.

I would say that I was at the bottom of the list of worthiness for such an office and my guess was that most of Empyrean agreed with me. I would have never dreamed it possible to receive such an appointment—talk about blindsided!

"I would be more nervous if you weren't afraid, Kendi. Every Shoer needs to have a healthy dose of fear to function effectively in this office. Without fear, you become reckless. And not only would you be risking your life, but the lives of all those who have no choice but to follow and to protect you," Tabbris explained.

"A healthy dose...what about paralyzing, gut-wrenching terror?" I chuckled without humor.

Tabbris reached out and took hold of my shoulder, pulled me to a stop, and turned me so that I was facing him.

"Tell me, why are you so petrified, son? One can overcome fear and still function. But what you are describing...what Reuel described to me...is completely something else. I need you to be transparent, or else I can't help you. No one is here but you and me, so tell me. What is it?"

Tabbris's directness brought me up short. I had spent the last few days wallowing in misery and grief. I hadn't thought out my reaction past the "woe is me" and "I'm going to get everyone killed" phases. I was kind of stuck in self-pity mode.

I spat out the first thing that came to mind.

"I don't want to be responsible for the lives of my fellow Guardian. I haven't even taken on that responsibility for myself yet. I'm sure you've heard about my glowing record. I'm 0–2 at the moment. Can't really say that I have lived up to the standard of a leader by any stretch of the imagination."

Just saying the words out loud made me even more ashamed to be standing with Tabbris.

"Stop right there. Are you listening to yourself? You just explained your own reaction."

I looked at him with one raised eyebrow, not knowing where he was going with this. He smiled in response to my expression and continued.

"And I quote, 'I don't want to be responsible…' The fact that Yah *created* you for the office of the Guardian makes that statement contrary. As a Guardian, your primary obligation is responsibility—responsibility for your assignments, responsibility to defend the gateways, responsibility to the Shoer, responsibility to your fellow Guardian. The list goes on and on.

"Kendi, you've been coddled for far too long. It's time that you experienced some tough love from someone other than just Yah.

"Until now, you have *chosen not* to be responsible, and it's a miracle that only two mortals have died because of your negligence. But there *is* a difference between an inability to handle responsibility and choosing to be irresponsible. Now that you know your appointment, that choice is no longer an option.

"Underneath all of the tears, the tantrums, and the wallowing is the fact that Yah eliminated your choice to be irresponsible when he appointed you to this office. There is no further decision to make. You must step into the role; it is your mandate. However, it will be up to you whether you live up to the expectation of the Host, the Guardian, and your team."

"What do you mean?"

"The office of the Shoer is appointed by Yah. But the Host chooses the Eklektos. *Eklektos* is a title of honor and respect coined by the Guardian. It is based on how you lead. You can choose to stand with integrity and honor and perform to the best of your ability, thus earning your place as Eklektos. Or you can simply stand as the Shoer until you are defeated and replaced—hopefully, you won't be killed in the process.

"The Guardian will follow you either by mandate or by choice. I prefer the latter. A soldier that respects his commander is far more passionate about the mission and defending the life of his leader. Don't you think?"

It suddenly dawned on me that no one to this point had called me Eklektos except for Malachi, and, as my Achim, he was probably obligated. That title had to be earned.

I couldn't disagree with anything that Tabbris had said. I never tried to take my rightful place in the Guardian. I'd spent all my time and energy trying to find an exit. And now Yah took away my option to exit. Was I capable of stepping into such a role if I put forth some effort?

"You would know far better than I, Eklektos. But I may never gain that kind of respect with all my screwing up. Most of the Guardian wouldn't follow me across the street—let alone into battle if given a choice."

"Well, Kendi, the fact is, they will not have a choice. So, it sounds as if you have a decision to make. I can certainly teach you the mechanics of the office, but beyond that, you will be on your own. *You* must decide that you are worthy of the calling to which you have been appointed and stand therein.

"Let me say this, Shoer—if you step up, the rest will fall into place."

I nodded. There was nothing Tabbris could say to make this any easier. I had a long, uphill battle to try to repair all the damage I had done and no idea where to start. It would take everything I had just to focus on the mechanics.

"So, what are the mechanics?" I asked, deliberately avoiding the obvious challenge that my election created.

Tabbris looked at me intently as if searching for an answer I had not yet formulated. After a long minute, the tiniest smile flitted at the corners of his mouth. I'm certain Tabbris didn't intend for me to notice.

I wanted to ask but thought better of it as he quickly rearranged his expression and began his explanation of the office of the Shoer.

"Each of the seven gateways was created in direct correlation to the seven deadly sins that plague the Earth. And there is a Dominion, a Legion regime head, that is the master of that sin—ruling not only the gateway but also the region of the world in which that gateway resides.

"For this reason, the only way to close the gateway is to defeat the Dominion that rules the region. Two of the gateways have been closed—Atsal and Zalal. Atsal was taken down in the Antarctic, and with it, Ascidia, who ruled the continent in slothfulness.

"And then there is Zalal—the gateway that I discovered in Australia. Djinn was set over the gateway there and contaminated the people with the sin of overindulgence. Djinn was a mighty warrior. He was yet another of Yah's Thrones who had rebelled with Lucifer; therefore, not easily defeated. Many of the Host were lost in the battle. I remember it as if it were yesterday."

Tabbris paused as he lamented the loss of his comrades. "Until that day, I didn't think I would be able to take the life of one of our own. I was sure that destroying the essence of an immortal being was completely beyond me. But there is another part of a Shoer's makeup that takes over during battle. It's the part of our essence that commands us to defend righteousness on the Earth. The Guardian has an inherent need to abolish the breach created so many millennia ago—once and for all. This need manifests itself in an overpowering way during battle. There is no way to fully explain this to you, Kendi. I am told it is second nature to the Guardian, and even more magnified in every Shoer."

Great. Now I had to worry about an instinct to kill as well.

"If you don't mind, I prefer to keep my murderous tendencies under wraps, for now, Eklektos. You said that you discovered the gate in Australia. How?" Tabbris laughed quietly.

"It would be easier for me to show you how to trap and destroy one of the Dominion, my friend."

"Locating the gateway in Charon will take tapping into your sixth sense, and the only way to accomplish this is to learn self-control. Not something that you are particularly known for, is it? I have been helping Malachi with this skill. I'd have to admit that he is a quick study."

"Wait a minute…Malachi?"

"Yes. As your Achim, Malachi must fully learn to utilize his sixth sense as well. It is the only way that he can effectively stand with you—to protect you.

"It is why Malachi was so persistent with Reuel a few days ago when you were in the reservoir. He knew you were in danger even when Reuel did not. How do you think he found you so quickly? He can sense when you need his help. Remember your first day of school when your anger almost got the best of you? Malachi is learning to *feel* you when you are not in his presence.

"You are not an exception to this skill, Kendi. As both an Achim and a Shoer, you have this ability as well. You and Malachi are extensions of one another. You can communicate at any time. You can feel what he feels and see what he sees, once you learn how to harness the authority that Yah has given to you. It takes patience and control—something that you are now going to have to take the time to learn. There are no shortcuts, no way around.

"This is the same power that will allow you to sense the location of the gateway in Charon. No other Guardian will have the same level of connection to the gate. The gate will *speak* to you."

Speak to me? Okay, maybe older members of the Host had the possibility of losing it after a certain number of years. Or perhaps there were only so many battles one could successfully handle before they completely lost their grip on reality.

"Tabbris…" I paused, not knowing how to begin questioning this insanity.

"Speak to you figuratively, Kendi. As you get closer to its location, there will be an unmistakable pull that you alone can feel. This ability will become part of your sixth sense. I know it all sounds foreign now. It will get easier. Reuel has spoken with Yah regarding my training you.

"I will be able to assist you, both here in Empyrean, and when you return to Danvers. Reuel has become quite fond of you, hasn't he?" he asked as he examined me from head to toe.

"I think he puts too much faith in me, considering my extreme lack of competence," I responded, lowering my voice as we approached the end of the path that entered Kahal.

"I think you could use some of Reuel's faith in yourself, Shoer." Tabbris quipped as we parted ways.

14

TRAINING DAY

The training field was about three football fields in length. Several separate groupings of the Host had already gathered. Farthest out in the field were Uriel, his team, and the extensions. Closest to my end was Reuel, Malachi, Raza, and Angelo. And in the center, were the instructors, the Thrones, including Ophan, who was literally glaring in my direction.

I hadn't seen Ophan since he'd learned of my betrayal in the high court several months ago. I was too ashamed to even make eye contact with him. Beyond that, his scowl was a quick reminder that I was still on his shit list.

"You know you must face Ophan eventually, right?" Tabbris remarked as I turned away from the field.

"I know. I just didn't think it would be today," I replied, gritting my teeth, trying to fight the anxiety that was knotting my stomach.

As we walked into the field, Reuel left the rest of our team and came to greet Tabbris and me. "Your Grace. Kendi."

"Hello, Reuel. Good to see you again."

"Likewise," Reuel added with a nod of his head and then turned to face me. "How are you?"

"I'm okay." I tried my best to smile, but it felt more like a grimace.

"Kendi, you and I will speak again soon," Tabbris concluded as he continued to the middle of the training field to meet the rest of the Thrones. There were six in all with Tabbris's arrival.

"How was your talk with Tabbris?" Reuel asked once Tabbris had walked away. "Informative yet...confusing," I replied truthfully.

"It will all become clearer soon. Don't worry."

"I'll take your word for it. What are we doing today?"

"Since we are on high alert, and Charon has been inundated with the

Guardian and some of the Thrones to assist, I thought it would be a good idea to have this meeting for both formal introductions and additional combat training. We can all use it," Reuel said as he placed a hand on my shoulder. I just nodded.

"You ready to join the others?"

"Not even close." I laughed despite myself.

We continued into Kahal. I stopped where I was most comfortable—with our team. "Hey, guys." I smiled, trying to put them at ease. "How's it going?"

They smiled back, although their eyes remained tight with concern.

"We're good, just ready to get some training in," Raza said in his usually overzealous tone, beaming. Reuel, Raza, and Angelo headed off to the center of the field, while Malachi hung back with me.

"Are you ready for this, brother?" he whispered.

"Hell no." I laughed. "But let's do it anyway."

"We'll do more information gathering today than anything. The battle skills come naturally when we need them, but information is power when dealing with the Legion. Just make sure you pay attention. I can help you with the battle logistics later. All right?"

I turned slightly in Malachi's direction. He looked tired and worried. After all Mal and I had been through, it was hard to comprehend the level to which we were now tied together. And even though the tethering was not his choice, the look in his eyes told me that he had come to terms with his placement. Malachi considered it an honor to stand with me. I was so undeserving of the level of commitment that was exuding from my Achim.

I nodded once in agreement.

We caught up with the rest of the team just as the meeting was called to order. "My friends, welcome to Kahal!" Tabbris's voice boomed across the field.

Simultaneously, all those that were gathered took a knee and bowed their heads, effectively giving Tabbris control of the meeting.

Tabbris began explaining the situation in our region, all of which I was far too familiar with. I had seen it unfold up close and personal over the last several days. Not only had the Legion invaded Charon, but somehow, they had also found out that I was the appointed Shoer and had placed a price on my head. I was now the target of every Dominion that had access because of that damned gateway.

Uriel had moved both his team and the extensions into the area, and Yah had commanded a small regime of Thrones—the five that stood with Tabbris midfield—to further protect the mortals, and to assist the rest of us in preparation for the impending battle. The Thrones would also stand with us in battle if necessary.

Battle was something I didn't want to think about. Any confidence I'd had in my skills or ability was literally beaten out of me back in Danvers. While I knew battle in my natural form would be completely different, my assurance had been shaken, and it would not be easy to settle back into the same brashness I'd once had. Tabbris rallied the troops. "The situation in Charon is urgent. Yet the Host will stand strong!" A rallying cry went up from the Guardian.

As he continued, I stole glances throughout the collection of angels present. Many I knew, or at least knew of. My reputation would be notorious here— which was more unfortunate for me than I cared to think about. Earning the respect of the Host at large would have to start with those that had been assigned to both protect and to follow me into battle. That meant this group.

My biggest two challenges were both here—Ophan and Uriel. I understood Ophan's aversion to me. But Uriel, I had never had any direct interaction with. He wanted nothing to do with me because of my debacle that implicated Malachi and, by default, him. Malachi had been one of his extensions at the time.

The gathered Thrones were Tabbris, Ophan, Cassiel, Xaphan, Mihr, and Gazardiel. Apart from Tabbris, they were the warriors Yah had appointed to watch over the region because of the impending battle. Tabbris had earned his right to choose where he would participate after his victory in Zalal. Everyone was familiar with this crew. No introductions were necessary.

I for one was certainly glad they were here.

Ophan was new to this grouping. He had replaced Naqam, who had been given a new assignment at Merkabah. I felt a pang of panic with his placement. I didn't like being so close to such a powerful being that had an ax to grind against me. At this point, I wasn't sure we were all fighting on the *same* side.

Gathered with Uriel were the twelve members of his elite team: Chamuel and Charoum (the twins), Urim, Sandalphon, Nisroc, Muriel, Isda, Forcus, Hael, Kutiel, Qaphsiel, and Gavreel. Again, I was familiar with this infamous bunch because of their reputations. If angels could be bad asses, these members of the Host would certainly qualify. However, I was not at all familiar with the others that lingered with the elite. The extensions changed frequently as Uriel deemed them unworthy for a spot on his team. I inconspicuously nudged Malachi for assistance.

"Who are these with Uriel? Not his team, but the others."

"Valoel, Jophiel, Elemiah, and Zuriel. The large one in the back is Liwet. He took my place after the...uh... incident."

"Ah...sorry, Mal." I realized then that I wasn't the only uncomfortable one here. When would I start thinking of more than just myself? Of course, Malachi would be anxious. How long had it been since he had to face Uriel and, worst yet, Liwet, who had been gunning for anyone's position at the first sign of trouble?

"Don't worry about it, Kendi. I'm fine." Malachi whispered, but I could see the tension in his eyes. Our attention was turned toward Tabbris, who began speaking.

"Friends, the time has come for us to stand together once again. The gate has been widened in Charon, and Abbadon is taking a stand. As we have done in times past, the Host will defend this region of the Earth. The gateway has not yet been located, but a new problem has arisen. The Legion has identified our Shoer and has marked him for destruction to preempt the gate's closing. This cannot be allowed to happen."

Damn. Tabbris was singling me out from the rest of the group. I could feel the eyes of my comrades, as they turned to inspect the newly appointed Shoer. I deliberately kept my focus on Tabbris, as I knew the scrutiny was not favorable. I could hear the low mumbles begin among the crowd as those who *knew* me began discussing the disaster that was my life.

The Eklektos allowed this to go on for several moments, and then called the congregation to order.

"Friends, come in closer. Our time today for training is limited. Let us make the most of the stint that we have been allotted."

With this, everyone moved to the center of the field. The divided groups effectively merged into one unit, and the Thrones took center stage facing the rest of us.

"First and foremost, know that both Abbadon and Azrael were Thrones prior to their dissension. So, everything that will be demonstrated here today can also be accomplished by them."

The five Thrones took to the skies, leaving Tabbris watching their illustration. One of the unique powers of the Thrones was the ability to control the atmosphere. They could conjure lightning and thunder and command the winds. They could also effectively block these same measures when defending against another Throne. The rest of us could only use evasive maneuvering.

I watched in awe as Gazardiel conjured a lightning bolt and hurled it toward Mihr. Mihr proceeded to launch himself at the fiery missile. As he approached the bolt, his already massive size expanded as he deflected it with his body and retaliated with a thunderous boom that sent Gazardiel into a tailspin spiraling toward Kahal. In a flash, Xaphan raced across the sky, holding his position in between Gazardiel and Mihr. He lifted one arm, and a great wind arose, wrapping around Gazardiel stopping his plummet. As Xaphan lifted the other arm, the wind threw Mihr across the sky. Ophan and Cassiel held their positions on the outskirts of the demonstration, observing as we did, as they were the newest of the assemblage.

I'd never seen such a display of power. How in the hell were we supposed to be able to defend against this? Let alone defeat a being who had mastered this kind of skill. With a gaping mouth, I stood watching.

This was the first time I had seen the Thrones in action. Was this demonstration supposed to help or hurt?

"Damn."

"They are something, aren't they?" Malachi agreed.

"Don't let this exhibition bother you too much. Thrones like to show off their strengths while hiding their weaknesses. They have limitations, Kendi. They aren't Yah."

Tabbris must have heard our exchange or anticipated how this showcase would make the rest of us feel.

"Uriel, Nisroc, please join our friends to further demonstrate," he requested.

Nisroc's countenance changed immediately. His hard expression became marred with a wide, mischievous grin. Uriel fared a bit better, keeping his eagerness undercover. The corner of his mouth twitched as he fought a smirk.

They took to the skies with an urgency that left me baffled. I would have been hesitant to engage these Thrones even in a mock battle. But Nisroc immediately confronted Gazardiel, and Uriel went after Mihr.

I fully expected both Thrones to again conjure the elements, but to my surprise, they both chose to engage in hand-to-hand combat. Why the lack of aggression now that others had joined the fight?

"Manipulating the elements takes great concentration and a tremendous amount of strength. It depletes their energy for a period. Therefore the Thrones often fight in pairs, so that if one is weakened, the other can protect. If there is not a protector, a weakened Throne can be brought down easily by a trained warrior."

Before Malachi could finish his explanation, Uriel struck Mihr with a blow that effectively crippled him. Mihr began falling from the sky. Before Mihr could regain his composure, Uriel slung his flaming bola and bound him from shoulders to torso—effectively limiting his flight. In a burst, Uriel swung in front of Mihr and grabbed him by the throat—the death-hold. He continued to drive Mihr toward Kahal until Xaphan struck him from behind. While Uriel attempted to recover, Xaphan freed Mihr from the bola.

Nisroc was not as quick to subdue Gazardiel, and they continued in hand-to-hand combat until Gazardiel reached both hands into the atmosphere and pulled out a blast of water that sent Nisroc into a tailspin.

"Notice you don't have a large window of time to take them down. You must be swift and precise. Time is of the essence when battling the Thrones," Malachi explained.

"How long is too long?" I wanted to know.

"It varies, Kendi. Based on how much of their strength is depleted. Their eyes are the best indicator. A Throne's eyes will become dim when their strength wanes. Once the glow is back, you're out of time."

I shook my head. That proximity was a little close for my taste.

Tabbris allowed the demonstration to continue for a while longer. I watched Uriel intently, as he was more skilled than his second-in-command. He quickly took advantage of the Thrones' weaknesses in every incident, prevailing in several altercations despite being outnumbered. There were effective demonstrations of each flaming weapon used in hand-to-hand combat: swords, bolas, mjolnirs, chained maces, and shields. When each of the Thrones had been defeated at least once, Tabbris called the exposition team back to Kahal.

"The next time we come together, which will be soon, we will rotate every regime into practical training with the Thrones. Make sure you each rehearse what you have witnessed today," Tabbris instructed.

"Before we disperse, there are a few other facts about the Thrones which will be helpful during either a chance encounter or in battle," he announced.

Tabbris gathered the group in closer, leaving only a small open circle in the center where he and the other Thrones stood. Everyone else was shuffled around to fill in the gaps as the congregation moved in for better vantage point. As I moved to my left, to avoid being buried in the crowd, others filed into the space between Malachi and me. The realignment pushed Reuel and the rest of the guys to the opposite side of the field while I was pressed into the midst of Uriel and his team. Wonderful.

I hoped to avoid any direct contact with Uriel, but it seemed that the movement had segued into several small conversations as everyone tried to get better acquainted with their new comrades.

Reluctantly, I glanced to my right and my left. Uriel was on one side, and Liwet was on the other. I tried, unsuccessfully, to suppress the heavy sigh before it escaped my lips.

"What, Shoer? Not happy to see me?"

My title sounded like an expletive coming from Uriel. I figured now was as good time as any to start trying to repair the breach my actions had created, because like it or not, I needed not only Uriel's help, but everyone else gathered at Kahal.

"Always good to see you, Uriel. Thanks for being here."

Uriel chuckled ominously. "Like we were given a choice." He said, looking at Liwet.

"This shouldn't take long with Abbadon and Azrael tracking. We'll be back in Teshukah soon enough, Uriel," Liwet snorted.

Despite my best effort, fury took over.

"What, Liwet? Looking to climb the food chain again by picking off one of your own, leech?" I spat at him.

"What was Yah thinking? Appointing Empyrean's resident delinquent to such a position. I promise you, boy, screw up on my watch and I'll feed you to Azrael myself!" Uriel had moved directly in front of me and was seething.

"Uriel, back away," I warned.

"Or what?" he taunted, moving in closer.

Without thinking, I exploded into combat form— flaming sword drawn and at Uriel's throat. Instantly there was a crowd. Malachi and Raza had flanked me, pulling me back, and Reuel had wedged himself in between Uriel and me. Liwet, Nisroc, and Gavreel had come to defend their leader.

While I remained enraged, Uriel began to laugh as he backed away.

"That temper will either serve you well or get you killed, Shoer. We'll see." Uriel retreated to the other side of the circle along with his cohorts.

"Settle down, Kendi," Reuel whispered. "We have to gather as much information as we can while here. There is no time to waste."

I was still in combat mode, hovering a foot from the ground—glowing and incensed. But Reuel was right. My time in Empyrean was almost over, and I was wasting it by allowing Uriel to push my buttons.

"You must learn to channel your temper so that it works to your advantage. Close your eyes. Bring it in." As Reuel continued speaking, I closed my eyes and allowed the burn of my rage to cool. I was coming down. As my feet again touched the grounds of Empyrean, I felt better.

Although the incident was over before it started, the crowd was aroused. Some seemed to be deciding if they should take sides, while others seemed to have come to the foregone conclusion that I was completely unworthy of following, and my display had just proved them right.

It was easy to see who stood where. Those standing with Uriel were hurling both verbal insults and visual threats my way. These included Liwet, Nisroc, Gavreel, and Forcus. These Guardians were more likely to hand me over to Abbadon than to defend me against him.

The remainder of Uriel's team and the extensions stood off to the side, observing the behavior of the other members of their team. As always, the Thrones seemed to be completely oblivious to the exchange. Of course, Reuel, Malachi, and the twins stood with me. I would be indebted to them for a millennium after all of this was over—assuming any of us actually survived.

Tabbris carefully observed the new groupings, and then called the crowd back to order without acknowledging the incident in any way.

"To effectively defend against the Thrones in the Earthen realm, there is one other fact that you must remember. Ophan, if you will kindly assist."

Ophan moved to stand next to Tabbris in the center of the audience.

"Thrones have one other unique ability that other members of the Host do not. Ophan."

"With your permission, Eklektos?" Ophan responded.

"Permission granted."

At Tabbris's word, Ophan's form began to morph until he no longer resembled a member of the angelic Host. He shifted onto all fours; fur grew out of his back and spread over his entire body. Ophan grew a muzzle, fangs, and a tail.

He had transformed into a large black dog—one with red glowing eyes.

"Thrones are shape-shifters, and all can transform in the Earthen realm. This activity is strictly forbidden in Empyrean. They can change their form into any animal; however, most have certain preferences that are easily recognized with practice."

Tabbris was still talking, but I was held captive in Ophan's sinister glare. He was growling, teeth bared—stalking toward me. His snarl turned upward into a perverse grin.

I took an unsteady step backward.

"This can't be right," I whispered, shaking my head. "The dogs...the reservoir. Why?" Malachi placed a hand on my shoulder to steady me. "Revenge. Thrones never forget."

15

DISTRACTIONS

Focus, Danielson, focus.

It seemed as if years had passed, rather than a couple of days, since our little mishap at the reservoir. Returning to school the next morning would be a chore. I had been so preoccupied that Danvers High hadn't even crossed my mind.

My nerves were on end. I still had so much to learn. And I had to couple the steep learning curve with beginning to create a relationship with Xavier, finding the gateway, watching out for the Dominion, and being cautious of an angry Throne that would probably annihilate me if given the opportunity. School was the last thing on my priority list, but I had to play my role, and play it well. Sort of like my life depended on it.

My body was exhausted. I had forgotten how much it took out of our human forms to astral travel. It was only 5:00 p.m. and I was completely wiped out. After leaving the training session at Kahal, I needed some time alone. So, when we got home, I stole away to my bedroom and turned on the TV. Though I wanted solitude, I didn't close the door. I couldn't risk alienating my family now—not when we were the key to each other's survival. There was no way for me to repay Reuel, Angelo, and Raza for their support. They were not tied to me like Malachi, yet they were no less supportive.

Sunday night football was on in the living room. This was traditionally "family bonding" time, but I knew everyone had other things on their minds this evening. Reuel was just trying to create some sense of normality in the midst of all that was going on. I wasn't bothering to watch either. The television was only providing background noise and dim lighting in my bedroom. I lay on the bed staring at the ceiling and allowing the events of the last few days to flood my thoughts. I was so distracted that the ring from my cell phone startled me.

I scurried off the bed and grabbed the phone from my desk. To my surprise, it was Sarielle. When Mr. Dubois made us partners in French class, we exchanged information, but neither of us had ever used it.

"Hello?" I was embarrassed by the gruffness of my voice.

I tried to clear my throat quietly. "Kendi? It's Elle."

"Hi, Sarielle. How are you?" I could hear her quiet sigh at the name.

"I'm...okay." She hesitated. "Thought you were going to get everyone together this weekend? Loser," she added sarcastically. I knew she was joking, but only just.

I had totally forgotten my comment to her as we parted ways the other day. Oops. "Yeah...sorry about that. My dad took us on an unexpected trip this weekend. We just got back not too long ago."

"Oh, cool. Where did you go?" Sarielle seemed cheered by the simple explanation. Interesting.

"We went to visit family in Maine."

"Gotcha. Hope it was fun?" Sarielle questioned. I hated lying to her, but what else could I do?

"Not really. More of a business trip for my dad actually."

I decided to change the subject before we got too deep into my cover story. "What did you do this weekend?"

"Not much. Lay around the house mostly. My mom found out I was at the hospital. One of her friends saw me in the ER and called to find out how I was doing. Xay saved the day as usual. He came up with a quick story about me feeling a little under the weather after school, and he swung me by to see Dr. Julie just as a precaution. I think she bought it, but I was still under house arrest all weekend. Totally sucks."

"Man...sorry to hear that. How *are* you feeling?" I thought this would be the perfect time to slip the question in.

"I'm all right, just sick of looking at the four walls of this house. Hey, what are you doing the rest of the afternoon?" Her mood perked up once again.

"Hadn't really thought about it. Why?"

"You promised me that we would hang out. Just trying to make an honest man out of you, Mr. Belling." I could hear the smirk in her voice.

"Oh, vraiment? Que proposez-vous?" I asked, instantly in a flirtatious mood. "Voulez-vous obtenir quelque chose à manger, et peutêtre aller au cinéma?"

"Something to eat sounds good, not really in the mood for a movie, though. We probably don't have enough time anyway—school tomorrow. Will your mom let you out of the house?"

"I'll tell her that we have a French assignment due or something. She'll be fine. What time are you coming to get me?"

"And you are supposing that I know where you live?" I chuckled.

"Tapleyville. The end of Adams Street, gray house with white trim."

"Yes, ma'am. Half an hour okay?"

"Sure is. See you in a few." She was attempting to hide her excitement. I smiled despite my somber mood. At least I seemed to brighten someone's day.

"See ya in a few."

I went to the bathroom to freshen up then pulled on a clean shirt with my jeans and grabbed a jacket.

Reuel and the guys were in the living room watching the same Patriots game that had been on in my room.

"Reuel, I'm going out for a while. Okay if I take the truck?"

"Absolutely. You sure you want to go alone?"

"I can come with you if you'd like," Malachi offered.

"Naw, I'll be fine. Just going to grab something to eat with Sarielle. She called."

"Oh. Okay. Just be...alert."

"I will. Thanks," I responded as I grabbed the keys from the board by the door.

The drive to Tapleyville took only about fifteen minutes, but I was extremely anxious when I turned onto Adams Street. I realized this was the first time I'd been alone in Danvers since finding out about the Dominion. Maybe I should have allowed Mal to come with me, but it was too late now, and I didn't want to disappoint Sarielle again. Plus, I was looking forward to her company. Perhaps she could get my mind off all the other crap going on.

I promptly dismissed the concern and parked the truck at the curb in front of the little gray house. Sarielle's car was in the driveway along with one other. It was a newer model Honda than the little red antique that she and Xavier drove to school every day. My muscles ached as I climbed out of the truck and headed up the walkway to the front door.

As I mounted the stairs, Sarielle peeked out from behind the white curtain in the front window.

The door popped open before I could reach the porch.

"I won't be gone long, Mom," Sarielle called over her shoulder and quickly closed the door.

She hurried down the stairs, grabbing my arm, and pulling me back up the walk toward the truck.

"In a hurry, are we?" I smiled down at her.

"Let's get out of here before she changes her mind!" Sarielle hissed.

"Okay, okay."

I opened the door for her, and after making sure she was secure, went around the truck and climbed in.

"So where to, Miss Breland?" I chuckled.

"Wherever, just drive." She seemed a little annoyed that I was so amused.

Sarielle was still glancing nervously at the front of the house. I started the truck and pulled off just to calm her down. I headed downtown so that we would have multiple choices of restaurants. "You didn't tell me that I was on a snatch-and-run mission. Why are you so nervous? Is your mom that much of a warden?"

"You have no idea. She means well, she really does, but Mom is a little overprotective. She worries a lot about Xay and me. Mom is going through a rough patch right now, and when she gets like this, she tends to throw all her attention in one direction. I think she just wants to keep herself preoccupied. Unfortunately, this weekend, I've been the target of her distraction.

"Every time I reached for medication or went to lie down, she was ready to go back to the hospital. She called Dr. Julie at least ten times—no joke. She's been smothering me and complaining about everything that Xay does or doesn't do. They have been arguing all weekend. I just can't stand it. They're driving me crazy. I needed a break. That's all. It'll get better...it always does."

I didn't expect the tirade. The last thing I wanted to do was to cause Sarielle more grief. If anyone knew the burden of too much all at once, it was me. I would make sure the time we spent together would be the break she was longing for. Xavier had told us that stress caused her condition to worsen. Couldn't her mom see that? I suddenly felt very protective of Sarielle.

I took a sideways glance at Sarielle. Her face was tired, drawn. Her normal color was not yet back in her cheeks though she had "rested" all weekend. As she lifted her hand to push back her hair, I saw that she was still trembling slightly. Yes, she definitely needed a break. I would try to take her mind off her family woes, if only for a couple of hours.

"Well, let's not worry about your mother or Xavier right now. It's just you and me, so let's find something to eat, huh? How about Goodies—food and dessert in one place?" I said, giving her a wink.

"Sounds good to me." Sarielle smiled and settled back into the seat and began to relax. I smiled in response, proud of myself.

Downtown was fairly crowded for a late Sunday afternoon, but I finally found a parking space a couple of blocks from Goodies and slid into it. I came around to assist Sarielle out of the truck. She took my hand and held it tightly as we walked toward the little shop. The air was brisk, as the sun was about to set. Sarielle shivered lightly as the wind began to blow.

"Are you cold?" I looked down at her, watching her soft, sandy curls blow away from her face.

"A little," she admitted. Sarielle was wearing jeans and a thin long-sleeved golden-colored shirt. It was truly her color. The shirt perfectly accented the gold undertones of her complexion but did little to protect her from the fall weather of Danvers. In her haste, she didn't think to grab a jacket, I guess. I pulled her to a stop, shrugged out of my jacket and held it out for her to put on.

"Won't you be cold?"

"Nah, I'm good. I dressed in layers. I'm fine."

Sarielle pulled the jacket close and pushed the sleeves back so that her hand would once again be free to take mine. She nestled just a little bit closer to my side. The warmth of her body felt good next to mine. The weather here, this time of year, was quite unforgiving.

Goodies was not crowded, and for that, I was grateful since I was starving. We went straight to the counter to order. Gus was there.

"Hey, kid. How's everything? Vanilla chai tea?" He smiled at me.

"Not today, Gus." I smiled, glad that I wasn't my normal, predictable self. "I'm hungry. Let me have a 2 Play with a Coke. Sarielle, what would you like?"

"Ummm…Toasted raviolis and water. Thanks."

"Aren't you going to eat more than that?" I could polish off two of the ravioli dishes in like five minutes, and it would only be an appetizer for me.

"Not much of an appetite right now…just enjoying the company." She grinned.

I paid Gus, ignoring the fact that he was now smirking at me in a very annoying way. There were a few booths open, as well as space at the counter. I would much rather sit in a booth, but figured I'd let Sarielle choose.

"Do you want to sit here at the counter, or grab a booth?"

Sarielle scanned the restaurant and headed for the booth in the back corner. We slid in to wait for our food.

"Thanks for coming to pick me up. You didn't have to. Hope I didn't make you feel too guilty," she added sheepishly.

"Not at all. I wasn't doing anything anyway. And trust me, I know the feeling of *too much* family bonding time. I was in my room, alone, with the TV on when you called. I needed a little space myself."

"See. I did bother you."

"Cut it out. If I didn't want to come, I would have said no. Trust me. I'm a big boy...and not the most polite. I'm sure you've noticed. I can't think of anyone at the moment that could guilt me into doing anything." I looked at her with a raised eyebrow as if to challenge her.

"We'll see now, won't we?" I liked the fact that she was not one to back down. While she had her brave face on, I could try to find out what was going on with her family.

"So, tell me, what's up with your mom and Xavier?" I had to figure him out and needed an "in" other than his sister. "Only if you don't mind talking about it," I added, not wanting to seem pushy.

"No, it's fine. I guess it would probably help to talk about it." She dropped her head and let out a heavy sigh, frowning again. Her anxiety had returned. I shouldn't have asked. This could have waited until another time.

I placed my hand under her chin and forced her to look at me. "What is it, Sarielle?" I encouraged.

"Mom just gives Xay such a hard time sometimes. I'm not sure why. Anytime she's upset, she lashes out at him. I think it's because he reminds her so much of Dad. They are so much alike. Or maybe she's just afraid to stress me out too much. I don't know. I don't think she means to play favorites, but that's just the way it seems, and it makes me feel awful for Xay."

"Didn't you tell me Xavier was your foster brother? He's adopted, right?"

"Yes, but so am I. Xay, and I were in the same foster home for about a year and a half before Mom and Dad adopted the both of us. He and I had become so close that they were afraid to separate us. We came sort of as a package deal, ya know?

"Things were great until our parents separated about three years ago. That's when Xay started acting out. I'm sure it was because Dad was gone. Xay felt abandoned all over again. To make matters worse, Dad moved to France shortly after the divorce for work.

"Dad and I were so close that I went to live with him for a while. I spent the better part of ninth grade and all of the tenth living with Dad, but Xay and Mom were having so much trouble, I came back. Someone needed to be here to run interference. I missed Xay terribly anyway. We only saw each other two or three times while I lived with Dad."

"Here you go. Can I get you anything else?" Gus interrupted to deliver our food to the table.

"No, I think we're good." I nodded to Gus.

Now I understood why Sarielle spoke French fluently while Xavier was completely clueless in the same class. Both adopted but sounded like Xavier was the one that always got the short end of the stick where his parents were concerned.

"What happened to your birth parents?" I thought better of the question a little too late. "I'm sorry. You don't have to answer that if you don't want to."

"No, it's okay. They died in a car wreck when I was about five. We were all in the car. I was the only one that survived the crash. A drunk driver hit us. A guy that was just passing by pulled me out of the car. He couldn't reach my parents in time.

"I don't remember them that clearly anymore—which kinda bothers me. I mean, I remember what they look like and all. I just don't remember much of my time with them. Just glimpses...bits and pieces. I remember feeling safe, warm...and knowing that I was loved.

"I know I have my mother's eyes. They were this odd hazel green too. I remember her smile and her hugs. I remember Daddy's beard. I used to play with the stubble on his face when I sat on his lap." Sarielle was smiling as she spoke tenderly about her birth parents.

"Wow, Sarielle. I'm really sorry." I couldn't help reaching across the table and taking her hand.

I felt like I should comfort her somehow, like I owed it to her.

"It's fine. It's been a long time. But that's how I found Xay. After the accident, there was no one to take care of me. I wound up in a foster home, scared to death, and not trusting anyone. I was too little to understand why Mommy and Daddy went to heaven and left me here alone. After all, we went everywhere together. Why was this time any different?" Sarielle chuckled at her lost innocence.

I didn't want to press her anymore on the topic of her parents, so I switched to what I hoped would be an easier topic.

"What about Xavier's parents?"

"That's a long story...with a not-so-happy ending," Sarielle responded with sadness in her voice. "Xay was abandoned as a newborn in a trash dumpster by his drug-addicted mother. When the police found Eileen, she was high out of her mind and had half bled to death from giving birth with no medical assistance. They locked her up for several months, and Xay was put into a foster home. By the time her trial rolled around, she was back on the wagon and swore off drugs.

"The judge sentenced Eileen to complete a rehab program and gave her visitation rights with Xay. Things were going well, and after about a year and a half, the judge granted Eileen's request for an overnight visit with Xay. She picked him up from the foster home on Friday and was supposed to bring him back by 6:00 p.m. on Saturday. She was a no-show. The foster home called the police around midnight because Eileen was not answering their calls."

Sarielle paused and turned away from me and stared out of the window. I squeezed her hand lightly to encourage her to continue.

"Did Eileen make a run for it with Xavier?" I speculated.

"No, Eileen didn't run. She fed him, changed him into his pajamas, put him to bed, and then she sat down and wrote a letter detailing why she couldn't take care of him...and then Eileen hung herself. Xay was three. He had woken up and was screaming for her by the time the police arrived.

"How do you explain to a three-year-old that your mommy decided to go away and leave you behind?" Sarielle turned back to me then with tears running down her face.

I got up and slid into the booth next to her. I put my arms around her and pulled her close to my side. She buried her head into my shoulder and let out a muffled sob.

"It's okay, Sarielle."

"No, it's not!" She made a futile attempt at pushing me away. "Nobody understands Xay the way that I do! I know he can come across as a jerk sometimes. But it's his defense mechanism. He won't allow anyone to get close to him because he's scared, he's afraid of being abandoned again. He told me he would be okay when I went with Dad. He lied. Xay went berserk. He doesn't think he deserves to be loved because his own mother dumped him in a trash can and then killed herself to get away from him. I know that feeling. I've lived through it too." Her voice broke at the end as she tried to stifle another sob. She was on the verge of hysterics.

I pulled her closer, rubbing her back, trying to soothe her. This spontaneous reconnaissance mission had turned out to be a really shitty idea. I didn't mean to upset her like this.

"Hey, Sarielle, shhhh...I do understand. Really. My mom died a few years ago too. We were really close. I took it even harder than the twins. I still haven't pulled it completely back together. It will get better for Xavier. I promise. I've been there." I hated lying to her, but it was the quickest way to divert her attention from Xavier and his emotional issues. "I'll talk to Xavier," I promised. "We have more in common than I realized." Never mind I had no choice.

Sarielle pulled away and grabbed a napkin to wipe her face. "Sorry for being so emotional. All of this just gets to me sometimes, that's all."

"No worries. Completely understandable. Are you okay?"

"Yeah. Better." She nodded.

"Good. Let's eat then. You haven't touched your food." All this drama couldn't be good for her. I moved back around to my side of the table so she would have room to eat.

We ate in silence for a few minutes. For one, I was extremely hungry, and secondly, I wanted to give her time to calm down. Overwhelming Sarielle this evening was not my intent.

I had finished devouring my meal and was ready to call Gus over to get dessert, but Sarielle was still picking at her ravioli. She had eaten only about half of the small portioned meal and had laid her fork aside to nurse the glass of water. I studied her for a few moments and then concluded that she was deep in a thought that had nothing to do with her food.

"Aren't you going to eat anymore?"

"Ummm...no, I think I'm done actually. My stomach is a little uneasy. Happens anytime I have to double up on meds." Sarielle shook her head in annoyance as she reached into her purse and pulled out a small pillbox.

"How are you feeling, really?"

"Not great." She let out a small sigh before throwing a couple of pills into her mouth and grabbing her water glass. "It'll take some time to get my strength back. No biggie, I'm used to it."

"All this drama doesn't help, does it?"

"Not really." Sarielle laughed quietly. "But I do most of it to myself, honestly. Xay would kill me himself if he knew how much I worried about him, about Mom, about Dad. But that's just how I am. I just want everyone to be okay. Ya know?"

"Yeah. I do. But it won't help any of them if you are in the hospital on some kind of drip keeping you alive. You've got to do a better job taking care of yourself. I saw Xavier's face when you collapsed, heard him pleading for you to wake up. He needs you, Sarielle. Which means you need to be healthy."

It was Sarielle who gave me the raised eyebrow this time.

"Since when do you care about what *Xavier* needs?" she asked sarcastically.

I had to laugh at her snarky grin. "Never said I did. However, I *do* care about his sister for some strange reason." I reached across the table and took her hand. "I like talking to you and hanging out with you. You remind me of one of my closest friends back home. I'd like you to be around for a while...got it?"

Sarielle nodded slowly as she stared into my eyes. Neither of us seemed to know what to say next. What was wrong with me? What the hell was I saying? Why did this human girl have to remind me so much of Eloa? The familiarity drew me to her like a magnet.

"Wanna share a banana split?" I asked, breaking the uncomfortable silence.

"Sure." Sarielle shrugged her shoulders. "Not like I'll have to eat much of it anyway. You eat like a horse, Kendi Belling."

"Ha ha, whatever." As I waved Gus over to place the order, Sarielle's cell phone rang. She retracted her hand and grabbed the phone from the side pocket of her purse. She looked at the caller ID. "Xay?"

I got up and went to the counter so that she would have some privacy. "What else can I get for you, kid?" Gus inquired.

"Banana split, two spoons." I wasn't sure on the toppings, and Sarielle was still on the phone, so I chose randomly, making sure that chocolate was included. I figured chocolate would be a safe bet for any teenage girl. Right?

"I'll bring it right over," Gus informed.

I walked slowly back to the corner booth, observing Sarielle as I went. Whatever she and Xavier were discussing seemed to be turning into an argument.

"You need to go home, Xay. Mom has been trying to call you for hours. Why aren't you answering your phone?" There was a brief pause.

"She didn't mean it. You know that. You both said things you didn't mean. No, I'm hanging out with Kendi. What's all that noise? Where are you? Ugh, Taylor...really? Just call Mom, okay? I gotta go...see you at home."

I slid back into the booth. Sarielle was returning the phone to her purse with an unsteady hand. "Everything okay?"

"I guess. Xay's on one of his rampages. He's angry with Mom, and he's hurting. It scares me when he gets like this. Xay can get reckless. Not sure where he is, and he's with Taylor, which *never* leads to anything good."

Taylor. Just the sound of his name still pissed me off.

Gus came over and put the banana split down. I handed a spoon to Sarielle.

"Let's pretend like it's nothing that a little ice cream with chocolate syrup can't fix." I winked at her.

She grinned, examining the ice cream. "Chocolate. How did you know?" I smirked, proud that my assumption was correct.

Goodies had the best ice cream in town. It didn't take long before I could see the bottom of the silver dish. Naturally, I had eaten most of the bowl. Sarielle had become very quiet since her phone call. She was worried.

Our little field trip seemed to be taking its toll on her strength. It was getting late anyway— plus we had school tomorrow. I dug into my pocket and pulled out a tip for Gus and slid it on the table.

"You look tired. Are you ready to go home?" I inquired, examining her face.

"I'm ready to go," Sarielle replied, making sure I heard the distinction.

I got up and took her by the hand to help her out of the booth. "See ya, Gus," I called over my shoulder as we went out the door.

The temperature had dropped even further as it was now dark. The streetlights had come on, and the once crowded streets were nearly empty.

"Would you like for me, to get the truck?" There were benches that lined the shops on Maple Street. Sarielle didn't look up to walking the two blocks. But I fully expected her to put on her brave face and deny that she was feeling weak.

"Sure," she replied, releasing my hand and lowering herself onto the nearest bench.

She was feeling worse than I thought. Since she was going to sit this one out, I could hurry. "Be right back." I hurried up the street toward the truck. The air was icy, and I didn't want

Sarielle uncomfortable any longer than necessary.

She had way too much on her shoulders for a seventeen-year-old girl. Sarielle had been through far more than I realized, and with her chronic illness, there seemed to be little space for escape. Her tendency to take care of everyone else while neglecting herself didn't sit well with me.

In more than three hundred years, I hadn't met many humans with a heart as pure as Sarielle.

She genuinely cared about other people more than herself. It was a rare trait.

As I crossed Cherry Street nearing Giovanni's, I heard a scuffle coming from the alley beside the shop. There was an argument in progress that seemed to be escalating quickly. Unfortunately, I recognized both the voices.

"You little shit. What do you mean you didn't get it?" The voice belonged to Taylor.

"He was taking too long. There wasn't enough time. I don't care what you say. It's not worth getting caught, man. Come on...don't be stupid!"

Damn it. Of course, Xavier would have to be involved.

Was this a test? I guess I would fail miserably if I crossed the street until I passed the alley and acted like I never heard a thing.

I passed Giovanni's and turned into the alley just as Taylor grabbed Xavier and slammed him into the wall.

"I'll break your neck, maggot. *You* don't get to question me. You'll do exactly what I tell you to do or else...," Taylor hissed.

"Or else what?" I asked, stepping out of the shadows.

I grabbed Taylor by the shoulder, flung him into the far wall, and stepped in front of Xavier.

"Kendi, what are you doing here?" Xavier said, surprised to see me.

"My truck is one block up across School Street. Go get in it. Now." I tossed him the keys and turned back to face Taylor. Xavier started to head out of the alley.

"You don't want to get involved in this," Xavier warned as he turned back toward me.

"I said go...now!" I was livid and not in the mood for discussion. Xavier rocked back on his heels, turned, and sprinted out of the alley.

Rage tore through me as Taylor gathered himself on the far side of the alley. With every heartbeat, strength surged into my muscles. Not just human strength, but the same kind of power I'd felt in the training field at Kahal. How was this possible?

"You're gonna eventually learn to mind your own business, Belling." Taylor stalked across the alley toward me.

I felt no urgency to avoid Taylor's advance. Angelic power was pulsating through my mortal body as if I would explode into my natural configuration.

This body was on fire, the rage consuming. If I struck Taylor now, he wouldn't survive.

Yah knew my temper, my lack of control. Why would he allow this kind of power to return to me now? Maybe the situation with the Dominion was more imminent than we knew? I should've known. Reuel would have never let me leave the house so easily—at least not without the guys to watch my back if he thought I wouldn't be able to defend myself.

Taylor didn't want to engage me right now. In my angelic form, battle was battle. And at this moment, angelic power was totally dominant. Part of me wanted to run so that I wouldn't hurt the arrogant idiot, but the other part of me wanted to crush his skull. I was in Shoer mode—kill or be killed.

Control, Kendi. This is not where you want to expend energy. Compose yourself.

Tabbris's voice brought me up short.

Taylor swung, but my senses were so heightened it was as if his fist was moving in slow motion. I caught his arm with no problem and pushed him back into the wall again. Even though I tried to temper the effort with which I shoved him, his back slammed into the concrete wall with enough force to knock the wind out of him. He came down on one knee as loose pieces of the cement wall rained down on his shoulders.

"Not today, Taylor. Trust me," I sneered, closing in on him. Rage seemed to propel me forward, toward my target, despite Tabbris's warning.

Walk away, Shoer. Now.

Taylor was still trying to catch his breath. It took everything in me, but I turned and walked out of the alley. He didn't follow, for which I was incredibly grateful. The restraint I had just exercised was about all I had. Another immediate encounter would not end well.

Xavier jumped out of the truck as soon as he saw me approaching.

"Xavier, what the hell?" I barked at him. "Get your ass back in the truck! Sarielle's waiting for me in front of Goodies… probably freezing.

"Don't you dare breathe a word of any of this to her. We just happened to run into each other. Do you hear me? She looks horrible and probably feels worse. Your sister doesn't need anything else to worry about tonight. She needs to rest. Not a word, do you understand me?"

"Got it," Xavier mumbled, climbing into the backseat.

"This isn't over. You will tell me what that shit was about," I threw over my shoulder pulling out of the parking space.

"Why's Elle out of the house anyway?" Xavier questioned. "She's supposed to be taking it easy."

"Well, seems like peace and quiet have been a little hard to come by this weekend with you and your mom going at each other's throats!" I was so angry I could chew nails.

"Elle told you that? She must be seriously upset. What happened? Where is she?" *Now* Xavier was anxious.

"Sarielle is all right. She just needs rest." I needed to calm down. We were pulling up in front of the ice cream shop, and I didn't want Sarielle to notice the drastic shift in my demeanor. I took several deep breaths before exiting the truck.

"Sorry, that took longer than I expected. I ran into Xavier down by Giovanni's. He's in the truck." I tried to smile to hide my aggravation.

"Oh. Okay." She seemed relieved to know where he was.

I opened the door and helped Sarielle into the truck. She was completely spent. I needed to get her home now.

"Xay, where were you?" she inquired over her shoulder. Her voice was so low, I wondered silently if he could even hear her.

"Ummm...just hanging out. Got hungry, so, I went to Giovanni's to grab a slice. I ran into Kendi on the way out."

"You really shouldn't ignore Mom's calls like that. You know she worries," Sarielle chastised as she let her head slump back on the headrest.

"I'll talk to Mom and apologize when we get home. Okay?"

"Thank you." She closed her eyes and went quiet. Xavier didn't say anything further either.

I was grateful for the silence. Sarielle needed to relax. She didn't open her eyes again until I stopped in front of their house, and Xavier popped the back door open.

"See you at school tomorrow, Kendi. Thanks, *uh*...for the ride." I nodded in response. Xavier glanced at Sarielle as he closed the door and proceeded up the walkway.

Sarielle was lingering. Good. I wanted a chance to say goodbye to her without Xavier around, and apparently so did she. Sarielle watched Xavier until he unlocked the door and went into the house, and then she turned to me.

"Thanks again for coming to get me. I didn't mean to be such a downer, but thanks for listening."

"Not a problem at all," I assured her. "You would do the same for me, wouldn't you?"

"You know it." She smiled.

"You really need to get some rest. Let me open the door for you."

I took her hand as she climbed down from the truck. She stumbled forward. I caught her in my arms. "You okay?"

"Yeah. Just a little off balance, that's all." I waited until she righted herself before releasing her shoulders and wrapping my arm tightly around her waist to walk her to the door.

The walkway was very dark as the streetlights didn't reach far into the yard. Xavier had turned on the porch light, so the small pool of light met us about a third of the way to the door. I supported Sarielle's weight as she leaned against me. What little strength she had earlier was completely exhausted.

We stepped onto the brightly lit porch, Sarielle paused at the door and turned to confront me. "Where did you really find my brother?" She was looking directly into my eyes. My resolve wavered, but I wouldn't allow her to be upset anymore tonight.

"Outside Giovanni's, just like Xavier said. Why?" I was trying my best to be convincing. Sarielle paused, giving me an opening to interrupt her trend of thought.

"Don't you think you've done enough worrying about your brother for one day? Xay is safely inside. You are only allowed to take care of Sarielle for the rest of the night. Understood?"

A grin began to slowly spread across her face, accentuating her dimples. She didn't say anything but nodded. I was curious about her pensive look, but I let it slide.

The wind started to blow. Sarielle tried to adjust quickly but shivered as the air blew her sandy hair back away from her face. Her eyes sparkled under the porch light as she continued to examine my face.

"It's getting really cold out here, and you need to get inside before your mom comes out here and kills both of us. Plus it's getting late, and my dad will start to wonder where I am."

Sarielle took a small step back shrugging out of my jacket. "Thanks for letting me borrow this." She handed it to me, and I slid the jacket on to free my hands. Her perfume wafted off the jacket, distracting me momentarily.

Sarielle stepped in closer and wrapped her arms around my waist, laying her head on my chest. "Thanks again for being my sounding board, and for whatever it was that you got Xay out of tonight." I chuckled and wrapped my arms around her in response. We hadn't fooled her one bit.

"You're welcome." I rubbed her back to create some warmth. "Sleep well, Sarielle. I'll see you tomorrow." I released her.

She took a step back, reached up and put her hands on the sides of my face, leaned in and pressed her lips to mine. "Good night, Kendi," she whispered intently.

Sarielle opened the door and slipped inside before I could process what had just happened.

I sauntered back up the darkening walkway with my mind filled with the happenings of the afternoon. My head swam as I considered the human girl who had just kissed me, definitely a first.

I sat in the truck absorbed in thoughts of Sarielle—her hair blowing in the breeze, the smell of her perfume, the intensity of those beautiful eyes, and the softness of her lips against mine. Just thinking of her stirred feelings that I didn't quite understand in this strange body. The time we spent together only made me more intrigued by her. Sarielle was a welcome diversion to the complexity I called my life.

As I started the truck to head for home, the familiar sound of a wind chime rang out in the distance—just a quick reminder that I couldn't afford the luxury of distraction. I had to be careful. Damn.

I sighed quietly, leaning across the steering wheel, letting any possibility fall from my mind.

Go home, Shoer.

I silently agreed with Tabbris, sat up, and shifted the truck into gear.

16
Dogs and Witches and Gates…
Oh, My!

Over the next couple of weeks, Tabbris visited as often as he could to work with me, both on my control issues and to teach me how to maximize my Achim. When Tabbris wasn't here, Mal was reassuring me that I would get the hang of it.

I had to learn how to fully function in my office and learn it fast. The Legion was not going to just wait around until I was adequately trained before trying to kill me.

More than ever before, I found myself wondering what it would be like if I failed—if I became a Shade. I made sure to keep these thoughts to myself, though. I couldn't dwell on the negative possibilities when Reuel and Malachi were around. I didn't want them any more worried about me than they already were. Reuel could read my thoughts, and I wasn't sure how much Malachi could *feel*.

I wouldn't wish this torment on my worst enemy. Being scared shitless was not the kind of thing that the troops needed to hear from their so-called leader. This was a weight that I would continue to carry alone.

I didn't have the luxury of spending precious time on the "what ifs." If I gave up, everyone connected to me would be doomed to an unwarranted death sentence. Tabbris made this very clear. So, I had to get my ass in gear. I would be responsible. The only place I knew to start was to cram three centuries of training into three weeks. While I knew this simple act wouldn't put a dent in the centuries of willful misconduct, but I would make up as much ground as I could.

The schedule I was keeping up was exhausting. I was in school all day and in training for most of the night. The long hours didn't have the same effect on the rest of the team. They were not trapped in a mortal body like me, but I wouldn't complain. Reuel was worried about how hard I was pushing myself, but I couldn't let up.

Now was the time to be strong. Not just for my family and myself, but for Xavier, Sarielle, and those that I had come to know as friends. Azrael would go after anyone he thought he could use to bring me down. Unfortunately, mortals made the easiest targets. I had to keep Xavier especially close. He was a self-destructive loose cannon, and I had to figure out how to control him. My hardest task would be protecting Xavier from himself. Of course, he had been strategically avoiding me since the night I found him in the alley with Taylor. He knew I would not rest until I found out exactly what was going on with him and his football buddy.

I was formulating a strategy of my own. I would find a way to get Xavier alone—away from both Sarielle and Taylor. I had to get him to trust me, show him that I could be a confidant. There was a reason he was jumping through hoops for Taylor, and I had to find out what it was before the situation was completely out of control. If it meant intertwining myself into his life, so be it.

The upside was having more time with Sarielle. The thought alone made me smile. But behind my smile, I was a little worried about her. She didn't seem to be recovering very well from her little episode at the reservoir. She had been in and out of school. Any time I asked, Xavier would say that she was at home resting. And when Sarielle was in school, she was not herself. So, my preoccupation was not only the Legion but also this girl that I couldn't seem to get out of my head.

"Daydream on your own time, Shoer. You ready to work?" Tabbris caught me off guard.

"Sure," I replied, pulling my weary frame up from the bed. I'd only been home from school for half an hour, and with only a couple hours' sleep the night before, I was beat.

"We'll work outside today. Grab your brother on your way out." Tabbris turned on his heels and headed for the stairs.

It never ceased to amaze me how he could appear out of thin air and make it seem as if he were here all along.

I went down the hall to retrieve Malachi. His door was open, so I stuck my head in.

"Tabbris is here. He wants to work outside today. Cool?"

"Sure." Malachi rose from his desk. "You all right, Kendi? You look worn out. I'm sure Tabbris would understand if you took a break today."

"Yeah right." I rolled my eyes. Tabbris had no sympathy where I was concerned. He stood as a constant reminder that I was unprepared because of my own negligence.

"You've been hitting it hard for nearly two weeks, kid. When was the last time you had more than two or three hours sleep? Remember, you're stuck in that human form. Your body is not self-generating like the rest of ours. You have to allow time to rest, or that body of yours will shut down."

"I know." I left it at that. I felt dead on my feet. If I were still for more than a few minutes, I would probably lapse into a coma.

"You two planning on getting started today?" Tabbris called from the stairway.

"Like I said, let's hit it." I smiled, punching Mal on the shoulder as we headed for stairs.

Once in the backyard, Tabbris launched into our mediation and control drills. I was trying to become more in tune with Malachi so that connecting would become second nature. It wasn't as easy as I'd hoped. To my chagrin, Malachi could only initiate a connection with me if I was in an emotionally heightened state—like my first day at school.

However, I had the ability to connect with Mal anytime—one of the fringe benefits of being the Shoer.

My patience was short today. We had been at it for more than an hour, and I had only connected with Malachi once, and then only for a few seconds. Tabbris sensed my frustration.

"Shoer, I know you are tired, but in your case, tired is good. You are less defiant when you're exhausted. Just relax and let it happen," Tabbris persuaded. "Face each other. Malachi, concentrate on opening up so that Kendi can connect."

Malachi proceeded to close his eyes, exhaling slowly. I could feel the draw as he welcomed my essence to connect with his. I closed my eyes in response and mentally searched for him, feeling my essence travel. It was a strange sensation. My norm was to rebuff anything foreign. But Tabbris was right. Today, I just didn't have the strength.

When I opened my eyes, I was looking at myself. Only, I was seeing myself through my brother's eyes. Damn, it worked!

I really did look like hell. I saw now why Mal was worried. "Weird, isn't it?" Malachi laughed as we thought in unison.

"Very."

"How are you still on your feet, man?" Now that we were connected, Malachi could feel my physical exhaustion. He went down on one knee as the fatigue settled into his body as well.

"You kinda get used to it after a while. I think I've been on autopilot for the last three days."

"Very good, Shoer. Hold the connection," Tabbris interrupted our banter. "Now, I want to teach you something new. Shoers have the ability to protect their Achim by blocking the connection that you two share. This is a very useful battle skill.

"If you are incapacitated, or worse, your Achim will be able to act independently. He will be able to intervene on your behalf until you regain strength and you can act as a team once again.

"Malachi cannot initiate blocking. So, it is something that you have to master, Kendi."

Malachi had no knowledge of this skill, and he was clearly displeased with my ability to separate myself from him in a crisis. Though, I was grateful Malachi would have a way of escape if things got out of hand.

"Concentrate. Focus on pulling everything into your center. You must forcibly break the connection."

I closed my eyes once again, pulling instead of pushing. As I concentrated on my center, I could feel strength building in my core. The sensation encouraged me to pull with greater force. The energy was a surge of power that snapped into place like a tightly stretched rubber band.

I opened my eyes, looking for Mal's approval, proud that I had finally accomplished a skill in one try, only to find my brother lying unconscious.

"Malachi!" I threw myself on the ground, lifting his head, shaking him. "What happened, Tabbris? What's wrong with him? What did I do wrong?"

"Calm down. He will be fine. Give him a minute. The extra surge of power you felt came from Malachi. A displacement of strength is what it takes to break the Achim's connection. With practice, you will be able to find the balance that won't drain so much from him while still severing the connection." As Tabbris spoke, Mal began to come around.

"Kendi? What happened?"

"Tabbris happened." I was more than a little irritated as Malachi sat up, regaining his bearings. "A little warning next time?" I threw in his direction as I pulled Mal up from the ground.

Tabbris ignored both of us and continued with his explanation of the technique.

"Blocking will only give you a small window of opportunity, Kendi. As your ability to block wanes, Malachi will regain strength, and again become connected to you if you're not careful. Blocking takes complete concentration and cannot be used in conjunction with any of your other powers.

"Only use blocking when absolutely necessary. When the connection is reestablished, the result can be an imbalance of power that has the potential to draw strength from both sides. It can take some time for both of you to recover from the transaction if you get it wrong."

"Tell me about it. I feel like I got hit by a truck," Malachi responded, taking a seat back on the ground.

"In battle, every second is precious. Once you perfect blocking, the connection will be severed, and your Achim will not be taken down in the process. You will also be able to reconnect without consequence."

I sat next to Mal, glowering at Tabbris who needed to work on the way he disseminated information.

"Are you okay?" I inquired.

"Yeah, just caught off guard is all. That was...strange. Let's not practice that skill any more today. Let a brother recover first. All right?" Malachi grinned.

"No disagreement here." Seeing Malachi incapacitated scared the hell out of me.

With all the connections broken, and me no longer blocking, I found myself back to my normal depleted self, and probably in worse shape than Mal. Tabbris noticed.

"While you two *recover*, let's maximize our time with a verbal lesson, shall we?" He seemed amused.

"Certainly, Eklektos," I responded, attempting to hide my frustration. "Topic?"

"I believe a history lesson is in order."

"A history lesson?" I replied with a raised eyebrow. "About?"

"This region. Charon. If you know what's gone on here, you can better prepare for what's coming."

I grimaced at the wrench in my gut but settled in to listen.

"The Dominion has long discovered that humans are easily manipulated. Mortals could be readily influenced if given the right motives—or the wrong ones, depending on how you look at it," Tabbris began.

"Influenced how?" Malachi questioned.

"Lucifer found that he could make connections with mortals who were looking to tap into the supernatural. Some were merely curious and became trapped by the prowess of the Dominion, yet there were others who were very willing participants in demonic activity. These mortals were deceived by the promises and lies that were made to them.

"The Dominion often made empty promises to these willing vessels and then used them to create unnecessary turmoil in the Earth. The willingness of these witches and warlocks resulted in the destruction of many of Yah's chosen."

"Hang on, Eklektos. Witches? Warlocks? Seriously?" I laughed.

"Yes, Shoer. The existence of mortals who lend themselves to the dark influence of the Dominion is very real. Mortals coined the titles. We simply acknowledge them.

"While we know Yah has not authorized such power in the Earth, the Dominion exploits humans who enable possession. They have found a way to pervert the power of Empyrean in this realm.

"So, to other mortals, it would seem that these people have extraordinary ability, but they are simply lending themselves as vessels to be used by the Dominion," Tabbris explained.

Possession...by the Dominion. Mal and I just looked at one another while Tabbris continued. "There is a specific incidence to note in this region. In the late 1600s, there was a young slave woman by the name of Tabitha. She was acquired by a minister in Barbados and was brought to Charon with his family when he was hired to preach in the village church.

"In Barbados, the Ta'avat region, Vohu was the Eklektos. Vohu had been overly vigilant of Tabitha because of her fascination with things of the spirit realm. Tabitha had a natural proclivity for tapping into the Empyreal realm, and Yah had chosen her as one of his messengers in the human realm.

"Unfortunately, Tabitha was not satisfied communicating only with Yah, and after being brought to Charon, she opened up herself to communion with many of the Dominion—Abbadon specifically. Abbadon was quickly able to corrupt the gift of prophecy that Yah had given her into fortunetelling and soothsaying. Her activity spiraled into self-possession and the entrancement of other young girls in her care. The bodily invasions of these mortals resulted in convulsions, self- mutilation, and other behaviors that were not easily explained. The girls' behavior was a result of rebelling against the forced possession.

"Of course, this activity did not go unnoticed, and Tabitha was taken into custody and questioned. She was beaten until she confessed to having conversations with dark spirits—the devil, she called him. She could detail her encounters with green-eyed men that could morph into animals—black dogs, cats, and wolves. Tabitha told stories of being transported on the wind when with these creatures. She was promptly labeled a witch and jailed by the town's authorities for the protection of the other citizens.

"At the coaxing of Abbadon, Tabitha began to accuse others of being involved in the same darkness. The innocents that she fingered were Yah's chosen. This had been the Dominion's plan all along—the destruction of the seed. The town descended into a chaos that is noted in history until this day."

"The Salem Witch Trials? Are you telling me that was all Abbadon?" I was staring wide-eyed at Tabbris.

"Abbadon with the assistance of Azrael and a few others," Tabbris confirmed. "Many innocent people died horrible deaths based on Tabitha's accusations. Some were hung, some were stoned, and still others died never being released from prison. The uprising lasted for months, during which time Abbadon saturated the region with Legion forces.

"In response, Anael was appointed as the Eklektos of Charon to search out and seal the gateway that had allowed for both the invasion and the corruption of so many people.

"It was not long before Anael located the gateway right in the middle of the very place where the Witch Trials began—a small township called Salem Village. The Shoer led a valiant battle against Abbadon. The encounter was one of the deadliest in Empyrean's history, and the closest that we have ever come to losing a Shoer. If it were not for the sacrifice of Orfiel, Anael would be in Sheol today." Tabbris paused in reverence for Orfiel.

"Orfiel was Anael's Achim," Malachi began. "I've heard the reports of his bravery—how he allowed himself to be captured and subsequently destroyed so that Anael would live."

"Yes, Malachi. This is the Orfiel of whom I speak." Tabbris continued with the lesson.

"The uprising ended almost as quickly as it began when the battle at

Charon was lost. This war claimed not only Orfiel but also many of the Dominion. Abbadon had to regroup quickly. The first thing he accomplished was the relocation of the gateway.

"Although the gateway was moved, the Legion's activity remains heaviest surrounding the original location. Many of the Dominion never moved on. And, unfortunately, we have yet to discover the new placement of the portal.

"This is the first time since Anael's defeat that a Shoer has been assigned to Charon."

Tabbris looked at me. The knot in my stomach tied itself tighter. I could have done without hearing about the war at Charon, specifically the part about the destruction of the Achim. Every time I thought about Mal sacrificing himself for me—which I knew he would do—it made me physically sick. "The original gate was in Salem Village. That township doesn't exist anymore. Where would that area of town be now?" I asked, redirecting the discussion.

"Salem Village is now the town of Danvers."

A string of profanities escaped my lips that should never be uttered in the presence of an Eklektos. I made a vain attempt to apologize while pulling myself together.

Yah! Damn it. What did he want from me? Would it not have been easier to give this detail to a Guardian who was far more prepared? Why would he put a rebellious, unprepared, selfish being like me in this Legion infested hotbed, and then appoint that same miscreant as the Shoer?

There was nothing I could say to Tabbris in response. I was disgusted.

Tabbris waited for additional questions or comments, and since I had none, he decided to proceed with the furtherance of the physical lesson.

"All right. You two should be well rested. On your feet, Guardian." Mal and I shrugged ourselves from the lawn and stood to face Tabbris.

"There is one other skill that I want to introduce today before I depart. Kendi, now that you have had success in connecting with your Achim, as well as blocking him, you now need to prepare yourself for coupling."

"Coupling?" I was afraid to ask.

"Coupling is the ability to channel both yours and Malachi's energy into the angelic realm so that you are able to search for the gateway. When you are successfully coupled, the gate's location will draw you.

"Malachi, you will only be able to feel the connection. You will not be able to aid in the search. It will be your job to keep the Shoer strengthened as he journeys in and out of the realm. Your priority is to watch while the Shoer searches. This activity is extremely taxing on the Shoer and can leave him weak and open to attack by the Dominion if they sense his presence and successfully find his location...in either realm.

"The Achim can break the connection, thus, ending the search. The two of you will need to work together to perfect this talent. The disconnection must be mutual. If the Achim disconnects too quickly, the Shoer could be left in the realm alone. This could prove disastrous.

"Malachi, be mindful that you will always sense danger as Kendi searches because he will be venturing into a realm that was never authorized by Yah. It is your task to distinguish between this natural sense of danger and any immediate threat to the Shoer."

Malachi nodded as he took in the words of the Eklektos.

"Shoer, once you are coupled with your Achim, you will feel his strength as when you were blocking. However, instead of continuing to pull that strength into yourself, you must allow the connection to remain so that you can draw on one another's strength. Coupling will take your connection to another level. It allows you to act as one being, though you have the strength of two.

"Once properly coupled, Kendi, you should be able to identify the pull of the gateway. I will warn you that the pull of the gateway can be...uncomfortable. The realm is cluttered with the presence of the Dominion. There is a unique buzz that will manifest when you enter the realm; however, the closer you get to the gateway, the buzz becomes a blaring that will try to pull you in. Kendi, you must find the entrance without being pulled through. Entering the gateway in this unconscious state means certain destruction. Lucifer's best warriors heavily guard the entrances. You can't go in without being fully corporeal and with your regime in tow.

"Find the location. Malachi will also be able to note its placement, so don't be worried if there is a level of disorientation as you work your way out of the realm in your non-corporeal form. Be cognizant of the fact that the Dominion patrols the area that leads to the gateway, and they are now on high alert because your identity has been revealed. They will be ready and waiting for you. On a positive note, you will be able to pinpoint the gate's location from quite a distance once you fully master the art of coupling." Tabbris smiled in encouragement. It wasn't working. "Any questions before we begin?"

"No, Eklektos." I kept my response limited for fear that my voice would expose my anxiety.

"No," Malachi echoed my response.

"Let's begin, then. Face one another. You two seem to have better success connecting this way. Remember, Kendi, don't continue to pull once you feel Malachi's strength."

I nodded, closing my eyes and centering myself to establish the connection with Malachi.

"*Are you ready for this, Kendi?*" Malachi questioned the moment we became linked, and Tabbris could no longer hear our silent conversation.

"*Of course not, but when will I ever be ready? Finding this gateway is the reason I'm here...no time like the present, right?*" I laughed nervously.

"*All right. Let's do this, but just so you know, I'm pulling out at the first sign of trouble. Got it? Your body is weak right now. The Dominion will take advantage of any weakness. I don't like this one bit. We shouldn't expose you like this.*"

"*You'll get no arguments from me, brother. First sign of trouble...*"

"All right, Kendi, I need you to begin pulling on Malachi's strength," Tabbris instructed. I tugged gently at the connection as to not block the bond. Malachi huffed.

"*You okay?*"

"*Yeah, fine. Keep going.*"

I carefully pulled harder until I felt tension in the rubber band.

"Ahhh," Malachi groaned. "*Can you hold it there? I don't think I will be able to hold you if you go farther.*"

I was having a hard time hearing Malachi. There was a low rumble in my ears that was distracting me.

"*Can you hear that, Mal?*" "*Hear what?*"

"*Be quiet for a minute. Listen.*"

As I floated, I intentionally turned and began moving in the direction of the hum. The sound intensified as if I had stumbled onto a large swarm of bees.

"*That...can you hear it now?*"

"*Yeah. I hear it. I guess we got the coupling right.*"

"*Guess so. That sound came immediately. Why do you think that is?*"

"*Not sure, but Tabbris did say the original gate was here in Danvers. Maybe Abbadon didn't move it far, especially with all of the Dominion activity in the region still.*"

"*Good point, we may be onto something. A little bit farther this way, then?*"

"*Carefully, brother.*"

Just as Malachi uttered his warning, the bees added a sting. "*Damn. Can you feel that?*"

"*Kind of. I feel it, but only through you…it's weird.*"

"*Guess we're getting warmer, huh? Where are we?*" I didn't recognize the area.

"*A few miles southwest of downtown Danvers.*"

"*You know what's out here?*"

"*Not too sure, but that's Proctor Street. There are a couple landmarks and a park of some sort, I think. Salem is south of here.*"

I pressed a little farther south toward the swarm against my better judgment. The stinging intensified until it felt like hundreds of needles pricking all at once.

"*Awwwwww. What the hell? Uncomfortable my ass! I don't want to know what Tabbris considers pain if this is discomfort.*"

"*Let's go back. Enough experimentation for one day.*"

"*Agreed. Let's get outta here.*"

I began to slowly release my connection to Malachi.

"*Wait a minute, Kendi. Did you see that?*"

"*See what?*"

"*That shadow to your left!*"

I turned in time to see the large black figure leap into my path. Tabbris said the Dominion would be ready and waiting.

"*Break the connect, Mal…break the connection! Now! We gotta get out of here!*"

The pain was intensifying. I felt like my skin was being pulled apart. I could feel the Dominion closing in. The atmosphere became dark with the evil presence. The air was no longer breathable. I began to hyperventilate, gasping as I remembered the dogs from the reservoir.

"*I'm trying, Kendi! Concentrate. Don't panic. We've got to disconnect from one another. I can't just snatch away. You'll be stuck!*"

Malachi's presence seemed to be fading. I couldn't tell which way I needed to go. Was I pulling or pushing now?

"*Concentrate, Shoer! Center yourself. Get control,*" Tabbris's voice was demanding.

I tried desperately to focus. I closed my eyes and inhaled, ignoring my immediate surroundings, and concentrated only on Malachi's presence.

"Now, Malachi! Get him out of there!"

I felt the connection as it severed, and we were once again in the backyard. I opened my eyes to see Malachi and Tabbris standing with me.

"Kendi, are you all right?" someone asked. It was as if I were listening through a long tunnel. I wanted to respond, but all my muscles were locked in place.

"Shoer?"

My muscles unlocked suddenly, and then there was nothing. The ground rushed up to meet me.

Darkness.

Out of night emerged the dark figure. It converged on me as I lay helpless on the ground. As it grew closer, it morphed, changed from dark to light—from an animal to one of my kind—angelic. This was not just an angel, but a Throne; the only beings of our kind that had the ability to shape-shift.

From my location on the damp earth, I couldn't discern my stalker. The glorious figure crept closer still—weapon drawn, ready to strike. The brilliant veil fell from his face revealing the huntsman. It wasn't the face that I expected. Not Abbadon or Azrael. The hunter was Ophan.

"A Throne never forgets, Shoer!" he roared as he drew back his flaming sword, ready to plunge the weapon through my core.

"Enough! Malachi, pull. You are still connected," Tabbris commanded. More darkness.

"Kendi? Can you hear me? Kendi!"

I opened my eyes to find Reuel shaking me. Malachi and Tabbris were both looking on. "Reuel?" I sat up, trying to steady myself. "What just happened?" I inquired looking to Tabbris for an answer.

"That, my friend, was your first journey into Sha'ar—the realm of the gateways. In your panic, you didn't fully journey out of the realm. It can be a little hard on the physical body. You'll be better able to tolerate the exit after a bit."

"Tabbris, this activity may be better practiced from Kahal, when Kendi is in his natural form and not so exposed, rather than here in Danvers. Don't you think?" Reuel made no attempt to disguise his anger.

"Perhaps. However, let's not forget how strong-willed our Shoer is. I find that Kendi absorbs the lessons faster when he is both in his human form and too exhausted to resist. I am here to prepare Kendi in the quickest and most effective manner possible. Not to coddle him. I fully intend to push him beyond the limits of his human form and will challenge what he can tolerate in his angelic form. We don't have time for pleasantries. I am only here to help, Reuel. The Legion will kill him given the first chance. Remember that. I will leave you to tend to Kendi." And with that, Tabbris was gone.

"Malachi, let's get him inside," Reuel instructed.

Even with Reuel and Mal supporting most of my weight, I found that I could barely stand. We entered the house, and I headed straight for the couch. I needed to rest before going any further.

"Is your strength returning?" Reuel inquired after a few moments.

My head was starting to clear. "I think so."

I turned to Malachi, who had been uncharacteristically quiet. "Mal, you okay?"

"Yeah. Sorry I couldn't get you out of there faster. I should have known you were still connected. I should have been able to sense that you weren't out. What if—"

I cut him off. "Stop. This was a first for both of us. We'll get the hang of it. I'm fine. You did nothing wrong," I encouraged.

This was going to be a huge problem. Malachi would never forgive himself now if something happened to me. The guilt was literally consuming him.

"Look, we're both new at this. We'll just watch each other's backs as best as we can. I have no doubt you will do everything you can to protect me. And please know that I will do everything in my power to never let you down again. I promise, brother."

"I've got you, Eklektos," Malachi responded, placing his hand on my shoulder as if to seal the vow.

"Hey, did I miss the part of Tabbris's lesson where he warned us about the hallucinations from this coupling stuff?" I tried to make light of what had just happened.

"Hallucinations? What did you see?" Reuel questioned.

"Ophan trying to kill me." I laughed out loud at how ridiculous this sounded. "You were unconscious. You saw Ophan?" Reuel and Malachi exchanged a look.

"You weren't hallucinating, Kendi. Ophan invaded the realm at your weakest point. You were still caught between Sha'ar and Charon. Tabbris intervened and sent him away," Malachi confirmed.

I could feel the color draining from my face as my blood ran cold. This time, I welcomed the darkness.

17
LET THE GAMES BEGIN

Something that once seemed so easy had now become my nemesis— school. It was aggravating to sit in classes all day and pretend that I was an insouciant teenager. But I had to play my role well now so that I could protect Xavier.

I found myself relying more on past knowledge to get through classes rather than trying to glean anything new. I just didn't have the capacity. During school, I found myself preoccupied with thoughts of evening training with Tabbris or Malachi and the guys. And I still had to deal with threats from Taylor and his buddies, so school was also a great place to practice meditation and self-control.

Malachi and I would connect frequently. This had become our way of communicating without involving the rest of the team. Though we needed to practice blocking, I shied away from it because of its effect on my brother. We tried again a few times, with marginally better results, but I still didn't like it.

And neither of us was particularly fond of coupling. The bodily effects were horrid—especially for me in my human form—and the impending danger from both Legion and Throne alike was enough to keep both of us at bay until we could train in the safety of Empyrean, or until Tabbris forced us into the skill. At least he would be on hand to intervene if necessary.

Another Monday morning at Danvers High and I was in no mood to endure an entire day of classes. I had more important things to do, although I was anxious to see Sarielle. She had been out of school a couple of days last week, and I was beginning to worry again. I hadn't reached out to her very much; just a random text message here and there. She had called a few times, but I let the phone go to voicemail. I felt awkward avoiding her, but I couldn't afford the distraction. I had to try to find a balance in the way I related to Sarielle. I should have never allowed her to get so close to me that evening. I had gotten caught up in the moment, but Tabbris was right. I had to focus on the task at hand. Daydreaming about a human girl was nothing but a useless complication. There were lives I was responsible for—both mortal and immortal.

"You're awfully quiet this morning," Mal observed as we headed to the Dunn Building.

"Yeah. Not feeling school today. It's kind of in the way right now, ya know?"

"I know but hang in there."

I gave him a half smile as we parted ways.

Sarielle was missing from English class again, and my mood deteriorated even further. I wouldn't see Xavier until lunch, and I was wound too tight this morning for that kind of patience. I waved at Rob as I stepped back out into the hallway and pulled my phone from my pocket. There were still a few minutes before the late bell.

The phone rang from behind me. I spun around to see Sarielle approaching. She glanced at the phone in her hand and then looked up at me.

"Looking for me?" She smiled. For the first time in a while, Sarielle looked more like herself.

"Sure was," I responded, extending my arms to embrace her. She nuzzled into me, laying her head on my chest, and wrapping her arms around my waist. I returned the gesture. We stayed this way for a long moment. I could feel the warmth of her body as she pressed close to me. It was strangely pleasant holding Sarielle this way. It was a sensation with which I was not familiar, but I liked it.

"What did you need?" Sarielle asked as she released me.

"Was just checking on you before the bell rang. I noticed you weren't here."

"Well, Mr. Belling, you act like you care or something," she teased.

"Who, me? Naah," I said, winking at her as we entered the classroom, and the late bell rang. Now that Sarielle was in school, the day passed more quickly. I felt better when she was where I could keep an eye on her. The entire crew was together at lunch for the first time in what seemed like forever. The weather had disintegrated as the day went along, and no one wanted to venture into the rain to grab lunch off campus. So, the cafeteria was crowded, stuffy, and smelly.

"Wish Renay would have packed lunches, cafeteria's a little tight today," Angelo said.

"Yeah, it is a little ripe in here too." Raz laughed. "Y'all wanna eat in the truck?"

I was still considering the idea when Xavier entered with Taylor and Rick. Why? What the heck was going on with this trio? Sarielle wouldn't like this. She wasn't yet here, and I didn't want her upset.

"Kendi, where are you going?" Malachi asked as I pushed away from the table. I nodded in the direction of the door. Both Malachi and the twins followed the direction of my glare and understood.

"Hey, Xavier," I called as I approached. "Saved seats for you and Sarielle. C'mon."

"Ah...hey, Kendi. Elle had an appointment at lunch. I was gonna—"

"Yeah. I want to ask you about that. Let's go. Your seat is there by Mal," I interrupted.

"Oh, okay." Xavier was caught off guard by my forcefulness. He turned to Taylor and Rick.

"Catch you guys later?"

"You know it," Rick replied.

I could feel Taylor's glare on my back as I spun Xavier around and headed to our table. Taylor despised me, but he was not as quick to act on his hatred since the night in the alley. He was still sizing me up, and me him. We pushed each other's buttons. Another blowup was inevitable.

"Where's Sarielle?" I asked, casually grabbing my burger.

"Checkup with Dr. Julie," Xavier replied, pulling open his lunch—intentionally avoiding my stare.

"Everything okay?"

"Yeah...just a scheduled check. She should be back by French."

Great. This was a perfect time to get some answers out of Xavier. With his sister gone, I could monopolize his free period. I only had to figure out a pretense before lunch ended, especially since he was now suspicious.

"Hey, everybody remembered your permissions slips for the field trip?" Lesley inquired after a couple minutes of silence. "Ms. Trap is a stickler when it comes to having them in on time."

Lesley's question effectively started a round of excited chatter. Everyone seemed to be looking forward to local history class today. Ms. Trap was covering a favorite—the Salem Witch Trials— in preparation for our Friday field trip. Was this just a coincidence or something more? With Yah, I could never tell.

I was eager to get to class for another reason altogether. I wanted to hear the Salem Witch Trial saga from the human perspective. Mal and I both wanted a chance to fill in the missing pieces in Tabbris's story. I also wanted to do some digging about Proctor Street, and what was located there.

The phone vibrated in my pocket. I pulled it out under the scrutiny of my brothers. It was Sarielle. Something was wrong.

"Sarielle?" Xavier looked up.

"Hey, Kendi. Sorry to bother you, but have you seen my brother? I've been trying to reach him." She was irritated.

"Xay's right here. We're in the cafe. You want to speak to him?"

"Please."

I handed the phone across the table. "Your sister." Now it was my turn to scrutinize.

"Elle?" Xavier paused. "I never heard my phone ring. Sorry. Everything okay?" Another pause. "Seriously? Where are you?" Xavier pushed away from the table, standing up. "Okay. I'm on the way." Xavier hung up the phone and handed it back to me.

"Rob, can I borrow your car? Elle's got a flat. She's stranded on Route 128." This was my way in.

"I'll take you. I can help since I have free next period."

"Thanks, man. Can we leave now? Elle's appointment is in a few minutes."

"No problem," I responded. "Raz?"

He tossed the keys across the table to me.

"Want me to ride, Kendi?" Malachi offered.

"Naah. Between Xavier and me, we should be able to get the tire changed and Sarielle to her appointment. I'll see you seventh period."

I opened up so that Malachi could connect. I was getting better at reading his eyes when he wanted a private conversation.

"You sure you want to go alone?"

"Yeah. I think I can handle it. I need a chance to speak with Xavier. It'll go better if we're alone."

"Gotcha. Just be careful and keep the channel open in case you need me."

"Will do."

The conversation passed between us in a microsecond. No one, not even the twins, would have noticed the pause. Mal and I were getting much better at this Achim stuff.

"See you guys later," I directed at Rob and Lesley.

As Xavier and I headed for the door, I was acutely aware of Taylor's curious eyes following the two of us. He was not particularly in favor of any kind of friendship that might be brewing between Xavier and me. Knowing that I was getting under his skin made me smirk as we passed his table.

I turned out of the parking lot headed toward Burley Street. Xavier hadn't said a word since we left the cafeteria—completely out of character for him. Normally, he would be chatting my ears off, annoying the shit out of me. I needed to get him talking. It wouldn't take long to get to Sarielle.

Being direct was all I knew. I wasn't exactly the "beat around the bush" kind of guy. I just didn't have the patience for that kind of nonsense. Besides, the tension in the truck made me uncomfortable, and I didn't like it.

"What's the deal with you and Taylor? I didn't say anything to Sarielle, but you still owe me an explanation. I haven't forgotten."

"Kendi…" He paused, shaking his head.

"Kendi, what? I want to know what's going on. You owe me an explanation, man. Don't you think?"

"Owe you—seriously? I told you not to get involved." Xavier stared out of the window.

"It's a little late for that, my friend. I would say I'm more than involved after body-slamming Taylor into a wall. You don't honestly think that he is going to let that go. Do you?"

"I didn't ask for your help. I could have handled Taylor myself." He was becoming irritated.

"Yeah, right. Sounded like you had it all under control. You were about to get your face smashed in, just standing there like an idiot! Why are you taking so much crap from that joker anyway?" I demanded.

"Now you sound like Elle. Back the hell off. Taylor and I are cool. We don't need a referee."

"That's complete bullshit, Xay, and you know it!"

This wasn't working. All I had succeeded in doing was making Xavier defensive, and me frustrated.

The rain had picked up, and it was getting harder to see. I flipped the wipers on high, squinting through the downpour. I took a silent breath to calm myself before beginning again.

"If I know what's going on, I can help."

"Just leave it alone, man." Xavier hesitated before turning to look at me. "You don't even like me. The only reason you even speak to me is because of my sister. You think I don't know that?"

I wished that were the only reason I was trying to form a friendship with him. No need to mention that my life depended on it.

His face was knotted in a scowl as he peered through the windshield at the rain, but he wasn't angry. His hurt expression confused me.

"Kendi, look out!" A car had stopped directly in front of us. The Rover fishtailed as I slammed on the brakes.

"Damn it!" I scrambled to regain control as I swerved around the stopped vehicle. This little incident effectively ended our banter. I had to pay attention to the road.

"Hey, pull over. There's Elle," Xavier announced after a couple minutes of silence.

I spotted the little red Honda at the same moment and pulled in behind it. Sarielle got out of the car as we did.

"You okay, Elle?"

"Yeah, stupid tire. My appointment is in ten minutes. Can you guys take me and then come back and deal with this?" Sarielle directed at Xavier. I answered for him.

"C'mon. Xay and I will come back and get the tire changed." I hoped my irritation with her brother didn't show as I spoke.

We dropped off Sarielle and headed back to Route 128. "There's a jack in the trunk. I'll grab it." Xavier jumped out of the truck before I could even get the car in park.

My annoyance with him was about to spill over. I sat in the truck for a moment and took a few deep breaths. The rain wasn't letting up, and I was in no way looking forward to getting drenched while we changed the tire.

"Everything all right, kid?"

I should have known Malachi would be drawn to me. It didn't take trouble for him to initiate connecting—just my amplified emotional state was enough.

"Yeah, Mal. Fine. Just annoyed with Xavier is all. I haven't managed to get squat out of him yet."

"Understand. Find a way to get him to trust you."

"Working on it." I hopped out of the truck into the downpour.

"Is there a full-sized tire or just a donut?" I questioned as I joined him at the back of the Honda.

"There's a real tire," he responded as he handed the jack to me and lifted the compartment to get the spare.

"Cool. Let's get this done. You can go pick up your sister, and I'll head back to school. I want to talk to Ms. Trap before class starts."

I went to the driver's side rear to jack up the car and get the blown tire off. The car's proximity to the highway made me nervous but changing the tire shouldn't take long—or so I thought. The bolts were rusted in place. After some persistence, I had freed four of the five bolts. But I had worked up such a sweat in the process that I couldn't get a good grip on the lug wrench to loosen the last bolt. The deluge of rain wasn't helping either.

"C'mon, man, let me try. We're getting soaked out here," Xavier complained, abruptly snapping the hood of his jacket up.

"Have at it." I dropped the lug wrench in the puddle at my feet and moved to the front end of the car.

Xavier strategically placed the wrench onto the last bolt so that the end of it was at a maximum height above the ground. He then proceeded to use his foot to apply pressure to jar the bolt loose. After a couple of quick stomps, it came off. I tried to ignore the snide grin as Xay bent down to remove the tire.

Why in the hell did I not think of doing it that way?

I was still sulking when I was startled by Malachi's voice screaming in my head.

"Kendi, Azrael is headed your way! Liwet is on his tail, but he is coming up fast."

My head snapped up, quickly surveying our surroundings. Nothing seemed out of order.

"Mal, help me out here. What should I be looking for?"

"Not sure. I'm sorry, Kendi. I should've come with you." I could hear the exasperation in his voice.

"Look, don't worry. We're okay. We'll be outta here and back on the road in just a sec."

I had barely thought the words when I heard the screech of tires against the wet pavement. A black SUV was skidding out of control and was headed directly at us, at Xavier in particular.

"Xay, look out!"

He turned in my direction but didn't move. He obviously didn't hear the skidding truck.

All I could do was launch myself at my assignment in hopes that I could knock him out of the way in time. In the split second I left my feet, Xavier saw the SUV approaching and jumped to his. As he did, I crashed into him, slamming him face forward into the Rover.

The SUV sideswiped the Honda and slammed into the guardrail a few feet in front of us, finally coming to a stop.

Wind chimes.

"Xay, are you all right?" I asked as I lifted myself from his back looking around.

"I think so."

But as he lifted himself from the ground, the blood began to flow from his forehead and started pooling on the ground at an alarming rate.

"Xay, sit back down. Stay still. You're bleeding…a lot." He looked dazed but did as I said. I opened the truck and grabbed a towel from the gym bag in the backseat.

"Hold this on your head. I need to get help."

"Mal, he's hurt. Xavier's hurt. There's blood everywhere!"

"I know. I saw everything. Stay calm. Reuel's on the way. He was closer to your location. Check the other driver and call 911. Azrael is gone. Liwet didn't catch him but did manage to deter him for now."

I reached into the truck to get my cell phone and dialed 911. While I was reporting the accident, I walked over to the SUV to see if the driver was injured. In my approach, I saw the extensive front-end damage to the vehicle, including a completely shattered windshield. The driver slowly opened the door and tried to climb out of the truck.

"Sir, are you all right?" I inquired.

"I–I–I'm so sorry. I don't know what happened. I must have fallen asleep or something," he began to apologize.

"It's all right. You need to stay still. I'm calling for help now." The man had multiple cuts on his face and forearms. I assumed from the shattered glass. The driver slumped back into the seat, disoriented.

I turned my attention back to Xavier, who was leaning against the truck with the towel held to his face.

"Xay, let me see your head."

As he moved the towel, I could momentarily see the depth of a gaping wound across his forehead before the fresh blood began to ooze. I was no doctor, but that was going to require stitches. Xavier was losing way too much blood.

"Here, let me hold that. I think I can apply more pressure until the paramedics get here."

Xavier didn't respond but moved his hand so that I could take the towel. His eyes were starting to lose focus as he slumped farther down the side of the truck.

"You hanging in there, man?" I wanted to keep him talking.

"Hmmm? Real dizzy. Think I'm gonna pass out."

"C'mon, Xay. Help's almost here."

I could hear the sirens in the distance. I craned my neck, looking over Xay's head, trying to see if the EMS was in view. I couldn't see the ambulance, but Reuel's car approaching. He came to a stop behind the truck and jumped out.

"Kendi!"

"I'm fine, Dad. My friend is hurt, though. The paramedics are on the way. The other driver is pretty cut up too."

Xay sagged. I caught his head before it hit the concrete.

"Xay!" His eyes fluttered and then closed. Reuel came to assist.

"I think he's okay. His breathing is even. He fainted from the loss of blood," Reuel explained.

"Liwet has Azrael on the run. He's long gone. The accident was Azrael's fault. He influenced the driver." Malachi was feeding me information as he gathered it.

"He can do that?"

"Unfortunately, he can. This man must have given Azrael a way in prior to today, and he took it. We may never know the source. It could be something as simple as voodoo and Ouiji boards, or as complicated as praying to Lucifer himself. I don't know ."

"What in the hell am I up against here, Mal? The Dominion can be anybody, anywhere. How can we even prepare for such a fight?"

"I don't know, brother. I don't know."

"Kendi?" Reuel noticed my pause.

"Azrael's gone. He had control of the other driver." Reuel said nothing but just shook his head in disgust.

The police and the ambulance pulled up at the same moment. The EMTs rushed to Xavier as he was unconscious. They moved me out of the way as they began working. "How long has he been out?"

"No more than two or three minutes," Reuel responded.

"Is he going to be okay?" I asked, moving closer.

"How'd this head injury happen?" the EMT asked without addressing my question.

"I pushed him out of the way of the SUV. He...he hit his head on the front of my truck. Please, is he going to be okay?" I had a horrible feeling in the pit of my stomach.

Reuel stepped in, placing a hand on my shoulder. "Let them work, son."

Reuel and I watched as the EMT got vitals, placed a pressure bandage on Xay's head, and started preparing him for transport. This guy was not working nearly fast enough for me. Granted, the other paramedic had gone to assist the police with the driver of the SUV. And the rain continued its steady downpour.

A second set of police had arrived and were cordoning off the accident scene. After setting up flares around the vehicles, one of the officers approached me.

"Young man, are you the one that called this in?"

"Yes."

"We are going to need to get a statement."

I was only partially listening. They were starting to load Xavier into the back of the ambulance. "Dad, I want to follow them to the hospital. I should make sure Xay is all right, and Sarielle is going to freak out. I need to be there to tell her what happened." The adrenalin was pumping. I was talking a mile a minute. My words were all one big jumble.

"Take a deep breath, Kendi. Stay calm."

"Officer, here is my card. I'm Nathan Belling, Criminal Attorney. My office is down on Maple Street. My son is rather upset about his friend. Can I bring him by the station tomorrow to give his statement?"

"Certainly, Mr. Belling, I thought I recognized you. I'm Officer Thomas. Just call me when you are ready, and we will take care of it. No problem." He handed Reuel a card.

"Are you okay to drive alone?" Reuel asked me.

"I'm fine. Let's go, they're leaving."

I started to call Sarielle on the way to the hospital but thought better of it after some consideration. I wanted to look her in the eyes and let her know her brother was all right. I didn't want her to go into panic mode. She would wind up on a stretcher next to him. And right now, I couldn't assure her with any level of confidence.

I used the OnStar system to contact Dr. Julie's office. If I told her what happened, she could bring Sarielle around to emergency. Luck would have it that I caught her before she went in to see Sarielle. She promised not to say anything to her until she knew more about Xavier's condition.

I pulled around the emergency loop and hopped out just as they were unloading Xay. He had still not come around.

The EMTs rushed the gurney past Reuel and me and into the emergency room. All we could do now was wait.

After about thirty minutes, a tall, slender woman hurried into the lobby and went straight to the desk.

"Xavier Breland, my son, is he here? I was told he was here. Where is he? Is he all right? Please tell me he is all right!"

"Calm down, ma'am. Your name?" the nurse replied.

The woman took a deep breath. "I'm sorry. Emily Breland. I'm looking for my son, Xavier Breland. I was told that he was brought in a few minutes ago."

"Yes, he's here. The doctors are with him now. I will let them know you are here. Someone will be out shortly to give you an update." The nurse turned and disappeared behind the double doors.

Emily turned toward the waiting room where Reuel and I sat. Her face was disfigured with worry. Reuel got up to meet Emily in the middle of the room. I followed.

"Ms. Breland? I'm Nathan Belling. This is my son, Kendi. He was with Xavier at the time of the accident."

Emily looked cautiously back and forth between the two of us trying to get a read as to the seriousness of the accident. But we knew only slightly more than she did.

"Oh, so you're Kendi. I've heard a lot about you." She smiled warmly. "It's nice to meet you both. I'm Emily Breland." She extended her hand first to Reuel and then to me.

"What happened?" Emily asked intently—never allowing her gaze to leave my eyes.

"Come on. Let's sit, Ms. Breland," Reuel instructed, ushering her to a seat in the corner of the room.

"Please call me Emily."

"Emily, have a seat. Let me start by saying I believe Xavier is going to be fine."

Emily turned to me, wanting details. "What happened?"

"Xay and I went to help Sarielle because she had a flat tire on Route 128. We dropped her off for her appointment and then went back to fix the tire. While Xay was putting the new tire on, a truck lost control in the rain and almost slammed into us. I pushed him out of the way, Xay fell forward and hit his head pretty hard on the front of my truck."

I didn't want to give too many details without the benefit of a doctor's report because I had no idea of how much damage my heroics had caused.

"How badly was he hurt?" Emily asked when I paused.

I wasn't sure how or if I wanted to continue. Reuel bailed me out.

"He has a cut on his forehead that will probably require stitches. He was bleeding quite a bit when I arrived. He lost consciousness shortly before the ambulance arrived."

"Oh my God…Xay." The tears started.

"Emily, Xavier will be all right." Reuel slid next to Emily and put his arm around her shoulder, handing her a handkerchief from his pocket. He was so much better at this stuff than the rest of us, especially me.

I felt bad for her, but I couldn't identify the source of my remorse. Was it simply because I had such a high stake in whether Xavier lived or died, or was it because I was beginning to care about these humans that I was sentenced to protect?

The awkward silence was nerve-racking. I got up and started to pace. The double doors opened, and Dr. Julie emerged. Emily nearly sprinted across the room.

"Julie! Where's Xavier? Is he all right?"

"Xay will be fine. He's awake. He needed fifteen stitches for the laceration to his forehead, and he has a concussion. We are going to keep him overnight just as a precaution. If he does well tonight, he will be released sometime tomorrow."

"Thank you so much. Can I see him?"

"They are getting him set up in a room now. Elle is with him. Give it about ten minutes, and then you will be able to go back."

The room breathed a collective sigh of relief.

"Kendi, you may have very well saved my son's life. Thank you."

"He would have done the same for me, Ms. Breland. I'm just glad Xay's all right. Do you mind if I stick around to see him?"

"Not at all. Please call me Emily."

"Emily." I smiled back at her. No one here would know how deep my relief ran, except Reuel. Dr. Julie nodded in my direction prior to retreating through the double doors. I could see why Sarielle and Xavier liked her so much. She was cool. Dr. Julie never let on that she already knew me, for which I was grateful. I certainly didn't want to explain to Emily the circumstances that led to our first encounter.

"I'm so glad that Xavier is okay, Emily. It was so nice to meet you." Reuel shook Emily's hand.

"You as well, Mr. Belling."

"Nathan."

"Nathan. You have a pretty special son there."

"Thank you. I agree." Reuel grinned, slapping me on the shoulder and pulling me in his direction very discreetly. He wanted to talk. "I hope to see you again soon, but under better circumstances." Reuel headed for the door.

"Absolutely," Emily responded.

I followed Reuel to the parking lot.

"Another close call. Abbadon is not going to let up. We've got to step up both our surveillance and our protection detail. Uriel and the extensions are setting up residences in Danvers and the surrounding area. We need them close. Xavier and his family are going to be under constant watch from now on. And you will not be alone anymore. Getting ambushed is not an option. Malachi will be with you from here on out."

"You'll get no argument from me. I'm tired of watching my life flash before my eyes. Thankfully this kid has nine lives, or we would both be toast by now."

"I'm heading over to the school to pick up the team. I will drop Malachi off here, just in case Azrael is still tracking you. Stay inside the hospital until he gets here. Understand?"

"Understood. Thanks, Reuel." I hung my head, feeling extremely unworthy of the team that Yah had placed around me—the chances they continued to take for me, putting themselves in harm's way and doing so as if it were a privilege.

"Look at me, Kendi. You must start believing in who Yah created you to be. Know that we will follow you either way, but a confident Shoer is a victorious Shoer."

"Why do you have so much faith in me when I have done nothing but let you down?"

"Son, I believe in grace—a grace that is continually renewed. And as long as we have this extension of grace, we have an opportunity to get it right. Who am I to say that tomorrow is not your day?" Reuel winked at me. "Or the next day, or the next day, or..." He chuckled.

"All right, all right. I get it. I just hope grace doesn't slam the door shut before I figure this out. My hourglass may be about empty."

"Don't count the sands of time out just yet."

"If you say so. I'll wait here for Mal. See you at home."

I watched Reuel until the gray Audi was out of sight. The air outside the hospital stirred suddenly, sending a shiver up my spine. I turned quickly and walked back into the warmth of the waiting room.

18
Turn Up the Heat

The screams were getting louder, closer as I ran. But the darkness was so daunting—closing in on me. My heart pounded in my chest as the sweat ran into my eyes. The night swallowed my hand as I lifted it to wipe my face. This was not normal. Terror began to overtake me. I couldn't think. Was I lost? I didn't recognize this place. My mind was clouded by fatigue. My body was drained as if I had been running for miles. I wanted to rest, but the screams... screams of someone familiar to me...propelled me farther into the darkness.

"Shoer! Get in there. He needs your help. Find him!" I was instantly alert as I received the mandate. The voice was weighted with authority, although I didn't know who was commanding me.

"I can't see. Where is he?" I pushed my way through the brush, hoping I was moving in the direction of the screams.

Suddenly, there in the darkness was a small spark— some sort of light. I ran harder, though my legs were about to give out. He needed my help. I was thankful for the light aiding my search, but it was changing. As I ran, the light grew, taking on its own personality. It consumed the darkness of the densely packed terrain. After a few more yards, the light was abruptly too much. It was too bright—blinding even. But I continued pressing my way toward the screams.

My discomfort multiplied as the brilliance took on another quality. It was hot! But the heat brought clarity to the scenario. The source of the light was fire—a fire that was quickly spreading. The inferno was the reason behind the panicked cries for help.

"Kendi! Over here...please...please help me!"

"Where are you? I can't see! Where are you?"

The voice grew silent. I could only hear gasping and coughing—someone choking on the dense smoke. My eyes, too, began to burn as the smoke filled them. A few more feet and the light abated, overtaken by smoke.

"Come on, Kendi—this way. I'll help."

A hand grabbed mine and pulled me deeper into the darkness. The forest was burning at an alarming rate. Only these weren't trees. I looked up above my head trying to see. What the hell? Corn stalks? I was in a cornfield.

"Kendi, we've got to hurry, or you'll be too late! He's over here." My chest hurt as the smoke began to fill my lungs, but I pushed my way through the tightly packed corn stalks until I was in a small clearing. I could see the person lying on the ground—but only just. I fell to my knees and crawled in the direction of the figure.

"Hey, are you all right?" When there was no response, I grabbed his shoulder and turned him over so that I could see his face.

Xavier. His face was ashen and unresponsive.

Panic gripped me. "Hey! Who's there? Help us! We need help!" The smoke seemed to triple in density. Everything blackened simultaneously. I reflexively threw myself across Xay to protect him from the advancing smoke.

"Help me! Where did you go? We gotta get outta here!"

There was an ominous chuckle from the darkness followed by a flash of light. "You sure you want my help?" Ophan jumped out of the blackness at me.

I shot up in bed covered in sweat, heart pounding.

A dream, it was only a dream.

"Are you sure about that, Shoer?" Ophan's voice came from the dark corner of my room.

"Awwwwh!" I screamed. Ophan laughed quietly and was gone.

"Kendi! What is it? Are you all right?" Malachi burst through the door, followed by Reuel and the twins. They were all alert and searching for any source of danger.

I scanned the room quickly trying to catch my breath. "Yeah, fine. Sorry, guys."

After a final glance around the room, although disturbed by my outburst, Reuel and the twins turned and left. Malachi lingered. He came and sat next to me on the bed and placed a hand on my shoulder. I knew he would be able to feel my body trembling.

"What's wrong? You're frightened—why?"

"It was just a bad dream. At least I think it was a dream."

"What do you mean?"

"It all just seemed so real, Mal. There was a fire, Xavier was trapped, and someone was trying to help us, then Ophan appeared out of nowhere. But when I awoke, he was...here."

"Who was here?" Malachi asked, looking around.

"Ophan was here in my room, taunting me. He's not going to let this go...is he? He won't stop until he feels like I've been punished for deceiving him." I paused and took a steadying breath before continuing.

"Why does he continue to mess with my head like this?" I looked up at the ceiling and spoke directly to Ophan. "Whatever you want to do to me, just do it and get it over with. Just kill me and get it over with if that's what you want to do! Why keep tormenting me? I can't deal with this right now!"

Malachi rose from the bed and started to pace during my rant.

"Calm down. Ophan can't kill you. Even the Thrones must follow Yah's orders. He can't touch you. But he can keep you distracted long enough for Abbadon to do the job for him. You can't let Ophan get to you."

He paced faster as he spoke, becoming increasingly more irritated as he considered my situation with Ophan.

"Tabbris was supposed to handle this. Ophan is crossing the line. You have enough to deal with preparing for Abbadon and the Legion. The Thrones and their pride, damn it! We'll all wind up in Sheol for it. Don't worry about it. I'll have a word with him."

Malachi was angry now. His hands were balled into tight fists.

I didn't want Mal to put himself in between an angry Throne and me. This was a problem that I had created, and I would have to deal with it.

"Mal, just leave it alone. Ophan is my headache. I'll figure something out."

"You don't get it, Kendi. The success of this assignment is bigger than you or me, and even Ophan. He's got to put this petty vendetta aside. I didn't plan on fighting both the Dominion and Ophan, but I will. Either he's with us, or he's against us. We can't afford to deal with these blurred lines anymore. Get some rest. I'll be back soon."

"Mal, no!" I reached for him. But, as quickly as Ophan had, Malachi was gone. I panicked, but there was nothing I could do. I couldn't follow.

Of all my mess-ups, Ophan may just be the biggest mistake I'd made so far. Being on the shit list of one of the Thrones was certainly detrimental to the completion of this assignment, both for the rest of the team and me.

I ran for the door. Reuel met me in the hallway; he had heard the commotion.

"Kendi? What's going on?"

"Malachi went after Ophan. You've got to stop him, Reuel. Please." I threw the words at him as if they were my only lifeline.

"Calm down. Nothing is going to happen to Malachi. I will bring him back."

And with that, Reuel was gone as well. The silence was deafening. All I could do was wait and hope that Reuel would successfully defuse the situation. I lay back on the bed and tried to relax my mind.

I thought of the one thing that I knew would calm me down—Sarielle. She was so delicate, so fragile, that I had to use restraint when I was around her. My natural inclination in her presence was to take it down a thousand. So, I concentrated on her face, her hair, the softness of her hand, and the sense of belonging I felt whenever I was with her. I could feel my tightly coiled muscles begin to loosen. A strange tranquility swept over me, and as the feelings of apprehension drifted away, I fell asleep.

Voices in the hallway broke through the carefully manufactured utopia I had conjured. Malachi and Reuel had returned. Though they were not shouting, the conversation was intense. Unfortunately, they kept their voices low enough that I couldn't hear. I was tempted to go and find out what had happened with Ophan but decided against it. The clock confirmed I had only slept an hour. Rolling over, I put the pillow over my head to further muffle the voices and thought of being with Sarielle the next day at school.

"Kendi, are you almost ready?" Raza questioned from the other side of the door. "Mal said he wants to leave early so you two can talk to Ms. Trap before school."

"Yeah. Be down in just a second."

I had gotten a late start this morning. Having only a few hours' sleep left me lethargic and in a foul mood. I wanted to pitch the alarm clock onto the front lawn after snoozing it three or four times.

Malachi volunteered to drive this morning, and Angelo had grabbed the front seat. Before long the normal banter started; however, Mal seemed quieter than normal.

"Mal, everything okay?" Ange questioned after a few minutes. I looked up from the backseat as Angelo nodded, and Mal glanced into the rearview mirror. He quickly diverted his eyes, but not without my noticing.

I pushed at Malachi to connect with him. *"Mal? What's going on?"*

Nothing.

"Malachi?"

Again, no response.

"Mal!"

Sigh. "Kendi, not now. We'll talk later." His eyes never left the road. He didn't want the twins to know we were having a conversation. I let it go.

We had a choice parking space this morning since we were so early.

"See you guys later. Salem should be…interesting. Wish we could go with you," Raz complained.

"Just stay alert in case something happens," Malachi said as we all rounded the back of the truck. "The Legion activity in that part of town is high. We may need your help."

"We'll be ready and waiting," Angelo replied.

"Here, take the keys, just in case." Malachi tossed the keys to Ange. "Come on, Kendi. Let's go find Ms. Trap."

I nodded to the twins as we turned for the Dunn Building. "What's bothering you? What happened last night with Ophan and Reuel?"

Malachi shook his head. His jaw tightened.

"Ophan swears he wasn't in your room last night. That he isn't harassing you. He said it must be guilt getting the best of you. I didn't handle Ophan very well. It could have gotten very ugly if Reuel and Tabbris hadn't shown up when they did. Thanks for sending Reuel. I guess you're not the only one with a hot head." Malachi laughed humorlessly.

"What were you and Ange talking about?"

"Reuel told the twins to watch me—to keep me away from Ophan. I agreed to be compliant."

"And will you?"

"Will I what?"

"Be compliant."

"My allegiance is to you, Eklektos. I will comply as long as it doesn't interfere with our assignment."

"Malachi," I started.

"Don't worry. I'll behave." He grinned and gave me a wink. "Great! Ms. Trap is here." Mal tapped on the door.

Ms. Trap looked up from her desk, smiled warmly, and waved us in.

"Good morning, gentlemen. You're here early. Afraid you'd miss the bus for the field trip?" She laughed. "We don't leave until after lunch."

"Naah. We wanted to ask some questions about the Salem Witch Trials. We were having a family discussion last night about it and wanted to get an opinion from a reputable, neutral source."

Damn, Mal was good at thinking on his feet.

"Oh, okay. What were you discussing?" Ms. Trap was genuinely curious.

"The witch trials occurred in Salem Village, and Salem Village is now Danvers. Correct?" he began.

"Yes. We discussed that in class." She looked puzzled.

"You said that the location of some of the landmarks associated with the Witch Trials is uncertain. Is there a way to pin any of those down?" Kendi asked.

"Are you referring to any landmark in particular?"

"Not really. But do you know what is out around Proctor Street, or what used to be there? Everything that we could find on the internet seemed to allude to a loss of factual data over the years."

"A loss of factual data…Kendi, you sound like an old man."

If only you knew…

"He is." Malachi laughed.

"Well, to be honest, no one really knows for certain. Despite all the records and documentation, the locations of many of the events surrounding the trials have been lost. The history has mostly been pieced together from family journals, word of mouth, and hand-drawn maps. Some historians believe that Proctor Street is the site of Gallows Hill."

"Gallows Hill?" Malachi repeated hesitantly.

"What is Gallows Hill?" I inquired, looking back and forth between the two.

"It's the place where the suspected witches were executed—death by hanging," Ms. Trap explained. "There has been a raging debate for years over the actual location. There was a historian in 1867, Charles Upham, who thought that Gallows Hill was the huge hill over on Langdon Street.

"But I believe he was discredited by journals and stories that have been passed down through the years. You see, the accused witches were taken to the execution site by horse-drawn carts. There is no way horses could get up that steep hill. Also, there is another story told about Benjamin Nurse, Rebecca's son, who rowed a small boat from the creek near their home into the North River and right up to the base of Gallows Hill to steal his mother's body so that he could give her a proper Christian burial. There have never been any waterways near the Langdon Street location.

"Some years later, in the late 1920s, a different historian, Sydney Perley, published an article containing clues that pointed to the Proctor Street location. He discovered that the North River used to spill into a large bay that pooled into Bickford's Pond. This pond has since been filled in, but, in 1692, it would have allowed Benjamin direct access to the small hill on Proctor Street. Most of the locals, including myself, believe that Proctor Street is the likely location."

"Ms. Trap, how do you know this stuff?"

She chuckled. "It's kind of my job, Kendi. Any other questions, guys? Homeroom is about to start."

"No, that was all. Thanks. We will see you this afternoon." We stepped into the hallway headed to our homeroom classes.

"You think Abbadon moved the gate from the center of town out to Gallows Hill?"

I thought it better to have this conversation silently just in case we were being tracked by the Dominion. Discovering the location of the gateway in Charon would make me more of a target than ever. Abbadon would not be able to relocate the portal again without first getting me out of the way.

"That would be my guess. We need to keep this between us until we can confirm and prepare."

Malachi glanced at me from the corner of his eye, trying to disguise the anxiety there.

While Malachi wasn't afraid of the impending battle, he was petrified that I wasn't ready to handle the imminent danger. He didn't have to voice his concern, I was learning to read my Achim.

"I'll be ready, Mal. Don't worry." I touched his shoulder to assure him as we continued down the hall.

When we turned the corner, I noticed Sarielle and Xay just outside the building. They were engaged in what seemed like a pretty intense argument.

"Hey, Mal..." I nodded toward the door, and we both headed outside to intervene.

"Get the hell off my back! I don't need you or Mom telling me what to do. Damn! You both are getting on my nerves. Just leave me alone, please!" Xay was screaming at Sarielle. He turned toward us as the door swung open.

"Hey, hey. What's going on? Everything okay here?" Mal asked, looking back and forth between the two.

"Yeah fine," Xavier snapped as he caught the door and attempted to brush past the both of us.

I caught him by the arm. "What's your problem, Xavier?" I probably had a tighter grip on him than I should have had, but it got his attention.

"Nothing. I have a headache is all." He snatched away from me and headed into the building.

I nodded at Mal to follow while I stayed with Sarielle. "Are you okay?"

"Not really." A tear ran down the left side of her cheek. She quickly lifted her hand to scrub it away.

"Come here." I pulled her into my arms as a sob broke free of her control. "Shhhh. It's okay. Come on, let's sit down." I led her around the side of the building to one of the benches. I held her for a minute until she calmed down.

"What's going on? What happened?" I inquired.

"Xay needs to be at home resting. He is not doing well, but he won't go back to the hospital. He is in a lot of pain and getting sick to his stomach...something's wrong. He told me he would go back to Beverly today if he wasn't feeling better. Then he got a call from Taylor this morning, and everything changed. Suddenly, he just can't miss the field trip. What's that all about?"

"I don't know, Sarielle, but I am trying to find out. Try not to worry. Mal and I will keep an eye on him. Okay?"

"Thanks, Kendi."

"No thanks necessary. That's what friends do, right?"

"Friends, huh?" She tried to give me a strained smile.

"What?"

"Nothing. Let's get inside before we're late for first period." I let it go, took her hand, and pulled her up from the bench.

The morning passed slowly as I thought through what Ms. Trap had said and what that meant for the team and me. Malachi was keeping an eye on Xay for me. He had been sick twice already, and his eyes weren't focusing. Sarielle had every reason to be worried. We all agreed to meet in the cafeteria for lunch since the bus was leaving immediately after for Salem. I met Sarielle in the hallway, and we walked to the cafe together.

"Xay looks horrible. Have you seen him?" Sarielle asked.

"Yeah. I know. We're watching him. The day is almost over. Mal and I will hog-tie him if need be and get him home after the field trip so you and your mom can get him to a doctor to get checked out."

"He's so stubborn. It may take hog-tying him for real." She laughed.

"You should smile more. You have such a beautiful smile," I complimented her without really thinking about it. She blushed.

"Thanks...friend." She laughed again as we entered the cafeteria and headed to the table where everyone else was starting to assemble.

Malachi wasn't here yet. Neither was Xay. I took a seat facing the door so that I could keep watch. After a couple of minutes, Xavier entered along with Taylor, Rick, and Corey. Mal was only a few steps behind.

"What's going on there?" I asked as Mal took a seat.

"Not sure. They have been speaking in code all morning, but something is certainly up. Taylor is determined to get Xay into Salem this afternoon."

"Interesting. You think we'll need the twins on standby to watch?"

"Probably not a bad idea. I'll fill them in."

We engaged in conversation at the table so that our silent dialogue wouldn't draw attention. Lunch passed quickly, and it was time to board the bus for Salem. Xavier immediately went to the back of the bus with the rest of his crew, sat down, put his head back, and closed his eyes. To Rob and Lesley's dismay, I followed suit, taking the seat directly in front of them and pulling Sarielle with me. Lesley and Rob grabbed the seats in front of me, and Malachi took the aisle seat across from me. It didn't take long before the generic insults began to hurl across the seat, clearly meant for me.

"Hey, Rick, you smell something?" Taylor asked.

"Yeah, smells like shitlocks."

My free hand curled into a fist. Sarielle squeezed the hand she was holding, probably hoping that I wouldn't start a fight.

"Ignore those idiots, Kendi."

I nodded my head enough for Malachi to know I was acknowledging him.

The insults continued in a similar fashion over the next few minutes until Xavier chimed in. "Guys, please. My head is pounding...give it a rest already."

"Sure, you're the boss." Rick laughed sarcastically, but the banter ended. I looked at Mal with a raised eyebrow. He shrugged.

The bus came to a stop near Essex Street where our outing would begin. The tour included stops at the Witch History Museum followed by the Witch House before visiting Gallows Hill Museum, the Witch Trials Memorial, and ending in Washington Square at the Salem Witch Museum.

Ms. Trap stood and began giving instructions regarding what notes would be important to recall later. Everyone started gathering their things, except Xay. He seemed to have fallen asleep in the few moments of silence.

"Xay? Hey, wake up." Sarielle reached over the seat and touched his shoulder. He startled awake and sat up with a moan. Bending forward, putting his head into his hands.

"You all right, man?" I asked.

"Fine," he retorted, scooting past us to follow Taylor up the aisle.

I shook my head, taking Sarielle's hand and followed the line of students unloading the bus.

We all gathered in the parking lot as Ms. Trap wrapped up her directions for the afternoon.

We paired off and headed for the Witch History Museum. Mal and I intentionally hung back so that Xay would be in front of us. He seemed unsteady to me.

"You think he's gonna make it, Mal?"

"Doesn't look like it. Why would he put himself through this?"

"Don't know. I guess we'll find out eventually."

We entered the Witch History Museum, and the costumed guide launched into her re-creation of the Salem Witch Trials. The exhibits were life-sized recreations of seventeenth-century Salem. Xavier stumbled along miserably. As we left the darkened forest scene and reentered a brightly lit room, Xay grimaced, abruptly cutting off the tour guide by asking for a bathroom.

"I got it." Mal followed Xavier. Sarielle's countenance fell.

"It's okay." I squeezed her hand.

They were back with the tour very quickly. Xay had splashed water on his face after dry heaving over a toilet. He pushed forward to catch up with Taylor.

"Hey, man. You got something I can take for this headache? I'm dying here."

Taylor reached into his pocket and pulled out an unmarked pill bottle and handed it to Xavier after grinning over his shoulder at Rick and Corey. Xay popped it open and threw two pills in his mouth.

Malachi pressed through the students between Xay and us. "Dude, what are you taking?" Xavier looked at Taylor for an answer.

"What are you? His mom? He said he had a headache." Mal and I shared a concerned glance, but let it go.

About an hour later, Xay seemed to be feeling better and had more energy. Whatever he took seemed to be working—at least temporarily. I was glad.

Xavier's change for the better made Sarielle's demeanor less somber as well. We had been to the Witch House and were leaving to go to the Gallows Museum when Ms. Trap announced that we were splitting up to cover the last two sites more efficiently.

Xavier had made his way to the front of the group, and we didn't crowd him since he seemed to be doing better. But now he was in the first group that was headed to the Salem Witch Museum, while Lesley, Mal, Sarielle, and I were headed to the Witch Trails Memorial over on Liberty Street. Fortunately, Rob wound up in the group with Xavier.

"Hey, Lesley, call Rob and ask him to keep an eye on Xay," I instructed.

"Sure thing. Probably a good idea."

"Mal, get Raz and Ange over here. We gotta keep a visual on him. A close one."

"Beat you to it. They're already en route. Raz will check in as soon as they have eyes on him." We watched Xavier walk away. Sarielle didn't like the fact that we were being separated either.

"I'm really starting to hate Taylor and company," she hissed.

"Just starting? Beat you to that long time ago." I laughed.

It was about a half-mile walk to the memorial; we were there in less than ten minutes. Ms. Trap gave us a brief introduction and then allowed us to move freely about the site. Sarielle and Lesley had partnered up and were engrossed in some girly conversation that had nothing to do with the tour. Mal and I strolled through the park, pretending to be interested while waiting to hear from Raza.

As we walked the grounds, I began to feel weird—almost light-headed. Mal noticed.

"What is that? You okay?"

While processing Mal's question, I felt myself searching, then pulling on Malachi.

"Hey, what are you doing?" Malachi staggered as I pulled on his strength.

"Mal, I'm not doing this. I don't know what's happening!" We were being coupled involuntarily. I pushed at the urge to continue pulling on Malachi's strength. I would have a hard time explaining why he was passed out on the ground. I pushed with everything I had while we pretended to be overly interested in the Giles Corey memorial which had a convenient ledge that we could cling on to. Mal sat on one side to regain his bearing. I began to drift.

"Mal, you're going to have to cover for me. Get me to a bathroom or something. We've gotta ride this out. The Hawthorne Hotel is right there. I don't know how

much longer I'll be able to control this body without taking you down with me."

Malachi pushed himself from the ledge and got the attention of Ms. Trap. I couldn't hear the excuse he made because the buzzing had begun as I was pulled farther into Sha'ar. The pain was not far behind. We made it to the family restroom, and Mal locked the door behind us before I completely lost control of my physical body, collapsing to the floor.

"Mal, what's going on?"

"Not really sure. The only one that has the authority to do this is Tabbris. I'm sure he has his reasons. We must be out of time to find that gateway. Concentrate, Kendi. We've got to get this done.

"I've contacted Reuel. He is going to find Tabbris to try to get him to break the connection, but you have to concentrate until I can get you out," Mal pleaded.

"Damn it, Tabbris! Malachi, I can't do this. The pain. Mal...I'm being ripped apart!"

"You can do this, Eklektos. You're designed for this. Concentrate. Where are you?"

As I rose into the realm, I opened my eyes. I was being pulled west from central Salem...toward Proctor Street.

"Proctor Street, Mal...Proctor Street."

"Okay. I see it. I've got you. I'm right here. Don't worry."

As we moved in closer, the pain began to subside, and I could better concentrate. The realm darkened abruptly, and a new sensation began to emerge—a bitter coldness. A strange strength began to rise in my core. I immediately became frightened for my Achim. Did I inadvertently pull strength from him in my moment of fear?

"Malachi?"

He understood my panic.

"I'm fine. That surge didn't come from me."

Whatever caused the surge was pushing me...propelling me forward into the darkness. I was almost to Gallows Hill.

I could see it just in the distance.

"Slow down, Kendi. We can't go there alone. If this is really the gateway, you can get pulled through. Stop!"

I could feel Malachi's mental restraint pulling me, but the unseen force continued pushing me in the direction that was supposed to be off-limits. In my mind, I knew I needed to go back, but my body was drawn to this place. There was anger and a new strength that was goading me on, closer to Gallows

Hill. It was as if I were entranced.

"Concentrate, Kendi. You've got to break the pull. We've got to go back. I can sense danger. Something's coming...something evil. I can feel it! The Legion is going to attack! It's a trap to pull you through the portal. Kendi...Kendi! Snap out of it! We've got to get outta here!"

As Malachi screamed at me, a dark mass emerged from behind Gallows Hill. The menacing figure let out a deafening roar. I should have been terrified, but the roar only made me angrier.

Enraged, I exploded into combat configuration—flaming swords drawn. There was no fear in me. I was set for battle. I readied myself to charge at the massive figure.

"Kendi! Noooo!"

As I charged, a streak of light obscured my path, slamming into me with such force I was sent into a tailspin. While trying to regain my composure, I was caught around the neck and incapacitated. I was driven to the ground in a death-hold.

"Control yourself, Shoer, or I'll do it for you!" Tabbris bellowed.

My instinct was to fight, to engage in battle. But this was Tabbris, my mentor, and, more importantly, an Eklektos and a Throne. I allowed myself to go limp as Tabbris drove me away from Gallows Hill and the imminent destruction that awaited me there.

"Didn't I tell you that the gateway was designed to draw you in? Abbadon was waiting there at the entrance to destroy you, boy. Are you that ready to die, to have this sentence over with? Why am I bothering with training if you won't listen to me?"

"Tabbris...I...I'm sorry. I wasn't prepared—"

Tabbris cut me off. *"Do you think Abbadon is going to wait for you to be prepared? You are fortunate that this was my test and I was prepared to intervene even before your precious Reuel came looking for me. Congratulations...you found the gateway but failed the test.*

"Achim! Get him out of here before I kill him myself!"

I could feel Malachi's tug. I didn't resist but closed my eyes and concentrated on the escape. Opening my eyes, Mal was there with hand extended to pull me up from the floor.

"Are you okay?"

"I'm sorry, Mal. I wasn't ready for that...but...but I should have been." I was disgusted with myself.

"Don't worry about it. Let's get out of here and find the others. Raza needs us to get to Xay," he responded, pulling me up from the floor. Before I could ask what was going on, my phone vibrated. As I looked down, blood began to pour from my nose and soak into my shirt.

"Damn it! What now?" I grabbed the phone from my pocket. "Shoot, it's Sarielle."

"Give me the phone. Get that blood stopped. I'll talk to her."

I grabbed some tissue from the counter and pinched the bridge of my nose, trying to stop both the blood flow and the dizziness that was beginning to set in.

"Elle?" Malachi answered the phone. Pause. "Yeah. Kendi's in the bathroom. What's wrong?" I turned toward Mal. "What did Rob say? Okay. I'm sure he's not far. We'll be there in a second." He hung up.

"Where's Xay? What's going on?"

"Rob just called Elle to let her know that he couldn't find Xay. Raz has eyes on him, but something's wrong. He is in the lower level bathroom in the museum. Raz said he thinks Xay is hallucinating. Apparently whatever Taylor gave him was a little stronger than aspirin."

"I'm gonna kill him! Let's go!"

We ran toward Washington Square.

19

THINGS THAT GO BUMP IN THE NIGHT

It was only a five-minute walk from the Hawthorne to the Salem Witch Museum, but because we were in a dead sprint, we made it there in less than two. We slowed our approach as we neared the front of the museum and Ms. Trap was entering with the group from the memorial park. Sarielle and Lesley were waiting by the door. Rob was still looking for Xavier inside the museum.

Sarielle concealed her panic until Ms. Trap was completely inside the building and out of earshot.

"Kendi! Mal! Xay just called me. He was babbling, not making any sense. Something about his mother being here and wanting him to go with her. He was losing it. What's wrong with him? He didn't tell me where he was. I don't know where he is! He was slurring…like he's drunk or something. Oh, God! I can't tell Ms. Trap. I can't. He'll get into trouble. He can't get into any more trouble. You've got to find him! You've got to!"

"It's going to be fine. We'll find him. Ms. Trap won't find out." Lesley was trying to comfort her.

"Elle calm down. We'll find him," Malachi echoed. "You two stay here with the tour. Kendi and I will find Rob and help look for Xay. I called the twins. They are on the way to pick us all up. We'll make some excuse to leave without Ms. Trap seeing him. Don't worry. It'll be fine. Trust me."

I squeezed her hand and gave her a quick smile as we entered the museum. I didn't dare unlock my jaw to try to speak to her. I was far too angry to disguise my utter disdain for Taylor and his cohorts right now.

We pushed our way past the crowd of people and found the far corner of the building as Raza led us. Rob was there, headed for the dark hallway. "Rob!"

He turned.

"Is Xay down there?" I asked.

"I hope so. It's the only place in the building I haven't been."

We didn't know what we were going to encounter when we found Xay. We needed a lookout. "Mal and I will check. Hang out here and make sure no one goes down there. Sarielle said Xay is pretty messed up from whatever he took. We don't need anyone else to see him. Call me if someone comes looking."

"Will do." Rob turned back toward the crowded room, attempting to blend in and not draw attention to the corner hallway.

The narrow hallway had a stairwell at the end. At the bottom of the stairs was a long corridor that was only illuminated by the light coming from under the bathroom door. This was obviously not a bathroom frequented by the public. We cautiously approached the door and tried the knob. It was locked. Malachi knocked.

"Xay? Are you in there? It's Malachi. Open the door." There was no response.

"Is he still in there?"

"Raz says he is. He's incoherent...semi-conscious."

"What now?"

"Raz and Ange are here. They're around the back of the building waiting in the truck. I'm going to have to break this door. We've got to get him out of the bathroom before someone comes down here."

Malachi grabbed the doorknob and pulled. He handed me the knob with the wood still attached while he reached through the gaping hole and unlocked the deadbolt. I tossed the knob into the trash in the corner and followed Mal into the bathroom.

Xay was sitting on the floor, slumped against the wall in a cold sweat. The mirror on the wall was broken, and Xay was clinging to a large shard of glass. His eyes were fixed on some object that neither of us could see, and he was speaking to the inanimate object in short gibberish like phrases.

"Don't...please don't. No, not again...don't go. You promised...I'll be good...I promise..." He whispered as he sobbed.

"Xay. Hey, man? You all right?" Malachi asked.

Xavier didn't acknowledge him in any way. He continued murmuring his private dialogue. His hand was starting to bleed as he clung to the glass with a death grip. He had several slashes on his left arm.

Malachi slowly walked up to Xay and placed a hand on his shoulder to get his attention. Xavier went berserk.

"Get away...get away from me! Please! Don't touch me! You said you would leave me alone if I went with her!" he screamed. His eyes were stretched wide. He was petrified. Xay cowered into the corner kicking and flailing, brandishing the glass shard as if trying to fend off an attacker.

"Xay, calm down! It's Malachi. See, there's Kendi. We aren't going to hurt you. We're here to help. It's going to be all right!"

Xavier scrambled to his feet and threw his body at Mal in a clumsy attempt to defend himself. He was swinging and shrieking at the top of his lungs. Malachi was calmly trying to talk him down while strategically blocking Xay's attack with the crude weapon.

What in the holy hell was wrong with this kid? Xavier was high as a kite. At the very least, he needed to be away from here to sleep the drugs off. At worst, this could be the beginning of an overdose. My heart hammered in my chest at the thought of possibly losing Xavier this way. We had to act quickly. The irritation I felt for Taylor boiled over. What a mess! Someone was going to hear this racket and come to investigate—Rob or no Rob. And there would be no way to explain this spectacle that wouldn't get us all in trouble.

I stepped in behind Xay and carefully pinched the carotid artery at the side of his neck, momentarily cutting off the blood and oxygen flow to his brain. He blacked out immediately. I caught him and lowered his body to the floor, kicking the glass out of his reach.

"Well, that's one way to fix the problem." Malachi looked critically at me.

"What? Would you rather his psychotic episode get us all caught?" I snapped.

My first thought was to punch him in the face. I figured this choice was the better of the two. I had to admit, I was almost as angry with Xavier as I was with Taylor. If he had listened to Sarielle, he would have been safely at home right now.

After a few seconds, Xay began to come around. He was still incoherent and talking to himself through clenched teeth. He was sweating profusely, his eyes were dilated, and his skin hot to the touch.

"What the hell did Taylor give him?" I asked rhetorically.

"No idea. But we should find out quickly. This kid is a wreck. I know Elle doesn't want him to get into trouble, but we may have to take him to the hospital. Maybe Dr. Julie will help us out. Let's try to cool him down. He's burning up."

I grabbed some paper towels from the dispenser and wet them with cold water. We stuffed them into his shirt and around his neck. I reached for my phone and called Angelo.

"Ange, we're about to bring Xay out. We are going to need some ice. Find as much as you can without raising suspicion. Mal is going to get him in the truck. Tell Raz to be ready. I'll have Sarielle meet us out front." I hung up and then called Rob.

"Rob. We've got Xay. Have Sarielle tell Ms. Trap that Xay got sick to his stomach and that her mom's picking them both up. Angelo will meet her out front in about five minutes." I didn't give him the opportunity to ask any questions. I shoved the phone back into my pocket and got up from the bathroom floor.

"Are you ready to move Xay to the truck? I'll make sure the coast is clear so you can teleport him. That will be the easiest way. He'll never remember it."

"Kendi, I need you to calm down." Malachi was scrutinizing my demeanor. He knew I was keeping a tight lid on the volcano that was my temper.

"I'm fine."

"Kendi."

"Mal, let's get Xay in the truck. We have to get him some help." I went to the corner of the hallway and pushed open the back door. Raza was there waiting. The alley was empty. Malachi scooped Xay up from the bathroom floor. I gave him a nod, and he and Xavier were gone. I felt the displacement of air as the pair passed by, and then they were in the third row of the truck.

"I'll be right back." I turned back up the dark hallway, headed for the stairs.

"Kendi, where are you going?" Mal called.

"I have to let Ms. Trap know we are leaving. I'll blame it on the nosebleed." I could be convincing enough with the fresh bloodstains on my shirt. "And then I'm going to find Taylor and beat the living shit out of him until he tells me what he gave Xay." The lid was coming off.

I ignored Mal's distant protest as I hurried back up the hallway.

Ms. Trap told me to feel better and that she would see Mal and me on Monday. It was easy to see why everyone liked her. She didn't treat us like two-year-olds but like young adults.

I scanned the museum quickly, looking for Taylor, Rick, or Corey, but didn't see them anywhere. Then I remembered that they were in the first group with Xay. They would have headed to memorial park for the last leg of the tour. Perfect. That meant no adult supervision.

I couldn't go out the front door. Lesley and Rob were waiting out front with Sarielle, and I didn't have time for explanations. I headed for the back door and raced up Hawthorne Boulevard toward the park. In my sprint, I connected with Mal.

"Get Sarielle and meet me back at the park," I barked.

"Kendi, don't do anything stupid. Please."

I didn't respond as I didn't want to make promises I had no intention of keeping. I entered the Liberty Street side of the park looking for Taylor and his minions. Luck would have it that they were separated from the group, not in the memorial itself but just outside of it, in the Burying Point Cemetery. Rick and Corey were hanging back just at the edge, while Taylor ventured farther into the cemetery. I stopped and walked around to the other side to get a better angle.

A tall man casually strolled over to Taylor and began having a conversation. They seemed to be discussing the tombstone in front of them. And then very inconspicuously, the man reached into his pocket, pulled something out, and shook it into Taylor's hand as he departed. Unbelievable. This was the same man I had seen with Taylor before his crew jumped me several months back. I would find out who he was, but right now I needed vital information from Taylor.

Taylor lingered in the cemetery as the man left. Rick and Corey rejoined the rest of their group in the memorial park. His back was to me as he continued to fabricate interest in the grave site. I quietly walked up behind him and grabbed him in the same hold that I had just used to take down Xavier. As he dropped, I flipped him over the rock wall that bordered the park, and then jumped over so that we were both out of sight. I straddled him as he came to.

"What...what are you doing, man?" Taylor tried unsuccessfully to push me off him. I dropped my forearm against his throat so that his windpipe would be compressed.

"I'm only going to ask you this once. What in the hell were those pills you gave to Xay?" I hissed.

Taylor chuckled defiantly. I pressed harder against his throat. He began to choke, so I let up, but only just.

"I'm serious, Taylor. I will break your damn neck and not think twice about it."

He began to struggle beneath me but didn't say anything. I could feel the supernatural strength building in my limbs as my rage increased. I used the additional strength to pin Taylor back to the ground.

"What was it? If we have to take him to the hospital, I swear the police will know exactly where the drugs came from. I'm sure they'll be very interested in your exchange here in the cemetery as well."

Taylor's lips were starting to discolor, so I let up off his throat again.

"I dare you. Go ahead and call the police." He coughed. "Try to explain to them how ya boy got X in his system, or better yet, how a stash of it got into his locker at school— him with a record and me squeaky clean. Call the police and let me know how that works out for him." He grinned evilly.

"You piece of trash!" I let go of his throat and punched him in the face. The one punch didn't nearly satisfy my lust for his blood, so I punched him again. My strength was building in unison with my rage. He tried to defend himself, but his attempt was futile. I punched again, and the blood spewed from his mouth into my face. I punched again. It felt good. The rage was being satiated.

A force knocked me from the top of the struggling, bloody teen. I turned to attack thinking it was Corey, Rick, or both.

But it was Raza who had launched himself at me. I was in kill mode. The warrior instinct wanted me to finish the job.

"Kendi! Control yourself. This kid is just a mortal, not the enemy. Stop!" Malachi was trying to talk me off the ledge.

In my pause, Raz got a tighter grip on me, and Angelo came to assist.

"Taylor, get out of here, now!" Raza roared as Ange helped hold me to the ground. Taylor scrambled to his feet and pulled himself back over the wall.

I was seething, but the rage was beginning to subside.

"Let me go, guys. I'm fine." They didn't loosen their grip but looked at the truck to get confirmation. Mal nodded, and they let me go.

"We need to call poison control. Those idiots gave Xavier Ecstasy. Stay here. I don't want Sarielle to freak out until we know what they say."

While Angelo made the call, I paced slowly, taking in slow deep breaths, trying to calm myself.

"Better?" Malachi asked.

"Slightly. I wanted to rip his head off his body. Literally. Tabbris wasn't joking about this warrior mode. It takes everything in me to turn it off. I could have killed him."

"But you didn't."

"This time."

"Poison control said it will take a minimum of five to six hours from the time of digestion for the effects of the drug to wear off. She said we needed to watch him closely and keep him cool. She recommended a cold shower or a tub full of cold water as long as we don't leave him alone in it. If he has trouble breathing or has a seizure, we need to get him to an ER," Angelo informed us as we walked back to the truck.

I slid in next to Sarielle on the second row.

"Taylor gave Xay Ecstasy. The good news is that it seemed to be only a small dose. He can probably just sleep it off," I informed Sarielle.

"Ecstasy? Oh, my God. Is he going to be okay?" She turned, trying to examine her brother.

"He'll be fine. We'll help you watch him just to make sure. Your mom is on second shift this week, right?"

"Yeah. She won't be home until early morning," Sarielle responded.

"Okay. Ange, head to Tapleyville." I smiled at Sarielle to reassure her. "Raz, call Rob and see if he and Lesley will come and help for a couple of hours as well."

"You've got that ice on Xay? It's a bad sign if he gets too hot, he could start to seize. We have no idea what the dose was on those pills." I mentally projected to Malachi so Sarielle wouldn't hear.

"Yeah. It's melting fast, though."

"We'll get him into a tub of cold water as soon as we get him home. We'll send the guys for more ice."

"Sounds like a plan."

We spent the next couple of hours taking turns watching Xavier in an ice bath, making sure that his head stayed above the water in his groggy state. He finally cooled off and seemed to be getting better, so Mal and I dried him off and got him into bed and left Sarielle and Lesley upstairs to watch him. We joined Rob, Angelo, and Raza in the living room.

We watched television and took turns sitting with Xay to relieve Sarielle. Around ten, he finally woke up enough to talk. Sarielle came downstairs and said Xavier was asking for Malachi and me. We headed up to his room.

Mal tapped on the door.

"Yeah...come in," Xay responded. I followed Malachi into the room.

"Hey, man. Feeling better?" Mal asked.

"I wish I could detach my head, it hurts so bad, but better. Thanks to you and Kendi." He looked back and forth between the two of us. "Thank you. I mean it. You could have just ratted me out to Ms. Trap and walked away. I owe you both big time."

"What you owe us is an explanation," I snapped. "What the hell are you doing taking pills from an unmarked bottle? And from Taylor nonetheless! You know damn well he's dealing, and don't tell me you didn't!"

"Kendi." Malachi interrupted.

"No, Mal. He's right. It was stupid, but I swear to you I didn't know I was taking X. I would never. Elle knows I would never mess with anything like that. You've got to believe me."

"Xay, you know that those guys are bad news. Why do you keep messing with them?" I asked point-blank.

"I can't tell you that. I can't. I'm sorry." He turned away from us.

"Then what in the hell are we doing up here? Mal, let's go!"

"Wait a minute," Malachi instructed. "Xay, why did you want to see us? What did you want to talk about?"

"I wanted to talk about what happened today...in the museum, I mean. I need to talk to somebody. I feel like I'm going crazy, but I don't want to worry Elle."

Malachi caught me by the arm and pulled me back from the doorway. "What is it? We're listening."

"I'm not sure where to start. Ever since that day at the reservoir, I have been having weird dreams. They're so real. I've never had the kind of dreams that I could wake up and recall every detail, until here recently. Sometimes the dreams are so real that I can't tell whether I am asleep or awake."

"What do you mean?" Mal asked.

"Kendi, do you remember I told you that I felt like someone pushed me from the pump house that day?" I nodded.

"Well, a few days after that day, I started having the same dream over and over. This...this...demon, I guess...I don't know what else to call it...is after me. I'm back at the reservoir, on top of the pump house watching you all swim, and I feel something coming up behind me. I turn, and this huge, black, lurking creature is coming for me. It's dark, and I can't really make out what it looks like, but I can always see its eyes—red and glowing."

"*Is this possible, Mal?*" I didn't dare look at him because I didn't want to tip Xay off.

"*I don't know...*"

"This thing picks me up and throws me into the reservoir and then stands there watching and laughing while I drown," Xavier continued. "I tried to pass it off as some post-traumatic symptom of drowning, until today."

"What happened today?" I tried hard to keep the tremble out of my voice. Mal noticed.

"I felt like I was losing it. I figured then that Taylor was getting his kicks by slipping me something, so I went into the bathroom to try and make myself throw up. I thought it would help. It didn't, and the X really kicked in. The bathroom got dark suddenly. And then the demon was there—the same one from my dreams. I think I broke the mirror to try to defend myself. I don't remember.

"But I do remember that the thing wanted me to hurt myself. It wanted me to try to kill myself. I told it that I wouldn't leave Elle. The demon got angry and kept sending snakes after me. I tried to use the glass to kill the snakes, but it wasn't working." Xavier's voice was shaking almost as much as his body as he recalled his ordeal.

One of the Dominion must be assigned to torment him. Abbadon is trying to get him to take himself out.

I nodded ever so slightly so that only my brother would notice.

"I remember cowering in the corner of the bathroom and then hearing a voice that I thought I recognized. My mom was there—my birth mom, Eileen. She was pleading with me to follow her to the top of the building. She said I could go with her and stay this time. I asked if Elle could come, and then she got angry. She started to leave. That's when you got there, and then Eileen was gone, and the demon was back.

"Am I going crazy? Should I tell Elle or Mom? I think I'm losing it."

Malachi stepped closer to the bed and put a hand on Xavier's shoulder. "I wouldn't worry your sister or your mom just yet. Ecstasy is a powerful hallucinogen. Nothing you experienced today was real. You'll be fine." He was trying hard to reassure Xay.

"What about the dreams?"

I jumped in. "You said it yourself, man. You almost drowned. Your sister collapsed right after. You honestly didn't have a space of time to deal with it. You were too worried about Sarielle. The mind has a crazy way of making us deal with stuff. Just talking about it today will probably help. I told you, Xay, I'm here, and contrary to what you believe, not just for your sister. You can talk to me."

"We both are," Malachi concurred.

"Thanks, guys. I mean that. Really." He put out his fist, and we sealed the conversation.

"Elle and your mom are taking you over to see Dr. Julie tomorrow," I informed Xay. "You shouldn't still be having these crazy headaches. You need to get checked."

"Okay." I think he felt just bad enough not to put up a fight.

"I'll grab you some Tylenol from the bathroom. Hopefully, it will help. You probably need to eat something too before you crash for the night. We'll go and grab something for you and Elle before we head home. Pizza?" We headed for the door.

"I'll eat anything right about now. I appreciate it, guys."

"Get some rest. We'll be back soon." I pulled the door closed. We stopped in the hallway.

"We need to meet with Tabbris. There has got to be a way to find out who is tormenting this kid before he jumps off a bridge or something. The Dominion is going all out on this one, huh? Is taking one Guardian down that important?"

"Apparently. We're going to have to engage Uriel now. Xavier is going to have to be covered twenty-four-seven until we figure this out. I know you're not fond of his team, but we have to use every available resource."

"Agreed. Let Reuel know we need to meet so that he can contact Uriel. Tabbris might still be pissed with me from this morning, but we need him as well."

"On it."

We headed downstairs to be normal teenage friends for a few more minutes before becoming immersed once again in the reality that I wished I could turn off. Permanently.

20
FEEL THE BURN

We said our good-byes to Sarielle and Xavier about an hour or so after dinner andpromised to drop by tomorrow to check on them. We were dropping Lesley at home, but Rob was going to stay awhile longer in case Sarielle needed any help.

After our conversation with Xavier, we wouldn't dare leave them uncovered while we met with Reuel and the others. Malachi coordinated with Liwet and Nisroc. They had the first watch. We passed them on the way out, casually nodding. I wouldn't pretend that I wanted to have anything to do with them other than the duties for which they were assigned.

Things in Danvers had certainly taken a turn for the worse. It was smart of Reuel to send Renay south to visit with her sister for a while. We would have to use the house as our central meeting spot. The extra company would be incredibly hard to explain.

When we arrived home, Reuel, Tabbris, and Uriel were waiting inside. Uriel's team was heavily guarding the outside. Tabbris wanted to be certain that this meeting would be secure. Angelo and Raza joined the troops outside.

We greeted one another cordially as everyone got settled so that we could rehash today's events.

I wanted to start with where my day took a nosedive. "Tabbris, why the random lesson this morning?"

"There was nothing random about it, Shoer. Did you and your Achim not suspect the gateway was at Gallows Hill?" he asked with a raised eyebrow, mocking me.

"You were spying on us?"

"Spying? It is my obligation as your mentor to keep an eye on you. It's also my job to push you harder and faster than you are willing to push yourself.

When did you plan to check out your theory? Tomorrow? Next week? Next month? The longer you wait, the more time the Dominion has to execute their plan to destroy you. We need to be ready to strike swiftly and with precision. We will not get a second chance. Understood?"

I knew Tabbris was right, but that didn't stop me from being ticked off. "I understand," I responded flatly.

"Abbadon didn't expect you to locate the gate so quickly. His conceit is what led him to relocate the portal only a few miles away from its original location. The Guardian is fully aware that all the gateways are located on sites where there has been some human tragedy. There are so many of those locations in this area that Abbadon took his chances. The locals have speculated for quite some time about the actual location of Gallows Hill. Abbadon thought he had sufficiently destroyed all evidence of its location in the fire of 1914. The Legion tried to burn Salem to the ground as a cover-up. They didn't count on stories being passed on from generation to generation. So now, he's not leaving anything to chance. Abbadon guarding that area himself confirms the gateway's there."

"So now what?" I wanted to know. "We know where the gateway is, so do we prepare to attack?"

"Not so fast. Locating the portal and entering it with an army of Guardian are two different things. We will need to devise a plan to draw the gatekeeper away. The only thing that will be tempting enough to Abbadon is the Shoer himself. If he feels like he has a good shot to take you down, he will take it." I could see Tabbris's wheels turning as he thought this through.

"Wait a minute. You want to use Kendi as bait!" Malachi was on his feet.

"Did you think your brother would be able to bring down Abbadon by hiding from him? The only way to close the gate in Charon is for the Shoer to defeat the gatekeeper. You know that, Malachi. What do you think we have been preparing him for?"

Malachi said nothing, but I could read everything he was thinking.

"Tabbris, you've spent quite a bit of time with Kendi over the last few weeks. Do you think he is ready to stand against Abbadon?" Reuel voiced what Mal wouldn't say.

"If the battle were today, no. That temper of his would certainly be his downfall. Kendi still needs to learn to control his rage so that it gives him an advantage in battle. Currently, it's still his greatest weakness."

"That's for certain," Uriel added.

There were no words to adequately describe the utter contempt that I felt for Uriel, but like him or not, we needed his team. I bit my tongue and said nothing.

"I have no doubt that our Shoer will be ready when the time comes. I have had a glimpse of what he is capable of. He'll be ready," Tabbris continued.

"Eklektos—" Malachi began, but I cut him off.

"It will be fine, Mal...really."

Mal said nothing further but looked at me trying to discern what I was thinking. I changed the subject.

"We had a conversation a couple of hours ago with Xavier Breland. It seems that one of the Dominion has found a way to draw him into our realm. He's being tormented. Can we find out who it is? And is there a way to stop it?"

"We don't have to look very far. It's Azrael. Abbadon has had his second-in-command on that kid for a while now. The only way to shut that door now is to take down Azrael." Uriel was beaming at the thought.

"Are you that anxious for bloodshed, Uriel?" Reuel seemed as irritated with his giddiness as I was with his presence.

"Is not that why you called me and the cavalry in, Reuel? If your, um, *team* can't handle the Dominion, then we will. Don't worry. Azrael will be far too occupied with my sword at his throat to be tormenting anyone from here on out. Yah wants this mess cleaned up. It's my job to deliver." Uriel shot a grin at Reuel.

"Is he always such an arrogant ass?"

"Yes, but he has a reason to be. He's the best there is at what he does, Kendi. That's why Yah sent him."

"I guess liking him is not a prerequisite to working with him. Jerk."

Malachi chuckled quietly. Tabbris shot us a look. My phone rang. It was Sarielle. What now? I walked into the kitchen to take the call. Mal followed.

"Sarielle? Everything okay?" I answered.

"No, Kendi. Taylor's here. I tried to stop him at the door, but he pushed right past me. Xay heard us arguing and told me to let him stay. After what he pulled today, I don't want him anywhere near Xay or me. I hate him! Why would Xay even speak with that idiot after what he did? I'm sorry. I know my brother is not your problem, but I didn't know who else to call. I'm sorry. I'm..." She was sobbing.

"Shhhh. Sarielle. It's okay. Calm down. Mal and I were still up anyway. Is

Rob gone?"

"Yeah. Taylor showed up about five minutes after he left. He was probably sitting outside waiting."

"Probably. Did Taylor say what he wanted? It's kinda late for a house call."

"Taylor doesn't talk to me. He knows I can't stand him. They went outside to sit on the porch."

"It'll be fine. Just keep an eye on them. We can't trust Taylor. He's proven that over and over."

"Tell me about it." Her voice trembled slightly. I could hear the extra movement and footsteps as she headed for the front of the house.

"What is he doing? Hell no! Xay!" Sarielle was screaming.

"What! What's going on? What is it?" I tried to get her attention.

"Elle, stop it. Go back in the house. Stop. Now." I could hear Xavier pleading through the connection.

"Sarielle? What's happening?" I asked again.

All I could hear was the commotion in the background—Sarielle and Xay yelling with an occasional interruption from Taylor.

"What's going on over there?" Mal inquired, moving closer to the phone.

Though she hadn't responded, I could make out the gist of the argument. Xavier was leaving with Taylor, and Sarielle was trying to stop him. Jackass!

"Taylor is taking Xay somewhere. Sarielle can't stop them by herself. Give Liwet a heads-up. We need eyes in the sky to find out where they are headed."

"On it." Malachi walked away to coordinate with the extensions.

I could hear an additional scuffle from the other side of the phone. The voices got quieter, but I could clearly hear other sounds now. Footsteps. The phone jostling more quickly. She was running, keys jingling, a door slamming.

What was she doing? "Sarielle...Sarielle...Sarielle!"

"He's leaving, Kendi. He's leaving with Taylor. He won't listen to me. I'm going after him. I have to bring him back. I can't just let him go!"

"Sarielle, wait a minute. I need you to stop for a minute and calm down. You don't need to be running around Danvers in a panic after your brother."

"I heard Taylor say something about the farm. I think I know where they are headed." She was not listening to my attempts to reason with her.

"The farm...Sarielle, what's that? You're not making any sense. Talk to me."

"I'll call you back."

"Wait!"

She was gone. "Damn it!" I hissed.

"What's happened?" Malachi asked.

"Sarielle went after Xay. That freakin' kid must have some kind of death wish. What's wrong with him? And now he's putting his sister in danger too. We gotta go after them. Running all over town in the dead of night with Azrael on the loose!"

"Liwet and Nisroc are following them. I need to get eyes on Elle too. I'll send Raz and Ange."

"Good idea. We've got to find out where they are going, now. More importantly, we need to find all of them before Azrael does."

"Agreed."

We headed back into the living room to inform the others, but Forcus entered the room at the same moment. He acknowledged Tabbris with a nod of his head.

"Your Grace. Azrael is on the move and has a contingent with him. We are tracking at least six."

"Where are they headed?" Tabbris replied.

"North toward Locust Street, but that's not all." He glanced at me. "His assignment just arrived at Connor Farm. Not far from the direction in which Azrael is headed."

"Damn it, Xavier!" I spat through my teeth.

"Some sort of trap?" Reuel directed at Tabbris.

"More than likely. Our Shoer will stay here. Uriel and a delegation of his choosing will handle it," Tabbris confirmed.

"Tabbris! He's my assignment! I am obligated to protect him!" My mind flooded with thoughts of all the catastrophes the Dominion could cause with three unsuspecting mortals. Not to mention someone as fragile as Sarielle.

"And we are obligated to protect you. Sit down," Tabbris demanded.

Defiance overtook my need for reason. It would not let me comply with Tabbris's command.

I didn't move.

"I said have a seat!" Tabbris moved closer.

"Trap or not, he's my responsibility, and I will not abandon him." We were standing toe to toe.

"Uriel, you've been given your charge. Take your leave." Tabbris didn't want an audience to my rebellion.

Uriel rose immediately. "Your Grace." He nodded as he left the house with

Forcus on his heels.

The door closed behind them, and Tabbris turned back to me. "Give us this room," Tabbris directed at Reuel and Malachi.

"Eklektos, Kendi was just..." Reuel began.

"The room. Now!"

Reuel grabbed Malachi's arm—he was stationary at my side—and led him from the living room.

Tabbris waited until they were completely out of sight before he began.

"Kendi, do you know why Yah agreed to my being your mentor?" He didn't wait for an answer. "It's because I can manage the big picture. Losing for me is not an option. Unlike Malachi, I am not obligated to you. And unlike Reuel, I'm not afraid to throw you over the edge only pulling you back if necessary. But most of all, you little urchin, I'm here to teach you some respect for this office in which you stand." Tabbris was speaking through his teeth, only an inch from my face.

"Yah has a certain partiality for Govad and myself. You see, we are the only two Shoers who have emerged victorious from Sha'ar thus far. And as such, we are granted special...abilities." Tabbris was circling behind me. I could feel the warmth of his breath on my neck as he spoke low and menacing.

Suddenly, Tabbris clamped down on the sides of my neck. The pressure paralyzed me. "Y–y–our Grace." I struggled to get the words out. "I c–can't breathe," I gasped.

"A little respect just might save your life, Shoer." Tabbris slid around to face me, but somehow, I still couldn't move. I was in a death-hold. Impossible.

Every warrior was trained in this battle maneuver. The death-hold could only be executed from a frontal approach. How did Tabbris accomplish this from behind me?

"You know, before I destroyed Djinn, I used this same death-hold to incapacitate him. But the hold had to be executed from the front so that the final blow would be effective. Finishing the job was...complicated. The maneuver was nearly impossible without the assistance of another warrior. But now..." Tabbris placed his hand about an inch from the center of my chest and slowly began to back away.

The room spun as my breath stopped momentarily. My chest heaved involuntarily while the breath was drawn from me. Then the pain came. It radiated from my core out to the tips of every limb. An internal explosion dropped me to my knees as I was depleted of my very being. All the while,

Tabbris's eyes were fixed, concentrated on my face—watching and waiting.

Death was coming. I was certain of it. My body convulsed helplessly, as I tried in vain to pull away from Tabbris's impalpable hold. I felt the essence leaving my body, and the terrifying emptiness being left in its stead, as Tabbris continued drawing the strength from my chest. The room darkened, I shrieked in pain, afraid for my life.

"Eklektos!" Reuel screamed.

Tabbris's resolve was unbroken. He was fixated on the task at hand. My hope was that he was concentrating on not accidentally killing me while teaching this lesson in obedience.

"Eklektos, please...please, stop!" It was Malachi's pleas this time. He was gasping as he attempted to control his connection to me as Tabbris took me down.

Tabbris looked up at Malachi, and the attack ceased. I collapsed to the floor, wallowing in pain. My muscles spasmed uncontrollably while the vacated part of my person rushed back into my body. Both Reuel and Malachi hurried to my side.

"Shoer, you will remain here with your Achim while Uriel handles the present situation. Understood?"

"Yes, Eklektos," I gasped. Tabbris nodded, smiling at my forced compliance.

Reuel stood to face Tabbris. "A word, Your Grace?"

"Your word must wait until I return. I have been summoned to Merkabah. See to your Shoer there." Tabbris turned and was gone.

Malachi lifted me from the floor and carried me to the couch. The room was silent for several minutes. Once my muscles stopped twitching, I slowly sat up.

"Well, that was fun," I said sarcastically.

"Tabbris had no right to do that to you, Kendi. He was out of line misusing his gifts in such a manner." Reuel was still angry.

"Agreed. It was a dick move, but it certainly got my attention. Lesson learned: don't challenge Tabbris's authority. He gets pissed."

Malachi was still silent. "Mal? You okay?"

"Not really." His voice was shaky.

"What's the matter? I'm all right, promise. It'll take more than a ticked-off Shoer to take me down permanently." I chuckled.

Malachi's countenance didn't change. "C'mon, Mal. I'm fine. Lighten up!"

Malachi shook his head. "Lighten up? That lesson wasn't just for you, brother. Tabbris wanted to make sure that I committed something to memory as well. I now know how it will feel if I fail in my mandate to protect you...if I let you die. And it's not funny." He looked me straight in the eye.

I didn't consider how deeply Tabbris' stunt would also affect my Achim. If I were to be destroyed, Malachi could certainly survive, but the deficit it would leave in his life would be devastating. I got up and went across the room to stand in front of him. I placed a hand on his shoulder. He was trembling as he had the day he revealed that he was my Achim.

"I'm so sorry, Mal. I wasn't thinking. I am fine, brother. Promise. We're okay. Nothing is going to happen to either of us. Got it?"

He smiled up at me. "Yeah. I got it. Are you sure you're recovered? Tabbris really flattened you." Malachi carefully inspected me. "Do me a favor? Try not to infuriate the most powerful beings in the universe please."

"I know, right. Hardhead, but the behind is definitely getting softer." We laughed together.

"No!" Reuel roared from the other side of the room.

We went to join him. "What is it?"

"We have a problem. The Legion set an ambush at Connor Farm for Kendi. Azrael has a contingent of about twenty. Uriel only took ten with him. Even with Raza and Angelo engaging, they are outnumbered."

"Wait a minute! The twins can't get into that fray. They are not ready for that kind of hand-to-hand combat!" Malachi warned.

"We can't let this happen, Reuel!" I concurred.

"There is no other choice, the twins have to engage. Uriel took all that was available, and unfortunately, the Legion has created a bigger problem. In the attempt to disguise the battle as a storm, a lightning strike has started a fire in the cornfield." Reuel looked at me. "Xavier, Taylor, and Elle are all in there."

The dream from a few nights prior came rushing back—the cornfield, the fire, and Xay being trapped, near death. Apparently, this was not just a dream after all. Yah must have been trying to warn me.

Malachi cringed suddenly. I connected with him, so I could see what was happening at the cornfield as well. It was mayhem. The darkened sky was filled with the Dominion and Uriel's team engaged in full-on battle.

While Uriel's team was very skilled, they were significantly outnumbered. The twins had joined the fight, strategically choosing to assist only in the battles where one of the Guardian was in trouble. They were young but very smart. Hand-to-hand combat with the older, stronger, and more skilled Dominion would not be wise.

Raz was also keeping an eye on Taylor and our friends, who were trying to find their way out of the cornfield. From above, I could see the intricacy of the patterns cut into the field. The Connor Farm Corn Maze was infamous for the inability of finding a way out. The maze was still intact from the Halloween celebration. Xay and Taylor were the farthest into the maze with Sarielle struggling to catch up. None of them realized a fire was raging at the edge of the cornfield and was quickly working its way in toward them.

"Reuel, we have got to get out there. None of them stand a chance. The Guardian is heavily outnumbered. It'll be a massacre, and the mortals will never make it out alive. By the time they figure out the danger they're in, it'll be too late! You've got to let me go. I know you want to protect me, but everything will be lost tonight if we don't get out there. If we go, at least we'll have a shot at turning this around. Please!"

I could feel the burn of the warrior fighting to break through the exterior façade of my human body. Once I was in my natural configuration, it would be next to impossible for Reuel to stop me, and he knew it. Reuel stepped forward, ready to subdue me.

I took a step back. Malachi was there blocking my escape. They had no intention of letting me go.

"Reuel! I've already seen this. I know I can get them out. The Guardian needs your help. Both you and Mal are skilled fighters. We can turn this thing around. I'll stay out of the battle. I promise. Just let me get Xavier and Sarielle out of there, please!"

Reuel was torn. I could see the deliberation in his eyes. He was my guardian and the only one who could agree to let me go. Like Tabbris, Yah had given Reuel both the authority and the power to subdue me. There would be nothing I could do without him agreeing to my request.

He exchanged a look with Malachi, who then took a step back.

"Kendi, you get the mortals out of there and leave. I will send the twins to cover you and Malachi, and I will help Uriel and his team. Understand?"

"Understood." I nodded in agreement as we burst into our natural configurations and took to the skies.

We were at the cornfield in what seemed like seconds. Seeing the chaos through my own eyes was completely different from the visual that Raza had given. The outer edge of the field was now an inferno. The fire had spread quickly, sending plumes of heavy black smoke into the air. Azrael had strategically covered up the battle under the guise of thunder and lightning. Every blow, every flaming sword, and every war cry would go unnoticed by any human scrutiny. Uriel was successfully holding off two of the Dominion, while Angelo was assisting Zuriel, who was not faring quite as well being outnumbered. I swiftly scanned the sky for my other gung-ho brother and found Raz paired with Nisroc. This made me feel better as Nisroc was a very learned warrior and would be able to protect Raz if he became overzealous.

I deliberately diverted my attention away from the battle as Reuel and Malachi raced in to engage the Dominion. I had to find Xavier and Sarielle, and the Dominion would surely send someone after me once they realized I was here. I had to hurry.

I first spotted Taylor at the far edge of the maze. He had successfully outrun the fire and had broken through the edge of the field back onto the Valley Road side where the cars were parked. He was choking and stumbling but seemed to be all right. Taylor turned back toward the fire briefly and then continued toward his car. Damn coward! He was leaving Xay, and now Sarielle too, behind to die.

I could barely see into the maze because of the smoke, but after a few frantic moments, I located Sarielle's small frame in the darkness. She had stopped running as the smoke had become too much. She was clinging onto the cornstalk closest to her, trying to keep herself upright as she gasped for air. I put myself down a few feet behind her.

"Sarielle!" I called to her.

"Kendi? Oh God! Kendi! You gotta get Xay. Xay..." Her voice trailed off into a choking cough as she reached for me.

"It's okay. I've got you." I caught her as she stumbled forward, collapsing into me.

"Xay...Xay!" she tried to call in between her choked coughs, frantically trying to see through the smoke. Her eyes were wild and unfocused, but she was determined. Sarielle would die trying to make sure Xavier was safe.

She was on the verge of losing consciousness from the lack of oxygen. I had to get her out of the maze before resuming my search for Xavier.

"Don't worry, sweetheart. I'll find Xay. I promise," I soothed her as I scooped her up into my arms. "You'll both be fine. Don't worry." I kissed her forehead as I pulled her in closer to my chest, protecting her from the smoke.

"Guys! I need some help! What's the quickest path out of this maze? I can't see

from the ground!"

"On my way, Kendi...on my way! I'll talk you out from the air," Angelo responded.

After several twists and turns and inhaling a lot of smoke, I broke through the edge of the cornfield with Sarielle in my arms. Her car was now the only one left in the parking lot. Taylor, being the stinking coward he was, had fled the scene. I crossed the road to the parking lot away from the fire before laying Sarielle on the ground next to her car. Her eyes were closed, and the color drained from her face.

"Sarielle. Can you hear me? Sarielle?" I tried to rouse her. She was breathing in short quick gasps.

"Sarielle...honey?" I brushed the wet hair away from her sweat-soaked face.

She moaned and began to cough, struggling to wake up. "Kendi," she whispered, choking back a sob. "Xay..."

"Shhhh. It's okay. You're safe. I won't let anything hurt you. I'll find Xay. I promise. It'll be fine," I soothed, holding her against my chest. "Just relax. Breathe. It's going to be all right.

"Raz! Where are you? I need you here now. I've got to get back into the maze to get Xay out!"

"Coming up behind you, brother. Right here." I turned to see Raz approaching.

"Raz, I need you to stay with Sarielle. We need to get her medical attention, and this fire has to be reported." I switched places on the ground with Raz. Opening the door of her Honda, I pulled her cell phone from the front seat and handed it to Raz.

"Call this in. I'm going to find Xavier."

"Be careful, Kendi," Raza warned. "They know you're here," he added inconspicuously, looking down at Sarielle. She was out of it and didn't notice.

"Ange, do you see him anywhere?"

"Not yet. Looking. The smoke is getting really thick up here."

"Okay. We'll have to search together. I can't wait here on the ground. Xay is running out of time. He won't survive in there much longer."

"Kendi! NO!" Malachi roared at me. *"Azrael is up here waiting for you. Angelo will find Xay and guide you from the ground. We can better conceal you if you stay grounded."*

"Mal, we're out of time. If I don't get Xavier out now, he's dead. It won't matter

then whether Azrael gets me or not. I'm going." And I was in the air.

My presence was immediately detected by the Dominion. One of Azrael's guards, Malak, was on me in a second.

"Ange! Kendi's got incoming. Get his flank. Now! I'll get there as soon as I can," Malachi ordered.

"I've got him, Mal, don't worry."

I turned to see Malak approaching from the west. The battle instinct kicked in immediately as I burst into warrior configuration, flaming sword in hand to defend my position. Just as in the training field in Empyrean, I felt an instant surge of power that radiated from my core. The added strength pulsated through every limb, causing me to feel invincible as I clashed with Malak.

The first blow with my sword was executed with such precision that Malak was thrust into a tailspin. I could have easily made my escape, but I wanted more. I wanted Malak destroyed. In my rage, I streaked across the sky, catching him by the throat in a death-hold. There was nothing he could do. I didn't hesitate, didn't think twice about delivering the final blow. I lifted my hand and struck the precise spot in the center of Malak's chest that would end his existence. His last cry was deafening as his eyes stared incredulously at the new Shoer who had ended his life in a mere two blows. I dropped his empty shell to the Earth. One of the guards of Sheol would be along to collect him soon enough.

The atmosphere reacted to the sudden loss of the immortal being. The heavens groaned with boisterous thunder, and the lightning was blinding.

"Kendi."

I wheeled around ready to attack again.

"Kendi, it's me!" Angelo said, throwing up his arms. I halted my advance.

In that same moment, Malachi came into my peripheral view. He watched, eyes wide, as Malak plummeted from the heavens, and then he turned to me.

"Eklektos. We should regroup for battle. Joining the others and me will best support you. Not here on the outskirts alone."

I was still too charged to speak.

"Xavier?" I thought.

"Angelo will find him." I simply nodded. Angelo promptly descended toward the burning field.

"Let's go," Malachi instructed.

"We are regrouping at the north end of the field. The Dominion halted their attack at the loss of Malak. They backed off but have not retreated. Azrael is not done. He is determined to take you down tonight. He wants to end this before you get anywhere near that gate."

The others were waiting as Mal said they would be. Uriel and his contingent of ten warriors including Forcus, Liwet, Gavreel, Nisroc, Isda, Zuriel, Urim, Muriel, Hael, and Sandalphon were there along with Reuel when we arrived.

"Shoer, I hope your sword is as ready as your temper," Uriel hissed at me. "Because now we stand and fight. Tabbris is sending Shopar and Naqam to help us. I hope they arrive before this is all over."

I said nothing but looked across the skies and could see the Dominion beginning their second approach. I briefly closed my eyes and concentrated on reining in the uncontrolled rage that would cause me to do something stupid. I took a deep breath and opened my eyes, turning toward Uriel.

"What are we facing? Are there fallen Thrones in this grouping?"

"Other than Azrael?" Liwet answered sarcastically.

"Sorath is here. See there in the middle on Azrael's left flank," Reuel informed. Just great. Though I'd had no previous interactions with Sorath, his ruthless reputation preceded him.

The anger that propelled me wanted to rip the Legion apart—one Dominion at a time. However, the discipline Tabbris had enforced during our practice sessions began to take over, and wisdom prevailed.

"Uriel, you are the most skilled warrior among us. Direct this congregation into battle, if you will, sir."

Uriel's eyes lit with surprise as I stood down. He said nothing but nodded in compliance. "The safest place for our Shoer is in the rear of the formation. We will formulate a wall of defense. Nisroc, Isda, Sandalphon, Forcus, and Gavreel, you will take the front line with me. Liwet, Muriel, Zuriel, Urim, and Hael take the middle. Malachi and Reuel, you will be the last line of defense for Kendi.

"Shoer, once the battle ensues, go find your assignment. We will keep the Legion busy. Malachi and Reuel will ensure that no one gets through."

The formation came together in an instant. Weapons were readied as the storm raged on. "Guardian, stand strong today and our Shoer doesn't fall!" Uriel roared as he lifted his sword and led the charge as we met the Legion in the air.

21
CLASH OF THE TITANS

Everything in me rebelled against leaving my comrades in battle; I was their leader. But if I didn't get on the ground and find Xavier, everything accomplished in the battle tonight would be for nothing. It was difficult blocking out the sounds of the fierce raging battle, but time was of the essence.

"Angelo! Do you have eyes on Xavier?"

"Not yet. I'm still looking. Wait, wait, there he is! I see him."

"Where are you?"

"East side of the field."

"Stay there. I'm coming to you. Don't let him out of your sight," I instructed.

"That won't be a problem. He's down, Kendi...and not moving."

I pushed myself to an unimaginable velocity to reach Angelo. Just as I did, the heavens echoed again with the sound of a fallen immortal. The thunder cracked in an unnatural way.

"Malachi! What happened?" There was no response. *"Mal, come on, please...talk to me. Mal!"*

It took only a few seconds of silence for the terror to set in.

"I'm here, Kendi. I'm all right, so is Reuel. Azrael just took down Zuriel."

"Zuriel?"

"No!" Angelo bowed his head in reverence to our fallen comrade.

It was irrational to think something had happened to Malachi. I would know physically if something happened to my Achim.

"Kendi, get Xavier. He doesn't have much time left. Get him and Sarielle out of here so that we can end this. Azrael won't stop until he's sure he can no longer get to you or your assignment."

"You're right, Mal. Angelo, I'll need you to lead me out."

"I've got you covered, Kendi. Go!"

I reached Xavier only seconds later. "Xay! Hey, Xavier!" I called to him as I made my approach. He didn't move.

I grabbed his shoulder and turned him over, and I relived my nightmare. Xay was breathing, but only just. He was in bad shape. I picked him up and tossed him over my shoulder.

"Ange, get us out of here." I continued to communicate silently so as not to draw the attention of the Dominion.

"Kendi, it's a long way out. I don't think Xavier will make it through all the smoke."

I deliberated briefly, but I knew what I had to do.

"Kendi, don't!" Reuel warned.

Neither teleporting nor taking to the skies with Xavier would go undetected by the Legion. The second I acted on this decision, my exact location would be revealed.

"Reuel, I don't have a choice. I've got to get Xavier out now. Tell the cavalry to get ready. I'm going to teleport him out, and then draw the Dominion away from him and Sarielle. I'll have no alternative then but to join you in combat.

"Reuel, I need your permission to do this. I can't teleport without your approval. Help me save him. Please."

"You have my permission to save him, son. Do what you have to do," Reuel complied.

"Ange, you stay with Raz to guard Sarielle and Xay," I directed.

"Kendi," Raza chimed in. *"Elle is waking up. She'll see you."*

"I'll have to fix that later, Raz. If I delay any longer, this kid is dead. This isn't about me anymore."

"Ready when you are, Eklektos." I could hear the pride in Angelo's response.

"Now!"

Instantly, Xay and I were on the other side of the road next to the little red Honda. Angelo joined me in the same instant. He assisted me in lowering Xavier to the ground.

His breathing was so shallow; I was afraid that it would stop at any moment. I had to get the smoke cleared from his lungs.

"Kendi? Where did you come from? What's going on?" Sarielle whispered. She was staring at us, trying to sit up.

"Kendi, your eyes," Raza warned.

I closed my eyes to cool the burn. In the dark night, and in this state, my eyes were probably somewhat frightening.

I couldn't completely abandon my supernatural configuration as I had to take care of Xavier. I bowed my head over him, placed my mouth a few centimeters from his, and began pulling. His body constricted as I drew the black smoke from his lungs. I continued to draw until his lungs were clear and then released the toxic smoke into the atmosphere in one big cloud in the darkness. My entire body was aglow at the completion of the task.

I pulled back to check Xay's condition. His color was returning, and his breathing was evening out. He was going to be fine. I was distracted suddenly by a gasping, ripping sound behind me. I turned toward the noise. Sarielle was in a full panic attack. She was shaking and gasping as the hysterics caused hyperventilation and near convulsions.

"Raz, move... move!" I slid over and took Sarielle into my arms.

"Shhhh! Sarielle, it's all right. You're fine. Both you and Xay are safe." Her body rocked violently with the tremors. I gently placed my hand on the side of her neck until the panic in her eyes subsided, and she slipped peacefully into unconsciousness.

"That's going to be difficult to explain," Angelo said, shaking his head.

"Tell me about it." Raz agreed.

The atmosphere was disrupted for a third time tonight. The crash of the thunder startled the three of us. Something was different. While we knew that another immortal had been lost, there was a visible edge to the violence of the climatic reaction this time. The lightning raced across the sky and struck the north end of the field, igniting an additional fire.

"Damn! What was that? Malachi, talk to me."

"Two of the Dominion just went down. Uriel and Liwet took out Raguel and Zadkiel. But the Legion isn't retreating. I think they just got angry. To borrow your words, *brother, they're pissed,"* Malachi responded.

"We've got incoming! The Legion just got reinforcements. Abbadon is here," Reuel announced.

"Did you say Abbadon?"

I looked to the skies for any sign of the Legion regime head. As I did, two blinding streaks of light obstructed my view of the night sky. Immediately, I exploded into battle configuration, taking to the heavens. If Abbadon was here, it was absolutely time for me to defend Charon. I wouldn't run, and I certainly wasn't going to hide.

As I flew, I snatched both flaming swords from the sheath on my back. "Abbadon! If you want me, here I am!" I bellowed.

They knew I was here. No need to be silent any longer. My strength had returned. I felt the supernatural ability pulsating through every fiber of my being. Any fear that was in me was swiftly replaced by a burning desire to avenge Charon in the name of Yah.

I halted my approach at the edge of the battle where the two streaks had appeared. I needed to identify friend or foe before I engaged.

It was Shopar and Naqam. The Thrones were here to help. "Shoer," Naqam greeted me.

"We've got your flank," Shopar added.

"Let's get in there." I took the lead.

The fighting was fierce in every area of the sky. The Legion had three Thrones among them. Abbadon, Azrael, and Sorath were all staying just on the edge of the fray—watching and waiting. The arrival of Naqam and Shopar helped to even the battle out significantly.

I scanned the skies for Malachi and Reuel and was relieved to see that they were paired in battle and had successfully pushed back two of the Dominion who were now fleeing back to their line of defense—the fallen Thrones—to regroup.

Malachi and Reuel joined our grouping, followed by Uriel and Liwet. We watched as the smaller battles all seemed to be going our way. But the Legion was still standing their ground. Odd.

"Well, this is an interesting turn of events." Uriel chuckled humorlessly as he stared across the battlefield at the opposing Thrones. "Why would Abbadon leave the gateway uncovered to show up here? Doesn't make sense. What is it between the two of you, Shoer? He's absolutely determined to have a personal hand in your destruction."

"As soon as I find that out, Uriel, you'll be the first to know. How about I go ask him?" I started into the field, but Naqam grabbed me by the arm.

"Wait a minute, Shoer. What are they doing?"

On the opposite side of the field, Abbadon, Azrael, and Sorath had formed a line, preparing to move as one. The Thrones along with Uriel immediately took my place on the front line. Liwet and Malachi took my flank, and Reuel had my back.

As they formed the new defensive line, the opposing Thrones reached into the atmosphere and pulled.

"Steady yourselves, Guardian!" Uriel warned. His voice echoed throughout the entire field.

Uriel's warning did little to prepare us for the torrents of wind and water that manifested out of the heavens at the command of the fallen Thrones. Our line of defense was instantaneously blown apart as we scrambled to regain our bearings.

Nisroc was in an uncontrolled tailspin, falling to Earth. One of the Dominion, Caim, seized the opportunity to attack. In an instant, Caim had Nisroc in a death-hold and was preparing his final blow. Shopar pulled his mjolnir and threw it with such force that the heavens thundered. The mjolnir's blow sent Caim plummeting toward the ground. Naqam then steadied Nisroc with the wind until he recovered from Caim's attack.

I remembered in the same moment that the opposing Thrones would have been weakened by their unanimous exploit. We could attack.

"Let's finish this!" I roared as the Guardian charged forward into battle.

The rain continued to fall in sheets while the thunder roared, and the lightning lit the night sky.

"Kendi, stay close. You hear me! Stay close," Malachi ordered. *"Don't do anything crazy. You have help. Got it?"*

I didn't get a chance to respond as Halpas tossed his flaming bolas to restrain me. I dodged the bolas, slicing it apart with my sword. Halpas took advantage of the distraction and attacked.

The anger raged from deep within me. I didn't have time for this menial distraction. My target was Abbadon, and I wanted him while he was still at a disadvantage. I channeled the rage into strength easily deflecting Halpas with my shield, sending him hurtling across the sky.

And then the skies exploded with Dominion. They were everywhere. The Guardian were all engaged in one-on-one battles. Some, like Uriel and the Thrones, were defending against multiple attackers.

I could see Abbadon on the far side of the field. The desire to take him down was the most overwhelming feeling I had experienced in over three hundred years. The need to destroy him and everything that he stood for served as fuel to my fury.

I battled my way across the sky, easily blocking and deflecting the attacks of the lesser Legion warriors. I could see Malachi and Liwet in my peripherals, still at my side, and Uriel and the Thrones plowing the road before me.

The Legion had layered their defenses with the lesser warriors on the exterior. As we made our way to their line of defense, the battles grew more intense. Suddenly, above the rush of the rain, I heard the clanging of chains. I wheeled toward the sound just in time to witness Sorath's chained maces lock with force around Isda's torso, incapacitating him.

"Isda...no!" Liwet yelled.

Uriel broke away from his opponent and raced across the sky toward his soldier, but Sorath was faster. He swooped in like a flash of light, executing the death-hold and delivering the final blow with a precision that bewildered us all. Isda's lifeless body fell to the Earth. Sorath then turned to Uriel to goad him on.

Uriel and Liwet charged Sorath simultaneously, leaving holes in my defensive line. Reuel moved to my side to replace Liwet, while Naqam and Shopar tightened up the frontal configuration. There was only one defender left in front of Abbadon, that being Azrael.

"Abbadon! Enough! You want me, come get some!" I was incensed.

"Be careful what you ask for, boy. Are you so ready to die? Ready to see more of your comrades fall?" Abbadon hissed.

"There is only one other life that needs to end today, Abbadon—yours!"

I charged with my weapons drawn, Malachi at my side. The heavens responded with the clashing of thunder as we came together. Azrael and Caim quickly engaged Shopar and Naqam.

Halpas hit Reuel with a crushing blow, leaving another hole in my defensive line.

"Reuel!"

"I'm fine, Kendi."

Abbadon was already a massive creature but expanded his size, even more, to take on both Malachi and me. It didn't help that he was as skilled with a sword and shield as both of us put together.

"How do you want to do this, brother?" Malachi huffed as he dodged a blow from Abbadon's shield.

"I'll keep him busy. Try to get behind him. Incapacitate him, and I will deliver the final blow."

But when Mal swung around behind Abbadon, he turned to engage him, leaving me at his back.

I charged in immediately immobilizing the demon. "Strike now, Mal. Strike now!"

As Malachi lifted his hand to deliver the final blow, I again heard the maces making an approach. The weapon locked me in its chains, spinning me around. I struggled uselessly and began descending from the sky. Sorath had broken free from Uriel long enough to hurl the weapon to contain me.

"Kendi!" Malachi realized that my hold on Abbadon had been broken.

Caim attacked while I was in descent, swooping in front of me to execute the death-hold. I immediately felt my strength wean, but my first thought was not for me but for my brother who was still fiercely battling Abbadon.

"Malachi get away from him. Now! Back away!" And, as Tabbris had taught, I blocked my connection with my Achim. If the Dominion got me, I'll be damned if they would get my brother as well. Malachi would survive this.

"Kendi, don't! Please let me help you," Malachi pleaded.

"Reuel! Reuel! Get Malachi away from the battle. I don't want him taken down with me. Get him out of here." I could feel myself fading, but not before I saw Reuel streak across the sky, grabbing hold of Mal. Reuel would keep him safely out of the battle at my request. I would not allow him to die with me.

My strength was fully depleted. Caim lifted his hand to deliver the deathblow. I began to close my eyes. I didn't want to see death when it came.

From the slits of my eyes, I saw the whirl of Shopar's mjolnir as it once again struck Caim. This time, the force of its blow sent us both in a downward spiral. Nisroc stopped my descent while Uriel cut away Sorath's maces.

"You aren't getting away from us that easy, Shoer!" Uriel chided. "Liwet! You and Nisroc are on guard until his strength returns. Ground him, he'll recover faster." Uriel sprinted back into the battle.

My head was spinning as my body attempted to recover. I couldn't seem to get my bearings.

"Shoer, we need to get you down," Nisroc instructed as he took me by the arm.

When my feet touched the ground, the pain of a thousand needles shot through both of my legs. "Awwwwh!" I shrieked, collapsing. "What the hell?"

"Like Uriel said, you'll recover faster down here. It just hurts like hell to do it." Liwet smirked.

"Reuel? Where are you?" I couldn't allow myself to reconnect with Malachi just yet. He would experience everything that I was feeling, and I wouldn't wish this pain on my worst enemy...well, maybe the worst ones.

"East side of the battle. The fighting has moved farther to the west. I wanted to give Malachi time to get back to full strength before we reengaged."

"Awwwwh...good idea," I moaned.

"Are you all right?"

"I will be. I'm grounded with Nisroc and Liwet waiting for the effects of the

death-hold to subside.”

“You know your brother is going to try to kill you himself once we get out of here, right?”

“Yeah, probably.” I laughed. I was already feeling better—almost back to normal.

“Kendi, we have a problem. Incoming, Sorath and Azrael are headed right for us!”

“Damn it! Liwet, Nisroc! The east side of the battle—go now! Reuel's got incoming, Azrael and Sorath!”

“We have instructions, we can't leave you unprotected,” Nisroc protested. “And now you have orders! Get in there. Now!”

Like lightning, they were gone. I lifted myself from the ground. While the pain was still noticeably there, it was tolerable. My legs were still wobbly, but I wouldn't need them in the air. I had to rejoin the battle.

“Reuel, I've sent Nisroc and Liwet to you. Hang in there. Help's coming.”

It frightened me that two Thrones were bearing down on Reuel. Mal was not yet at full strength, and the Legion would certainly take advantage. I rose cautiously into the air, as I was blind. I didn't dare take the risk of connecting with Mal and further weakening him, and Reuel didn't need the added distraction of me in his head.

Luck would have it that I rose behind the battle, completely unnoticed— just the way I needed it. Reuel and Malachi were holding off Sorath while Liwet and Nisroc engaged Azrael.

Liwet was a quick warrior. His strike was like that of a snake—agile and executed with great precision. He moved in a dart of light about the night sky with such speed that he was not easy to track. Nisroc was more deliberate in his battle style, methodically calculating each move. The pair effectively kept Azrael off balance.

Malachi and Reuel were faring just as well. They had a level of communication and trust that made for a great pairing. Because I knew Malachi well, I recognized his struggle to stay ahead of the battle, but Reuel had it under control. He was a learned warrior who had been defending against this Dominion since the insurrection.

After a minute, the atmosphere became oddly still. The rain slowed, and the wind quieted. I wasn't the only one to notice; Guardian and Legion alike paused to observe the occurrence. All but one—Abbadon. It was a trick.

Abbadon had created the illusion, pulling the elements into himself as he expanded. I readied myself to attack as my strength had returned, and I knew he would be weakened. A sudden crack of thunder interrupted my ascent. The small grouping with my brother, my leader, and my new comrades was blown apart by the blast. In the same moment, Sorath swept in behind Malachi and Azrael behind Liwet, incapacitating them while Reuel and Nisroc continued to plummet earthward, trapped in Halpas's bolas.

The explosion was a planned distraction. My approach back into the battle had not gone unnoticed at all. Abbadon was ready and waiting.

"Shoer!" he bellowed across the battlefield. "Let's not cause the unnecessary destruction of any further immortals today. Surrender to me now, and we can end this farce."

I quickly scanned the field. The battle had turned in the favor of the Legion. Uriel had a sword to his throat; Forcus, Hael, and Gavreel were all being bested in their fights; Reuel and Nisroc were caught in Halpas's dragnet, effectively removing them from the present battle; and, worst of all, Malachi was a single strike from being destroyed. If I was going to surrender, now was the time to do it.

I bowed my head and considered taking a knee before Abbadon. Somehow, I knew it would come to this. Yah had to see this coming when he appointed me—a rogue Guardian that had done nothing but fail thus far.

The Legion knew they had a young, inexperienced target that would likely fall without much resistance. It was for this moment that I had warned Reuel when he took me under his charge. I was not worthy of this appointment or of his confidence.

I raised my head to look at Malachi—the one person I vowed would survive this sentence. The light was leaving his eyes as Sorath tightened his grip.

"You can still do this, Eklektos. This moment is what I'll gladly give my life for. Take him down, brother. Seal the gate." Malachi's eyes pleaded with me.

As I looked into the eyes of my Achim, power began to build in my core. The strength was inflamed by the resentment I felt for being forced into this position. I didn't want this role or the responsibility of so many lives being placed in my hands. It incensed me. I could feel the surge of power as the rage emptied into my being. My chest seemed to expand with the added capacity. In this moment, I could either reject Yah's plan for me or finally embrace it. My hands curled into tight fists as I accepted the new influence. Tonight, I *would* allow a death to occur—just, not the one everyone expected. Tonight, *I* would die to self and step into my office—reborn the Shoer of Charon.

I knew what I needed to do.

"Uriel. I hope you're as good as everyone thinks you are." I could see him in my peripherals.

"Better." He nodded with a smirk.

"Urim, Sandalphon, be ready." I could see them coming around the edge of the battlefield. *"Malachi...forgive me."* I watched as his eyes stretched wide with disbelief.

Then I bowed my head and opened my connection with him further than I had ever done—past communication, past blocking. I coupled with him, pulling with all my strength so that our power would instantly become one. His body contorted violently as he shrieked with the pain caused by my sudden invasion. And then his body went limp. Sorath released him.

"Now!" I roared at Uriel.

In my increased strength, I bounded across the sky straight for Azrael. Uriel flipped around Ipas and struck his captor with a blow that sent him hurling. He then raced in after Sorath.

"Urim! Release Reuel and Nisroc!" I barked. *"Sandalphon, protect my brother with your life."*

I cringed internally at having taken down Malachi in such a violent manner.

I sliced through the air with a speed and force I had never imagined being capable of. I slammed into Azrael, forcing him to release a weakened Liwet. Azrael attempted to regain his hold, but I struck him with my sword, spinning him to face me.

"So, this is the best Yah can do these days?" He laughed defiantly, which only enraged me further.

I quickly replaced my sword in its sheath to free my hands. Everything in me wanted to rip Azrael's head from his shoulders. This vile, evil being that had tortured both Xavier and me and thought he was justified in doing so. I attacked.

Even with the added strength, Azrael would not go down easily. He was an ancient Throne and had the experience of thousands of years and just as many battles. His pride would not allow him to retreat. This battle would only end when one voice was permanently silenced.

Azrael landed a punch that spun me back several feet. I had to regroup.

Uriel had successfully disarmed Sorath. Sorath was retreating, with Urim and Liwet in pursuit.

As he fled, Uriel swooped in to help me.

"Move, Shoer. I've got this."

"Azrael is mine, Uriel!" I spat through my teeth as I grabbed both swords from my back.

I spun in, striking Azrael, sending him into a spin. Mid-spin, Uriel caught him in a chokehold before he could right himself.

"You want him, Shoer, take him!" Uriel swiftly adjusted his hold until Azrael was incapacitated.

I flew directly in front of Azrael so that I could see his eyes.

"What do you think about Yah's choice now, demon?" He stared defiantly at me but kept his silence.

I reached back and struck Azrael's core, snatching the light from his eyes. "That was for Zuriel," I added.

Uriel released his shell as a sonic boom shook the heavens. A Throne had fallen. I immediately looked across the field to locate Abbadon. He was gone, and the remaining Dominion retreating. This battle was over.

Uriel and I looked at one another for a long moment. He said nothing but nodded once and headed across the field to gather what remained of his contingent.

The power surge was subsiding, which allowed me to think past the battle and warrior mode. My mind flooded with concern for Malachi and the rest of our family, not to mention Xavier and Sarielle.

There was still a mess that needed cleaning up. My attention turned to the blaring sirens and flashing lights in the distance. I looked to the ground. The emergency vehicles were approaching. I had to hurry.

Reuel was in a clearing of the cornfield with Sandalphon and Malachi—who was lying motionless. "Reuel! Is Mal all right?" I hollered, rushing to them.

"He should be okay. His body needs time to recover, though. He's vulnerable out here. We should get him under better cover until he is fully restored."

Mal's face was so lifeless. I reached out and touched his chest. I needed to make sure for myself that he was still with me.

"Let's take him home," I suggested. Reuel nodded. We teleported Malachi safely to the house. "We have to get back. The twins can't deal with the mess out there. Humans will be all over that scene in the next couple of minutes."

"Angelo? Raza? Are Sarielle and Xavier still unaware?" Reuel questioned.

"Yes, but Elle is starting to come around," Raz confirmed.

"You and Angelo get here to the house. Keep an eye on Malachi. Kendi and I are coming back there now."

"On our way," Angelo agreed.

"Let's go, Kendi," Reuel started.

I took him by the arm. "I need your help, Reuel. Sarielle saw me in my natural form while I was healing Xay. She was petrified."

Reuel looked into my eyes for a long moment, seeming to consider some internal dilemma, but then placed a hand on my shoulder.

"I'll take care of it, son. Don't worry." He smiled at me, and we were back on Valley Road.

Neither Sarielle nor Xavier was alert enough to notice our return.

Reuel went and knelt beside Sarielle and took her by the hand. With a low moan, she turned toward his touch, and her eyes fluttered open. When she noticed me standing beside Reuel, she dragged in a ragged breath, shrinking away from us. She remembered what she had seen.

"Sarielle, it's okay," I began. Reuel raised his hand to quiet me. He gently placed his hands on either side of her face, forcing her to look directly into his eyes. Reuel's eyes began to glow as he connected with her on another level. Sarielle would have been screaming hysterically if Reuel had not had her entranced. After several seconds, he bowed his head and closed his eyes, mentally releasing her from his hold. Her eyes rolled into the back of her head and then closed.

In the few seconds that it took for her to recover, Reuel and I had switched places. I slid onto the ground next to her and carefully pulled her into my arms. With the back of my hand, I began gently stroking her cheek. Her face was so cold. I pulled her in closer to the warmth of my body.

"Sarielle, can you hear me? Sarielle?" I rubbed her arm, trying to create warmth.

She opened her eyes, looking around. She immediately noticed her brother lying a few feet away from her.

"Xay?" I loosened my hold as she tried to reach for him. She only sat halfway up before slumping back into me.

"Take it easy. Xay is going to be fine. My dad and I got him out of the fire in time. He is going to be okay. Help is almost here. Try to rest."

She was too exhausted to resist. She lay back into my arms, staring up at me.

"I love you, Kendi," she whispered, and her eyes closed again. I looked up at Reuel. He said nothing, but his eyes were genuinely concerned.

The fire trucks and the ambulances pulled up simultaneously. I reflexively pulled Sarielle in closer, protecting her, as a surge of heat welled up inside my chest. It was a different kind of heat—one that had nothing to do with the fire or my internal rage.

22
The Fallen

I wanted to ride in the ambulance with Sarielle, but Reuel advised against it. The paramedics immediately administered a high dosage of steroids to Sarielle once I mentioned her condition. She opened her eyes briefly as they loaded her onto the stretcher, but they thought it best to sedate her to make sure she stayed calm.

Xavier was immediately given oxygen to help rouse him; his oxygen saturation had been very low upon initial examination. He too was beginning to come around by the time he was loaded into the second ambulance.

Reuel and I followed the siblings to the hospital in their Honda. On the way, we devised an acceptable story for the authorities, and for Emily. She was going to start thinking that the Bellings were just magnets for disaster. Every time we met, unfortunately, it was in the emergency room.

Malachi had recovered from my little coupling experiment and was meeting us at the hospital while the twins went to connect with Uriel's team to get an assessment of the evening's battle.

We told Emily the same story we planned to tell the police. It was Taylor Thomas who had taken Xay to the cornfield, and Sarielle had followed to bring her sick brother back home. However, when she arrived at the farm, the boys were already in the maze. In her panic, she called me for help locating them. They were deep in the maze when the lightning strike started the fire. We had arrived just in time to see Taylor abandoning them to save his own ass.

Emily was livid and vowed she was going to press charges. Even after all we'd been through tonight, the thought of Taylor behind bars brought a huge smile to my face. She had also called her ex-husband, who was boarding a plane heading for the States. I guess she needed the support. This had indeed been a rough season for her and her children.

Malachi arrived just as Emily was allowed back to see Sarielle and Xavier. They were both being admitted. Emily thanked Reuel and me once again on behalf of her family and disappeared behind the double doors.

We moved to the far end of the waiting room to talk without being overheard. Once we were in an unpopulated corner of the room, I turned to inspect Malachi, hoping I had not caused permanent injury with my latest exploit.

"Mal, I'm so sorry…"

He cut me off. "Kendi, I'm fine though you could try to warn a brother next time." He laughed. "Didn't know my little brother could pack such a punch."

I grinned, though I didn't find the same level of humor in almost losing my brother. Mal felt my anxiety. He reached for me and pulled me into a strong embrace.

"I'm all right, man, really." He released me but held onto my shoulder. "I'm proud of you. You led us well, Eklektos."

Reuel smiled at our private exchange, and then suddenly stiffened at our side.

We stepped in closer protecting our leader from the unseen danger. Reuel loosened his stance, bowing his head in acknowledgment. Someone was communicating with him. After a few moments, he opened his eyes. Something wasn't right. His eyes no longer held the same light they did a minute ago. The flat, distant look in his eyes frightened me. The information exchange was not good news—I could feel it.

"Reuel, what is it?" Malachi whispered. His voice trembled slightly. He was feeling a similar dread.

Reuel shook his head as if to clear his thoughts. "Everything's going to be fine," he responded. "I've been summoned to Merkabah. I'll be leaving as soon as I make sure that the imminent danger here has subsided…even if only momentarily."

His response was off, too formal. This wasn't the Reuel I had come to know and respect.

"What's happening, Reuel?" I tried to push him silently. Without acknowledging my attempt, he started a different conversation.

"Kendi, today you exemplified the attributes of the leader, the warrior, I knew you were created to be. I was honored to stand at your side, Eklektos." He bowed his head, acknowledging my office. "You handled yourself well." I saw pride clouded by worry in his eyes.

"Reuel? What's the matter?" I tried again. The shift in his demeanor was concerning.

I stared at him while he silently communicated with Malachi. Mal gave one quick nod in agreement while I watched.

"Make sure Elle and Xavier are okay and then head home. Not too long, okay?" We both agreed.

"The battle was won today but know that Abbadon's already planning for war and he won't be easily defeated. Understand?"

"Yes, sir," I acknowledged his warning.

"Stay alert." Reuel looked back and forth between us and then turned and left.

"What the hell was that all about?"

"Not completely sure, Kendi...not completely sure." Malachi shook his head.

We waited for a little more than an hour before Emily came out and informed us that we could go back. Xavier was admitted to a regular room, but Sarielle was in the ICU on Dr. Julie's floor so that she could be closely watched through the night. Sarielle would only be allowed one visitor at a time. Mal and I decided to split up so that we could see both of our friends before we left.

I headed to see Xay first. As I approached, two police officers were leaving his room. I waited until they passed the nurse's station before continuing to the door. It was cracked open, but I knocked anyway.

"Yeah," Xay responded, so I pushed the door open and went in. His countenance fell as soon as he saw me. I pretended not to notice.

I would take it easy on him. He looked like hell, and I'm sure he felt just as bad. Xavier had an oxygen tube in his nose, and a couple of IV drips. I guess almost being cooked to death has a way of severely dehydrating the body.

"Hey, man. Just wanted to stop by and see how you were doing before heading home. How are you feeling?"

"Like I got hit by a bus and had it back up and roll over me a second time just for shits and giggles. But I guess I'll live...that's what they tell me anyway."

"Well then, I guess you pretty much feel like you look, huh?" I teased, sitting on the side of his bed. "You know, I could really make some money if I start charging a service fee for saving your ass."

He smiled and then laughed weakly, embarrassed.

"The police were just in here," he started. He knew the questions were coming. "I told them I couldn't remember what happened at Connor Farm, Kendi. That's the truth. I remember Taylor and I leaving the house after fighting with Elle. I remember being irritated when I realized that she followed us, and Taylor thought it was funny to go farther into the maze just to piss her off.

"But then we all got lost. I felt like crap. My head was pounding, I was off balance, and I couldn't keep up with Taylor. Next thing I know, I was in the back of an ambulance."

"You don't remember the fire, or your BFF leaving you and your sister there to die, just to cover his ass?" I spat sarcastically.

"I don't remember a fire. And that's what I told the police. And that's what I told Taylor when he stopped by before they did." Damn it! Taylor had already gotten to him. "Taylor said that he was ready to go, but I wanted to stay and find Elle so we could ride back home together, so he left. He said that he didn't see any signs of a fire when he rolled out. Elle's car was parked right next to his, so he figured we were okay. He came to the hospital after seeing the fire on the news and Elle's car was still on the side of the road in the mix with the fire trucks."

"Taylor said? He's lying, Xay. He left you there, both of you! If it were not for my brothers and my dad, I would have never been able to find you both in time." I stopped to take a breath to calm myself. I was shouting. Now wasn't a good time to discuss Taylor.

"I'm not going to push the issue tonight. You need to rest. I just wanted to point out yet another reason why you need to stay the hell away from that piece of trash."

"I agree he can be a prick, but he wouldn't—"

I interrupted him. "He did, Xay...trust me, he did."

Xavier sighed, leaning his head back into the pillow, closing his eyes tightly; he pulled his hands to either side of his head. He was in pain.

"Head still hurting?"

"Like I took a bullet to the brain, man."

"You want me to send the nurse in? I'm gonna go so you can rest."

"Please," he responded without ever opening his eyes.

"Feel better, Xay." I closed the door quietly.

After stopping by the nurse's station for Xay, I headed toward the ICU, connecting with Mal on the way. *"I hope Sarielle's in better shape than her brother."*

"Actually, she's okay. A little groggy from her meds, but otherwise, I think she's fine. She's asking for you."

Why did Sarielle asking for me make me so nervous?

"What's going on with Xay?" Mal wanted to know.

"He's in a lot of pain. The nurse was headed in to medicate him when I left. I'm sure he'll be out for the rest of the night."

"That's probably best. He never did allow himself time to recover from that concussion. He won't have a choice now."

"Exactly."

"Well, I suppose I'll just hang out in the waiting area while you visit with Elle. Then we can head home. We still need to debrief with Uriel."

"Sounds like a plan."

The intensive care unit was eerily quiet. The continuous beeping of random heart monitors was the only sound.

"Which room is it, Mal?"

"Come to the end of the hall and make a left. It's the third room on the right side. I'll step out into the hallway."

When I rounded the corner, Mal was waiting as promised. "You look tired," he observed as I approached.

"Yeah, rough day."

"That's an understatement if I ever heard one." Malachi shook his head. "I think I'll go see Xavier anyway. I know he's in a rough shape, but I'll just sit with him for a few while you see Elle."

"Meet you in the lobby in ten minutes?"

"That works."

I watched Mal leave before approaching Sarielle's room. I peeked through the open door. Sarielle's eyes were closed. I slipped in quietly and crept to her bedside. Her hair fanned out wildly across the pillow in a mass of golden-brown curls. The color had returned to her cheeks. She looked peaceful, better. It made me feel less anxious.

As a Guardian, I had spent much of my existence with humans. And until this assignment, I had successfully managed to stay aloof, doing the bare minimum to complete the job so that I could move on as quickly as possible. I didn't care, and I didn't get involved. Tonight made me realize why this time was so different. It was because of the fragile girl lying in this hospital bed in front of me. Somehow, she had silently disarmed my defenses, breaking through my impenetrable tough exterior, and found my soul.

I reached out my hand and gently stroked her cheek. Sarielle sighed quietly and opened her eyes.

"Kendi," she whispered with a smile. I opened my hand cradling her cheek.

"Hey there, beautiful." I smiled in response. I let go of her face and took her hand, sitting on the side of the bed, careful not to get tangled in the tubes from her IV.

"How are you?"

"I'm fine...just really tired."

"Well, I'm glad you are okay, so I won't feel guilty yelling at you.

"What in the world were you thinking? Running out in the middle of the night after your brother like that! You didn't tell me where you were going, and then you didn't even call me back! You scared me half to death. You know that?"

She tilted her head to one side looking me in the eye.

"I'm sorry. I didn't mean to upset you, but I couldn't just let them leave."

"You could have waited for me. I would have found Xay without you putting yourself in danger, Sarielle. Seeing you lying there, unconscious like that..." I shook my head to clear the visual. "It made me feel so helpless."

While I stared into her golden eyes, the same warmth that radiated through me earlier tonight began to overtake me again. It was the same feeling that made me want to protect her, to shield her from anything that would harm her or upset her. It was the feeling that drove me to look for her every day at school and to think of her all the time. I didn't know why, but I *needed* Sarielle. I grimaced as the thought of losing her brought physical pain.

Sarielle reached out to caress my face. With the tips of her fingers, she gently traced along the lines of my jaw. Her touch electrified my entire body, causing my breath to quicken as her fingers moved to my lips.

"I'm fine, Kendi. How about you? You look exhausted." Her fingers moved to the circles under my eyes. I closed them and was momentarily free from the trance in which she held me.

"I know you're not wasting your energy worrying about me," I said quietly.

"You aren't the only one that's allowed to worry, Mr. Belling." Her tone caused me to open my eyes. Sarielle was only inches from my face now.

"Kendi, you're worth loving too." Her warm breath brushed my face, and my heart melted. It ached in a way that was completely foreign to me; the human heart I should have never been given.

"Sarielle," I challenged, attempting to back away. I couldn't allow anyone, and especially not her, so close to me. Malachi being tethered to me was a constant source of torment. And tonight, it was brutally clear that Abbadon would use whomever he could to get to me. I refused to be the cause of someone's death.

I started to get up from the bed. She caught me by the hand and wouldn't let me go. "Please don't push me away, Kendi. Let me be here for you," she whispered intently.

The pain in her eyes was easy to read. She perceived my response as rejection—the rejection of someone she dared to love. A tear ran down her cheek. I lifted my hand and gently wiped it away.

"You make me feel safe and loved. Let me do the same for you." Her eyes wouldn't release me.

Sarielle had such a hold on me. I couldn't think straight with her so close to me. Without permission, my hand left her cheek, slid behind her neck, and pulled her into me. My lips lightly met hers, and my heart sped out of control as her lips parted, crushing to mine. The excitement coursed through every fiber of my body becoming more heightened the longer her lips were on mine. My other hand reached greedily for her face as I moved in closer.

Any ability I had to resist this girl was gone. My willpower had crumbled.

Her warm body pressed against mine as the electric tension whipped around us, attempting to bind us together. My body reacted in ways that were completely foreign. My stomach tightened to the point of pain. All the while, I wanted more. Sarielle lay back into the pillows.

I followed.

"Kendi...NO! What are you doing? We need to go. Now," Malachi screamed in my head.

I gently pulled away from Sarielle and stood up. "I have to go. Malachi's waiting for me in the lobby."

"Okay," she stammered, attempting to hide the same excitement that was raging within me. "Will you come back tomorrow?" She pleaded.

"You know I will." I stroked her cheek one last time and leaned in to kiss her forehead. "Promise me you'll rest?"

"Promise." She relaxed back into her pillow.

"Good night, Sarielle," I whispered, staring at her for a long moment before pulling the door closed behind me.

I walked slowly through the quiet corridors rehearsing my visit with Sarielle. I knew it was wrong to kiss her, but I couldn't make myself regret it. Given another opportunity, things would have probably played out the same way, and that bothered me tremendously.

What would make me act in such a manner? Sarielle was only human. What made her so different than the countless thousands, maybe even millions, of humans I had encountered over the centuries? I tossed that question over and over in my mind as I approached the lobby knowing I would have to face Malachi.

I hated that he was—and probably always would be—a front-row witness to all my missteps.

Malachi was standing next to the exit. I braced myself for the tirade, but it didn't come.

"Ready to go?" Mal asked as I approached.

I simply nodded and followed him out the door. The look in Mal's eyes forced my silence. It was not the anger or the disappointment I expected but one of pity. Malachi looked as if he had just been devastated by some bad news.

We rode silently through the deserted streets of Danvers toward home. I leaned my head back, closing my eyes, trying to clear my mind, but thoughts of Sarielle continued to flood my consciousness. Every time I thought of the moment our lips met, it did strange things to me. The thoughts would awaken every nerve ending in my body. I felt Malachi wince quietly from the driver's seat as we pulled into the driveway.

As we walked toward the front door, I pulled Malachi to a stop.

"Mal, talk to me. You haven't said two words since we left the hospital." He sighed and shook his head.

"There's so much going on right now, and Yah seems to have opened the floodgates. Our assignment here has morphed into this...this conundrum that continues to throw me for a loop. It's my job to protect you, to stand with you, and I will to my dying breath, but there are some things I can't protect you from, brother."

The same pained look Mal had at the hospital had returned.

"What are you talking about?" I responded as he continued toward the front door.

"I'm talking about Elle."

"Why would you need to protect me from Sarielle?" I questioned.

She was one of the most gentle, vulnerable human beings I'd ever met. One who constantly put everyone else's needs before her own. She had a heart of gold. Mal didn't need to protect me from her. And tonight, I realized that I would give my life to keep anything from harming her.

"You don't even know what's happening to you... what's already happened to you...do you?" Malachi stared at me incredulously.

"What are you talking about?"

"Kendi, you've fallen in love with her. You *are* in love with Sarielle." He pushed open the front door and walked into the house.

I followed Mal into the living room, dazed. I didn't know what to make of his revelation. I didn't even know what it meant to be *in love*. This was a human emotion that, until recently, I wasn't capable of processing.

"Mal, Kendi, we were just about to call you," Raz greeted us, Angelo at his side.

"We were making sure Xay and Elle were okay. Reuel told us we would need to meet with Uriel for a debriefing," Mal started, and then looked back at me.

I'm sure the look on my face resembled the gut punch I had just received. I couldn't think now.

"Yes, we do. We have to talk." There was sternness to Raza's tone that was very unlike him. "I think it can wait for a few hours. Kendi needs time to recover from tonight. He's back in his human form and is spent. It's been a long day. I'll connect with Uriel to make the arrangements. We should wait for Reuel to return from Empyrean to have the discussion anyway."

"I don't think that's going to be possible," Angelo chimed in.

"Why not? What's going on?" Mal and I looked back and forth between the twins.

"Reuel wasn't summoned to Empyrean, guys. He was escorted to Merkabah by Agat and Bahram," Raz explained.

"Why would the Authorities come for Reuel? Why is he being confined?" I demanded.

"Calm down, Kendi. Reuel will get this sorted out. I'm sure he'll be back soon to let us know what's going on," Malachi tried to reassure me. "He asked me to hold things down here until he returned. He'll be back soon."

Malachi's confidence wavered as he repeated himself. Reuel had only told us what he wanted us to know. His being arrested was a consequence of helping me. Reuel had crossed the line one time too many on my behalf. I felt it in my gut.

My legs suddenly felt hollow. I needed to sit. Heading for the couch, my legs seemed to be getting heavier with each step. All the events of this evening were a burden that my human form was not suited to carry.

"Mal, I don't think Reuel is coming back anytime soon. Yah has appointed a replacement."

I stopped short of the couch and stared blankly at Raza. "A replacement?"

The weight of the past twenty-four hours came crashing down on me. I felt as though Abbadon had pulled my spine out through my nose. Reaching for the couch, I fell to my knees... as Uriel walked in from the kitchen.

Epilogue

"Reuel, how are you?"

"It's good to see you. Yah allowed you to visit?"

"No." Eloa smiled timidly. "The Authorities owe me a few favors."

"I see." Reuel chuckled. "I know you're keeping watch over Kendi. How is he?"

"He is putting on a brave face for the team, only Malachi knows he is coming apart at the seams. He blames himself for your confinement. Kendi's having trouble moving past the incident at the cornfield. Uriel is a warrior, not a protector like you. He has been...severe with Kendi, trying to get him to re-engage."

"Severe?"

"Uriel only sees the need to get the gateway closed. So, he pushes Kendi in unproductive ways. Abbadon has appointed a new second-in-command. Sorath has promised to avenge Azrael, and he has widened the gateway, flooding Charon with Dominion presence. The region is coming under extreme attack. To make matters worse, Abbadon's pulling together an army of mortals who have opened themselves up to be influenced. The attacks will come from mortal and immortal alike.

"So, you see, Uriel has an urgency for the warrior in Kendi to take a stand. He doesn't have the patience to deal with Kendi's remorse."

"I made my choices with full knowledge of the consequences, Eloa."

"I know. But Kendi is ambivalent right now. He is not thinking clearly. He hates himself for letting you down, and he's looking for solace."

"Ambivalent?"

"He's found love for a mortal. Kendi is starting to fulfill Yah's plan for him."

"How does that make him ambivalent?"

"We'll have to see what he does with that love, Reuel."

GLOSSARY OF TERMS

Achim—Celestial brother created from the same essence as the Shoer; protector of Shoer

Atsal—Continent of Antarctica governed by the spirit of Slothfulness; gateway closed by Govad

Charon—Continent of North America governed by the spirit of Wrath

Dominion—Fallen Angels; those who have rebelled against Yah

Eklektos—Title of respect, meaning *chosen*, given to deserving Shoers by the Guardian

Empyrean—Home of the Angelic Host

Erehwon—Realm of Empyrean where deceased mortals reside

Gaavah—Continent of Africa governed by the spirit of Pride

Gateways—Seven portals torn between Empyrean and Earth by Lucifer and his regime heads; one located on each continent of the Earth

Kahal—Meeting place of the Angelic Host in Empyrean

Legion—Dominion army

Merkabah—Palace, sanctuary in Empyrean; place of the Throne Room of Yah

Qinah—Continent of Asia governed by the spirit of Envy

Sha'ar—The forbidden realm of the gateways between Empyrean and Earth

Sheol—Realm of Empyrean where destroyed immortals reside

Shoer—Highest rank of the Guardian; gatekeepers assigned the task of locating and sealing the gateways

Ta'avat—Continent of South America governed by the spirit of Greed

Teomim—Celestial twin

Teshukah—Continent of Europe governed by the spirit of Lust

Zalal—Continent of Australia governed by the spirit of Gluttony; gateway closed by Tabbris

LIST OF ANGELS

THE RULING JUDGES

Haamiah—Judge of Integrity
Johoel—Mediator of the Host
Maion—Angel of Discipline and Self-Control
Micah—Angel of Destiny
Paschar—Angel of Vision
Qadhi—Angel of Justice (against mankind)
Ramiel—Angel of Hope
Rashnu—Angel of Judgment (against mankind)
Reuel—Overseer and Guardian Team Leader in Charon
Sammael—Escort of souls to Empyrean
Sraosha—Angel of Obedience

SHOERS

Anael—Shoer at Charon; defeated in battle by Abbadon; replaced by Kendi
Govad—Shoer at Atsal; defeated Ascidia
Haram—Shoer at Gaavah
Kendi—Shoer at Charon
Omniel—Shoer at Teshuka
Ruach—Shoer at Qinah
Tabbris—Shoer at Zalal; defeated Djinn; closing the gateway at Zalal; Throne
Vohu—Shoer at Ta'avat

ADVOCATES (of Mankind)

Elijah—Human that never died
Enoch—Human that never died

THE GUARDIAN

Agla—Govad's Achim
Angelo—Reuel's Team, Raza's Teomim (twin)
Barrattiel—Haram's Achim
Chamuel—Uriel's Elite Team
Charoum—Uriel's Elite Team
Elemiah—Extension to Uriel's Team
Forcus—Uriel's Elite Team
Gavreel—Uriel's Elite Team
Hael—Uriel's Elite Team
Hozi—Tabbris's Achim
Isda—Uriel's Elite Team
Jophiel—Extension to Uriel's Team
Kutiel—Uriel's Elite Team
Leo—Omniel's Achim
Liwet—Extension to Uriel's Team; replaced Malachi
Malachi—Reuel's Team, Kendi's Achim
Muriel—Uriel's Elite Team
Nisroc—Uriel's Elite Team
Orfiel—Anael's Achim; destroyed by Abbadon
Peliel—Vohu's Achim
Qaphsiel—Uriel's Elite Team
Raza—Reuel's Team; Angelo's Teomim (twin)
Sablo—Ruach's Achim
Sandalphon—Uriel's Elite Team
Uriel—Team Leader in Teshukah
Urim—Uriel's Elite Team
Valoel—Extension to Uriel's Team
Zuriel—Extension to Uriel's Team; destroyed by Azrael

THRONES

Cassiel—Assigned to defend Charon

Charam—Led the Host on Yah's behalf at the Insurrection

Gazardiel—Assigned to defend Charon

Mihr—Assigned to defend Charon

Naqam—Guard at Merkabah

Naasir—Assigned to Sheol as a guard and escort (as punishment)

Ophan—Newly created; betrayed by Kendi

Scorpio—Guard at Merkabah

Shopar—Guard at Merkabah

Xaphan—Assigned to defend Charon

THE DOMINION

Abbadon—Angel of Death and Legion Regime Head; fallen Throne

Ascidia—Ruler of gateway at Atsal; defeated by Govad

Azrael—Angel of Destruction; second-in-command to Abbadon; fallen Throne; destroyed by Kendi

Berith—Governor of the Legion; fallen Throne

Caim—Dominion soldier

Djinn—Ruler of gateway at Zalal; defeated by Tabbris

Eligor—Dominion soldier

Halpas—Dominion soldier

Ipos—Dominion soldier

Lahash—Interferer of divine will; fallen Throne

Lucifer—Led the first Insurrection; fallen Throne

Malak—Member of Abbadon's guard; destroyed by Kendi

Malpas—Dominion soldier

Raguel—Member of Abbadon's guard; destroyed by Uriel

Ruax—Dominion soldier

Soqed—Destroyed by Uriel in a battle at Teshukah

Sorath—False bearer of light; fallen Throne

Zadkiel—Member of Abbadon's guard; destroyed by Liwet

Zagan—Angel of Deception

OTHER MEMBERS OF THE HOST

Agat—Authority
Bahram—Authority
Eloa—Angel of Compassion
Yah—Supreme Ruler

About the Author

Ella Clarke is an imaginative urban fantasy author who resides in Central North Carolina. With a deep-rooted love for the wondrous and a mind brimming with possibilities, Ella weaves intricate tales that transport readers to untouched realms. Armed with a degree in chemistry and a minor in mathematics, she skillfully merges the realms of science and fascination, infusing her narratives with a unique blend of logic and wonder. Ella's stories explore the uncharted territories of imagination, where ordinary lives collide with extraordinary destinies. Her writing is a brilliant concoction of vibrant world-building, complex characters, and compelling plotlines.

When not crafting fantastical tales, Ella is a corporate executive in the medical device industry. She and her husband have four wonderful children and are enjoying empty nester status with their fur babies.

NOTE FROM ELLA CLARKE

Word-of-mouth is crucial for any author to succeed. If you enjoyed *{Book Title}*, please leave a review online—anywhere you are able. Even if it's just a sentence or two. It would make all the difference and would be very much appreciated.

Thanks!
Ella Clarke